Critical Acclaim for Stina Leicht's
Of Blood and Honey

"Riveting. A remarkable thriller that brings together the personal and the political and uses the fantastic to examine the forces that have driven the recent history of the troubles in Northern Ireland. An extraordinarily exciting read that makes me want to use phrases like fast-paced, spell-binding, and couldn't put it down."

—Eileen Gunn, author of *Stable Strategies and Others*

"Of Blood and Honey is remarkable! It was a compulsive read—I had to finish it as fast as possible and will be waiting impatiently for the next."

—Kat Richardson, author of *Greywalker*

"Set in the Ireland of the Troubles, before the recent détente, this fraught debut captures the backdrop of tension and choosing sides that overlays even the smallest act. The lingering effects of the Kesh and Malone prisons are gut-wrenchingly convincing."

—*Publishers Weekly*

"With an expert blend of classic Irish fantasy tropes and a gritty, realistic portrayal of the IRA circa early 1970s, Leicht offers one of the more distinctive and powerful novels of the young decade."

—Jeff VanderMeer, author of *City of Saints and Madmen*

"Stina Leicht's *Of Blood and Honey* is a captivating debut that seamlessly blends together historical drama with supernatural horror and dark fantasy, bringing to mind the excellent Danilov Quintet by Jasper Kent... a dazzling debut that will hopefully receive the attention and praise that it deserves."

—Robert Thompson, *Fantasy Literature.com*

Critical Acclaim for Stina Leicht's
Of Blood and Honey
(continued...)

"...a novel you can't quite call traditional fantasy, nor urban fantasy, nor alternate history. Whatever you call it, *Of Blood and Honey* doesn't mess around. It comes at you like a car bomb. This is fantasy by way of Ken Loach, not Peter Jackson."

—*SF Reviews.net*

"The pacing and atmosphere of *Of Blood and Honey* are truly phenomenal, making it a contender for 2011's best debut."

—*Ranting Dragon*

"It's a rough read. Brutal in spots. Surprisingly tender in others. As a debut goes for Stina Leicht, it's a marvelous one."

—Josh Vogt, *Examiner.com*

"Not since Jim Butcher's *Storm Front* have I read an Urban Fantasy that has felt so relevant to the overall discussion of Fantasy literature. *Of Blood and Honey* is Fantasy that deserves to stand alongside the best that authors like Powers, Gaiman and De Lint have to offer.... If you're bored of the same ol' Epic Fantasy, or you need a break from spaceships, hyperdrives and anti-grav suits, cleanse your palette with *Of Blood and Honey* and find out just how good Urban Fantasy can be."

—Aidan Moher, Best Speculative Fiction Blog nominee
for *A Dribble of Ink*

"*Of Blood & Honey* offer[s] truly well-crafted and yes, original and imaginative takes on familiar tropes.... We tell the same tales forever and again, and call them myths, or in the case of these books, fine novels."

—*Agony Column News*

"*Of Blood and Honey* is Leicht's début novel and it is one of the better novels I have read this year."

—Rob Weber, *Fantasy Book Critic*

"*Of Blood and Honey* isn't one of those happy-go-lucky stories where everything is roses and the hero wins everything he ever dreamed of. It is one of those books that pulls you forward from chapter to chapter until you reach the end."

—Rie Sheridan Rose, author of *The Luckless Prince*

"This book won't make you happy and will, in all likelihood, make you want to cry, but when you've finished it, you'll be glad that you decided to read it."

—*Lost in a Good Book*

"The writing is smooth and assured, and the plot is thriller-oriented with plenty of action. You shouldn't think that means the characters are neglected. They aren't, and they're all vivid and well rendered. Since this is obviously the first book in a series, there's more to look forward to from Leicht, who I hope is working on the sequel."

—Bill Crider, author of the Sheriff Dan Rhodes series

and BLUE SKIES
from PAIN

and BLUE SKIES
from PAIN

A BOOK OF THE FEY AND THE FALLEN

stina leicht

night shade books
san francisco

Night Shade Books
http://www.nightshadebooks.com

To Dane Caruthers
As you wish.

Also, to my Mom who taught me the words
"persistence" and "subversion."

The Nephilim were on earth in those days (and even after-wards) when the sons of God resorted to the women, and had children by them. These were the heroes of days gone by, men of renown.

—Genesis 6:4

According to adherents of the fallen-angel story, fairies are, by nature, indiscriminate in their favours and lacking all moral proportion, sometimes helping and sometimes hindering hu-mankind. Fairy activities, never genuinely evil, are dismissed as capricious whims of morally deficient creatures. Necessarily, Christianity has a vested interest in this fallen-angel view.

—from *A History of Irish Fairies*
by Carolyn White

Prologue

Waterford, County Waterford, Ireland
September 1967

An agony-laced shriek reverberated up the narrow stairwell, freezing a hard knot in Probationary Guardian Joseph Murray's stomach. The lingering scream was unmistakably male. Concern for the other members of his field unit flashed to mind. *Father Drager? Father Wright? Father Jackson? Or is it someone else?* As the distant cry faded, he struggled against a powerful urge to rush down the rough-hewn stairs. *Remember the emergency protocols, Joseph,* he thought. *You've strayed enough from procedure as it is.* With one year remaining of seminary school and only a few months of field training, it was still difficult to think of himself in the same terms as the others. Unlike them, he'd never intended to become a priest, let alone a soldier. His degrees were in pre-medical science and psychology, not the preternatural. He'd been very much in love, even engaged to be married. It was shocking how much one's life could change in a matter of moments. His parents, siblings and friends weren't aware of the true nature of his new vocation or the reasons behind it. If he told them demons and fallen angels walked the earth unnoticed by all except for an unlucky few, they would've had him committed—well, again, and on a more permanent basis.

1

The Order of Milites Dei had saved him in more ways than one.

Careful and quiet wins out. Stay calm. Don't do anything rash. The enemy doesn't know you're here.

Because you were ordered to guard the entrance, you idiot. Don't be rash? Have you not already been so? Guilt tugged at his heart. He'd been a member of the Order for almost six months. This was his first field assignment and here he was disobeying orders like one of those angry young men the Americans made so many films about lately. *You're thirty-two, Joseph. Far too old for this kind of thing.* However, Father Drager had missed his last radio check-in. And the jittery feeling in his gut told him something was very wrong. Hadn't Father Jackson encouraged him to trust his instincts? So it was that Joseph found himself abandoning his post to radio Waterford. As a result another Guardian unit would arrive within twenty minutes.

You should've stayed at your post. The others are prepared for this. You aren't.

What if twenty minutes is too late?

What if I've done something stupid?

Even with the aid of a flashlight, it was too dark to see more than a few feet ahead. The light-beam trembled on the stone steps. He took a deep breath to steady himself and pressed on. The long dagger's leather grip felt reassuring in his right hand. His mouth was dry, and his senses seemed sharper than usual. This close to the Irish coast the chilled subterranean air reeked of sour earth and stagnant sea water. Moisture dripped, echoing in the otherwise silent darkness. Each step down seemed to give the shadows more solidity. The flashlight's beam dimmed as if the darkness was feeding off the light. He shook the flashlight, and the batteries inside rattled. The sound was huge. Pointing the flashlight back down the passage, the small circle of yellowish light brightened and revealed a section of bare earth floor at the bottom of the crude stairs. He edged down the last steps with his back to the wall. Searching for possible enemies, he waited until he was sure it was safe before proceeding into the orphanage's cramped root cellar. He looked down at the floor and stopped.

A small child's coat lay discarded in a heap. The faded pale blue wool was torn and stained with blood. Given the briefing, he shouldn't have been surprised. Still, it was a shock. He swallowed the sudden rush of anger and willed his heart to slow.

Demons. Spawn of fallen angels.

Empty shelves lined the walls. A crude wooden door was half hidden by a filthy curtain. He moved closer and paused to listen. Switching the flashlight to his knife hand, he gently tugged the door open left-handed. The hinges made very little sound as he slipped through. He returned the flashlight to his left hand and found himself in a primitive hallway with four doors—two on each side—nearest to the entrance. Peering inside the first on the left, he discovered it was being used as a supply cupboard. A shovel, broom, and several buckets as well as coiled rope and rolls of thick tape were neatly arranged against the wall. Cleaning supplies and jars of murky unknowable liquids were stacked on the shelves. He entered the second little room on the left and was almost overcome with the stench of human excrement. The room was empty but for a set of child-sized manacles fixed to chains bolted into the stone wall. A bucket in the corner was the source of the stink. That and the dark stains in the hard-packed dirt floor were all that remained of the room's former occupant. Narrow lines had been repeatedly clawed into the earth around the steel drain sunk into the floor, traces left by small bloody fingers. Combined with the coat, the scene was too easy to imagine.

He fled the room, eyes stinging. He leaned against the closed door and wiped his face in an attempt to rid himself of the images. He'd been warned, but he hadn't thought it would hit him this hard. He swallowed his emotions—*now isn't the time*—and wiped his face again, centering on the reality of beard stubble scraping against his palm. *Calm yourself. Think of the others. Think of Mary.* With a last steadying breath, he nodded to himself and then investigated the other two rooms. They contained trash and clothing remnants. A half-burned doll stared up out of the mess. Still disturbed by what he'd found earlier, he purposely didn't study the contents—merely checked to see if either room was occupied and continued on.

The rough corridor appeared to join a naturally formed tunnel located underneath the orphanage. Sharp, man-made cuts gave way to smooth water-worn walls. Ten feet down the passage another harrowing scream raked his nerves. "Oh, Jesus! No!"

Cruel laughter echoed up from the end of the hallway.

Demons will prey upon your darkest fears. He closed his eyes and swallowed his terror again. It tasted of bile.

A majority of what he knew about the Fallen consisted of what he'd read and heard from the others. His only actual experience had been that fateful night, years ago. In truth, it hadn't lasted long. Others had more harrowing stories. Everyone within the Order had a tale to tell—if it could be told at all. The Order only recruited those whose lives had already been destroyed by demons or their spawn.

He kept his pace slow and careful. Dingy light flickered ahead, and now he could hear the whispering roar of butane camp lanterns and the distant boom of the surf slamming the cliffs outside along with the sounds of the enemy intent upon torture. The ground had grown damp and felt slightly sticky under the soles of his combat boots. A new smell reached his nose, overshadowing the others. *Fresh blood. Vomit.*

The passage curved to the left. He placed his back against the left wall and put away the flashlight before continuing to inch forward. The rough surface was cold against his back—even through the thickness of his anorak. Soon he came upon another door. Checking, he found it locked. He was unable to secure it, and so, he moved on. The tunnel walls widened, eventually becoming a cave. He'd gotten almost to the end of the passage when the soft sound of nearby movement froze him in place with a shuddering heart.

Someone grabbed his right arm. Turning, he tensed for a fight. The hand trapping his bicep released it, then made the signal for silence in front of a shadowy face. Joseph got the impression of light military-cropped hair, sharp features, and an aristocratic nose in the gloom. Recognition flooded in along side a surge of relief. *Father Jackson.*

Father Jackson gestured for him to retreat. Joseph followed orders, slowly shifting back down the hallway until he was instructed to stop with a hand signal. He opened his mouth to whisper an explanation, but Father Jackson again signalled for silence.

"We're all that's left, I'm afraid," Father Jackson said, speaking quietly in his ear. "You're a trainee and aren't cleared for field duty. Not yet. Therefore, you've the option to refuse—"

"I'm ready," Joseph whispered. *This is what I've waited for. Ever since Mary—*

"Knew I could count on you," Father Jackson said. A relieved expression flashed across his aquiline features in the dim light. "The door behind us leads to an observation area. Take your position there. I'll handle the situation down here."

"Don't you need my assistance?"

"I need you in that observation room," Father Jackson said. His dark eyes were sharp. "After a count of one hundred, I'll throw a stun grenade. Then I'll go in. If it's necessary, I'll give you a signal when to start firing. Whatever you do, don't reveal your presence unless you absolutely must. Wait for my signal. Understood?"

"But how is that—"

"Am I understood, Probationary Guardian Murray?"

Sighing, Joseph nodded. *He knows what he's doing. You don't.* Frustration tightened his jaw. *Be patient. One day. Soon.*

A passage from the Bible came to mind. *Whoever exacts vengeance will experience the vengeance of the Lord, who keeps strict account of sin.*

A thirst for revenge is the easiest means for a demon to get through to you.

"You're only to observe," Father Jackson said. "It's possible I can handle this alone. If so, I will. Don't take any unnecessary risks. Someone has to survive this mess and report. Where's your rifle?"

Internally, Joseph cursed. "Father Drager told me to leave it in the van. Didn't think it would be necessary when I went back. But I should've—"

"It's all right. None of us expected this."

"I've my pistol." Joseph sheathed the dagger and then drew his 9mm Browning left-handed. Although he'd worked right-handed since his first day in grammar school, he was still a slightly better shot with his left—particularly under stressful conditions. He glanced at his wristwatch. "The range isn't as good as the rifle's but—"

"It's good enough." Father Jackson started to move away.

Joseph stopped him with a hand on his shoulder. "I've radioed for help. They should arrive in ten minutes, Father. It isn't proper procedure but—"

"That was wise. I'm glad you did so." Father Jackson gave him a curt nod of approval and then signalled that he was ready. Holding up his index finger, he started the count. *1–2–3....*

Joseph reached into his pocket and continued the silent count by fingering the beads of his rosary right-handed. He trailed behind his mentor, gun at the ready. When they reached the door leading to the observation room, Father Jackson gave him a silent blessing and then gestured for him to go in. *20–21–22...*

God go with you too, Father, Joseph thought and headed up the tunnel.

The observation room was a small open balcony looking down upon the area below. It also contained a desk, a chair, several television monitors, and the body of a man dressed in a dark suit. His throat had been cut, and the cooling blood was forming a large puddle on the stone floor. Arterial spray coated much of the far wall. *42–43–44....* Looking down at the monitors he felt a chill. One of the screens showed the very hallway he'd just travelled down.

They would've had me too.

He checked his pistol to see it was loaded. Save for the color, the custom-made ammunition appeared normal. However, each silver-coated hollow-point bullet housed a blessed rosary bead made of jet. Taking care not to be seen, Joseph risked peeking over the ledge. He got the impression of a gloomy thirty-foot by fifty-foot room with a tall ceiling, rough concrete floor, pink fiberglass insulation, and half-finished cinderblock walls. *59–60–61....* With the second glance he noted a large white bathtub near where the tunnel emptied into the room. Next to it were several buckets, chains and manacles as well as a coiled water hose. A body lay sprawled in the center of the floor. Based on the clothing, Joseph was fairly certain it was either Father Drager or Father Wright, but the head and face were lost in a mass of gore. Another priest hung suspended by his feet. Joseph wasn't sure whether the man was still alive or not. *86–87–88....* His targets were at his far right, tearing at the hanging priest. Joseph swallowed an urge to kill all three at once and then looked away.

A bright flash lit up the room.

When he peered over the ledge he spied Father Jackson hiding behind the cover provided by the large cast-iron bathtub. He kicked at the tin buckets. They rolled away, banging and clattering against the concrete floor. The men—*Fallen, they're Fallen*—were dressed as orphanage attendants. One wore a priest's collar. However, the words they shouted at Father Jackson were foul and in Latin. New to the Order and the priesthood, Joseph wasn't quite proficient enough in Latin yet to translate. He had a feeling he didn't really want to understand anyway.

Father Jackson aimed his pistol around the edge of the tub, squeezing the trigger twice in quick succession. One of the Fallen dropped. Its screams of agony filled up the room and echoed through the tunnels. Joseph watched the demon convulse on the concrete until its body dissolved into so much ash and smoke.

"Stop this, priest!" The demon's voice was heavily accented with Eastern European and difficult to understand, but the force of command behind it was powerful enough that it gave Joseph a start. Although tall, its back was bent with a large hunch, and its movements were short and jerky like that of an animal's. Unnatural. "You are alone. We have your friend. Do you not see this?"

The other remaining demon rotated the hanging priest on the rope so that his bloodied and bruised face was revealed.

It's Father Drager, Joseph thought.

Father Drager's shirt was gone, and blood oozed from several wounds in his arms, stomach, and chest. One arm hung at a bad, twisted angle. He was breathing and flinched when the man with the Eastern European accent placed a curved knife to his throat, but his eyes were wide and blind with internal horror.

"Put down your weapons, or I will kill him," the taller demon said.

"You have no hope of leaving this place. Reinforcements are on the way," Father Jackson said.

"Reinforcements?" The tall demon in the priest's collar laughed. "Isn't that wonderful? More human fodder." It stepped toward Father Jackson. "So fragile. So easy to manipulate." It muttered something under its breath. Once again, Joseph couldn't understand the words—this time because he couldn't hear. "You and your friend on the rope will be long dead. Or...." It cocked its head as if listening. "Ahhhh, I see." It held out a hand and muttered something again. "Some things can't be forgiven. Stand, and together, we'll make everyone pay."

Father Jackson stood.

"Drop your weapons," the tall demon said.

To Joseph's horror, he watched as Father Jackson did exactly that. *They use your weaknesses against you,* Joseph thought. A chill shivered through him, and he finally understood why Father Jackson had sent him upstairs.

Kill the half-demon first. Joseph settled into position, assuming a two-handed stabilizing grip on the pistol and then carefully aimed the Browning at the Fallen armed with the dagger. He didn't want to risk missing. He was near the limits of the pistol's range. So, he aimed for the chest. *I can do this.* He'd scored quite high in marksmanship from the start, surprising even himself. However, this was the first time he'd actually pointed a weapon at a human be—*Fallen. It's a demon. It isn't human.* He took a deep breath, hesitating for an instant. *This is it. There is no going back after this. I'll have taken a life.* He thought of the worst night of his life in spite of himself—*this is why I lived and she didn't*—and slowly squeezed the trigger.

The effect was instantaneous. The recoil sent a shock up his left wrist and arm. At the same time, the creature stumbled. Bright red blood splashed the wall behind it. Its knife fell away from Father Drager's throat and clattered to the floor. Joseph didn't wait. He placed two more shots—a second one in the chest and one in the head—then changed targets. The full-blooded Fallen whirled, searching for the source of the shots. There wasn't much time. Joseph knew he'd be spotted in seconds. If the thing could control Father Jackson so easily, then he was certainly no match for it. Joseph steadied himself as best he could and fired another four rounds. The first went wide. The second clipped the demon on the shoulder. The last two struck home, creating dark patches on the creature's chest.

Six shots remaining.

The demon looked up at him and grinned. Joseph fired twice more, hitting the creature again in the chest. It laughed. Someone screamed. Father Jackson hurled himself at the thing. Unwilling to risk being controlled or shooting Father Jackson, Joseph lifted the barrel of the Browning and dropped behind the balcony wall. He scurried in a crouch to a new position and peered over the ledge.

Father Jackson had brought the thing down with a full body tackle. He lifted a fist and punched the demon in the face. The fallen angel didn't resist. It laughed as its blackening face smoldered. Father Jackson hit it again and again. Its laughter didn't cease even as the smoke thickened and dark red embers flickered underneath its cracking skin.

Joseph scanned the area. Unable to spy any other targets, he decided it was safe enough to risk leaving his position. *Something is wrong.* He sprinted as fast as he could. By the time he reached Father Jackson the demon was a pile of stinking ash and burned clothing. Father Jackson knelt in the dust, blistered hands clenched around fistfuls of filthy rags.

"Father?" Joseph asked. There were three doors along the wall to his left and two more on the right. He needed to secure them, but he was worried about Father Jackson. "It's gone now. Dead. Father?"

Father Jackson turned and wiped his face with a wince, leaving a smudge of foul ash on his wet cheeks. His eyes were distant. He blinked.

"Father?"

Father Jackson's eyes began to slowly focus. "Joseph?"

"Yes, Father. It's me."

Father Jackson blinked again. Then he shook his head as if to clear it. "Yes." He coughed and sniffed and wiped his hands on his shirt. Again he flinched. "Have you secured the perimeter?" He stumbled to his feet. The mask of professionalism had shifted back into place. His clothes were thick with dark grey dust but not burned. Apparently, the only skin affected was in direct contact with the demon.

"No, Father. I—"

A loud crash from the original passage caused them both to turn. The thump-thump of heavy footsteps were accompanied by the rattle and clink of military-grade weapons and equipment. "Father Drager? Father Jackson? Are you here?"

"Here!" Father Jackson attempted to slap the dust off and winced with a hiss of pain. Gazing down at himself, he sighed. "Help me see to Father Drager."

Joseph nodded. *They use your weaknesses to control you.* So he'd been told. Now he knew.

Four Guardians emerged from the passage. Two rushed to treat Father Jackson's burned hands and help with Father Drager while the others began a search of the area. It took some time, but they were finally able to get Father Drager free without hurting him. His arm was badly broken, and he'd suffered a number of bad cuts. None appeared bad enough to account for the state of catatonic shock, however. He stared, sightless into a distant past or a horror-filled future, alive but unresponsive. A stretcher was sent for and brought in. One of the others presided over Father Wright, giving the mangled corpse the Last Rites. While Father Drager was being tended, Joseph decided to help investigate the other rooms.

He entered the remaining unchecked room and regretted it almost at once. The stench was terrific. Coughing, he struggled to maintain control over his stomach. Four children blinked up at him from the darkness, their frail hands held up to shield their eyes from the abrupt invasion of light. They appeared to range in ages from four to twelve or thirteen. Starved, half-naked, filthy and bruised, it was almost impossible to tell boys from girls. Each was chained to the wall by the ankles. He would've mistaken them for human but for the predator's eyes reflecting the light pouring into the tiny room with a reddish-yellow glow. He was about to turn away when he spied a silvery sheen to the third child's eyes. Thinking it might be a trick of the light, he looked closer. It was subtle and could've easily been missed, but the silver glint remained. He studied and compared the other children.

"The light hurts," a six-year-old said, shying away.

"Shhh. I'm sorry. It will be all right. I need to see your eyes," Joseph said.

"Don't you believe him," the oldest boy said, lisping through broken teeth.

Father Murray discovered that three of the four children's eyes reacted in the same odd way—again, only if he searched for it and only if the light struck their irises at a particular angle. However, the last child's didn't. *Interesting. I wonder if anyone has noticed this before?* The boy with the broken teeth appeared to be the oldest, and he stared back at Joseph with a face filled with hate.

They aren't human, Joseph thought, knowing full well each of their bruised faces would be with him to the end of his days in spite of that fact. *But does that excuse what was done to them?*

As if in answer to the questions rising in Joseph's mind, one of the other Guardians spoke behind him. "Demon spawn. All of them."

Jesus Christ, look at them, Joseph thought. *Does it matter what they are? They suffer. They feel pain.* The Fallen had been present in this place. So it had been reported. *But the creatures weren't in charge. Who could knowingly do this to them? And beneath one of our own orphanages?* He was about to voice his objections when the doorway darkened.

"What is that trainee doing here?"

Joseph turned to face an angry Guardian with greying brown hair, a thin nose and square face. The accent was definitely Limerick. The Order of Milites Dei operated in secrecy. Therefore, there was no such thing as a uniform for Guardians nor recognizable markers of rank. The priest's attitude was enough to command respect, however.

"I'm Probationary Guardian Joseph Murray, Father," Joseph said. "I've been assigned to Guardian Jackson."

The priest from Limerick glared at him. "Benjamin?"

It took several minutes, but Father Jackson finally appeared. Both of his hands were swathed in thick bandages.

"Yes, Monsignor Paul," Father Jackson said.

"Why did you bring a trainee into a combat area?" Monsignor Paul asked.

Joseph watched Father Jackson's face for some clue as to his fate. *I disobeyed my orders. Will I be barred?*

"With respect, Monsignor Paul, I don't believe that now is the appropriate time or place for this discussion," Father Jackson said.

"I understand he was ordered to stand guard at the entrance to the root cellar," Monsignor Paul said.

Father Jackson lowered his head. "That was the original order given. However, circumstances—"

"Did you order him to leave his post?"

Father Jackson sighed. "He took it upon himself to do so."

"Very well," Monsignor Paul said. "We will address this issue later. For now, Probationary Guardian Joseph Murray, you will be placed on suspension. Upon completion of this field assignment, you will report to the facility in Waterford for an examination and a tribunal. Understand?"

Joseph felt the blood drain from his upper body down into his feet. *A tribunal?*

"With respect, isn't that somewhat harsh? He saved my life as well as the life of Father Drager."

"Enough," Monsignor Paul said. "We will discuss this later. For now, he'll assist with the clean up." With that, Monsignor Paul turned and walked away.

"Father, I don't understand—"

Father Jackson lowered his voice. "Joseph, there is more going on here than you know." He sighed. "We'll discuss it later. Try not to worry. For now, we've much to do."

The orphanage was evacuated, the staff removed for questioning, and the evidence in the dungeon below destroyed. So it happened that an hour before dawn, Joseph stood exhausted in the field outside and watched the orphanage burn. He tried not to think of the blood on his hands or the faces of the ones laid to rest. The *Gardai Siochána*, as the constabulary were called in the south, would report the victims as casualties of a tragic fire caused by faulty electrical wiring. *It was a mercy,* Joseph reassured himself. Upwind from the smoke, he breathed in clean sea air and struggled with doubts. *A mercy.*

Movement in the flickering semi-darkness caught his eye, and he spotted a wounded boy fleeing the burning building. The boy stopped, his singed face reflecting the flames of terror and hate. Joseph looked into the lad's eyes and recognized him as the oldest boy from that tiny room. It was then that Joseph understood something about himself. They stared at one another for seven heartbeats—the boy, poised to sprint for his life, and Joseph, waiting for some sort of sign from God. At the last, Joseph was unable to stand the thought of another murder. He looked the other way while the boy escaped into the open field.

Joseph told no one, but every night he dreamed.

Chapter 1

Somewhere Outside Ballynahatty,
County Down, Northern Ireland
November 1977

L iam Kelly stood in the middle of a starlit dooryard with his hands in the air and cursed the day he'd met Father Murray.

"What are you doing here?" the farmer asked from shadows cast by the light pouring out of an open cottage door.

As threats went, the hayfork in the farmer's palsied hands could be categorized in the vicinity of worrisome. In Liam's specific case, however, it could be argued whether the real danger was in the old iron used by four generations of farmers or the remote possibility of tetanus. Regardless, both risks were considerably outranked by the three hastily dressed men lurking in the shadows near the barn—three men who obviously didn't belong on a farm.

"Sorry to be disturbing you. I lost my way, is all," Liam said, again cursing Father Murray, not that the situation was actually the priest's fault. Liam was the one who'd decided to get some air. Naturally, he'd been in a rage at the time. He'd argued with Father Murray about the current plan to forge a peace agreement between the Catholic Church and the Fey. At the last, Father Murray had been giving him shite about how he, Liam,

13

needed to take control of his life and stop running from one bad situation and into another. Now that Liam had cooled off he was beginning to rethink matters.

The presence of deadly weapons tended to do that to him.

"On your way somewhere, is it?" the youngest of the three asked and stepped into the shaft of light. It darkened his features and outlined his form in gold. He held a Kalashnikov at the ready and was wearing a long brown leather coat with a fur collar the likes of which would've easily fit in on an American television program featuring pimps named after affectionate ursines. The lad looked to be about sixteen. *Which,* Liam thought, *would explain the atrocious taste in outdoor apparel.*

For fuck's sake, he hasn't outgrown the spots on his face.

"Do we know you?" the spotty boy asked. His accent made Liam think of Derry.

"Don't think you do," Liam said. *At least, I fucking hope not,* he thought. *Things are complicated enough as it is.* Although Derry had been home for most of his life, he'd been away for five years if one counted the prison time. He hoped that absence, combined with the new beard and punk-cropped hair, would serve as a sufficient disguise in the darkness.

Against his better judgment, he gave the men closer scrutiny. He didn't recognize any of them, which was good. It was a cold night, but he could see that one of them was barefoot and the second hadn't had time to button his shirt and coat. The third, the speaker, was fully dressed and alert.

The sentry, Liam thought.

"And what is your name, then?" The spotty boy's voice cracked with the tension, making him sound about twelve.

Although there was little in the way of light, Liam made out part of a tattoo on the tallest man's chest. It appeared to be a banner. The script scrawled inside was impossible to read—half concealed as it was, but Liam decided to bet his life that if it contained a date, that date was Easter 1916 and not July 1690. Liam addressed the two men in the shadows and attempted to use the Belfast in his voice to camouflage the Derry. "I'm Liam from Andytown." Liam was a common enough name among Catholics, and Andersonstown was a Nationalist estate.

"You're a long fucking way from West Belfast, son." It came as no surprise that the older, more authoritative voice came from the taller man with the tattoo. His tone was hard and neutral with a hint of disapproval but that was to be expected.

There'll be more of them. All are sure to be armed, Liam thought. *So, where are they?* "Aye. So what?"

"And what's your business here, Liam from Andytown?" the authoritative man with the tattoo asked. His clipped Derry working-class dialect matched the kid's.

The real question was, what were the three men doing here? Were they paramilitaries or were they smugglers? They weren't Loyalists otherwise they'd have shot him dead the instant he'd revealed himself for a Catholic. On the other hand, the likelihood of a Republican recruit getting the piss knocked out of him for dressing like an American pimp was high—too high to make either the Provisional or even the Official IRA a sensible option. Liam glanced again at the boy in the fur-collared coat. His face was set in a determined expression.

This is going to go bad, Liam thought. "Been visiting a friend a few miles from here. Couldn't sleep. Went for a walk. Took a short cut through your fields, and got turned around. As I said, I didn't mean to disturb you. I'm sorry, sir."

"He's seen us," the spotty boy said. "He'll have to be done for."

Well, now. Aren't you the wee hard man? Liam swallowed the retort. At twenty-two, technically he wasn't much older than the boy. *But Jesus, was I ever that much of a tosser?* Liam had to admit he probably had been and possibly still was. He had, after all, walked straight into this mess. *Me and my fucking temper.* Father Murray had warned him not to leave, but he hadn't listened. That was generally the way of things, and generally, the way Liam liked it. On this side of the situation, however, it seemed a wee bit predictable. Once, he wouldn't have cared, but lately he was considering the advantage in other behavioral options.

Will you look at that? Maturity, that is. Mary Kate would've laughed, but Mary Kate wasn't there. She was dead, and he was about to join her if he didn't talk fast. "Look, mate, I don't know or care who you are, or what you're doing. Let me go back to where I came from, and I'll leave you to your business."

"Shut it, you," the spotty boy said.

A big lorry pulled up to the gate and stopped. Liam's stomach did a queasy jolt when he saw that its headlights were off. The sentry signaled to the driver, and the gate let out a groan as it was pushed open by one of the lorry's passengers. Liam mentally cursed a third time when the man with the tattoo signaled to the others with a quick glance and a nod.

"Come with me," the spotty boy said.

My fucking luck, Liam thought with his heart slamming in his ears. He wondered whether they were smuggling whiskey, cigarettes or guns. If he was headed for a bullet in the skull, it'd be nice to know. He took a deep breath as the lorry approached, relying on his unusually powerful sense of smell to glean the answer. *Petrol. Smugglers then. Not paramilitaries.*

Since he'd "retired" from the Provisionals under less than ideal circumstances, he was relieved to have his suspicions confirmed. If they'd turned out to be Provos and found out who he was, they'd contact HQ and then his future—however short—would most likely involve a thorough hiding, a great deal of screaming and a blowtorch for good measure. On the other hand, Provos had a certain reputation even among smugglers. He'd decided to reveal himself for a Provo and pointedly draw the conclusion that it would be best to let him go his way unmolested, when he spotted a Glasgow Rangers stocking cap on one of the men who had hopped out of the truck. Liam's blood froze. *Loyalist smugglers. Shite.*

Before he had time to wonder how he'd been so far wrong something heavy slammed into the side of his head, and the ground came up fast. Dazed, he felt himself lifted but couldn't protest. He watched the gravel and then the grass pass under his dragging feet and contemplated the situation. He discovered he had few feelings on the subject of dying as the two men carried him through a break in the thick hedge at the far end of the dooryard.

"I've no time to be dealing with this. I'm for heading back. So, we're trusting you," one of the men whispered. "Don't be fucking this up. You hear?"

"Yes, sir."

"Do it fast. Get back to the lorry. We'll tidy up after."

Liam wondered if he'd see Mary Kate again. The prospect was somewhat comforting. His wife had been dead for well over a year, and although the sharp pain of grief was fading, there were still moments when the guilt and loneliness ambushed him. A strange sort of confusion set in. Not long ago he'd wanted nothing more than to die and couldn't. It was odd that his time should come now when his prospects were better, and for doing something so stupid as not watching where he was going.

Feeling the curious emptiness in the back of his skull—a void he'd fought so hard for much of his adult life to create—he suddenly regretted the lack. *Father Murray's little hypnosis experiment would take now of all times.* Liam considered calling the monster up out of his subconscious where it'd been banished for the time being but wasn't confident he could, regardless of Father Murray insisting it was possible. Liam decided against the attempt when he remembered the rest of the priest's plan and how it was likely to end. *Best to die now and get it over with, then.*

"This will do."

They'd dragged him to a secluded area shielded by a rock wall and the thick hedge. It was far enough from the house that the others couldn't see what was happening and close enough that reinforcements were at hand if called. He was dropped, and the older man left. Liam couldn't help remembering the last time he'd been in a similar situation—only he'd been the one holding the gun and his best mate, Oran, had been facing the bullet. Liam rolled onto his back. A piercing headache punched its way through the numbness. His palms were stinging. The side of his face felt cool and sticky. *Blood.* He blinked, gazing up into the night sky. In the northeast, the light from Belfast overwhelmed the stars. There were no clouds, the rain having stopped earlier in the day.

Clear night in spite of the cold. No moon, he thought. He discovered that he felt nothing—no fear, no anger—at the prospect of dying, which seemed a wee bit unusual upon closer inspection.

The spotty boy with the Kalashnikov kicked him. "Up on your knees, taig."

At that moment Liam's temper flared up, and he clamped down on an urge to fall upon his captor and rip the boy's throat out. The anger transformed from red hot lava to polar ice in a second. "This is fucking pointless. I said I'll not tell anyone what you are doing here."

"Shut up! Get on your knees!"

"That's a bleeding automatic rifle, mate. You hit me with that thing it'll make a real mess."

"Why do you think we dragged you out here? Get on your knees, or I'll plug you now."

Fucker. Liam gave an exaggerated sigh. "Fine. Fine. I merely wanted to point out that a man with a coat as nice as that might not want to muck it up." He didn't understand why he was taking the piss. The boy wouldn't react well, but Liam couldn't stop himself. He staggered to his feet and considered his options, but it was difficult to think past the ache in his head and the frozen rage.

The boy paused and frowned. "Turn around. Then get on your knees. Now. I'll not tell you again." The rifle was shoved into Liam's chest for emphasis.

The damp cold seeped through Liam's jeans as the wet grass soaked his knees. The icy rifle barrel was balanced against the back of his neck. Without thinking, he jerked away and was rewarded with a sharp blow to the back of the head. Pain exploded behind his eyes.

"Don't move."

The gun barrel was replaced, and Liam attempted not to shiver lest sudden movement cause the gun to go off. He sensed what was most certainly the boy removing his precious leather coat one-handed. If Liam was to do something to save himself, now was the time, but with the rifle barrel where it was, all the kid needed to do was twitch and Liam would be decapitated in a stream of bullets. *Shite.* He'd been counting on the wee fuck bollocksing up. *Calm yourself. You're alive yet. There's still time. Think.* His skull remained empty of all but the feel of the gun barrel, the doubled pain and the drumming of his heart.

A gust of wind jostled the hedge. Liam heard something else too—stealthy movement in the dark. A chill went through him, and his stomach did a lazy flip. *They've sent someone to check up on the wee shite. Fuck. Well, that's that.* Taking a slow careful breath, cold, sharp air filled his lungs as he attempted to remember a final prayer. It's what one did, right? Pray? He almost didn't see the point. Filled with cold, his chest hurt. *Our Father, who art in heaven—*

The ache in his head thudded with the beat of his heart, and his senses grew impossibly sharp. He again looked up into the sky. Faded as they were, the stars were beautiful, and as he watched, a lone rebel unbolted itself from its place in the firmament and streaked across the blackness in a graceful arc. As last sights went, it really wasn't bad. He took in another slow breath to prepare himself and almost tasted grass, damp earth and the spotty boy's stinking aftershave mixed with the smell of stale cigarettes.

Cigarettes. He opened his mouth to request a smoke—an attempt at one last chance for life—when he heard a soft sound, and the gun was snatched from the back of his neck. He turned just as the spotty boy dropped to the ground.

"I ainm Danu, cad atá ar siúl agat?" In Danu's name, what are you doing?

Liam turned his head to see the speaker. A tall man with shoulder-length blond hair exited the hedge. There was no point of entry or exit at the spot where he had appeared. This, of course, wasn't the only thing that was out of the ordinary about him. He was also dressed in clothes that belonged in a university history textbook and was armed with a bronze-tipped spear. A round shield looped over one shoulder by the leather strap completed the ensemble.

Liam feigned a casual attitude regarding his uncle's dramatic entrance while a rush of emotions flooded his brain—anger, disappointment and shame. Gazing down at the spotty boy, he asked in Irish, "Did you kill him?"

"What would I do a stupid thing like that for?" Sceolán asked. "It's asleep, he is. He'll be fine when he wakes."

Staggering to his feet, Liam gave the limp form two good solid kicks. "Perhaps not as fine as all that."

"Stop that now," Sceolán said. "We'll be late as it is."

"You took your time in coming." Picking up the rifle, Liam searched his former captor's pockets for a second clip and was rewarded. He pocketed it and slung the Kalashnikov over his shoulder.

"Was looking for you back at the priest's house where you'd called out. If you'd had any patience at all I'd have found you there and not here on the verge of getting your brains blown out. Crossed foolish of you. You are half mortal, you know. There's no promise you'll come back from it, and you'll not impress the Fianna, acting the hot-headed wean."

Liam hid his embarrassment and anger by glaring at the ground.

"You've no worry. I'll not breathe a word of this foolishness. Although, I should, and the tongue-lashing you would get for it would serve you right."

Accepting the cloth his uncle held out, Liam wiped the blood from the side of his face. "Aye, well… thanks."

"You're welcome." Sceolán pointed to the rifle. "I thought you'd retired from the fighting."

"The wee fuck will have an easier time explaining if the gun is missing. They might not even shoot him." Liam straightened and then joined Sceolán at the stone wall. "Anyway, it may come in handy."

Sceolán turned, giving him a raised eyebrow. "I thought this was to be a negotiation?"

"Aye. Well, I've had dealings with the Bishop's lads before. They're not much for listening without strong motivation."

Liam watched Sceolán scramble up and over the wall, exhibiting a grace that wouldn't normally have been seen in someone his age, but then, a mortal Uncle Sceolán's age was normally moldering in a thousand-year-old burial mound. Liam climbed the wall with far less skill and ease. His collar bone was still healing, and it ached from time to time—particularly if he wasn't careful and, truth be told, he hadn't been careful over the past hour or so.

"Can I ask you a question?" Liam asked, finally working up the nerve. There wasn't much time. Soon he'd be living in what equated to a prison cell for an indefinite period of time, being examined by surgeons who weren't certain he was human. When he thought about it, that wasn't terribly different from Long Kesh, and here he was volunteering for it. He shuddered. "There's something I need to know. Was the reason I'd called for you."

Sceolán nodded.

"Do you dream?" Liam asked.

Pausing, Sceolán glanced over his shoulder with an amused expression. "What kind of a question is that?"

Liam felt his cheeks burn. He didn't know the simplest things about his father's people beyond the stories his aunt Sheila had told him, and so far, more than half of those had been proven to be either outright falsehoods or exaggerations.

Sceolán shrugged. "As much as anyone, I suppose."

"When someone like you—I mean, me—us…. Are they only dreams?"

"Depends. It could be, or it could be a portent or a message."

Liam squinted into the darkness and debated whether or not to go on. He took a deep breath. "How do you know if it's important?"

"By the feel of it in my skull."

"Oh."

Sceolán gave him another long look. "Is that all?"

Liam wanted to continue. An entire catalog of questions had formed a queue in his brain over the past two weeks. Unfortunately, there hadn't been an appropriate moment for personal questions the three times he'd seen his father since the incident at Raven's Hill—or so Liam had told himself. Now certainly wasn't the time. In any case, he'd already made a fool of himself twice and that was enough for one evening. "Aye. That's all."

"Then I've a question for you as well." Sceolán continued on a few paces before saying anything. "I'll not go against Bran or you in this peace agreement of yours. But I will say you two have far more belief in it succeeding than I do."

"I wouldn't be so sure."

"Is that so?"

"Aye. Well, I wasn't staring down the honor of meeting an Inquisitor when we first discussed it, was I?" *At least not without the monster to even the odds if needed,* Liam thought. It'd been the main reason he'd argued with Father Murray. Dangerous as it was, Liam didn't like the idea of going in without the ability to shape shift. However, he couldn't always control himself when he became the Hound and that had been the very reason why Father Murray had insisted on keeping the hypnotic muzzle in place when it'd proved to work.

Sceolán stopped where he was. "Are you saying you don't trust your friend, the priest?"

"I trust him." Liam paused. "For the most part, but there are about a hundred different ways this thing could go wrong. Not the least of which is me ending on a dissection table or in the Kesh."

"You don't have to give yourself over to them. We can call the whole thing off."

Liam watched his uncle navigate around a cowpat in the pitch black field—a thing no mortal could've done—and was reassured. Not being the only one who could see in the dark made him feel normal. "Terms of the truce. Better me than one of you. I'm half mortal. Father Murray says the Inquisitor will show restraint for that reason alone."

"Are you certain of that?"

Nervous, Liam paused and combed his fingers through his hair. "To tell you the truth... well... no."

"Then don't do it."

"The Church must have their proof that the Fey are not one in the same as the Fallen. Without that, they'll never stop the killing. Think of the weans they've murdered." *My own included.* Liam wanted to be angry, but nothing came. He sensed a whisper stir in the back of his brain. Whether it was the spark of rage or the beast in its uneasy rest he couldn't be sure. He felt odd. *Too distant.* The emptiness was disconcerting.

"Was this insanity your idea or the priest's?"

Best get this done with, Liam thought. "Father Murray's." He stole a glance at his watch and began to walk faster.

"I don't like it."

"He'll be with me the entire time. Wouldn't agree to it otherwise."

"What good will that do? It's not as if the man has any authority among them."

"True enough," Liam said. "But he can summon my father and therefore, the rest of you if it should happen that I'm not able to do so myself. I don't think the Bishop would want the Fianna showing up for Sunday mass ready for a fight."

Uncle Sceolán looked thoughtful. "They could quietly get rid of you both while you're in their hands. Catch your Father Murray unaware. Wouldn't take much to make it look like you killed the priest. Problem solved. No need for inconvenient truths or admissions of guilt. Everything back to the way it was. Simpler."

"I really wish you wouldn't say things like that."

"Aye, well." Uncle Sceolán hefted his spear. "I been at the warring a long time, you know?"

Taking a route parallel to the Ballynahatty lane and through fallow hay fields, Liam followed Sceolán to the northeast edge of the Giant's Ring—the agreed-upon meeting place. It consisted of a flattened hill with a four-meter-high earthen ridge running in a two hundred-meter circle around the top. The grass was worn bare around the inside and close to the ancient ridge where the local people had held horse races in the 1800s.

According to Uncle Sceolán, the Fey still did so. Near the center was a small tomb formed from standing stones. The Ring was bordered on the outside by a few trees, the hay field, a car park to the east, and a small but dense wood to the south. The place fairly vibrated with power. Liam could feel the tingling of it radiating through his feet and his skin, and the air grew heavier the closer he came.

Shouts echoed across the empty field.

"Sounds like they started without us," Liam said.

"We'd best get there before the fighting breaks out." Uncle Sceolán winked. "Didn't think Cathal was going to lose that bet this soon."

Trotting to the northern-most entrance, Liam passed through the break in the earthen bank. A camp table was set up near the rock tomb and a few papers rested in a neat arrangement on top. At the moment both table and papers had been abandoned and men were shouting and gesticulating at one another to the side. It took Liam several seconds to spy Father Murray in the cluster of modern Catholic priests surrounding two ancient Irish warriors. He was standing in the middle of the verbal fray with his hands held out as if shielding the two Fey warriors behind him. In spite of the stated agreement of no more than three representatives to each side, Liam counted no less than twelve heavily armed priests in addition to Father Murray and the Bishop.

Fucking typical, that, Liam thought.

However, it was obvious that the Fey had kept their word. Liam's father, Bran, stood at the center of the mob, back to back with a member of the Fianna Liam didn't recognize. Liam wasn't sure who Father Murray thought he was attempting to protect—whether it was the Church's assassins or the Fey warriors. Either way, Liam had the feeling Father Murray was going to end up on the bad side of it. Sometimes Liam wondered if the priest had any sense at all.

He attempted to make himself heard over the shouting. "Have you signed the truce already?"

Father Murray turned. "Where have you been? I began to think you'd changed your mind."

"Needed to clear my head. Went for a short run. Got turned around on the way back, but Uncle Sceolán set me to rights," Liam said. "Although, it would've been easy enough to find you by the ruckus. It's a wonder the

Fallen, the British Army or the RUC haven't turned up too." Not that Liam had much faith in the RUC. The Royal Ulster Constabulary operated more like bully boys than police in Liam's experience.

One of the priests burst from the group surrounding the Fey. He was short and had an ugly scar across the bridge of his nose. Limping, he drew a long dagger. Liam remembered the Kalashnikov in time to bring the rifle to bear. Several priests scurried out of the way. Others shouted warnings. There came the clatter of weapons being drawn as the others prepared for the fight. Spotting the rifle at last, the limping priest came to an abrupt stop. "Demon!"

"Evening, Father Dominic," Liam said. "How's the leg?"

Father Dominic muttered something very un-priest-like.

"Liam!" It was Father Murray. "Put down that rifle!"

"Be happy to." Liam poked the barrel of the Kalashnikov at Father Dominic. "However, I wasn't the one who drew first."

One of the other priest-assassins muttered, "As if a blade warrants an automatic weapon."

"Poisoned blade. Therefore, I beg to differ," Liam said and then paused. "Then again, when assessing the danger I should've factored in who was wielding the bloody thing." He shouldered the rifle.

The insult took several heartbeats to register on Father Dominic's face. He growled and charged, raising the dirk. Liam stepped out of the priest's path at the last instant. Father Dominic shot past before stumbling to a halt. He prepared for another charge.

"Bernard!" An older man who Liam assumed was Bishop Avery pushed his way through the protective circle of priests.

Father Dominic's face contorted with rage. "This... creature maimed Father Christopher."

"You ambushed me," Liam said, feeling his anger rise. "I could've killed you, and I didn't."

"Everyone, please," Father Murray said. "This is no way to begin. I thought we agreed to a peaceful meeting?"

Bran stood at the ready, bronze-tipped spear in hand. "It is they who have not kept to their word. Your holy man brought yon army."

Bishop Avery gaped. "Too many times we've been met with treachery—"

"Not at the hands of the Fianna," Uncle Sceolán said, edging his way past angry priests to take his place at Bran's side.

Father Murray sighed. "Look, we'll get nowhere like this. There must be something we can agree upon. Anything?"

"Is there?" Bran asked.

"Ireland will be lost if we refuse to cooperate with one another," Father Murray said. "Can we at least agree to that?"

"We are the Fianna," Uncle Sceolán said, "and we'll not be defeated."

"Then why are you here?" Father Murray asked.

Uncle Sceolán looked to Bran, opened his mouth and then shut it.

Bran straightened. "We are here because there is need. We cannot fight two wars at once."

Uncle Sceolán harrumphed.

The ghost of a smile brushed Bran's lips, and his eyes glittered with what might have been a red reflection. "Well, not with ease."

"And Your Grace?" Father Murray asked.

Bishop Avery sighed. "The situation could be better."

"There. We agree on something. So, please, everyone. Stay calm," Father Murray said. "We're here to talk."

"Put away the blade, Bernard. Now," Bishop Avery said. "Come here."

"Yes, Bernard," Liam said. "Do as you're told."

"Liam, quit it," Father Murray said.

Father Dominic leaned close enough for Liam to smell the whiskey on his breath and whispered, "I'll sort you out later, demon. Best watch yourself." He sheathed the dagger and went to the Bishop.

"Liam, the gun," Father Murray said, holding out a hand. He looked angry, and Liam couldn't help being a wee bit glad.

Bran said, "Best do as he says, son."

"Are you?" Liam asked his father.

Bran glanced at Bishop Avery and then put his spear on the ground. "We are here to negotiate a truce, not start another war. If your Father Murray feels the Bishop is here in earnest, I'll not refuse."

Not seeing another choice, Liam handed the rifle to Father Murray.

"All right, then," Father Murray said once he'd placed the rifle under the table out of easy reach. "Let's begin." He picked up the papers and distributed copies to both Bishop Avery and Bran. "The Roman Catholic Church agrees to a temporary cease-fire between Herself and the Fey for the duration of one week within the confines of the Diocese of Raphoe, Derry, Down and Connor, Armagh, Dromore, Clogher, Kilmore, Ardagh and Clonmacnoise, and Meath."

Bran frowned at the paper in his hand. "What is this? The truce was to include all of Ireland for a month."

"Bishop Avery is only authorized to make this offer for the Archdiocese of Armagh," one of the Church clerks said in a thick Kerry accent.

"I'm giving you my son," Bran said, dropping the agreement onto the table in disgust. "You ask me to risk him for this?"

Father Murray laid a hand on Bran's arm. "A lasting trust is built with small steps."

"He's my son. I'd hardly count that a small step."

"Then have another take his place," Bishop Avery said. "We are offering a hostage in exchange. Father Franklin will go with you. That's all I can offer."

For a brief moment, Liam wondered if he'd be consulted at all or if they'd continue to discuss him as if he weren't present.

Father Murray lowered his voice. "Liam will be safe. I swear it."

Bran turned and gave Liam a long look. "It's your neck. You've the last word. What do you say?"

Here's your chance, Liam thought. *Tell them all to sod off.* He held his father's gaze and thought of Mary Kate, Oran and everyone else who'd suffered. He thought of the baby that would've lived. Mary Kate's baby. *Our son.* It was easier, somehow, to summon up Mary Kate's smile on a child's face. *Daughter. We could've had a daughter.* That ghost of a feeling stirred again inside his chest. It took an instant to recognize it at last, and suddenly nothing else mattered.

"I'm in," Liam said.

Bran nodded, went to the table and signed the truce with the pen Father Murray offered. Looking up from the agreement, Bran stared at Bishop Avery. "If anything happens to my son—if he's harmed in any way, you'll not make old bones. I'll see to it myself. I don't care where you hide. Me and mine will find you. Do you understand me, Robert Avery, priest?"

Bishop Avery swallowed. "I do." And with a nervous pause, he signed the document.

Chapter 2

Belfast, County Antrim, Northern Ireland
November 1977

"Remove your clothes," the Church Inquisitor said.

Liam bit down an urge to tell the man to go fuck himself and settled on a hard stare instead.

It was small relief that the Inquisitor looked nowhere near as intimidating as his title implied. He was average height, small in build and although he'd tucked it behind his ears, it was obvious he hadn't cut his hair in months. A stained lab coat partially covered his clerical shirt and priest collar. The black badge pinned above the right pocket was engraved with the name "Father Gerard Conroy, MD" in white block letters. His freshly shaved face was carefully set in an expression that could at worst be described as professional curiosity. There were no blood-red hoods, hot pokers or thumbscrews in evidence. However, a quick inventory of the medical tray the man was holding caused Liam to revise his initial impression.

He waited five rushed heartbeats in an effort to hide his anxiety before looking to Father Murray. "Is it to be another strip search, then?" In spite of reassurances that a thorough search was standard procedure when entering a high-security facility, Liam had struggled to get through the pat down without acting on the urge to kill someone.

"This is a medical examination. Undressing is standard procedure," Father Conroy said with a friendly smile clearly intended for Father Murray's benefit.

Liam caught the severe lines beneath the Inquisitor's facade at once.

The Inquisitor set the tray on the built-in desk to the right. The desk, along with the examination table and the wheeled office chair, comprised all the furnishings in the room. "I need baseline vital statistics. A comparison will be made to those of a human's."

"Get my records from the infirmary at Long Kesh or Malone, if you've the need," Liam said.

"Liam—"

"Everyone knew me for a mortal until a few weeks ago. Including myself. If there were a difference a surgeon could catch, they would've noticed long before now."

"He does have a point," Father Murray said.

Father Conroy frowned. "Records can be falsified."

"Why the fuck would a prison surgeon go to the trouble?" Liam asked.

Father Murray shot him a stern glance, and Liam once more reminded himself to keep his temper in check.

"Father Conroy is due respect," Father Murray whispered. "He has done nothing to warrant—"

"I know. I know. Sorry, Father." Liam left it up to interpretation as for which priest the apology was intended.

Father Conroy spoke to Father Murray again. "I must have the data before we begin."

"Begin what, exactly?" Liam asked.

Father Conroy blinked. "The process of verifying the truth, of course."

"And what truth is that?" Liam asked.

"Liam, please. This is why we're here," Father Murray said, pushing his horn-rimmed glasses up the bridge of his nose.

Again taking in the medical tray with its store of needles, surgical knives and bandages, Liam said, "I didn't agree to being cut up like a wee lab rat."

"That isn't the plan," Father Murray said. "Why would you think such a thing?"

"Oh, I don't know. This is only a medical exam at the hands of a priest who calls himself an 'Inquisitor.' A man, I might add, who has more than a few scalpels at hand," Liam said, allowing his anger to seep out in sarcasm. "Why should I anticipate a problem?"

"I must collect samples," Father Conroy said in a mild tone.

Liam bolted off the examination table and set his back to the farthest wall. He then gave the Inquisitor the two fingers. "Sample this."

"Liam, calm yourself. This is for the peace agreement," Father Murray said, his voice acquiring the all-too-familiar tone seemingly reserved for frightened children and out-of-control idiots.

"I won't be cut up. Not even for the peace." Scanning the white cinderblock walls, Liam realized the examination room lacked everyday objects one might normally find in a doctor's office—charts, cabinets, photos of family. It occurred to Liam that the room also lacked anything that might be used in defense. *There's always a scalpel. If I can get to one of the fucking things before he does.* A surge of panic tensed his muscles. *And the chair. There's the chair.*

"I'm prepared to drug it—I mean, him." Father Conroy corrected himself when Father Murray opened his mouth to protest. Reaching for his tray, Father Conroy picked up a pre-prepared syringe loaded with a clear substance.

Liam scanned the room for an escape route. They were underground. There were no windows and only the one door. "I'll not let you near me with that—"

"Security can restrain the creature if necessary while I drug it," the Inquisitor said, moving toward the phone.

Father Murray said, "There's no need."

"Don't call me a fucking creature. I'm Liam Kelly. You'd think you could read that off your fucking charts."

"Liam, this isn't what you think," Father Murray said.

"Why did I let you talk me into this?" Liam edged to the door with his heart slamming in his ears and his stomach rolling. The door lock was a standard deadbolt. He might be able to force it open with a couple of kicks. The idea of throwing his shoulder against it made him wince, but left with no other choice he'd risk re-breaking his collarbone. Unfortunately, the complex was well designed as far as security went. Located underneath a Catholic Church-owned building near Queen's University, the examination room was secure. The only access to the surface was through an elevator guarded by surveillance cameras and manned by armed and combat-trained priests.

Aye. And no one above can hear the screaming from here, either. Awful convenient, that, when you think about it. Liam felt his chest constrict. It became hard to breathe.

Father Murray said, "You're safe here."

"Are you mental?" *Can't defend myself,* Liam thought. *Can't shape-shift. Trapped. Was stupid to have come here.* A powerful need to run tightened his muscles. The reasonable part of himself knew he was over-reacting. Why was he so terrified of an Inquisitor and not the spotty boy with the Kalashnikov? Then it came to him. Loyalist hatred was mundane. Terrible as it was, he understood it. Loyalists hated anyone who wasn't a Loyalist. Every Irish Catholic knew that. He'd grown up with such things. On the other hand, murderous Inquisitors, demons, and Fey were aspects of a strange world he knew little about—a world with rules he didn't know, a world he'd been dragged into against his will.

Father Murray whispered to the Inquisitor, "Leave us for a few minutes."

Father Conroy paused and then shrugged. "I'll be outside with security if you need me. Knock when you're ready."

Waiting until the keys finished rattling in the lock, Father Murray took a deep breath. His shoulders dropped, and he seemed to relax a bit. He moved away from the door. "I'm watching over everything they do. I won't allow them to hurt you."

"More like I won't." In Liam's experience, it didn't take strength to wield a knife with deadly force—only the knowledge of where it was best employed. "And I'd be able to see to that for certain if you hadn't—"

Father Murray shushed him and gave the door a meaningful glance.

Liam pointed to the tray and whispered, "I know what torture looks like, Father. And from where I'm sitting it looks like that. At least, until the bleeding and screaming. And I'm not about to let it get that far."

"You're free to go any time. You do understand that was part of the agreement?" Father Murray asked. "Your father is proud of you for volunteering for this. We all are. It's a brave thing, agreeing to come here. But you've lived through a great deal—"

"No more than anyone else."

"—too much if you ask me. So, tell me you can't do this. I'll get you out of here. Right now. But if you can endure it—Liam, think of the lives that can be saved. Remember why you're here."

Liam stared at the tray and swallowed. His mouth was dry. His tongue scratched against the roof of his mouth.

"Can you trust me?" Father Murray asked.

Liam pushed a hand through his hair. He couldn't help noticing the tremor in his fingers as he did so. He told himself it was the chill in the air. "Aye," he said. "I will—I can." He wasn't about to admit to fear within Father Conroy's hearing. "Scalpels make me a wee bit nervous."

"I can't blame you." Father Murray sighed. "Would it help with the anxiety if you had detailed descriptions of the procedures to be performed?"

"Aye, it might."

"Then, I'll see what I can do."

Resigning himself, Liam slipped out of his anorak, tugged his sweater off over his head and began to undo the buttons on his shirt. Within a few minutes he was sitting on the examination table once more—this time, dressed in his underpants and a fervent wish that he were anywhere else. The stomach-churning stench of antiseptic, mold, and cleansers was impossible to ignore. The paper covering the examination table's brown vinyl padding crackled underneath him. His skin prickled in the cold, musty, recycled air. He'd grown so accustomed to a tingling sensation preceding a shape change that while Father Murray's back was turned Liam automatically gripped the edge of the steel examination table and was disappointed when the goose bumps on his arms didn't instantly fade.

Fucking hypnosis.

You can negate the effects any time you wish. Father Murray said as much. What if I've angered the monster? What if it refuses to come when called?

Father Murray signaled for the Inquisitor to return. Upon entering, Father Conroy appeared surprised that Liam had agreed to continue without extreme coercion. With a small nod, the Inquisitor went to the desk and picked up a new Polaroid camera from the tray.

"Stand, please."

Liam bit back another retort and slid from the table. Under Father Conroy's intense gaze, Liam struggled with shame. *This is nothing,* he told himself. *I've been through worse, so I have. But if he touches me, I'll fucking knock him flat.*

Father Conroy snapped photographs while Liam turned, front, sides and back. The Inquisitor took a closeup of the commemorative Bloody Sunday tattoo on Liam's upper arm and paused when he spied Liam's back and shoulder. "What is this scarring from?"

"What's it fucking look like?" Liam asked.

Father Murray cleared his throat and gave him the look he usually saved for unruly school boys—a stare that Liam was intimately familiar with. "Liam was injured by a car bomb. He was hit with shrapnel," Father Murray said.

Liam noted the half-truth and found it reassuring to see that Father Murray didn't trust the Inquisitor either.

"It was injured?"

"Please, Father Conroy. His name is Liam."

"Oh. Yes," Father Conroy said, pausing. "Was… did Liam sustain severe injuries?" He gave the name emphasis as evidence of his compliance.

"Again, what the fuck—"

"Liam." Father Murray frowned.

Liam inhaled and held his breath. He waited until he was sure his heart had slowed, and then he spoke. "Sorry, Father."

Father Murray took over, reciting a list of broken bones and hurts that Liam hadn't been aware of. *A lacerated spleen? I had a lacerated spleen?*

"How long ago was this?" Father Conroy asked.

Again, Liam let Father Murray answer. "Last month."

"The burns look as if they healed several years ago."

"He heals fast," Father Murray said.

"Interesting." Father Conroy returned to his cart and made some notes on his clipboard. "How fast?"

"Three days. That time. There are exceptions. But I'm at a loss as to the mitigating factor. He suffered a broken collarbone several weeks ago. It's still not completely healed."

Liam couldn't decide if that statement was strictly a lie or not. His father had explained in no uncertain terms that impulsively throwing oneself against a one ton limestone boulder that later turns out to be made of meteoric iron ore anchored in place by powerful druids is not exactly the brightest idea—not that there'd been other options at the time. Liam allowed Father Murray's half-truths to slip by and focused on the cinderblock wall while the two priests discussed the details of his medical history—that is, the details Father Murray was willing to give. After the conversation ended, Liam feigned patience while his temperature was taken and his eyes, ears, nose and throat were checked. Father Conroy's movements were precise and professional, but Liam remained vigilant. Everything was going smoothly enough until Father Conroy's stethoscope made contact with Liam's naked chest.

Liam flinched with a yelp. "Where do you keep that fucking thing? The icebox?"

Father Conroy leaned backward with an apologetic smile. "I always forget about that. I'm sorry." He breathed on the end a few times and then rubbed it on his lab coat before trying again. "Is that better?"

Liam blinked at the display of sympathy. "Aye."

Resuming his professional attitude, Father Conroy parroted standard requests for deep breaths. Then he looped the stethoscope around his neck and made a few notes. "Now. Open your mouth again, please."

Liam cooperated. Father Conroy swabbed the inside of his cheek and then painted the sample on the surface of a Petri dish. With that done, Father Conroy selected a scalpel from the tray. Liam tried not to shy away from the blade as Father Conroy gently scraped the back of his hand. The results were transferred to a second Petri dish. Next, Father Conroy took his pulse, frowned to himself while jotting down the result and then picked up a blood pressure cuff.

After much fussing with the cuff's bulb and the chilly stethoscope, Father Conroy sat back. "Interesting. I'll have to bring this to the Bishop's attention."

"Is there a problem?" Father Murray asked.

Liam swallowed a spike of terror. *Is it something everyone else missed? Something else I wasn't told?*

"The creature's blood pressure and heart rate are unusually elevated. I mean, compared to a human at rest—that is—"

"Is *his* blood pressure at a dangerous or abnormal level?" Father Murray asked, clearly angry. "For a *human* under any circumstance?"

"Ah. No, but I—"

"Are there not perfectly logical and normal reasons for a human being to exhibit a rapid heart rate and high blood pressure? Strong emotion, perhaps?" Father Murray asked.

"Ah." Father Conroy blinked several times. "In cases of—of undue stress—"

Relieved, Liam kept his expression blank.

"Yes," Father Murray said. "In cases of undue stress. Yes." He paused. "You and I both know the Order accepts only the best, most qualified, highly intelligent and skilled for service. You've been entrusted with a grave responsibility. As such is the case, I assume you are good at your job. What is your specialty, by the way?"

Father Conroy looked confused. Liam couldn't blame him. It was as if a mask had been lifted. He hadn't seen this side of Father Murray before and couldn't shake the feeling that he was about to witness a dressing-down.

"Medical research focusing in hematology and genetics with an interest in biochemistry," Father Conroy said.

Nodding, Father Murray said, "In case you were curious, my specialty of expertise is psychology and medical biology. It is my duty to observe others—my brothers within the Order as well as those outside it—for certain mental influences and…" He paused. "…weaknesses. In the case of my brothers, this includes weaknesses which might affect the accuracy of their work. Ours is a hazardous calling, after all."

Liam thought he perceived a minute shift in Father Conroy's careful expression.

"You're familiar with the scientific method?" Father Murray asked.

Father Conroy frowned. "Of course. I—"

"Of course," Father Murray said. "It's a basic concept and employed across multiple scientific disciplines. In your experience, have you witnessed an instance of an observer's bias effecting data outcome?"

Father Conroy blinked but didn't answer.

"We all have. To disastrous results," Father Murray said. "So. With all these things in mind, wouldn't it best serve the Order to make observations from a less assuming, perhaps even neutral, position?"

Swallowing, Father Conroy said, "Well, perhaps."

"Good," Father Murray said. "I'm sure Bishop Avery and the Grand Inquisitor would both be reassured by your devotion to accuracy."

Father Conroy nodded and returned to his work with an altered attitude. As Liam was weighed and measured in more ways than he thought necessary, Father Conroy filled in several pages of forms and charts. When that was done he picked up an empty syringe and said he needed to collect a blood sample. Liam looked once more to Father Murray who nodded encouragement.

Liam sighed and gave the Inquisitor his left arm. The man gazed down at Liam's inner elbow and paused.

"You've scar tissue here."

"Aye. A fucking Peeler got fucking careless with his fucking questions," Liam said. "What the fuck does it matter to you?"

"May I have the other arm?"

Liam gave Father Conroy his right arm and gritted his teeth. Father Conroy took the blood sample, taped the puncture wound, gathered his paperwork and left.

Slipping into his jeans, Liam said, "Thanks."

"For what?" Father Murray asked.

"For taking a stand with that fuck. But what I don't understand is why he took a tongue lashing from you?"

"I reminded him that while he may be an Inquisitor, I am a Guardian. Which means that it is not only my duty to spot and report demons and Fallen outside the Church. It's also my responsibility to watch for suspect behavior from within the Order as well. In case of demonic influence."

Liam felt his mouth drop open. "You threatened to report him for one of the Fallen?"

"I merely pointed out that it might best serve his interests to be cautious in his conclusions. Otherwise, it could bring up certain doubts."

Fucking brutal, that is. Pulling on his socks, Liam said, "I'm glad you're on my side."

"You're welcome."

"Will there be more of that shite? The needles and such?"

"I'm afraid so," Father Murray said. "But that's all for today."

Liam finished tying his boot laces and grabbed his sweater and shirt from the desk. "Let's get out of here. It's fucking late. I'm knackered."

"The Bishop arranged for accommodations. A suite of rooms. Should be comfortable enough."

Jamming his arms into his shirt, Liam said, "As comfortable as a prison can be."

"This is a research facility. They are trying to make this as easy on you as they can."

"Sure, Father." He pulled his sweater on over his unbuttoned shirt. The layer of scratchy wool between the chilly air and his bare skin did its work. "As long as you're here to witness it."

Notably, Father Murray didn't argue the point. He brought out a set of keys from his coat pocket and opened the door. An armed priest in a guard uniform stood in the narrow hall nearby. The guard waited until they passed, tugged on the doorknob to see that it was secure and then stepped in place behind them. Father Murray stopped and turned to confront him.

"There is no need for an escort," Father Murray said. "I know where our rooms are."

"I've orders," the screw said, one hand on his pistol. "He's not to roam free."

Liam opened his mouth to object, but Father Murray spoke first. "Are we in danger, then? From whom?"

An uneasy expression passed over the guard's grim face. "I've orders—"

"Prison," Liam whispered.

Father Murray sighed. "Come on, Liam."

As Liam followed Father Murray down the hallway lined with sealed doors, the claustrophobic feeling worsened. Liam didn't like the smell of the place. Something somewhere was rotting. It was faint, but very much present. In spite of the late hour, medical staff passed by with a business-like air—all of them priests of varying ages dressed in lab coats or guard uniforms. All of them carrying weapons. A number of them carried on animated conversations in Latin. There were no female nurses—no nuns—anywhere to be seen.

It wasn't long before Father Murray stopped at a grey door with the label "Observation Room" bolted in the center. Liam attempted to suppress a shiver. Father Murray produced the key ring again and after searching for the correct key, unlocked the door. To Liam's relief, the guard didn't follow them inside.

The furnishings weren't much different from the rectory in Derry. The sitting room furniture was well-worn but tasteful. An overstuffed sofa was arranged to the left. A thick rug covered the floor, and a landscape painting hung on the wall over the sofa. A large crucifix was tacked up next to the door. Liam noted the lack of a television or record player and considered asking Father Murray if a radio might be arranged. *Can you get a radio signal underground?* Shelves lined with books provided some potential relief from boredom. A kitchenette branched off the back of the sitting room. There were two doors—one on either side of the kitchenette.

Father Murray motioned to the door on the left. "Your room is there. I'll be staying over here."

Liam peered through the doorway into his room and saw it was furnished in a similar fashion as the rest of the suite. However, unlike the rest of the underground floor, the builder had left a window. Liam entered the room to have a closer look. When he pulled back the curtains he was granted a view of blank wall and a fluorescent light—currently off. Whether it was intended to reflect the time of day, he wouldn't know until dawn. He took a deep breath, scenting the air. All in all, it would've been welcoming, but for the cameras mounted in the ceiling and the underlying reek of old blood not quite concealed by furniture polish, mold, and pine-scented disinfectant. The cocktail of smells did nothing for the knots in his stomach.

Pointing upward, Liam asked, "Is that necessary?"

"You should know you'll be filmed. Sound will be recorded as well."

"On second thought, this is worse. At least a prison doesn't pretend to be something it isn't."

"Your things are on the bed. You'll find everything you need in the washroom and the kitchen. If you want extra blankets, or if they missed something, let me know. I'll make the arrangements."

Liam went to the old laundry bag resting on top of the bed. Loosening the square knot in the drawstring, it became obvious that someone had searched its contents. He'd been angry when he'd packed—more like terrified, not to put too fine a point on it. As a result, he'd stuffed his clothes in the bag without bothering about the wrinkles. Now they were neatly folded. He considered complaining, but nothing appeared to be missing. Retrieving the light blue flannel pajamas Father Murray had provided, Liam left them on the bed, tightened the drawstring on the bag and tossed it onto the floor. There was a chest of drawers made of a dark wood, but he wasn't about to use it.

He straightened and took a long, deep breath to clear his head. Once again the scent of old blood haunted his nose. That's when he noticed that Father Murray hadn't moved from the doorway. Glancing over his shoulder, Liam wondered if the priest smelled it too, but it was clear by his expression there was another reason he was waiting.

"I must leave you here. Only for a little while," Father Murray said.

"If I'm staying, so are you."

"I'll be back. I've a short conference with Bishop Avery."

Liam's eyes narrowed.

"It's nothing. A briefing. Mere formality. He wanted to see me before tomorrow. While I'm there I'll ask for a copy of the examination and testing schedule. It's better this way. I don't trust Father Conroy will take such requests seriously."

"You're going to leave me in this stinking place?"

"What are you afraid of?"

"Can't you smell the blood?"

Father Murray's eyes narrowed. "Blood?"

"Aye. Was quite a lot too." Liam took another deep, slow breath. "Was some time ago. A month? Maybe two. Hard to tell, given what they cleaned it up with. Bleach. Something that smells like pine to cover. Doesn't help much."

"Interesting." Father Murray looked uneasy. "I'll keep it short. Less than an hour."

Liam felt his jaw and shoulders tighten. His eyes burned from exhaustion, and he stifled a yawn. There were no clocks that he could see, but they hadn't taken his watch from him, and he knew it was close to two in the morning.

"You look exhausted. Try to get some sleep," Father Murray said.

"And if you don't come back?"

"Stop your worrying." Father Murray smiled but Liam sensed nervousness beneath. "I'll see you in the morning." Then Father Murray shut the door.

Liam listened for the lock and didn't hear it. To be sure, he went to the bedroom door and opened it in time to see Father Murray exit the suite.

Liam caught a glimpse of the guards in the hallway outside. Keys jangled, and the loud click-thump of the locking mechanism spiked Liam's anxiety. Tired as he was, he didn't think he could sleep. There was no television, no radio. Walking to the bookshelves in desperation, he examined the titles. All appeared to be of a religious nature. So, he returned to his room, defeated.

The only lock on the bedroom door was a deadbolt that required a key which he didn't have. He considered jamming a chair under the bedroom doorknob for privacy, but neither the chairs nor the doorknob were designed in a way that would make that feasible. With nothing to serve as a distraction, he put on the pajamas, brushed his teeth, climbed into bed and tried not to think. Lying in the dim light emitted by security lamps, he rolled over on his side and turned his back on the camera's staring red dot. With his face to the wall, it wasn't long before he grew tired of the flowered wallpaper. He turned on the bedside lamp and searched through the laundry bag.

A cup of tea would be nice, but he didn't trust that the kitchen's stores hadn't been tampered with. Reaching into his coat pocket, he pulled out an old photograph of his father and mother. The photo was, along with his wedding ring, one of his few remaining possessions. He supposed he should've left it with his mother in Derry where it would have been safe, but for now he was glad to have it with him.

Studying the black-and-white image, once again Liam noted that although Bran was immortal, he'd aged. In the photo, he could've been twenty years old at the most. Liam thought his father now looked to be around forty—only slightly older than Liam's mother. His uncle Sceolán was Bran's twin brother. Bran had said as much. However, Sceolán could've easily passed for twenty or twenty-five. What all that meant, Liam couldn't have said.

He couldn't help thinking it ironic. Everything he knew about his father and his father's people was almost entirely comprised of fiction. Yet, the reason for giving himself over to the Inquisitor was so that the Church could learn about the Fey. In truth, he probably knew less than the Catholic Church did, and they didn't even believe in the Fey. It occurred to Liam that maybe that was another reason why his father had risked sending him—he didn't know enough to reveal anything important. The realization gave Liam a chill.

Rubbing his eyes, he lay back on the soft feather pillows. The tension from the day had snarled his muscles into painful knots. He couldn't get comfortable. As a last resort, he grabbed a volume from the bookshelf and read for a time but found he couldn't focus on the page. He wouldn't let himself sleep—couldn't until he knew that Father Murray had returned. However, he did permit his eyes the briefest of rests from time to time. Once. Twice. And then he passed into a fitful sleep.

Chapter 3

"So, you finally have what you wanted, Joseph," Father Thomas said. "I sincerely hope you know what you're doing."

Although Father Thomas was his direct supervisor, Father Murray knew better than to take the remark as anything other than what it was—a symptom of exhaustion and frustration. The peace initiative had gotten a rough start. It'd been a long day, and this was just the beginning. Unfortunately, there were a long series of even longer days ahead, and they both knew it.

"To tell the truth, there are those among the Order who firmly believe you've lost your damned mind," Father Thomas said.

"Are you among them?" Father Murray followed Father Thomas's bulky form into the steel elevator and attempted to dismiss a sense of foreboding. It didn't help that the dull ache behind his left eye was showing signs of becoming a rather nasty headache.

Father Thomas shook his head. "You should know better than that. You've my full support. If there's even a small chance you're correct..." He sighed. "Innocents mistakenly murdered for centuries. I half hope you're wrong."

"I'm right in this."

"I believe that you believe, and that's enough for me," Father Thomas said. "But take care how you proceed, and who you push. There are those who want to see you fail. They'll do anything to prove you wrong. Remember what happened after Waterford."

Father Murray swallowed. *That was a mess. Three dead when it was finally done. One in mental hospital. Two weeks of suspension.* He'd very nearly been suspended permanently. *But I was proved right, was I not?* He wasn't always right. No one was, but he liked to think himself wise enough to concede when it became clear otherwise. *Except when it came to Mary Kate, is that not so? How wrong were you then?* "I'll be careful," Father Murray said.

"I'm serious this time, Joseph. The slightest mistake could land you in a containment room. Possibly to the end of your days. Do you understand?"

"I do." The headache decided to quit lurking and get serious.

"Bishop Avery is taking a big risk. We all are."

Not as big as I am, apparently. Father Murray said, "I can only do my best."

"The Bishop has faith in you, Joseph. Keep that in mind. No matter what happens. He believes in this investigation. But there are other considerations. Considerations you're unaware of."

"What considerations?" Father Murray felt his stomach tighten in a cold knot.

Father Thomas paused before stepping out of the elevator. "Considerations."

"Shouldn't I know what's going on?"

"Not now." Father Thomas shot a meaningful glance up at the camera mounted near the ceiling.

Father Murray nodded.

This wasn't his first visit to the Belfast facility—more like the hundredth, but it was the first time he'd entered it since he'd resigned from the Order of Milites Dei. Nothing seemed to have changed over the past month. The hallway was identical to the one on the underground floor—sterile white walls, grey steel doors and matching flecked-grey tile. Black numbers were etched on the three-by-five-inch steel plates bolted to each door at eye height. The second floor, the one they were currently on, consisted primarily of security, administrative offices, a few apartments reserved for important guests and record storage. The labs, infirmary, kitchen, chapel, medical staff, supplies and two morgues were located on the floors above. The observation room and two examination rooms existed underneath the building. A third set of cellar rooms existed, he knew. They were located on the eastern side of the building, but he'd never been unlucky enough to visit them.

There's still time, Joseph.

He kept his voice low to prevent it from echoing. "Has something changed since yesterday?"

Father Thomas whispered, "Later." He opened the door to Bishop Avery's office and ushered him in.

Entering the dark-paneled room, Father Murray steeled himself against mounting trepidation. The faint aroma of frankincense, normally comforting, didn't help. Three hours into the peace agreement, he already didn't like where things were headed. He'd known the situation would be challenging, given Liam's authority issues and the overall sentiment within the Order toward the Fey, but he hadn't thought it would metastasize this quickly. He prepared for another fight and scanned the photos of the Order's heroic casualties—their simple black frames hung in precise rows like tombstones. A thick brown curtain was drawn over the windows to the left.

"Hello, Joseph. Have a seat," Bishop Avery said, looking up from his paperwork. "Declan, would you mind bringing in some tea?"

"Not at all, Your Grace," Father Thomas said.

"Two cups, please? That is, if Joseph will be joining me?"

"Yes. Thank you, Your Grace," Father Murray said.

"Thank you, Declan. That will be all for now."

Father Thomas nodded and shut the door.

"I understand you've settled into your rooms. Is everything in order?" Bishop Avery asked.

"With respect, Your Grace, it would be best if I could take Liam to and from appointments without restraints or an armed escort."

Bishop Avery put down his pen. "Request denied."

"Damn it, we must show good faith or the peace process is doomed."

Bishop Avery frowned.

"I apologize, Your Grace." Father Murray pushed up his glasses and pinched the bridge of his nose. His head was pounding. He didn't do well on shorted sleep—never had, and it was only getting worse as he got older. *Don't fuck this up. Do you want to end up in that padded room?* "It's been a difficult day."

"Heightened security levels are in effect for your safety. The fact that you're living in that suite against my better judgment is concession enough."

"Liam has resided at my sister's house for two weeks. There's not been a single incident. Not one. I've observed him since he was a lad of thirteen. I'm in no danger."

Bishop Avery folded his hands together on top of the heavy oak desk. "Why is this issue so important?"

"He was interred in Long Kesh and at Malone. Psychologically—"

"I've read the reports," Bishop Avery said. "I still don't understand the problem."

Have you not visited the prisons? Do you not have the slightest idea of what they're like? Father Murray paused to get some control over his emotions. Certain newscasters liked to compare the facilities where Irish political prisoners were kept to comfortable hotels, but he didn't know of anyone who could do so after looking into the eyes of anyone unfortunate enough to have been interred in one of them for any length of time. "If he is treated like a prisoner it will affect the results."

"You assured me that the strip search incident was an unusual circumstance."

Father Murray said, "My recommendations shouldn't have been ignored. I told them not to do it."

"That was an unfortunate error. However, Father Conroy has since reported that Mr. Kelly was agitated and confrontational during the medical examination."

"He was terrified. I'd be frightened too if I'd gone through what he has," Father Murray said. "Could someone please speak to Gerry about his bedside manner? He threatened to sedate the lad against his will. I understand Gerry isn't used to dealing with the living, but that was too far even for him."

"All right. I'll have Declan talk to him."

"Thank you, Your Grace," Father Murray said. "I've another request."

"Yes?"

"I'd like a list of the tests to be performed. It will decrease the lad's anxiety."

"Why?"

There came a knock on the door and Father Thomas entered with a tray containing a teapot covered with a brown cosy, sugar and milk, spoons and two white porcelain cups with saucers. He set the tray on top of Bishop Avery's desk and asked, "Will you need anything else, Your Grace?"

"I believe that is everything. Thank you," Bishop Avery said.

"Then, I'll see you in the morning."

"Goodnight, Declan," Bishop Avery said.

Father Murray exchanged nods with Father Thomas and waited until the door clicked closed to continue. "It has been demonstrated that the Fey cannot be photographed without their consent. We don't know whether or not other results can be affected. We must have Liam's full cooperation if we're to get useful data."

"Has Mr. Kelly indicated that he won't cooperate?" Bishop Avery poured milk into the first cup and paused with a questioning look.

Father Murray declined with a shake of the head. "I didn't say that." He sighed. "Look, we must admit that we don't know what we're doing. The Fey are not the Fallen."

"Perhaps." Bishop Avery picked up the white porcelain teapot. Steam arose from the spout as he poured, and the scent of strong black tea soon joined that of the incense. "However, our policy in the past has been that they be numbered among the angelic host who chose to remain neutral in Heaven's conflict with Lucifer. That they were banished to earth as a result." Bishop Avery offered a steaming cup of tea. "Therefore, there are those who say the Fey are justifiably classified as Fallen. Neutrality in God's war is much the same as supporting evil. If God saw fit to cast them out of Heaven, then the answer is obvious. Regrettable, perhaps, but obvious."

Father Murray accepted the cup and focused on adding sugar to his tea to buy a short pause. "That is one theory," he said, taking a sip and feeling the warm liquid make its way to his stomach. He felt better already. "However, the Fey don't regard themselves as angels. Nor do they mention having been cast from Heaven, let alone that they might have ever seen it. Surely if—"

"If the Fey are designated a new category of lesser Fallen, then a gradual policy change is possible without the drastic consequences of an open admission of wrong-doing. This has been posed by members of the council as the solution to the dilemma the Church now faces."

"Is it a solution we seek? Or the truth?"

Bishop Avery's cup let out a hard clink as it hit the saucer resting on his desk. "This is a very delicate matter, Joseph. All the options must be carefully considered. A case-by-case plea for mercy can be posited for judgments upon the Fey. The peace agreement could have a chance of going forward. Also, if it is found that the children of the Fey can accept God's grace, their status can be altered. They can be counted human should they convert and remain active members of the Church."

"With due respect, Your Grace, what does that mean?"

"It means we must remember our priorities. Saving lives and souls, the welfare of nations as well as the Holy Mother Church are all far more important than a debate over semantics."

Am I actually hearing this? Father Murray thought. *From Bishop Avery of all people?* "Semantics? You honestly believe I retired from my position over semantics?"

Bishop Avery took another sip of tea. His expression was carefully controlled. That alone was a signal to Father Murray that Bishop Avery didn't actually approve of the proposal any more than he did. "No, I don't believe you retired over semantics," Bishop Avery said. "You are—were one of the best Guardians we've ever had. It would be foolish to dismiss your theory outright." He looked up from his tea. "There is something I wish to divulge. Alone and in this room. May I count upon your discretion?"

"Of course."

"I grew up in a small village in County Down. My father kept sheep in the Mourne Mountains, you know. Like many boys, I spent more than one rough night alone with the flock in the hills as a lad. I've seen things. As we all have. But I'm almost certain I met a púca one night. I'd heard things earlier in the night and was frightened. A tall, dark-man appeared out of the gloom. It was a relief. Friendly, he was. Joined me at my fire. I shared what little food I had. We swapped stories for hours. Then he left, and I never saw him again. Until yesterday evening, that is. At the Giant's Ring."

"You recognized him? Who was it?"

Bishop Avery sipped his tea. "Bran. I'm certain of it."

"Then why let others force us to abandon the spirit of what we're doing before we've even begun? Why put Liam Kelly through any of this, if the decision is already made?"

"Don't worry. Nothing has been formalized. As you say, we have no solid information—only fiction and myth, which makes this study vital. We must take advantage of the opportunities we have. However, I don't wish you to be disappointed should the ultimate outcome not be exactly what you hoped."

"Your Grace, I'm not the one you should be concerned about disappointing. It's the Fey. We don't want the Fianna for an enemy."

"I've no intention of making them so," Bishop Avery said, taking a sip of tea. He changed his tone as if he were starting an unrelated conversation. "I've held a leadership role within the Order for some time. Some might say... too long."

Father Murray froze, his cup halfway to his lips. He felt a chill. "Are you considering retirement?"

"We both know that choice isn't always a factor," Bishop Avery said. His gaze was intense over the edge of his cup.

The warm tea didn't dispel the cold. A long silence stretched out, leaving a void occupied only by the ticking of a clock.

Bishop Avery cleared his throat and returned to the previous subject. "Change is possible, but the Church does not make rapid change. Some would say it is our greatest virtue."

"Others would say it is a deadly flaw."

"Take courage, Joseph. We aren't beaten yet. We have more than a few allies among the College of Cardinals. I merely wished to be as forthright as you have been with me," Bishop Avery said. He finished his tea and placed cup and saucer on the tray. "The security detail will remain in place. However, restraints will not be used—provided there is no further trouble from your Mr. Kelly."

That's something. Father Murray said, "Thank you."

"As for the procedure schedule... Have you considered that pre-knowledge might allow Mr. Kelly to affect the data results?"

I should have thought of that. "I will devise a double-blind test to check for such a response first."

"Meet with Father Stevenson tomorrow. He can help."

"Thaddeus is here?"

Bishop Avery leaned back in his padded leather chair and folded his hands across his stomach. "I thought you might feel more comfortable working with someone you could trust, given the circumstances."

"Thank you." Father Murray finished his tea and set the empty cup with the other tea things.

"Once you're certain the test results won't be tampered with, I'll have Declan provide a list of procedures," Bishop Avery said.

"Thank you, Your Grace." Father Murray paused a second time, uncertain how to proceed. "May I ask an unrelated question?"

Bishop Avery nodded.

"Was anyone killed or injured in that suite recently?"

Bishop Avery froze. Father Murray had worked with the Bishop for most of his career. He knew him well enough to know for the most part when the man was lying or hiding something—or in this case, surprised. Father Murray had to admit it was one of the reasons he liked working for him. In a profession where much depended upon intuition, it was a relief to work with someone who was easy to read.

"A week ago a spawn of the Fallen was brought in for observation as a trial run for your experiment," Bishop Avery said. "The demon killed the assigned observer and four of the security staff before we were able to put it down."

Ah, that explains it, Father Murray thought.

"How did you know?"

"Liam smelled the blood."

"He did what?"

"He has an extremely keen sense of smell, Your Grace."

"I see." The worry line deepened between Bishop Avery's eyebrows. "Does he have any other unusual... talents we should be aware of?"

"He has inherited certain qualities from his father, Your Grace. However, I'm unaware of anything beyond what I've listed in my reports."

"Anything that might prove a security problem?"

"He isn't dangerous. I'd bet my life on it."

"You are," Bishop Avery said, "and I don't like it."

"We're doing the right thing, Your Grace. You must trust me."

"I do. It's one of the reasons I'm giving this harebrained idea of yours a chance," Bishop Avery said. "Your instincts are impeccable. One hundred twenty-three demon spawn processed with minimal human casualties and property loss. No other Guardian has had a record like that in a hundred years." He glanced at the photos of the dead lining the wall. "Are you sure I can't convince you to return to active service?"

One hundred twenty-three dead. And I'll never know for certain if all of them were demons. Babes, most of them. Babes and children. The unborn. Father Murray swallowed. "No, Your Grace. Thank you, but no," he said. "I'll serve as my conscience will allow. But I can't return to my former role."

"Our loss. And God's."

"The peace agreement is more important, Your Grace."

"I hope you're right. One more thing," Bishop Avery said. "Security reported activity outside this facility half an hour ago." He reached into a drawer and pulled out a black and white photograph. He turned it and then pushed it across the desk. "Do you know who this is?"

Father Murray looked down at the surveillance photograph and recognized the man in the image at once. He was a little surprised that Bishop Avery didn't, since Liam's uncle, Sceolán, had been present at the negotiations only a few hours before. Six foot two inches tall with thick shoulder-length blond hair, Sceolán was difficult to miss. However, in the grainy photograph he was dressed in a wool knit cap, flared jeans, a Pink Floyd t-shirt and a dark anorak. He could've passed for any number of university students who roamed the area but for the silver glint in his eyes. In the photo he was staring directly into the camera, a knowing smile on his face that spoke of mischief.

"He's Bran's twin brother," Father Murray said. "Is something wrong?"

"Not at the moment. But security is keeping an eye on him."

I'm sure Sceolán is keeping an eye on them too, Father Murray thought. *And with better success.*

"We're prepared for trouble," Bishop Avery said.

"I wouldn't expect any. He's probably only keeping watch over his nephew. The Fey demonstrate strong family ties. There were no provisions made against a presence outside the facility. Expect him to remain until

Liam is returned," Father Murray said. "Would you prefer if I spoke with him? If he were more discreet, it might prevent trouble—"

"There's no need," Bishop Avery said. "It's late. You should go to bed."

"One last request," Father Murray said. "Liam will need access to an exercise yard or a track. He prefers to run in the mornings."

"Impossible."

"Exercise reduces stress. If you insist on keeping him under lock and key, I'd recommend allowing him freedom to vent his anxiety in a positive manner. He has claustrophobic tendencies. It's only a matter of time before the pressure will become too much."

Bishop Avery paused, obviously giving the matter some thought. "All right. There's a private track located on the roof. I'll arrange for access. But you will be escorted by guards, and you will remain with him at all times."

"Thank you, Your Grace."

Chapter 4

Liam found himself in a field edged with ancient oak trees and carpeted with soft grass. A half moon drifted in the cloud-tattered sky, and soft mist obscured the ground. Getting to his feet—*paws*—he had a strange feeling he'd been in the place before. *But when?* A northern breeze shoved its way through the woods, bringing with it a deepening cold, the rustling of leaves and the warning scent of early snow. His senses were sharper in wolfhound form, and the intensity of perception was as intoxicating as ever. Breathing deep, there came a rush of information in subtle layers. Something wrong in the wind caused him to hunch inside his own fur. Mixed among the sharp pepper and cinnamon of green things rooting in the dirt and the musk of animal spore, he detected a fragile aroma that didn't belong.

Memories of safety and acceptance surfaced. *Love.* He knew it then for soap set off by the warmth of mortal skin—and not just any soap, a particular brand. The spectre of deep grief stirred within his chest. Filled with dread, he waited for details to emerge, but was distracted by another combination of olfactory clues more easily identified: stale cigarette smoke, gun oil, greasy chips, and the acrid scent of heroin—or at least, the acid that heroin was so often cut with to make it mix with water when heated.

The monster growled within Liam's skull.

Detective Inspector Haddock.

All at once, revulsion fought with need. It'd been at least eight months since heroin had surged through Liam's veins. Eight months of forced sobriety, mind-numbing fear and nightmares. Eight months of yearning. The monster raged from the darkest corners of his mind in a series of machine gun thoughts. *Find Haddock. He'll have the smack. Rip his throat out. We'll take what we want. Think of it. A fix. We need it. We can kill him. Kill him now.*

Liam licked his lips. *Heroin will keep the pain*—grief—*away.* Catching himself before he could yield, he shook his head. *I'm done with the killing. Done with the smack. Done with you too, you fuck.*

The monster didn't answer, but Liam knew the creature waited in smug silence. That the monster was awake again was bad enough. What was much worse was the queasy knowledge that this wasn't the first time he'd run across Haddock's scent in recent weeks.

Can't be, Liam thought. *I did for him. Haddock is fucking dead.*

A sigh whispered on the back of the freshening wind. Liam's ears pricked. The snap of a twig brought him to sharp attention. Sensing movement to his left, he turned and spotted a large white shape as it flitted behind a tree trunk.

The monster whispered, *Prey,* and the word sent a shiver of anticipation through Liam's body.

A low, mournful horn note stretched across the night sky and then dissipated, leaving a residue of foreboding. Liam sensed the white shape in the woods as it started and then froze. Liam and the monster inside him joined in the listening. When the call wasn't repeated Liam dared edge sideways, moving in silence until he spied a beautiful white doe—the largest he'd seen in his life.

She was graceful and delicate regardless of her size. Her eyes, nose and hooves were an inky black, and her coat darkened at the tips of her ears and at her hooves. Wary, the doe stood twitching—perched on the edge of flight. He held his breath, listening to his heart slam inside his chest. When there came no new sign she relaxed and resumed grazing. He inched a wee bit closer while the monster whispered a susurrus of bloodlust, restless for the pursuit. Determined to keep control, Liam set his jaw. The desire to lose himself in the giddy freedom of speed built up in his muscles.

In the distance the horn sounded a second time.

Kill her, the monster thought. *Now!*

As if hearing the creature, the doe bolted. The monster sprinted after, slipping the bounds of Liam's will. The horn blared a third time—louder, longer and closer. It sang of murder and terror and—

The hunt.

The monster's blood burned with the desire to shred flesh and rip sinew. Liam rode along—dizzy in the flood of sensation, unable to stop the creature occupying his body and not wanting to, even if he could. Unseen others may have joined the chase, but he'd spotted her first, and the monster was fast. The others were too far away to catch up. The creature plunged into a dead run, ripping through foliage and darting around the trunks of trees the size of black taxis. Before long, the monster-Hound came to a stream and inwardly shrank from the sight of it, slowing. The doe shot down the path at the water's edge. The stream was ten or fifteen feet across and didn't appear deep. Yet, Liam knew this for an illusion. Something moved in the false shallows. A premonition of death hung on the air, and the monster kept to the far side of the path—away from the water—as it continued on.

Liam lost sight of the doe when the trail took a sharp bend to the left, circumventing a huge deadfall. Again, the monster slowed. The hunt was drawing closer, and Liam could make out baying hounds and short horn blasts interspaced with the crash of rapid-flowing water. Glancing to his right, he saw the stream had joined forces with a second body of water. The monster wasn't far from the fallen tree when a sharp cry and the crunch of broken forest debris brought him up short.

The stream flowed over a steep waterfall and gathered in a deep black pool at the bottom. He craned his neck to see over the spilling water. The doe lay below at the edge of the pool, struggling to get to her feet. The rich scent of blood sent him charging around the dead tree and down the steep slope. He noticed the abrupt drop-off just before he plunged over it. The mad scramble to save himself sent dead leaves and dirt sliding off into nothingness. He waited until he was sure he had good purchase and backed himself away from danger. Gasping, his heart hammered in his ears. Then the doe's bleats of pain and another, closer horn blast spurred him to his feet. He searched and found a second way down the slope. Upon finally reaching the bottom, he looked for her, and his heart stopped.

The doe was gone. Mary Kate sat at the riverbank, clutching her wounded ankle. Her light brown hair, once beautiful, was now dirty and tangled with twigs and leaves. Her slim legs and graceful feet were bare, scratched and bleeding and caked with mud. The hem of her white dress was in shreds. Her skin was so pallid it was almost blue with the chill. She was shivering as she let out a sob. Lifting her head, she pushed filthy hair from her face. Guilt tangled with love and missing memories as Liam remembered it all: the blood, the last ride to hospital, the waiting room, the awful feel of her final breath against his cheek.

Mary Kate.

Jesus Christ, it's really you. His shock came out in a series of barks and yelps. *You're alive!* He didn't know how it could be, and he didn't care. He hopped with joy. He trembled with the need to gather her in his arms and kiss the pain away. A twisted ankle was nothing. He could deal with that—they could handle anything together. Mary Kate was the strong one. Always was. And she was back. He'd never leave her alone again. She'd be safe. He'd see to it. He'd protect her with his life's blood.

Understanding he meant to go to her, she let out a short scream. There was no sign of recognition in her face, only terror. She scooted back, away from him.

He froze. *Please, Mary Kate,* he thought to her. *It's only me. I'm here to help.*

She held up a hand as if to shoo him away.

I'm the fucking Hound. Shame extinguished his elation. *She knew about the monster but never saw it. Not like this. Why would she know me as I am now? And here I've frightened her.* He made a conscious effort to return to mortal form but couldn't. There wasn't even the slightest tingle along his skin to indicate he'd made the attempt. It made sense. The change was more difficult to control when he was under stress, and he'd just had the shock of his life. *She's alive!* He barked, happy, and once again forgetting himself.

Mary Kate dragged herself closer to the water.

Wait. I'll not hurt you. Again, he thought at her, wishing with all his might for a human voice. He sat on his haunches and tried to appear as non-threatening as possible. He stared into her terrified eyes and willed her to understand. *It's only me, Mary Kate. Your Liam.*

I think not. The monster—the one Father Murray had magicked away with his hypnotism—mocked. *You're not you. You're me.*

Liam thought back at the creature, *Leave us be. Mary Kate and I, we can be together again.*

Horn calls and triumphant howls came from the woods above. The other hunters weren't far now. Mary Kate bit her lip. A fearful whine escaped her throat and an overwhelming need to protect her left Liam breathless.

It's all right, love. Stay as you are, he thought at her. *I'm here. I'll take care of it.*

Sod off! The monster snarled. *You've no say. None I don't grant you. Not in this place. How does it feel to be the one left watching? You have no power here.* Liam felt a growl rumble deep in the back of his throat. He struggled to force the creature back into unconsciousness, but it had control of the body now. Helpless, Liam felt his own haunches bunch, gathering energy for an attack.

I'm here, the monster thought—its internal voice a mockery of Liam's own. *It's all right, love.*

Mary Kate's hand splashed into the water. Discomfort flashed across her face in response. It was clear she didn't like the pond any more than he did, but she'd fling herself into the water if she must.

No, Mary Kate! Don't! It's not safe! Liam looked at the water. The thing that had stalked him to this place was down there—he didn't need to see it. He knew. *Stop this,* he thought at the monster. *Please don't hurt her.*

You let that priest put me away, the creature thought back. *You'd banish me? Fuck you. I'll have my fun. And there's not a fucking thing you can do about it.*

A splash drew his attention again to the pond. A sickly grey-green shape neared the surface and then vanished. Whatever it was, its shadow stretched six feet. A low animal sound halfway between a whale's moan and an insect's staccato vibration broke free of the water. It was joined by

Mary Kate's terrified keen.

The other hunters had reached the fallen tree. He could hear them making their way down the broken path. Trapped between the thing in the water, the hunters and the wolfhound, Liam watched Mary Kate search for escape.

Yes, the monster thought. *Run.*

Oh, Christ. I won't let you do this. Let her go. Liam again fought for control but knew he couldn't without iron or steel.

Mary Kate looked into the woods beyond the monster-Hound and screamed.

"Hello, sweetheart. Glad to see me?"

Liam felt a cold hand slam between his shoulders. He darted from under the hand's grip and whirled, snarling. Detective Inspector Haddock laughed and brought up a gun.

The monster staggered backward, slipped in the mud, and landed in the pond with a splash. As the water closed over Liam's head, bone-deep cold smashed into him and for a moment he couldn't think, let alone breathe. In an instant he lost all sense of direction. The water was deep, too deep to find the bottom. His lungs began their demand for air. Mary Kate's muffled screams filtered through the painful cold. Then something slimy and sharp grasped one of his hind legs and yanked. He yelped in shock and most of his precious air supply sped to the surface in a gush of bubbles. He was pulled down deeper into the darkness. Mary Kate was in trouble. He could hear her. He fought the thing that held him, kicking and biting. He *would* save her. He didn't care what he had to do. Haddock was up there. He had to—

"Liam!"

A bearded man dressed in red plaid flannel pajamas was shaking him. The man's brown hair was disheveled and his horn-rimmed glasses were askew. It took a moment before recognition set in, and Liam remembered where he was.

"Father?"

"You were screaming. Are you all right?"

Somewhere outside the flat an alarm shrieked, muted by thick concrete and stone. Liam sat up, rubbing his face. The beard itched. A powerful sense of relief blurred his vision. "A dream. Was only a dream." He blinked back raw emotions, suddenly remembering the cameras mounted in the ceiling.

Father Murray whispered, "You were calling out for Mary Kate. That's the fifth time this week."

Same dream for weeks. That thing in the water. Mary Kate. Was all so real. Never saw Haddock before. What does it mean? Or is it only a nightmare? It wasn't all that unusual, having the bad dreams. Liam had had them from the time he was a child. Now that he was an adult, he had nightmares so often that he'd become immune to their well-worn horrors. Occasionally, he'd have the bad night—maybe once or twice a week, but this—

Someone in heavy boots was running in the hall outside, several some-ones to be exact. Guards, he assumed. The alarm was still whooping on the other side of the thick cinderblock wall. Father Murray didn't seem to hear it.

"You should talk to someone about this. If not me, then someone else."

Father Murray and his fucking psychology, Liam thought. *Always digging.* "It's nothing. Only a dream."

"Right." Father Murray smoothed sleep-tousled hair. "Care for a cup of tea?" It was obvious he hadn't given up on the fight—only delayed it.

Liam grabbed his watch from the nightstand and slipped it on. The feel of cold steel against his bare skin was a comfort. "It's four in the morning, Father. Anyway, don't you think you should answer that?"

"Answer what?"

The screws began shouting and pounding against the front door.

So, you're having a wee problem with your fucking door, are you? Liam couldn't stop a small smile.

"Ah. I see." Father Murray went to the bedroom door, checked the sit-ting room and sighed. "Meet me in the kitchen after they've gone."

A loud bang and crash from the sitting room announced the arrival of the screws. Booted feet thundered across the floor. Guns clattered. "Guardian Murray!"

"I'm here! I'm here! Everything is fine. I have everything in hand. Re-turn to your post."

"The creature, is it secured?"

Father Murray shut the bedroom door with a firm slam.

Shifting to the edge of the bed and grabbing a shirt to cover his bare chest, Liam listened. Screws were screws and unlike Father Murray, Liam understood how the game was played. The only factor was how far the Church's screws were prepared to go. In Her Majesty's prisons, a Republican's life wasn't worth much. Here? The Church was the Church after all. On the other hand, he was here because they suspected him for a demon which was a far cry from an ordinary Republican—even among Loyalists.

Wouldn't take much to make it look like you killed the priest. Liam fervently wished his Uncle hadn't planted that worry in his mind.

"His name is Liam Kelly, not 'creature.' Can't you lot remember that? I said everything was fine. Why don't you clear out so we can get some sleep?"

"Sorry, Guardian, but we have our orders. Can you explain why the door was jammed?"

Unable to lock his own door, Liam hadn't been able to sleep—not well and not for long. Unlike his bedroom, the suite's outer door was fitted with a normal knob. Therefore, he'd set a kitchen chair against the outer door after Father Murray had returned from his meeting and gone to bed. Liam supposed he should've told Father Murray about it but didn't think it would come up until the morning.

Father Murray sighed. "That's my fault. I didn't trust we'd be left to sleep in peace. Apparently, I was correct."

Another lie? Father, that's getting to be a bad habit, Liam thought. He searched for some socks to serve as slippers. Based on what he could hear, he guessed there were six screws. *Six? Do they not have anything else to do?*

"The alarm activated. We must perform a visual check of the creature—"

Father Murray interrupted the screw. "He can hear you, you know."

"Security procedure must be followed. Need I remind you that the rules are not only for your own safety but for the operational integrity of this facility, Father?"

Liam wasn't sure but he thought there might have been a hint of fear in the screw's voice.

Father Murray sighed again. "Get on with it."

The bedroom door flew open. For a moment, Liam was overwhelmed as a multitude of scents filled his nose—some mundane and others less so: the sweat of excitement; coffee; pipe tobacco; milky tea; whiskey; spearmint and underneath it all a horrible stench of burned decay. His heart jolted with recognition. He knew that odor. He'd sensed it in the past whenever the Fallen were near. However, before he could note which smells originated from which guard, he was dragged from the bed and thrown against the wall face-first. His lower lip split open, caught between his teeth and the wall. He tasted blood, and his eyes watered with the sharp pain.

"What were you up to, demon? Why did you jam the door?"

Liam reached a hand to his bleeding mouth, but it was slapped away. Pain exploded in his right kidney. *Ah,* he thought, gasping. *It's to be a hiding, then.*

Another punch landed in his back and another. They knew what they were about. Three blows and he couldn't breathe. With the exception of the face to the wall all the hits had landed where it would show the least. He was released, and he dropped to the floor.

"What the hell are you doing?" Father Murray asked.

One of the screws reiterated the need for safety procedures and regulations. A rough pat down commenced, and Liam gritted his teeth against rising panic. He lost track of what the others were doing. He tried to ignore the hands on his body, but couldn't. *This is nothing,* Liam thought, reassuring himself. *Stay calm. It's only a quick search. Happens every day on the outside. No more strip searches. Father Murray promised. A brush down. That's all. No sense in over-reacting—*

The guard slid his hands all the way up Liam's leg to the inside of his thigh, and the panic took over. He reacted without thinking. Shame heating his face, he yanked an arm free and elbowed the offending screw in the head as hard as he could.

"Shite! My nose!"

"I'll kill you! Don't you fucking touch me!" Two more screws rushed in to pin Liam's arms, and a steel cuff locked around his right wrist.

"What the hell are you doing?" It was Father Murray.

"Don't move!" One of the two scrabbled for Liam's left wrist.

"Get them the fuck off me!" The cuff was jerked, and it bit into Liam's arm. "Get them off!"

A screw yelled in Liam's ear. "Stop fighting, damn it!"

"Fucking kill you! I'll rip—" Liam felt a knee in the middle of his back. "Don't you fucking touch me!" He fought with everything he had, striking out whenever he could get a limb free. He made contact a number of times and was rewarded with a few grunts. "Let go! Let me go! Get off—" A boot caught him in the face and another in the thigh. The rest was lost in the fog of adrenaline. In short order the pain began to build enough to be felt beyond the general numbness, and he hoped he wasn't going to lose any teeth or an eye. Then his right arm was painfully twisted up his back, and a hard kick landed on his weakened right shoulder. The bone gave way in a burst of white-hot pain, and he thought he was going to pass out.

"Stop! You're killing him!"

"I said freeze!"

Someone was screaming. Liam realized it was himself.

"Don't shoot! Don't shoot!" Again, it was Father Murray.

"He broke my nose!"

"Get Williams to the infirmary! Get out of here!"

"Yes, sir!"

Father Murray said, "Wait! Don't shoot!"

"It attacked Father Westbrook," a guard said.

"He's not fighting," Father Murray said. "Can't you see? Don't shoot!"

Liam felt more than saw all but one of the guards move back. Deep pain beat time with his heart. Someone laid a hand on his shoulder, and agony forced the little breath he had remaining from his lungs.

"Liam? Liam? Are you all right?" It was Father Murray.

Liam gasped for air and was sorry for it at once. "Shoulder. Jesus. Oh, fuck. My shoulder." Everything was blurry.

"Get Father Conroy! Now!" Father Murray again.

"The Inquisitor?" one of the screws asked.

Father Murray sounded angrier than Liam remembered ever hearing before. "Are you going to make the fucking call or am I? He needs medical attention. Now."

"The demon?"

"He's a young man who was left in your charge who you nearly beat to death. If he were a spawn of the Fallen, he would have killed at least two or three of you. Don't you think? Get the cuffs off him. And put the gun away. Now," Father Murray said. "He's no threat to you."

Blinking, Liam noticed the screw standing over him was holding a loaded syringe. A second screw was pointing a gun at him. Another jolt of panic surged through Liam's system numbing the pain for a brief moment.

"He injured Father Williams as well. I'm not authorised to—"

"Then damn well get someone in here who is!"

"According to procedure, I must sedate the subject when it's agitated."

"*He's* perfectly fine," Father Murray said. "You're the ones who could use sedation!"

"He appeared calm before and then attacked Father Williams. He's dangerous. And—"

"Only after your man used excessive force," Father Murray said.

"The alarm sounded. There was screaming. For all we knew—"

"The lad had a bad dream. Check the tapes if you don't believe me," Father Murray said. "In all your dealings with demons, have you ever known one of *them* to have a nightmare?"

The screw armed with the syringe hesitated.

"Neither have I." Father Murray sighed. "Look, I understand everyone is under a great deal of pressure. But do you honestly think this is the appropriate response?"

The screw armed with the syringe said, "It's best not to take chances."

"Are you a trained Guardian?" Father Murray asked.

"No, sir. But—"

"I am. And I'm telling you he isn't a threat. I had the situation under control. In fact, everything was perfectly fine until you and your team kicked in the door."

The screw armed with the syringe turned to one of the others. "Father Jensen, get over here and hold this." He handed off the syringe. "Watch him. He so much as coughs without permission, stick him."

"Yes, sir."

Then he brought out a key from his pocket and removed the cuffs.

"Liam, can you stand?" Father Murray asked.

Liam risked a nod. It seemed to take an eternity, and twice he had to pause while the room faded in and out of focus, but he was able to get to his feet without fainting and without needing too much help from Father Murray. However, if there was anything else required of him—and Liam had a terrible feeling there would be—he wasn't sure he'd last it. He shivered. It was suddenly very cold.

"We have to get you to the examination room. It's down the hall. Do you think you can make it?"

Liam gave the screws a hard stare. It wasn't easy, and he had to squint because of his bruised face, but it was worth the trouble. None of them had moved to the phone at any point in the proceedings. Some had their hands to their weapons but hadn't drawn. The burned rot stink was stronger now, but he still couldn't pinpoint where it came from. Something wasn't right about the screws. *One of them is Fallen. Has to be.* But none had the characteristic hunched back. Still, they were too excited. Their expressions reminded him of a scene from a documentary he'd seen years ago about a pack of jackals. He had an uneasy feeling at that moment that if he or Father Murray showed any sign of weakness then they were both fucked. He swallowed and lifted his chin in defiance. The screws glared back at him with an equal amount of disdain.

"Liam?"

Do I say anything now? Or wait? Which is less likely to get us killed? Liam took a careful, shuddering breath. His teeth painfully clattered together. *Not now.* "Aye. I'll do."

"There's a lad." Father Murray pointed to the bed. "Get me that blanket. He's going into shock."

Liam felt a bit better the instant the blanket was wrapped around him. He leaned against the wall for support. Father Murray positioned himself to get under Liam's left shoulder in order to help him walk. A nameless unease had settled into the empty place in the back of his brain where the monster normally lived. He wanted out of that room and away from the screws as soon as possible. Again, he thought of circling jackals.

A screw stood in their path and bared his teeth in a fierce grin.

Father Murray said, "Get out of the way. Please."

Not moving, the screw said, "We've orders—"

"You've no wish to let the others down. I understand. We must protect friends, loved ones. More than their lives—their souls. With so much at stake, it's easy to forget ourselves. But shouldn't our own humanity be a part of the humanity we protect?" Father Murray asked. "You're a priest. One of God's own. We end suffering. We don't cause it. Please."

One of the guards looked away and then the tension was gone.

The screw in charge said, "Let them pass. We'll follow them to the examination room." He spoke without moving his gaze from Father Murray. "Father Jenson, call the Inquisitor and tell him we're on the way."

Liam felt Father Murray's steady presence under his left shoulder.

"Come on, Liam."

They staggered past the screws and through the door. Once they were out into the hall, Liam whispered, "Nice wee speech, Father."

"Save your breath," Father Murray muttered back, returning the humor. "You're going to need it."

Liam whispered again, "Watch yourself. The guards. Something stinks like Raven's Hill."

Father Murray's eyes widened and then he gave a brief nod.

Focused on warning Father Murray, Liam stumbled and squeezed his eyes shut against the flash of paralyzing pain gripping his shoulder and chest. Father Murray paused until Liam signaled he could continue. The screws gathered around, watchful.

He didn't know how he made it to the examination room, but he did. Father Conroy was standing outside with a smug look.

"What happened?" Father Conroy asked.

"Why don't I give you a copy of my report?" Father Murray asked.

Liam remembered stepping up to the examination table and at some point he'd lain down, that was obvious, but he couldn't have said when. That moment and a few others were lost in a fog of pain. The next time he opened his eyes the screws were gone. *That's something.* The where and why didn't so much matter at present. The blanket was tugged out of his grip. Cold air brushed against his skin as his shirt was opened. He shivered.

"Interesting."

"Is that all you can say? The guards almost killed him."

A drawer slammed. Metal clinked against metal. "Then perhaps your experiment shouldn't have tampered with the security system."

"He tucked a chair under a doorknob. Does that warrant this kind of reaction, Gerry? Do you understand what will happen when Bran sees what they've done?"

The sharp smell of rubbing alcohol invaded Liam's nose. A cold cloth wiped at his cheek. Someone was cleaning the blood from his face—

Father Conroy, he assumed.

"Ask him why he did it," Father Conroy said.

Liam tried to answer, but his mouth didn't respond right away. His tongue felt too big for his mouth.

"What did he say?" Father Conroy asked.

"Liam?" Father Murray asked.

"Couldn't sleep," Liam said. The words came out in a lisp. He tried to open his eyes and couldn't for the most part. The left one was now swollen shut, and the right one wasn't much better. He could only see through one watery slit. Both priests were very close. Father Conroy held a bloody bit of cotton wool in his hand. Liam stopped trying to see.

"There," Father Murray said. "He did it so he could sleep."

"You know that wasn't the reason, Joseph."

"What's it going to take to convince you he's human?"

More movement. A drawer slammed again. Papers fluttered. A ballpoint pen clicked.

"What are you doing?" Father Murray asked.

"We're finished here. I've cleaned the wounds. Photographed and measured everything. Now we wait."

"Wait for what?"

"Didn't you say he heals for himself? I need to record how long it takes."

"You can't be serious," Father Murray said. "You're not going to set the shoulder? Or give him something for the pain?"

"I assume that would not only be a waste of materials but also might interfere with the results."

"Help him, damn you! If you don't, I'm taking him out of here right now! I'm calling off this whole thing!"

"Don't be so hasty. There's so much to learn."

"Do it! Now!"

It was Father Conroy's turn to sigh. There was another bout of metallic noises, the clink of glass. Liam felt a needle stab in his right arm, and by the time the shirt was cut from him the pain had grown distant. He could breathe again. He remembered something with a jolt of panic.

"Lighter."

"What is it, Liam?"

"In my pocket. My lighter. I need it."

A cold steel rectangle was pressed into his palm.

"Try to sleep, Liam," Father Murray said. "Father Conroy is going to set your shoulder. This is going to hurt."

Chapter 5

Belfast, County Antrim, Northern Ireland
November 1977

"Put the scalpel away, Gerry," Father Murray said as another sobering jolt of adrenaline seared the last remnants of sleep from his system. *Is Gerry safe? What if those guards aren't the only ones affected? Why didn't I notice something was wrong until Liam said something? Is it because I've wanted this so much?* He assumed a protective stance between Father Conroy and the now unconscious Liam. *How far has the contamination gone? Surely it can't have gone far without someone noticing? What if it's reached Bishop Avery? Am I losing my ability to judge the difference between human and demon?* "You've set his shoulder. Thank you. Now, we'll be leaving." The prospects of fighting his way out of a high-security facility weren't good, even if waking Liam was an option. On the other hand, leaving him behind was unthinkable.

"This will only take a moment. He won't feel a thing," Father Conroy said. "I need fresh tissue samples. Larger than yesterday's. The samples were useless before I could analyze them. Even you must admit that's unusual, if not impossible for a human."

"Impossible?" Father Murray blinked. "Slides can be mixed up, mislabeled, or tainted. You know that. It's happened before and—"

66

"One live tissue sample is all I need to prove otherwise."

Shocked, Father Murray felt the corners of his mouth tug downward as hopelessness and desperation set in. The room seemed suddenly colder and Gerry's focused expression acquired a sinister quality. "I gave him my word that no one would do such a thing."

"He won't even notice, given the extent of his injuries."

"That isn't the point, and you know it. He's not one of your lab animals. I'll not let you dissect him."

"It wouldn't require that much tissue to solve the mystery. Then security can bring a gurney, and you can escort him to the observation room for a rest."

"As far as I'm concerned the agreement is terminated."

"You can't mean that!"

Father Murray shifted so that he had a better view of the exit, and his left arm was clear. If the guards heard Father Conroy's protests and suspected anything out of the ordinary, there would be a fight. The examination room wouldn't provide much maneuver room. *The best option would be to incapacitate Gerry now before anyone senses a problem, but how to keep security from alerting the others?* Father Murray didn't want to use deadly force—he couldn't. At this stage, there was no way of telling if anyone was beyond helping or not, and without being certain his conscience wouldn't allow it.

Can you be confident of anything anymore? How many have you murdered in error? He swallowed. *I'm not imagining the contamination and neither was Liam. Be certain of Gerry first. Then decide what to do.* Father Murray took a chance and looked into Father Conroy's eyes. It was hard to say under the circumstances, but his pupils appeared normal. *Good.*

Father Conroy continued his protests. "I can't let you leave. I—"

"Do you have your rosary?"

"Of course."

"May I see it?"

Unbuttoning his white lab coat, Father Conroy revealed a hand-knitted brown pullover sweater vest layered over a black priest's shirt. He dug inside his right trouser pocket and fished out a jet bead rosary. "What's wrong?"

"Hold up the crucifix."

Father Conroy followed instructions without hesitation. His pupils remained stable nor did he flinch.

"Is it blessed?" Father Murray asked.

"Every day. According to procedure." Father Conroy's face grew pale, and he glanced down at Liam. "You suspect contamination?"

"Put out your hand." Father Murray brought out his own rosary beads. They were warm from resting inside his own trousers pocket.

Again, Father Conroy did as asked. Pressing the crucifix into Father Conroy's palm, Father Murray studied the other priest's reactions and again found no negative reaction.

Thank God, Father Murray thought.

"Should we proceed to the next step?" Father Conroy asked.

"It isn't necessary." Father Murray put away his rosary beads. "That's enough for me."

"Please forgive me," Father Conroy said. "But you've been in closer contact with the subject than I have. And I understand you didn't attend mass yesterday."

"There wasn't time. Not after the screening, and you know it," Father Murray said. "Liam isn't the source of the taint." Nonetheless, he put out his hand and accepted the touch of Father Conroy's rosary crucifix without further protest.

"From the moment your friend entered this facility, I've counted no less than three security alarms," Father Conroy said, pocketing his rosary beads. "Three in less than twenty-four hours. I'd say that was a fairly direct causality."

"Circumstantial evidence."

"If you say so. Are you going to explain?"

"This facility's security has been breached."

Father Conroy's expression transformed from caution to scepticism. "That isn't possible."

"Have you not heard of Sarajevo? December of 1913? Budapest and Vienna in 1914? How about Munich in 1920? That contamination caused factors which led to World War II. The facility in Rome had to be abandoned until 1945. Remember? Or do they not review the Order's history with recruits anymore?"

Father Conroy shrugged. "Procedures have been set in place since then and have stood the test. There hasn't been a recurrence in decades. We learned from those mistakes."

"And who is to say the Fallen haven't as well?"

"Don't be preposterous!"

"I'm bloody serious and lower your voice," Father Murray whispered. "I'm warning you. The security team outside that door have been contaminated."

"Your evidence?"

"Is that not evidence enough?" Father Murray asked, pointing at Liam. "Or does it have to be you or me before you'll admit something is wrong?" He sighed and pushed up his glasses. He was tired, his head ached and his eyes burned. "There's no time for this. If you'll not accept the word of a Guardian—"

"A retired Guardian," Father Conroy interrupted, "who resigned under unusual circumstances."

"If you'll not report the breach, then, fine. All I ask is that you'll give us a quarter hour to get out of here."

"I can't do that. Not without Bishop Avery's approval."

"Then ring him. Or give an alert about that security team. Do what you think is right. I don't care which. The longer you argue with me, the less time either of us has to survive."

Father Conroy paused and then crossed over to the built-in desk. He picked up the phone receiver and dialled a series of numbers. Several moments passed before the phone was finally answered. "Your Grace, we have a problem."

Father Murray didn't bother listening. Any member of the Order who spent time serving in the field knew the lowest of demons was capable of out-witting a human being. Even those who never saw field work were aware of what was at stake. Over-confidence could mean death or worse, damnation. However, Father Conroy was right on one point. The Order had learned much since the first Inquisition instigated by Pope Lucius in the late 1100s. *But we've been wrong about the Fey. For centuries. Could it be that the Fallen only allow us to think our security procedures work?* Although fallible, demons were immortal. They had the advantage of the broader perspective immortality brings and were known to plan accordingly. It was one the many aspects of demons that made them such a formidable enemy. *Where else might we be mistaken?*

Ask one question and there came twenty more. It was understood that demons had no power over the faithful. Hold fast to purity, the grace of God and belief, and you were safe. No demon could withstand the grace of God. But were human beings actually capable of remaining in a perpetual state of grace? He'd had enough experience to think otherwise. Six months retired, and he wasn't familiar with the roster anymore. Who could he trust? What could he believe?

There is always God, Father Murray thought. *Jesus, his son, Mother Mary, and the saints. No matter the frailty of human beings certain things remain steadfast.*

Right?

This isn't the time for a crisis of faith, Joe.

The bang-ring of the receiver clattering against the telephone base brought Father Murray back to the present situation.

"The Bishop is on his way," Father Conroy said.

Lowering his voice, Father Murray asked, "And did you warn him?"

Father Conroy glanced to the door, nodded and whispered, "Better to be safe than sorry, I suppose."

Relief loosened the tension in Father Murray's neck a notch. A Level Three lock-down alarm sounded, but another quarter of an hour passed before the anticipated knock on the door finally came. He stopped Father Conroy from answering with a hand on his arm.

"Best let me," Father Murray whispered. He moved into a defensible position next to the door and gripped the pistol he'd hidden under his jacket. Bullets didn't differentiate between humans and the preternatural—even blessed ones, but it would have to do. He'd left his blade with his sister for fear of it being reclaimed by the Order when he'd entered the Belfast facility. "Yes?"

"Guardian Murray?" The question, phrased in Latin, resonated with authority.

He recognized the sonorous voice with its Limerick accent and unease displaced relief. *That explains a few things.* He answered in the Latin as well. It was customary since members of the Order originated from all over the world. Latin was often the only language anyone had in common. "I've retired, Monsignor Paul."

"So I've heard," Monsignor Clarence Paul, the Grand Inquisitor for all

Catholic dioceses within the Northern Hemisphere said. "However, your actions would speak otherwise."

Father Murray hesitated. If the Grand Inquisitor were present, then matters were serious indeed. It explained Father Thomas's trepidation and Bishop Avery's fear.

"Are you going to let us in?" Monsignor Paul asked.

"That depends. Has the previous security team been relieved of duty?" Father Murray asked.

"They have," Monsignor Paul said.

Upon opening the door, Father Murray saw that the guards had indeed been replaced by a new, unfamiliar group. They were accompanied by one hastily dressed Bishop Avery, an armed and bullet-proof-armoured Father Thomas, and one Monsignor Paul whose frayed bath robe and worn slippers belied his lofty and most independent status. Leaving the security team in the hallway, the others entered the examination room. Father Thomas nodded a greeting after assuring himself that Liam was unconscious. However, he didn't seem to relax his guard and kept his dagger at the ready.

"All right, Joseph. We're all here. Would you mind telling us why it was necessary to call us out of bed?" Monsignor Paul asked. "After the mess in Jerusalem, I was rather hoping for some undisrupted sleep. I assume the issue is serious?" With wispy, thinning white hair and a thick well-trimmed beard, there was something about him that reminded Father Murray of an aged Richard Harris. He supposed it was the aristocratic nose and the deep, theatrical voice with its English school polish not quite disguising the Irish West Country.

Father Murray said, "Re-screen those guards and everyone who has had contact with them."

"That will take considerable time and resources. You're certain of this?" Monsignor Paul asked.

"When were they last screened?" Father Murray asked.

"A month ago," Father Thomas said. "They were scheduled for relief on Friday and haven't left the building since."

"Shite. Then we're later in catching the problem than I'd hoped," Father Murray said. "Unless... is there someone new that they came in contact with?"

Father Thomas tilted his head down and peered over the top of his round, wire frame spectacles. "Besides yourself and your charge?"

"I know what this looks like. But if it were so, why would Liam Kelly have waited until we entered a high security facility? Until he was alone? Wouldn't it have been better to have murdered one and all at the Giant's Ring?" Father Murray asked and made a silent plea to St. Francis for patience. "You don't have to agree with me to see the necessity in clearing—"

"Take it easy, Joseph. The security team will be screened," Bishop Avery said. "However, you're asking us to shut down operations for an entire day. We need to know the specifics of what triggered the incident report. What did you see?"

"The security team which arrived in answer to an earlier alarm was agitated and violent. And then there was the deciding factor."

"And that was?" Monsignor Paul asked.

Taking a deep breath, Father Murray hoped he wasn't betraying a confidence. "Simply put—Liam sensed the problem before I did."

"What?" Father Thomas asked. "How?"

"He said they smelled… wrong," Father Murray said.

"Smelled?" Father Conroy asked.

"You've not mentioned this ability before," Bishop Avery said with a frown. "It isn't listed in any of your reports."

"I did tell you his senses were more keen than average, Your Grace," Father Murray said.

"You've had several interactions with that security team," Father Thomas said. "Why didn't he notice it before?"

"I'm not certain he didn't," Father Murray said. "However, he didn't tell me about it until after the beating."

"He can smell demons?" Father Conroy asked.

"Are you certain?" Bishop Avery asked.

"Liam is," Father Murray said. "Think of it. How useful would it be to detect demonic presence or contamination without lengthy screenings? How much easier to know our enemies from our friends?"

"Provided we can trust his claims," Father Conroy said. "Or trust that he'd tell us the truth, if he does hold such abilities."

"We should recruit him," Father Thomas said.

"Unlike the Dominicans, there are no lay people among our numbers and never have been," said Monsignor Paul. "He would have to be ordained to be considered."

"Have you spoken to him?" Father Conroy asked. "I've never seen a less likely candidate in my life."

Gerry is not far wrong there, Father Murray thought, but he couldn't stop himself from pushing the issue a bit. "Oh, I'm sure I can think of a few worse."

"Regardless, we have yet to determine whether he's human or not," said Father Conroy, giving him a reproachful look.

Father Thomas said, "And why should that matter, if it's his help we're asking for?"

"I'd say it rather does," said Father Conroy. "Do non-humans have souls? If so, can a non-human receive the sacraments, let alone dispense them?"

Bishop Avery held up a hand. "We'll debate the issue later. We have more urgent concerns. This facility may be contaminated. Declan, call security. Tell them to prolong the lockdown until otherwise notified."

Father Thomas nodded and went to the phone.

Monsignor Paul turned to Father Conroy. "Have you finished the report I asked for?"

"Yes, Monsignor Paul," Father Conroy said.

"And do you believe Father Murray to be free from demonic taint at this time?" Monsignor Paul asked.

Father Murray returned Father Conroy's judging look. He did his best not to take it personally. They were all exhausted for one reason or another, and it was a valid question, given the circumstances.

"I believe so," Father Conroy said. "But I have reservations."

"Reservations?" Father Murray asked.

Father Conroy frowned. "You have a bias—"

"I'd rather hope so," Father Murray said. "In any case, why should it matter if I've retired?"

Father Conroy opened his mouth to answer but stopped when Bishop Avery held up a hand. "That's enough." He turned away and stepped to the examination table. "Have you reached any conclusions regarding the subject?"

"The results are… inconclusive," Father Conroy said. "He passed the holy water test previous to entering the facility."

"What test?" Father Murray asked.

Father Conroy looked away.

Father Thomas asked, "Do you remember the glass of water we served him before the search?"

"You didn't—" Father Murray said. "Why the hell didn't you tell me?"

An embarrassed expression passed over Father Thomas's chubby features. "We considered it. But it was thought that you'd object on the grounds that it would risk your charge dying in a flash of brimstone."

"Not at all," Father Murray said. "If you'd asked me, I could have told you he's taken Holy Communion every Sunday since he was a child. With the exception of the years he served in prison, of course. I administered it myself from the time he was but a lad of thirteen. That is, until a little over two years ago. You would've known that if you'd bothered to read the entire report."

"And why did you stop?" Monsignor Paul asked.

"It was the death of his wife," Father Murray said, withholding information he felt was too personal. "The murder was never solved. It was hard on him."

"He blamed God?" Father Conroy asked.

"It's a common enough—a *human* enough response. Is it not?" Father Murray asked. "You'd know that if you'd lost a loved one yourself."

The room grew silent. Monsignor Paul's disapproval was clear, and Bishop Avery gave him a reproachful look.

"I apologise, Gerry," Father Murray said. "I've not had much sleep over the past week."

Father Conroy's jaw was tight, but he nodded an acceptance, nonetheless.

"You've had two days," Bishop Avery said to Father Conroy. "We've only the five remaining."

Father Conroy said, "I was about to take a live sample but—"

"Your Grace," Father Murray interrupted. "We can't continue to hold Liam in good faith."

"If issue was due to the security team being tainted, how is there a problem?" Monsignor Paul asked. "The issue is being corrected in a prompt manner."

Father Murray bit back a second remark that could easily land him in circumstances he'd later regret—regardless of the fact that Monsignor Paul no longer had any direct power over him. *Not as a member of the Order anyway.* "Liam was attacked while in our custody. We promised his father that he would be safe. The man isn't going to be happy when he finds out what happened."

"All the more reason for damage control," Monsignor Paul said.

"Damage control?" Father Murray asked. "We must tell the Fey, and extend our sincere apologies. And we must do it now."

"We should get all the information we can. Once the truce is called off, it isn't likely that there'll be another chance," Father Conroy said.

"I can't agree to a continuation of testing. Not without a guarantee of Liam's safety," Father Murray said. "I'm responsible. His father will come to me."

"You owe allegiance to the Mother Church," Father Conroy said. "Not some demon—"

"Enough!" Bishop Avery sighed. "There's no covering up this mess, Monsignor Paul. The lad will talk the moment he wakes. And who could blame him? We've given him no reason to trust us. When he sees his father, the Fey will know, and that will be the end of it."

Monsignor Paul said, "Give me some time. A few days—"

"You heard. We can't," Bishop Avery said.

"Perhaps if we drugged him—" Father Conroy said.

"No!"

"Joseph, please," Father Thomas said. "Calm down. Maybe you could talk to him when he wakes. Explain that it wasn't our fault?"

Father Murray shook his head. "We are responsible."

"Nonetheless, the guards were contaminated. We can't be blamed for the actions of the Fallen," Father Thomas said. "Can we? Surely, the Fey will see that."

Father Conroy said, "We were in as much danger as he was—perhaps more."

"More?" Father Murray asked. "No one else in this room sustained injuries. Explain again how we were in more danger?"

Father Conroy said, "If he isn't human, then he doesn't have a soul. And therefore—"

"Again, enough!" Bishop Avery sighed. "There is no point in continuing with speculation. We must wait until we have facts."

"I will not authorize further testing. I can't, Your Grace," Father Murray said, folding his arms across his chest. "Not when what Gerry is proposing amounts to vivisecting a living being."

Bishop Avery held up a hand, effectively silencing a fresh explosion of arguments and protests. "Gerry, Declan, Monsignor Paul, would you give me a moment alone with Joseph?"

Father Conroy nodded and went to the door. Monsignor Paul and Father Thomas paused.

"Are you sure this is wise, Your Grace?" Father Thomas glanced at Liam's unconscious form.

"He's been drugged," Bishop Avery said. "And is likely to remain that way for hours, is he not?"

Father Conroy shrugged. "Given the dosage, the subject should be unconscious for at least an hour. I took the precaution of administering a non-human dose."

"What? That might kill him!" Father Murray said.

"I rather doubt it," Father Conroy said. "Given what we know, it's safe to assume he metabolizes medications at a faster rate. And in any case, I've gathered enough data to determine that the subject isn't entirely human. Even you admit that is so."

"Nonetheless," Bishop Avery said, loud enough to drown out further protests. "I will be safe for a few minutes. You'll not be far."

"But, Your Grace—"

"Don't insult me by insisting, Declan," Bishop Avery said.

Father Thomas's shoulders dropped. "Yes, Your Grace." He slipped out last, behind Monsignor Paul, but paused to give a meaningful glance that seemed to say, *I'm leaving under protest. The Bishop's life is in your hands now.*

Father Murray nodded in answer. Waiting until the door clicked shut, he released the breath he was holding, but he knew the battle was far from over.

"Gerry took a hell of a chance with the dosage. Was that an act of good faith, do you think? And why is Monsignor Paul here?" he asked. "Who called him in? Was it you?"

"Frankly, I thought we had enough problems. No, Monsignor Paul heard about the situation from Cardinal Wilkinson, and travelled here on his own. There's been a recent development you should be aware of, Joseph," Bishop Avery said.

"Go on," Father Murray said.

"The Prelate has agreed to send his Secretary to observe the situation for himself," Bishop Avery said. "He's taking your hypothesis under serious consideration. I've been granted the authority to extend the truce should your theory prove sound."

Father Murray blinked. "This is what I've been praying for."

"Yes, I know," Bishop Avery said. "If the Prelate's Secretary is sufficiently convinced then I'm to meet with His Holiness, himself. Joseph, much hinges on how this is handled."

Nodding, Father Murray felt conflicted. "But we can't guarantee Liam's safety."

"There is a danger, I admit. But it existed from the start. You both knew that before you came here."

Father Murray looked down at Liam. The lad twitched in his sleep, and Father Murray wondered what demons walked in Liam's dreams. Whatever it was seemed to be more than a lengthy prison stay could account for. However, he couldn't help if Liam refused to talk. *What would he say to this? Would he take another chance? Or would he withdraw?* Father Murray sighed. "I can't make this decision for him, Your Grace. No matter what Gerry says, Liam is human. And as such, he has the right to choose. I won't take that away from him—no matter how important I might think the reason."

"All right," Bishop Avery said. "When he wakes, ask him if he wishes to proceed. Until then, I won't approve any further testing."

"Thank you, Your Grace."

"But you must decide whether or not to stay in the meantime."

Father Murray took a deep breath. There was a possibility that this would be his only chance of getting Liam out of the Belfast facility alive. On the other hand, there was the possibility that the truce could be extended, that the Pope might agree to acknowledge the Fey. It'd only been five years since alterations in Church doctrine had been made that most felt were impossible. Did he dare accept this risk for Liam, if even for a few hours?

It's everything I've prayed for. If we leave now it's all over. Bran was willing to take the risk. The Fey understand what's at stake. All those lives. "We'll stay."

"Very good, Joseph," Bishop Avery said. "Thank you."

"On two conditions."

"They are?"

"That Liam be treated as a human being until absolutely proven otherwise."

"What exactly do you mean?"

"No more threats. No more beatings. He should be addressed by his name, with respect due any other person, and if medical care is required there should be no delays." Father Murray watched as his words sunk in.

"Why should there be a delay?"

"Before you arrived, Gerry wanted to record the length of time required for Liam to heal without medical assistance. Then he administered a potentially lethal dose of a narcotic without my knowledge," Father Murray said. "What are we running? A torture chamber?"

"I was unaware that he'd withheld medical assistance."

"His behaviour today has been reprehensible. Let alone irresponsible. You heard him. He claims he isn't certain what Liam is. This is what uncertainty looks like? Which brings me to the second condition."

"Yes?"

"I want Gerry replaced. He's dangerously biased. And I can't trust him to not poison the lad before my very eyes."

Bishop Avery's eyes narrowed and the lines around his frown pulled deeper. "We've only five days remaining. Even if there were time, it's impossible," Bishop Avery said. "Father Gerry Conroy's scientific credentials are unique. It's why he was selected for this project. It would require three specialists to replace him. That would mean three more technicians would be aware of the doubt surrounding the Fey. The Church wants this issue kept localized until more is known. The security issues alone…." He made a gesture with his hands as if helpless.

"You say you trust me. That you believe in what I'm doing."

"I do."

"Gerry Conroy will kill Liam Kelly if we leave him in his care."

Drawing in a deep breath, Bishop Avery looked down at the sleeping Liam. "If we were to assign a medical technician to stand in for Gerry whenever patient interaction is required, would that suffice?"

"I don't believe that assigning a nurse with no oversight power is enough, Your Grace."

"All right." Bishop Avery paused. "He's well aware that as a doctor he lacks patient rapport. I can cite that as the reason for the change to Monsignor Paul. Then whoever is assigned as medical technician will be placed under your supervision. Is that enough?"

"Yes, Your Grace."

"All right," Bishop Avery said. "Your demands are granted."

"Thank you."

"Have you given much consideration as to what happens once your friend leaves the premises without being declared completely human?"

"I'm sorry? I don't understand."

"The Order is aware of Mr. Kelly's existence. He's been categorized as a potential threat. Your position within the Order shielded him in the past. Now..." Bishop Avery said and shrugged. "Now is a different situation entirely."

"Is that a threat?"

"I don't intend it as such. With the Grand Inquisitor present... you need to be aware how your status affects Mr. Kelly—should it continue as it is."

"You want me back in, is that it?"

"Joseph, listen—"

"I told you I'm no good to you as a Guardian."

"Please listen," Bishop Avery said. "We need you every bit as much as you need us. I'm aware of it, if you aren't. You won't make much headway if your loyalties are being questioned at every turn."

"That doesn't change my feelings on—"

"I understand your misgivings. They're perfectly valid. However, does this mean you aren't willing to use maximum force in the field, if it should be required?"

Father Murray swallowed and thought about the moments before the Bishop had arrived. "Ah, no."

"I thought not," Bishop Avery said and paused to blow air out of his cheeks. "There are consequences to your having resigned. For example, the weapons registered to you must be turned in. You'll be defenceless, as will your charge. Do you understand?"

"I do."

"If you remain outside the Order, I can't help you—much as I wish otherwise. I've already much to explain to the Prelate."

Liam muttered in his sleep. He looked distressed. Certain it was another nightmare, Father Murray put a hand on his shoulder to reassure him, but Liam cried out and jerked away. The stained paper cover on the examination table crackled beneath him.

What else can I do? Father Murray thought. *We need the Church's resources. But returning to active service will grant the Church authority over me and my actions. If forced to choose, would I side with the Church? Without the Church, what can I believe in? What chance do we have? Two against thousands?* "All right."

"Good. As of this moment you're reinstated as a Guardian."

"But I can't promise—"

"You have independent status and a special assignment," Bishop Avery said. "Liam Kelly and the Fey are to be your sole concern. Report directly to me. Father Thomas will stand in as needed from time to time, and I recommend keeping him informed. He will be signing your requisitions, after all. However, I want regular reports. Recommendations too. You're the only one who can gain their trust. You're the only one we've had close enough."

"And Monsignor Paul?"

"The Grand Inquisitor reports solely to the Pope himself. You know that." Bishop Avery held up a hand. "I'll keep him directed elsewhere as much as possible and for as long as I can."

"Thank you."

"Do what you can. Convince the Fey to continue working with us. But remember there isn't much time."

"They aren't going to like what I have to report."

"They're soldiers, and they're at war as we are," Bishop Avery said. "I suspect they'll understand."

"I hope you're right."

Chapter 6

The sky above Queen's University had brightened to a dull grey by the time Father Murray stepped onto the cement walk outside the Order's Belfast facility. Pulling his black wool overcoat tight, he breathed out white clouds that vanished an instant after forming. Several army vehicles thundered past. He turned up his coat collar and missed the gloves he'd forgotten in his rush to find Sceolán. The wind was up. A stray bit of newspaper rode gritty wind gusts, whirling like a lonely *céilí* dancer abandoned by his partner. Father Murray's chest ached with the bitter cold. The sharp scent of winter reminded him that it'd be December soon—the Christmas season, a time filled with love, hope and anticipation for some, isolation for others.

He scanned the empty street where Sceolán had been last captured by the Order's expensive surveillance cameras but didn't see anyone. The Fey came and went for reasons of their own. That much was consistent with the old tales. Father Murray had recently observed that, unlike the Fallen, the Fey seemed reluctant to frequent city environments—although he couldn't have said why. When left with no alternative, they tended to restrict their visits to terse whispered messages in empty gardens or church yards. In his experience, they didn't make actual appearances in the city. If Sceolán had spent two days haunting a busy street, it was worth noting.

Not wishing to disturb the sleeping neighborhood, Father Murray waited twenty minutes before resorting to the only method he'd known to work. "Sceolán," he said in a loud whisper. "I've news of your nephew. We must speak."

A fresh blast of night air rustled down the street, setting the battered bit of newspaper on another forlorn dance.

"What is it, priest?" the question floated on the wind in a hollow echo.

What are the Fey? Are they specters that mirror centuries of legend? Earth-bound ghosts trapped into echoing traumatic events in specific places? Father Murray thought. *Will we ever know?* "Something has happened."

The street remained empty.

"If speak we must, then speak," came a quiet reply that could have easily been mistaken for the wind.

Father Murray reached inside his overcoat and under his shirt, tugging at the leather thong hanging around his neck until the ordinary-looking river stone looped on it emerged. He held the stone up to his right eye and scanned the area through the hole in the center while keeping his back to the surveillance camera. He spied Sceolán in front of a university building across the street. He was dressed as he'd been in the Bishop's photo, casually leaning against a brick wall as if it were perfectly normal for a student to loiter on the street at this hour. He didn't seem much bothered by cold or wind. His anorak gaped open, revealing the front of a dark t-shirt. The words *Wish You Were Here* were visible in large pink letters across the front.

No, not spirits tied to the past, Father Murray thought. *If that were so, would Sceolán know of Pink Floyd? Or does he? Is it merely a disguise he puts on to pass for mortal when the need arises?*

"Ah, now, that's hardly playing fair," Sceolán said. His lanky frame straightened, and he tapped his cheek below one eye with an index finger.

"I prefer to see the person I'm addressing," Father Murray said and put away the holey stone. "Besides, I'd rather not wake those in much need of rest with unnecessary shouting."

"Fair enough." Sceolán shrugged and crossed the street.

Father Murray noted how solid Sceolán appeared for someone who'd

"Interesting."

"Such things run in mortal families. It's one of the many reasons worthy mortals are brought across and counted among our numbers. When a child is born of one of us and a mortal who holds power—any sort of power... well... there's no knowing how it might come out. But sometimes he's gifted with talents from both parents."

"I see," Father Murray said. "Wait. From both parents, you say?"

Sceolán nodded.

"Mrs. Kelly. I remember something Bran told me once. He said she had prevented him from seeing his son. That Mrs. Kelly had put a geas on him. I thought he'd meant only that she'd extracted an oath from him. There was more to it?"

"Powerful, she is," Sceolán said with a smile. "Much to my brother's frequent consternation. Keeps him on a tight lead, that one." He shook his head. "It isn't only the love that does it, you know. Otherwise, he'd have stolen his son from this place long ago. No matter the wishes of the mother. The mortal world holds great danger for our kind. There is a balance to such things. This place holds no love for that which does not belong, even if it once did. Much sorrow can come of it."

"Oh," Father Murray said, thinking. "Can Mrs. Kelly sense the Fallen as Liam does?"

"You'd have to ask her," Sceolán said. "But I'm not certain she knows her own strength. She doesn't seem to use it for anything but making my brother miserable." He let out a short laugh. "Women. Aye?"

"So, Liam's ability to smell the Fallen is unique?"

Sceolán frowned in thought. "He wouldn't be the first púca with such a nose. But we've not seen the like among our ranks in quite a long time. If what you say is true, then our Liam has great value for our people."

"For mortals as well." *Mrs. Kelly has some sort of power,* Father Murray thought. *And it runs in families. What of Liam's siblings?*

"Who is this... Thomas?"

"Father Declan Thomas is a friend," Father Murray said. "I trust him."

"And those who gave Liam the beating? What is to become of them?" Sceolán asked. His expression was unreadable, but the flicker of red in his eyes had returned.

"They're being decontaminated."

"Ah." Sceolán looked down at the pavement. "This can be done?"

"With mortals. Yes," Father Murray said. "Not with—"

"The Fallen?" Sceolán's eyes narrowed.

"No. Not with them," Father Murray said, making a point to emphasize the last word.

Sceolán nodded. "There'll be a price. Liam will see it paid."

"What do you mean by that?"

"I must go now," Sceolán said. "I'll bring my brother your news. He'll let you know where things stand on the peace agreement." He turned and started down the walk.

"Wait! You didn't answer my question."

Speaking over his shoulder, Sceolán said, "I told you I was here to get information. Not give it. Be glad I've seen fit to grant you what I have."

Father Murray trotted down the walk to catch up. "But how will I know that the agreement is still in effect?"

"We will leave you a sign," Sceolán said, taking a quick turn at the corner before Father Murray could reach it. "And should that sign be one of your own without his head... well... that should be easy enough to interpret, don't you think?"

Father Murray ran to the end of the street. He arrived only moments after Sceolán, but by the time he got there Sceolán was gone.

Chapter 7

Belfast, County Antrim, Northern Ireland
November 1977

"Hello, sweetheart. Glad to see me?"

Liam sat bolt upright in bed, heart slamming his breastbone like a rioter. That voice with its Liverpool accent brought the hairs on the back of his neck to full attention. *Another fucking dream,* he thought, breathing heavy. He focused on calming himself. He didn't want the cameras picking up yet another embarrassing moment, but it was then that he registered the balding figure standing at the foot of the bed and choked.

"Jesus fucking Christ!" An electric charge of terror knifed Liam in the heart. "You're dead!"

"Right you are," said Detective Inspector Haddock. "Not much gets past you, does it?"

"How—what are you doing here?" Liam glanced at the door. It was shut. He hadn't heard it open. *Am I dreaming?*

"Your slow Paddy brain just can't comprehend the situation, is that it? Let's review, shall we? I'm dead. You killed me. Therefore, the term for my condition is 'ghost.' As for what I'm doing," Haddock moved to the side of the bed. "Was never much for superstitious rot, but I believe they call it haunting."

D.I. Haddock didn't appear even remotely specter-like. If anything, the bent Peeler was downright opaque. Light from the security lamps cast soft shadows on the blue wool blanket. Liam reached out to touch the rough surface of the cloth, avoiding Haddock's silhouette. "You're no shade. You're lying."

Making a clucking sound in the back of his throat, Haddock pointed to the camera bolted above the washroom door. "Now, now. Keep that up and someone's likely to take notice. And I'd prefer to have you to myself for the time being."

Liam would've been fine with the screws showing up even if it meant another hiding. It would settle the question of whether or not he'd gone mad or Haddock was real. *And if something is wrong and others are made aware of it? What then?*

Turning away from the camera, Liam whispered, "What the fuck do you want?"

"That is the question, isn't it?" Haddock walked to the center of the room and surveyed his surroundings. He gave off an air of arrogant satisfaction. With a slow nod, he turned and smiled his shark's smile. To Liam's thinking, the expression had been bad enough before, but something about this version of Haddock lent it even more menace. "Nice place you got here. A bloke in my condition could get real comfortable like."

"The fuck away with y—"

"Shhhhhh." Haddock pointed to the camera a second time. "They can't see or hear me, but they can certainly see and hear you."

Running his left hand through his hair, Liam reached a decision. He climbed out of bed somewhat awkwardly due to the sling on his right arm and limped to the washroom. Without closing the door—there was none to close—he turned on the faucet and then let the water run in the sink as if he were waiting for it to heat up. He had hoped the dream or hallucination or whatever it was would stop once he'd gotten out of bed, but Haddock's face appeared in the mirror behind him. The apparition, if apparition it was, was so real Liam could smell the man's aftershave.

"Why are you here?" Liam asked, dreading the answer.

"Been asking myself the very same question. Came up with a few answers. Want to know what I've discovered?"

Liam washed his face with the warm water and pretended to check the state of the bruises. The image staring back at him with its bed-rumpled hair, blackened eyes and swollen nose reminded him of a bare-knuckle boxer after a match. *A losing match*, he thought, and waited for Haddock to get on with it.

"It's your fucking fault," Haddock said, taking in the washroom's decor. He touched an empty shelf and made a disapproving sound as if he'd found the level of cleanliness not to his liking. "Not that I can think of anywhere better to be. The entertainment potential alone. Brilliant."

"This isn't happening." Dread twisted in Liam's stomach.

"Oh, let me assure you. It is."

"I'm dreaming."

"I don't think so."

"Then I'm mad."

"Highly likely, given the state of the inside of your cracked Fenian skull," Haddock said. "Then again, you're a fucking addict. You might be high."

"Fuck you. It's clean, I am." The words were out like a cry of pain in response to a roughly probed wound. The guilt made no sense. Liam didn't give a shite what the fuck Haddock thought, but there it was, nonetheless.

"Do you really want to be? That shit the surgeon gave you was better than anything I ever had on hand. Medical-grade morphine. Want to bet there's more where that came from?"

"Fuck you."

"Your conversation skills haven't improved. Remember when Nigel Johnston pounded the shit out of you? He could teach this lot a few things. Ah, those were the days."

Liam closed his eyes. He felt fuzzy but blessedly pain-free. He didn't know what the Inquisitor had injected him with. Whatever it was, Haddock was right on that count. It had been really good, not that he'd noticed at the time. Perhaps it was still in effect? He didn't know how long he'd been unconscious. The Inquisitor might have dosed him again, must have. The shoulder didn't hurt. Liam turned the water off. Checking his watch, he saw it was six o'clock. Whether it was morning or night or even what day it was, he wasn't sure. He would've thought the time loss disconcerting except that Haddock's presence was far, far worse.

"What to do? What to do?" Haddock asked. "So much to catch up on."

Ignoring Haddock, Liam went back to bed and shut his eyes. *Please let this be a hallucination,* he thought. "Go the fuck away."

"Had an interesting conversation with your wife," Haddock said.

Liam's eyes snapped open, and Haddock's cold hand clamped down on his mouth.

"Call me curious. Did you kill her too?" Haddock asked, standing over him. "Murdered your only friend and then your wife? Doesn't pay to stick around you does it?"

Liam's reply was muffled by Haddock's palm. *I didn't kill her!*

"You are one sad sack of worthless shit. Paddies." With the fingers of his right hand, Haddock pinched Liam's nose shut. "You are useful for one thing, however."

Unable to breathe, Liam dug at Haddock's hands but couldn't do much one-handed. Liam twisted and writhed on the mattress heedless of his bruised nose. Black spots stained his vision. The room grew dim. His lungs burned for air. Haddock's palm was corpse-cold against his face, and the stench of death lodged itself in the back of Liam's throat. Somewhere the now familiar alarm whooped. Gagging, he tore at Haddock with both hands now, forgetting his broken shoulder.

"Liam?" Father Murray knocked on the door. "Is something wrong? Liam?" The door opened.

Haddock vanished, and Liam was left gasping. His vision brightened with the flood of oxygen. Father Murray rushed to his bedside. The telephone rang from Father Murray's room.

"What's wrong?"

Liam sat up and scanned the area for any sign of Haddock.

"Liam?"

He slumped in relief. "Dream. That's all. It was a dream."

"I'll call off the alarm and get some water."

"Don't leave!"

Father Murray paused, a concerned, uneasy expression on his face.

He thinks I'm off my nut, Liam thought. *Fuck. Maybe I am.* His shoulder started hurting, the pain ramping up into something huge. He needed to get his arm back in the sling, but the fucking thing was bunched into a snarled mess, and he couldn't get it sorted one-handed. Even so, he was shaking so bad that the cloth slipped out of his hand twice.

Father Murray reached over to help without being asked.

"All right." Once the sling was put right, he collected the only chair in the room and deposited it next to the bed. "I'm here. Talk."

Liam waited until his heart slowed, and his breathing normalized. Calm, he instantly felt foolish. None of the past twenty minutes made any sense. It was the drugs. *Had to be.* He'd been dreaming of Haddock on and off for a week at least. What had happened was only more of the same. If he were free, he'd go for a run to clear his head, but he wasn't free. He was locked away in this place until the Church was done with him, and he'd been the one to let them do it. Conflicting needs battled for attention: a deep desire to run; the hunger for heroin; the faded yearning for Mary Kate accompanied by an ache of refreshed grief.

Footsteps thudded in the hall outside.

"Tea. I want some tea." Left-handed, Liam patted the pocket of the shirt he'd taken to sleeping in, checking that the steel lighter was still there. Then he got out of bed and limped to the kitchen.

Father Murray followed. "Are you going to tell me what happened?"

"You'll think me mad," Liam whispered and then filled the electric tea kettle with fresh water and plugged it in. *Shite. The cameras. They'll have it all on film.*

"Tell me anyway," Father Murray said.

Security pounded on the door. Father Murray left him in order to answer it. Liam tensed up in anticipation of another beating. On impulse, he opened the cabinet containing the mugs and grabbed one. If Father Murray pressed him afterward, he decided to say he'd been readying it for tea and not the guards. Although Liam wasn't exactly certain of his ability to throw left-handed, a token resistance was better than none at all. However, when Father Murray opened the door the guards didn't force themselves inside. The tea kettle gave off a loud pop, punctuating the whispered exchange at the door. Liam ignored the conversation, loitering at the open cabinet until the door thumped shut. With that done, he watched Father Murray rush to the next room. The telephone stopped its protests and not long after the alarm ceased its squalling.

Uneasy, Liam continued with the process of making tea. He was slowly getting used to navigating the world left-handed. On his feet again, he already felt better. The pain living in his right shoulder was passing into another fitful sleep. Already it registered as little more than a vague ache. His face—all but the freshly bruised nose—was healing, and his ribs felt fine. The bandages would be off soon, probably later in the day. That is, provided there were no more confrontations.

With the immediate threat resolved, his thoughts drifted back to Haddock. *My fault, he said. What did he mean by that? Was it only a dream? Am I going mad?*

The last question had been asked so often since the monster first came to him that it lurked in the back of his brain like a Loyalist thug waiting for an opportunity at a soft target. *Am I mad?* Liam wanted the answer, but just as soon as he prepared himself to ask the question and face the truth he shied away from it. The consequences were too frightening. There was nothing in which he could trust. He didn't know the simplest things about himself, his Fey heritage, and what any of it might mean. He had so many questions for his father and uncle. However, there were no means for answers until he was free. What day was it? Tuesday? If they sensed something wrong in him, would the Order insist on keeping him longer than originally agreed? The walls pressed in and the compulsion to run made him twitch. He actually abandoned the tea and took three steps toward the door before he stopped himself short.

Father Murray emerged from his bedroom at that moment, his concerned expression deepened.

"What day is it?" Liam asked.

"Tuesday. You slept most of the day through. You needed it. Healing well by the look of it."

"Oh."

"We must talk."

"Aye?" Unease settled into Liam's shoulders. He turned his back on Father Murray and returned to the kitchenette.

"It's about the peace agreement. Then we'll address what just happened."

The tea had steeped a bit too long in the mug. In spite of the milk it was dark enough to pass for coffee—if the coffee in question had an orange tint. Acting against years of poverty's training in thrift, Liam poured the mess out in the sink, rinsed out the mug and started the tea kettle once more.

"You're not obligated to stay. Not after what those guards did to you," Father Murray said.

"You're not bloody serious."

"The Order failed to keep its promise. Now it's up to you to decide whether or not you'll stay."

Liam swallowed. "I can leave?"

"Yes."

"Now? And no one will stop me?"

"The choice is yours, Liam. However, I wish you would consider staying."

"Ah," Liam said, with a sinking feeling in his gut. *There would be a fucking catch.* "All right. Let's hear it. Your grand noble reasons to remain a hostage and trust the nice murdering bigots."

"It's not like that."

"It fucking is," Liam said. "There's always some fucking grand reason why I must turn the other cheek, aye? Act the fucking saint. But those bastards don't have to be remotely sorry for whatever it is they've done. Hell, they don't have to bother admitting a fucking thing. Can't have them inconvenienced, you know. So, what's it to be this time, Father? Let's hear it."

Father Murray looked away. It almost made Liam sorry for taking out his frustrations on him. *Almost.*

"There will be changes. If you choose to stay," Father Murray said, appearing to speak to the tile floor. "Do you wish to hear the offer?"

"As if I have a fucking choice."

"You do. I'm very serious about this. They tried to get me to make the decision for you, but I refused. As much as this means to me, it isn't my life at stake. Not now. All this time others have chosen for you. Whether because you were a child or because you were a prisoner. Well, that time is over. You're a man grown. The time has come to stop reacting and start acting. You're a free man. It's time to behave as one."

Liam blinked twice and swallowed. He opened his mouth to speak but his voice caught, and he coughed. "I'll hear it." The answer came out in a croak. "The offer."

"You're to be treated with courtesy by the staff. No more abuse."

A derisive retort lodged in the back of Liam's throat, but he let it be.

Father Murray continued. "Also, as of this moment you'll be granted private access to the Order's gym as needed. There's an outdoor track on the roof. You'll be able to run whenever you like, provided advance notice is given to the staff."

"And?"

"That's all I have. But if you've other demands I'll take them to Bishop Avery. He's open to anything within reason." Father Murray's tone was careful. He seemed to be making it clear who held the power in the situation.

"I see." Liam didn't know what to make of the change. Father Murray wasn't attempting to influence the outcome as he usually did. No guilty ploys. No appeals to his better nature. Nothing. "And the reasons for staying are the same, I suppose?"

"Actually, no," Father Murray said. "But should the results prove you're human—and we both know they will—the Church will extend the truce with the Fey. During that time, the Bishop is to accompany the Prelate and meet with His Holiness, the Pope, to discuss a policy change."

"They're serious?"

"Yes."

Liam paused. "They'll not go back on it?"

Deep regret passed over Father Murray's features. "I understand your mistrust. But as far as I can tell, the offer is being made in earnest. In fact, a representative from the Prelate's office is on his way and should arrive this evening. The Grand Inquisitor of the Northern Hemisphere is already here."

"Grand Inquisitor? Sorry, Father, but that does not in any fashion sound good."

"To be honest," Father Murray said. "I'm not sure it is. But his stated reasons for being present are to see to it that the tests are scientifically accurate by Church standards. If nothing else, his presence means my proposal for a new category of preternatural being is no longer being considered an outlandish suggestion from a battle-fatigued Guardian. The matter is under serious debate."

"Your proposal?"

Father Murray nodded. "Well? What's your answer to be?" During the entire conversation he had restricted his gaze to the floor as if he were afraid.

Liam weighed the situation and for the first time felt he had a real choice that would alter not only his life but the lives of others in a positive way. However, he had to admit that with the exception of Father Murray, he didn't trust anyone in the fucking building.

On second thought, sometimes he didn't trust Father Murray either.

A Grand Inquisitor for fuck's sake. Liam shivered. The Fey needed the truce. That hadn't changed. *What would Mary Kate have said to this?* That was easy. His Mary Kate, in spite of the temper she'd had on her—perhaps even because of it—had been for peace and civil rights. She'd have done anything to make a positive change. She was brave and fierce, was his Mary Kate. *Not like me.*

This is a real chance to get away out of here. No more locks and guards. He needed out, to breathe free air. *Leave it to someone else. Another of the Fey could take his place. Let them pay the price in blood.* But which? His da?

You're a coward.

I'm not. I've done my bit.

Four more days. Four. It seemed like forever.

His choice. His chance. He thought again of Mary Kate. "All right," Liam said. "I'll stay."

Father Murray finally shifted his gaze from the floor. His relief was obvious. "Thank you, Liam."

A shift had taken place. One Liam wasn't entirely clear on, but he could feel it. For the moment, he wasn't a wee piece of a greater plan—a broken pawn that could easily be discarded for little cost. He was an equal. It felt fine. "Can I ask for something?"

"Of course."

"Is there any way of getting music in this place? A radio? Or a record player? I'm dead bored."

"I'll arrange it." Father Murray went to the cabinet, fetched a second mug and took over making the tea. "Now tell me about what just happened." He retrieved the milk from the refrigerator.

"It won't make any sense."

"It's all right. Go on." Worry carved a deep line between Father Murray's eyes.

And just like that, the feeling of wholeness vanished. Liam swallowed rising anger. It left a bitter taste on his tongue. The water in the electric kettle roared ever louder until Father Murray switched it off. He finished with the tea and handed Liam the second steaming mug. The taste of freshly brewed tea was some comfort. Liam latched onto it like an anchor while he attempted to think of an intelligent way to explain. When the silence stretched a wee bit long he gave up. "I'm… going off my nut," he whispered. "Was Haddock. He's here."

Father Murray sat at the table with his tea. "He's dead."

"Aye, so I told him." Liam laughed and hated the raw terror that escaped his throat in the sound.

"It was a nightmare."

"Right. A fucking nightmare that almost smothered me in my bed." Liam took a sip from a shaking cup.

"You're serious."

"Can ghosts haunt people, Father?"

"It's possible, I suppose."

Gazing into the steaming cup, Liam attempted not to think about the things Haddock had said and failed.

Father Murray said, "I'll check on a few things. And let you know. In the meantime, try not to worry."

Easy enough for you to say. Liam nodded.

"How about some breakfast?" Father Murray asked. "You've not eaten in some time."

"I'm not hungry."

"I'll make toast."

Liam rushed through the afternoon's battery of psychological tests as fast as he could. It was hard to not think of the consequences weighing on his answers. Once or twice he thought he spied Haddock's ghost, but each time he checked there was nothing there. Father Stevenson, the priest who had administered the new series of examinations, seemed not to take notice.

Stevenson's American accent reminded Liam of a mixture of cowboy films and Elvis Presley. He was also suffering from a bad cold which unfortunately made him more difficult to understand. He was thin and wore a beard like Father Murray. However, while Father Murray had a studious fisherman's air about him, Father Stevenson would've passed for a New York Beatnik but for the layers of wool, the mildly aristocratic John Wayne accent, and the friendly smile. Strangely, that smile only made Liam trust him less.

When the tests were finally done three armed guards escorted Liam and

Father Stevenson down the hallway back to the observation room. Liam thought the inconsistency of the security measures bordered on comical. Why so many guards and yet rely upon simple locks and steel doors to keep him confined? They seemed unable to make up their minds whether he was more powerful than a normal human being or not. Liam kept an eye out for Haddock, but he didn't make another appearance. When Father Stevenson opened the Observation Room door, Liam entered first and spied Father Murray sitting at the table in the kitchenette, having a cup of tea. He'd returned from whatever errand had called him away that morning.

"Afternoon, Joseph," Father Stevenson said.

"Thaddeus." Father Murray smiled and nodded. He abandoned his tea and entered the sitting room.

Feeling anxious, Liam went to his room. He'd had enough of being poked, prodded and observed. He needed a run and decided to talk to Father Murray about going up to the roof. Liam heard quiet murmuring from the sitting room but ignored the conversation. Father Murray would let him know the results soon enough. Once more, Liam struggled with the urge for certainty and the comfort of ignorance. Bored, he looked for something suitable for a run and noted he was down to the last clean shirt. Either he would have to start doing his washing in the tub or it was time to ask Father Murray if there was a laundry service. *Bet they're experts at removing bloodstains. Bastards.*

"Liam?"

"Yes, Father?" Liam returned to the sitting room. Father Stevenson was gone. Liam noticed a cardboard box resting on the table next to the sofa. "What's this?"

"A record player. Compliments of Bishop Avery," Father Murray said. "Give me a moment. I need to ring someone."

"All right."

"In the meantime, why don't you set up the record player?"

Liam nodded, picked up the cardboard box and then took it to his room. He set the box on the built-in desk and opened it. He was shocked to find several albums from his and Mary Kate's former record collection. All six record albums were used and a bit scratched. Their collection had consisted of older Rolling Stones, Bad Company, Thin Lizzy, and Rory

Gallagher for the most part because most had been gifts from Oran who didn't venture much beyond the bounds of hard rock. Still, it was good stuff. Retrieving the first album from the box, a copy of Rolling Stones's *Sticky Fingers*, Liam touched its surface and read Mary Kate's handwriting on the edge with something approaching awe. *Our first record! With love, Mary Kate.* It still smelled of their flat, and he was immediately transported to a happier time. Mary Kate had splurged and bought the record new. It had been her favourite, and she'd played the thing over and over for a week when she'd first gotten it. Not that he'd minded, of course, particularly when she'd done him a strip tease to "Can't You Hear Me Knocking."

A slow smile crept across his face at the memory.

He ripped into the rest of the contents one-handed, discovering a black, square record player with a big speaker in the front panel. Getting it out of the box wasn't easy, and he supposed he should've asked for help rather than risking dropping the thing, but he couldn't bring himself to wait. He plugged it into an electrical socket, and then popped the silver latches on the sides. The lid yawned open, releasing the scent of plastic and factory glue. While it wasn't what one would call top of the line, it was a much nicer model than the one he and Mary Kate had owned. For one thing, it was new and for another, it was possible to stack more than one album on the spindle.

Carefully placing the needle on the fourth track of *Sticky Fingers*, he turned up the volume to its maximum. The speaker let out a few hisses, pops and crackles to let him know it was in working order. Then he threw himself onto the bed, got comfortable and closed his eyes. The opening guitar riffs blasted into the room, and Mick Jagger launched into "Can't You Hear Me Knocking." Taking a deep breath, a strange sensation surfaced. It was almost as if the memory of Mary Kate were someone else's. So much had happened. In spite of everything, he'd been so happy. He'd had everything he could've wanted, and he hadn't even known it at the time. Grief ambushed him, snagging his chest in a crushing grip.

He felt more than heard someone walk across the room. Opening wet eyes, he sat up in time to see a frowning Father Murray lift the needle from the record.

"Is there a problem, Father?"

"I said turn it down," Father Murray said.

"Sorry. Didn't hear you."

"You'll not make me regret this, will you?"

"You're going to tell me you don't care for the Stones?"

"I don't care for anything at that volume."

"Ah, now, that thing, good as it is, doesn't put out nearly the sound the speakers at The Harp and Drum did," Liam said. "I know you survived that."

"This isn't an underground bar."

"Well, we are underground."

"Liam—"

"—and I don't think the sound travels upstairs from here much. Do you?"

"Promise me you'll keep the volume to a manageable level."

Liam nodded, knowing full well that their definitions of manageable might differ. "Of course, Father."

"I need some tea. Join me?"

"Aye." Liam slid off the bed and followed Father Murray to the kitchenette. "Where did you find the records?"

"Don't you recognize them?" Father Murray started the kettle and then sat down at the table. He produced a pen from a pocket and began writing on a yellow legal pad.

"They're mine and Mary Kate's." Liam went to the refrigerator, got out the milk bottle and placed it on the table next to the sugar. "But everything was gone after—after I got back from Ballymena."

"While you were away your mother and I salvaged what we could. She's been holding on to the things she felt you might need or want. I asked her to send the records while we were at my sister's. I thought they'd bring you some comfort." Father Murray indicated he should sit in the chair on the far right side of the table. The pad of paper was resting in front of it. A message was printed on its surface in Father Murray's careful handwriting.

There are blind spots. Places the cameras can't see, it read. *The right side of the kitchen table is one. Security can record the conversation, but at least we've this. I want you to talk about the things you need to say without feeling judged.*

"*An bfhuil aon Gaeilge agat?*" Liam asked, keeping his voice low. *Do you have any Irish?* It was the first solution to come to mind. Irish had long been used in the prisons whenever the Nationalist prisoners didn't want the screws to understand.

Father Murray got up and went to the cabinet next to the sink, returning with two cups. One corner of his mouth twitched upward. "*Tá. Beagán.*" A little.

"*Maith thú.*" *Good.* Liam smiled. It was obvious Father Murray had more Irish than he'd started with. While passing notes was certainly a good solution to the problem, it wasn't optimal. Liam's ability to read had improved, but he was still slow at it, and the state of his handwriting was embarrassing. He continued in Irish at a whisper. "Do *they* have any Irish, do you think?" He had to repeat it slower before Father Murray understood.

Shaking his head, Father Murray reached for the notepad.

"That'll be useful, then," Liam said, watching as Father Murray gently tore the note free, folded it and then dropped it into the sink.

Father Murray returned to making the tea. "Unfortunately, it wouldn't take long to find a translator," he whispered. "Even with relations between the Church and the Nationalists the way they are."

Liam sighed.

Father Murray wrote, *There are ways of getting around the surveillance. It's not impossible.* He waited until Liam finished reading and then proceeded to rip both notes into tiny pieces and drop them into the sink, rinsing them down the drain. He picked up a dirty plate from breakfast and began washing it. The sound of his voice wasn't quite loud enough to be heard over the running water. "I've done it many times, myself."

Liam moved to Father Murray's side and blinked. "Why would you know how to do a thing like that?" He grabbed a kitchen towel.

"You think you're the only one who's ever been under observation?" Father Murray asked, handing off the plate and starting in on a dirty mug. "Everyone who joins the Order is screened. Not only at the start, but every time there's thought to be just cause."

"Oh."

"However, we must let them think they're getting everything even if they are not. Do you understand?"

Liam nodded.

Chapter 8

"Hope you don't mind my saying," Father Stevenson said in his slow Texas drawl made stuffy by a head cold. Sitting hunched over a cup of hot cocoa in a buttoned overcoat and wool neck scarf, he was overdressed for an indoor table at the commissary. Father Murray assumed it was because of the illness. "You're taking a mighty big risk with that kid. Have you given any consideration to what happens if he cracks?"

Father Murray looked up from his own cup and tried not to show his unease. In an attempt at holiday festivity, someone had decorated the room using red and gold ropes of tinsel. It only made the white walls and empty plastic chairs appear more desolate.

In his rush to architect the peace agreement, he hadn't considered what might happen if Liam was diagnosed with a personality disorder. He hadn't pried, believing that Liam deserved at least that small amount of dignity. *Maybe I should have. If I'd been the one to find a problem it wouldn't have had so many repercussions. Why didn't I consider that?* Sipping his tea, he swallowed a feeling that he may have let Liam down at the expense of his own ambitions. *So many lives in the balance, God help me.* "I warned you that he had some… unusual traits. Quirks."

Father Stevenson lowered his voice. "I saw the tape. He was talking to thin air. That's quite a bit more than a quirk, Joe."

"Then it's to be a psychotic disorder diagnosis, is it?"

It was late, and the commissary was empty of anyone except for the janitorial staff. The kitchen was closed, but hot beverages were available for those working through the night. A faint ghost of the roast beef that had been served for the dinner haunted the air. The commissary had the advantage of being free of cameras or listening devices, and as such, this had been the main reason he'd chosen it as a meeting place. If he'd elected to meet off the grounds, reports would be filed, and he wanted to hear Father Stevenson's conclusions without the worry of interference.

"He displays symptoms, but that isn't what's bothering me," Father Stevenson said with a sniff. "We've discovered physical anomalies—rapid healing, elevated heart rate, metabolism, kinesthetic responses and the lower body temperature that Father Conroy discussed with you earlier. The good news is he passed all the usual tests without complications. Hell, I watched him drink three glasses of holy water with no hesitation and no ill effects. As far as I can determine, he's not one of the Nephilim as Father Conroy suspects. If he is, he's of a type not on record. Sure, he exhibits high levels of aggression. But hell, antagonism toward authority is a natural psychological reaction to abuse. You say it was his stepfather?"

Father Murray nodded. "One of the reasons why I hesitated to act when I was first given the field assignment. If a demon spawn is injured or harmed in any way, the perceived perpetrator is killed or injured instantly. Patrick Kelly was never harmed."

"Interesting." Father Stevenson blew his nose.

"Have you come to any conclusions in regards to his… status, yet?"

"Frankly, he's either a human with unusually fast reflexes and a few physical anomalies or another type of preternatural creature. Although, I need more evidence to support the second theory."

"In your professional opinion?" Father Murray asked with a certain amount of relief.

"I'm absolutely certain he's not a full-fledged demon. As for a Nephilim? Nephilim have been known to get past the holy water test, but never in that quantity. Not without discomfort and not voluntarily. They certainly sense its presence. The kid had no idea. I was watching."

"He's been Confirmed."

"No shit?" Both of Father Stevenson's eyebrows shot up.

"First Communion and Confession," Father Murray said. "I checked the records. He's never had a problem with any of the sacraments."

"Well, how about that?" Father Stevenson wiped under his reddened nose and pocketed his handkerchief. "Must say, as charming as the Nephilim can be, I've yet to meet one I've actually liked."

Father Murray smiled.

"Also, the tests indicate he carries far too much anxiety. I've yet to see a Nephilim clever enough to fake that," Father Stevenson said. "By the way, is there some significance to that cigarette lighter he carries around?"

"It belonged to his wife. Other than that, I don't think so. Why?"

"Seems to touch it when upset or antagonized."

A twinge of guilt surfaced. *He needs real help. You should be paying attention, Joe. It's not like the lad has anyone else to look out for him outside of his mother.* He remembered Bran and reconsidered. *Well, no one mortal, anyway.* "I hadn't noticed."

"The test results indicate he is highly intelligent. However, he is suffering from depressive neurosis as you suspected." Father Stevenson flipped through his notes. "There are indications of obsessive compulsive disorder, phobic or anxiety neurosis, hysterical disassociation, aggressive personality, drug dependence, psychophysiological symptoms, sexual trauma and transient situational disturbance."

"That's a long list."

"Take it easy. I'm sure you'd be hard-pressed to find anyone around here who didn't exhibit quite a few of those symptoms. That said, we should give serious consideration to cognitive therapy if you think he'll respond. Medication too. As soon as the biological data is complete. We've got to get him stabilized before he does something stupid. And trust me, he will do something self-destructive—maybe even suicidal if he hasn't already. He'll use whatever is at hand. And that means—"

"The guards." Father Murray felt a chill settle into his stomach. *Mary, Mother of God, what was I thinking?* "I'll watch him."

"He sets his mind to it, well… I'm not sure you'll be able to stop him."

"I know."

"One more thing," Father Stevenson said. "You understand if that kid is declared human, he's in deep trouble?"

Father Murray blinked. "Why?"

"You might not hold a grudge over Waterford, but one thing is for certain, the Grand Inquisitor sure as hell does."

"Do you think that's why he's here?"

"What do you think?" Father Stevenson whispered. "He's gunning for you." He blew his nose into a white handkerchief again.

"He was running experiments on children."

"Spawn of the Fallen."

"The administrative staff were contaminated."

"That wasn't his fault."

"Are you telling me that you believe Monsignor Paul wasn't aware of what they were up to? He had full medical records on every one of them. They were running child prostitution—"

"The records were lost in the fire. You've no proof."

"I was right about Father Davidson," Father Murray said. "Father Jackson and the others would still be alive if someone had listened to me."

"I know." Father Stevenson sighed. "Look, I'm on your side in this. I saw what Father Davidson did. I was there."

"Why now?" Father Murray asked. "It's been years."

"I wish I knew," Father Stevenson said. "But I gotta warn you. That kid gets declared human and stays here? He's headed for hard time in the pokey for membership in an illegal organization first chance Monsignor Paul gets. You damn well know which illegal organization I'm talking about. You won't be looking at much better. You get my drift?"

"There's no proof."

"The kid's word against theirs. Even I know how that one comes out."

"Thanks for the warning."

"Not a problem." Father Stevenson closed his little black notebook. "Now, I've told you everything I know. It's your turn."

"You haven't told me all of what is bothering you."

"We'll address that after you tell me what's going on."

Father Murray stared into his tea again. He'd known Father Thaddeus Stevenson on and off for five years. They'd met shortly after Waterford. In spite of the risks, Father Stevenson had taken his side against Monsignor

Paul's allegations and had given a solid recommendation as well. Father Stevenson had eventually been transferred to South Africa as a result. Father Murray knew he needed to trust someone. Father Stevenson was worth trusting. "You said Liam was talking to someone who wasn't there. Were there indications of another presence?"

Leaning closer, Father Stevenson said, "Fine. If we continue on the assumption that the kid isn't psychotic. And if what you propose is true…" He paused and shrugged. "Then a presence is possible."

"Right."

"But here's where I hope you're wrong." Father Stevenson sighed. "Because if there is an entity in the complex that no one but that kid has detected then security isn't what it should be. If that doesn't scare you, it sure as shit scares me."

"The Bishop isn't going to like this."

Father Stevenson drank his hot cocoa and grimaced. "Security will like it less."

"Would you do me a favor?" Father Murray asked. "Don't mention this conversation to anyone. Not yet."

"Bishop Avery is expecting an overview of the test results tomorrow afternoon."

"It's important that we get our facts straight before security is involved. You know how they'll react. The agreement will blow apart."

Father Stevenson sighed. "Okay. You got one more day. I'll make up some excuse. But you know we're cutting it awful fine. There are only three days left."

"Have you ever read a report that indicated a bad smell associated with the Fallen? The only demons that I've been able to find such an association with would definitely be incapable of getting past the security measures."

Father Stevenson shook his head. "Have you smelled something?"

"Not me. No," Father Murray said. "But Liam has."

"Do you think it's associated with whatever it was he saw?"

"I don't think so," Father Murray said. "But I'm going to find out."

Chapter 9

"This is a dream, so it is," Oran said in his I'm-older-and-wiser voice.

Oh, for fuck's sake, Liam thought, rolling his eyes. Admittedly, compared to Oran, Liam hadn't seen much of the world beyond the confines of Derry and Belfast. Oran had worked on a fishing trawler before marrying Elizabeth and had visited many distant sea ports, if the stories were true. Also, unlike Oran, Liam had had sex with only one woman in his whole life and that one woman was his wife, Mary Kate. According to some people—that is, Oran—that meant he might as well be a virgin on top of everything else. "Oh, aye?" Liam asked. "So, you're wanting to talk that solipsism shite, then?"

It was summer. The evening was nice and warm, and they were sitting on the steps outside the apartment building near the car park, having a few pints and a smoke before it was time to go home for dinner. Across the street, four British soldiers had three lads up against a wall and were patting down the poor bastards while a small crowd looked on.

"Solip-what?"

"Solipsism," Liam said, keeping his tone casual. He got out his cigarettes and offered one to Oran before continuing. "A philosophical theory based on the concept that nothing but the self exists." Tossing out words Oran didn't know was Liam's way of evening the score.

"Where the fuck did you hear a shite word like that?"

"Read it in one of Mary Kate's textbooks last week," Liam said, lighting a cigarette and blowing out the smoke in one big, warm cloud. It was hard not to smile and ruin the effect.

Mary Kate hadn't come home from University yet, but he wasn't expecting her to show for another hour. He could feel the grease under his nails and the grit in his hair from lying on the ground. He'd changed the oil and had spent a couple hours tinkering with the taxi's engine. Oran was a professional mechanic, and he was present for company, moral support, and if Liam was perfectly honest, insurance against his freshman efforts banjaxing the engine.

Oran's face went red. "I'm fucking serious, you bog idiot."

Liam blinked. It usually took three or four attempts at winding Oran up to get a response.

"Oh." Liam took a couple swallows of scrumpy and waited for Oran to get to the point. Oran being Oran, that could take a while.

"There's no time for this," Oran said, throwing his empty at a pile of rubbish that had collected on the edge of the car park. He missed, and the bottle shattered in a spray of broken glass on the pavement a foot short. He got up. "Fuck you."

"Don't go."

Oran's brows pressed together in an angry line. "Will you listen? Or are you for playing games?"

"I'm listening." Liam wondered if it was something to do with the next bank job. Oran tended to get twitchy when a new one was in the works. Liam was usually the last in the unit to know. Of course, they had to give him enough notice to start shopping for a likely car. If a new job was being planned, it meant it was time to tour the Loyalist areas again. He wondered how long he'd have to lift the car? He'd need to replace the spark plugs and tires—

"This is a dream, mate," Oran said. "A dream."

—and make the necessary adjustments to the alignment. "I hear you."

"No, you don't." Oran sighed. "Look. We're not outside your flat, planning a job. This isn't the summer of 1976. It's more than a year later. You're in hospital being studied like a rat in a cage. I'm dead. You shot me. This is a dream."

A bad feeling solidified in Liam's gut and twisted. "Don't say shite like that. I'd die before I'd do for you! And you know it!" Liam's throat ached. Such a thing wasn't fucking possible, but the knot in his insides hinted at an unwanted truth and if he wasn't careful it'd ruin a perfectly pleasant afternoon. Maybe it already had.

Oran bent enough to lay a gentle hand on his shoulder. Now that his face was closer Liam noticed a small pale and round dent on Oran's forehead just above his right eyebrow.

That wasn't there before.

"Listen, mate," Oran said. "It's all right. I'm your friend. I always will be. Nothing will change that. Nothing. You did me a good turn. No matter how much it hurt for you to do it. I owe you."

Why would Oran think I'd do for him? Why would he even say a thing like that? "I didn't—"

"You did what I asked of you. And you kept my name clean in Elizabeth's eyes. So I'm here to help. And here I'll stay. You're not alone. Understand?"

Liam blinked. Oran wasn't making any sense at all.

"Something bad is about to happen. And it's very important that I give you an understanding of things before you wake up."

It's the monster in you, Liam thought. *That's why he thinks I've done for him. He fucking sees it. That fucking creature. They all do. But I wouldn't let—*

"Shut your fucking gob!"

Liam hadn't understood that he'd been slabbering out loud until Oran's punch landed. Liam felt the dull smack in his jaw, and his head rocked back far enough to hit the cinderblock wall behind him.

"Shite! Why the fuck do you have to make it so fucking difficult to help you?" Oran shook out his fist and moved his fingers to make certain his knuckles were sound. "You're going to wake, and you'll remember. I want you to remember. It's important."

Liam stared up at Oran, not believing.

"You must find Mary Kate. You need her. And she needs you. Be careful. You can't go and scare her. She'll rabbit off. And she'll not find her way to you again. If that happens, you're both fucked. Do you hear?"

"Aye."

"And never you mind that fuck, Haddock."

"Wait. Haddock?"

"Listen to me." Oran blew air out of his cheeks. "He's not as powerful as he wants you to think. Fucking bent Peeler. He has limits, so he does. You watch for them. You'll see. Can only go at you for so long. Takes too much energy over there. Are you listening?"

"I am."

"One more thing," Oran said. "That priest may be keeping you from shifting for now, but you're not helpless. You have other resources, you know. Use what you have. Think. I know you have it in you. There'll come a time when you'll need to, and soon. Understand?"

"What the fuck are you on about?" Liam asked.

"Just do as I say. Don't be such a stubborn idiot. Think before you act. And don't you dare kill yourself, you hear?"

"What?"

"I know you want to. The fucking drugs," Oran said, glaring. "I know it fucking hurts, mate. You don't want to feel anymore. I understand. But that's a coward's way, and I know you're no coward."

Liam looked away and ran his fingers through his hair. His face was hot, but his chest was cold. He didn't know Oran could see so much. *Must be obvious to everyone.* "Don't know what you mean."

"You do. I know you do. I saw. What the fuck were you thinking? That wee bastard with the spots might have killed you."

"He didn't."

"There's things you must face, *mo chara*. Otherwise, that fucking monster in your head will have you," Oran said. "And you'll not find Mary Kate. You'll be fucked, and there'll be no saving you. Do you hear? You have to find her before it does."

"Before what does? The monster?"

Oran shook his head and turned, starting his way home.

"Wait!" Liam stood up, but the scrumpy had more of a kick than he'd anticipated. He was drunk and dizzy and had to put a hand against the wall to keep from falling. "I don't understand! Don't go!"

Oran shouted from across the car park. "You're a smart lad even if you are mule stubborn. So I told Éamon, and so it is. You'll figure it out. Solipsism. Fuck. The cheek on you." He snorted. "Well, I'm off. I should look in on Elizabeth and the little ones. Wee Brian is too clever for his own good. Making mischief most likely. Gets it from his ma." Oran winked.

Liam discovered he was paralyzed. Worse, he couldn't breathe. He forced air through his throat to call Oran back, but all that came out was a hiss. He tried again and again until his voice cracked through the invisible barrier, and he screamed. "Oran!"

He woke with tears on his face and a painful lump in his throat. *Christ, why the fuck did I have to be the one to live? Why me and not you?*

You're nothing but a junkie. Elizabeth's last words to him echoed up from the past. The wee red light near the ceiling glowered at him in the half-light, reminding Liam of where he was. *Fucking cameras.* He took in a slow breath. Wiping his face with the inside of his shirt sleeve, he coughed and then took a slow breath to bury the grief down deep where it belonged—where the cameras couldn't record it.

Find Mary Kate, he thought. *Before it finds her. What the fuck did Oran mean by that?* Liam didn't care what happened to himself when it came down to it, but Mary Kate was another matter.

When did I last check on Oran's family? Shite. Three weeks? A month? I promised to look after them. What if they need something? What if the weans are in trouble? He cursed himself for wallowing in his grief. He had responsibilities. *No time for this shite.*

Get out of here. Have to get out of here. I must.

If he were above ground, he'd grab his trainers and go for a run to Oran's for a quick check on Elizabeth and the weans, but he couldn't, not yet. Suddenly the walls pressed in and then all at once his chest seized up, and he couldn't move or breathe due to a mind-stunning pain in the middle of his back. It spread to his ribs. His muscles felt like they were knotting on their own, twisting, shredding, ripping themselves from his bones. It wasn't like the shape-shifting. That was about reconfiguring and changing. This was about destruction. Panic set in. He was going to suffocate if he didn't breathe soon. Then the fit passed as quickly as it'd come. It left behind a tingling sensation along the backs of his arms not entirely because of the cold.

Gingerly, he sat up and swung his legs over the side of the bed. The room was freezing.

That isn't good. Should tell Father Murray about that.

What if he tells the fucking Inquisitor? I'm fucked. Looking up at the cameras, Liam wondered why no one had come to look in on him when clearly he'd had some sort of attack. *Bastards.* He checked the time. It was three o'clock in the morning. He needed to run so bad he could almost taste it. How many tons of dirt, steel, concrete, and stone weighed above his head? *The roof.* There was the track on the roof. His ribs ached with the specter of distant pain—an unwelcome visitor who could return at any moment. *Can't think about that. Stop it. Now.*

He heard a thump from the other room and paused, listening. When it wasn't repeated he convinced himself it was nothing. Getting out of bed, he decided on a cup of tea.

Thump. Thump. Shuffle.

Rushing across the room, he grabbed the door handle. The door didn't budge.

Locked. It's locked. Father Murray locked me in. Why? Terror surged through his system.

Another thump was followed by a crash and a muffled shout. His fear of being trapped was forgotten in a frozen spasm of dread.

Something bad is about to happen.

"Father?!" Liam grabbed at the doorknob again, rattling it. It didn't budge. He went to the bed, quickly pulled on a pair of discarded socks and jammed on his work boots. Then he rushed at the door, giving it a good kick and then another, leaving a grey boot print on the pristine white paint. The steel door shuddered inside its wooden frame. The door frame splintered and cracked. Another muted shout filtered in from the other side of the wall.

"I'm coming, Father!" He stepped back and smashed the sole of his boot on the space next to the doorknob a third time. The lock's steel bolt shredded the door frame. He shoved through the narrow space and staggered into the sitting room, scraping his arms and back in the process. His shirt tore, but he didn't notice it much because of the stench of week-old burned corpse.

The door to Father Murray's room gaped. Liam rushed to help but stopped when he saw the blond screw named Father Jensen crash into a bookshelf. The bookcase teetered, and a cascade of books dropped to the floor of Father Murray's room. A picture smashed, shattering glass all over the rug. Dressed only in brown plaid flannel pajamas, no shoes and unarmed, Father Murray closed on Jensen. As Liam watched, the priest executed a head butt that would've been at home in any bar fight. Liam winced at the crunch of bone and cartilage as Jensen's nose was pulped. Blood gushed down the screw's face. Father Murray followed that move up with a knee to the groin, and Liam was impressed with the priest's utter lack of scruples when it came to a fist-fight. Father Murray then dove for a pistol lying on the floor, but Jensen moved with an unnatural speed and grace for a man of his size. Darting over to the gun, Jensen kicked it out of Father Murray's reach. The priest rolled onto his back. Jensen stomped on Father Murray's chest, pinning him under a big black boot.

Do something, you idiot. Liam bolted into the room. Spying the pistol on the rug near the chest of drawers, he picked it up and without conscious thought, checked the safety and then pointed it at Jensen. "Get the fuck off him!" He paused, considering whether or not to fire the Browning. *I gave up the fighting. I swore I would. Toss it to Father Murray. Jensen is a priest. And fucking screw or no, I can't murder a priest.*

At that moment, Father Murray snatched up a piece of splintered furniture leg and stabbed Father Jensen in the calf. Father Jensen screamed. Father Murray swung the piece of wood again—this time with both hands and a great deal of force. Father Jensen stumbled. Father Murray was free and on his feet again.

"Run, Liam! Get out of here!" Father Murray waved him out of the room.

Father Jensen whirled. To Liam's surprise, the screw charged at him with a snarl. Father Jensen reached for the pistol. Liam's reflexes made the decision for him. His finger twitched against the trigger. In the same instant, Father Jensen slapped the gun barrel. The gun went off. Liam smelled blood mixed in with the smoke of spent cartridge but didn't take the time to see if he'd hit his target. He ducked under Father Jensen's arm and darted past. However, Liam was brought up short by the sight of Father Murray sprawled on the floor near the washroom. A small bottle of clear fluid was on the carpet next to his hand. A dark stain expanded in the carpet underneath him. With a blink, Liam knew it to be blood.

It had soaked through the right side of Father Murray's pajama top and splattered the wall. The priest's brown eyes stared up at Liam, wide with shock. Liam's heart stopped, frozen solid.

Oh, fuck. I've done for him, he thought. Dropping to his knees, Liam put a hand to the wound to stop the bleeding.

Jensen trotted to the telephone that had been upended on the floor and pushed the button a couple times to ring off before dialing. "Hello? This is security." His accent was layered with something foreign that Liam couldn't identify. "The creature in OR has escaped. It killed everyone on this level. It's armed. Get help down here." Jensen slammed the receiver onto the base with a smile, and with a salute, he fled the room.

The alarms started their whooping.

Liam automatically wiped his prints from the gun before dropping it onto the carpet.

Father Murray wheezed. His mouth moved to form words, but nothing came out. His eyes squeezed shut against a spasm of pain. He sputtered.

"Father?"

"Go, Liam. After him."

"But—"

"Keys. They're on the chest of drawers." He seemed to take in as much air as the hurt would let him. "Follow him. Find out where he goes."

"I shot you."

"Was an accident. I'll explain."

Father Murray didn't look much like he was going to live to do much explaining. If that were the case, it'd be Liam's word against Father Jensen's phone call. *The camera. Is there a fucking camera in this room?* Liam searched the ceiling and found the damned thing smashed.

Father Murray grabbed his arm and tugged, bringing Liam back to the problem at hand. "After him. Ring for me at St. Agnes. Leave a message. Trust only me, Father Thomas, or Bishop Avery. No one else. Got it?"

"You'll bleed to death."

"I'll be fine. It's only the shock setting in. Go."

Liam got up from the floor. The screw was long gone. It was too late to follow him. How much longer before the others showed up? Liam needed a few things if he was to get far. It'd been freezing the last time he'd been outside. He couldn't go dressed in his pajamas. He pulled the blanket from the bed and draped it over Father Murray. Then Liam grabbed the keys from the top of the chest of drawers and ran back to his room. He shoved the warped door on its now twisted hinges. It made an awful sound as it gave away. His laundry bag was where he'd left it, leaning against the foot of the bed. Stuffing clothes lying scattered on the floor back into the bag, he jerked the string tight and secured it with a quick knot. That done, he slipped into his anorak and then shouldered the laundry bag. Two kicks forced the door open wide enough for him to exit with the awkward burden balanced on his left shoulder. Pausing to look in at the priest one last time, he saw that Father Murray appeared to be unconscious. Liam prayed that help would arrive in time and trotted to the outer door. The alarm's whoops were loud enough to hurt his ears.

The short hallway was empty of guards, and he wouldn't have known they'd been there at all save for the drying crimson stains and lumps of flesh decorating the white cinderblock walls. Smudged lines of blood traced a path to the bodies, or what Liam assumed were bodies. Two legs jutted out of an open supply closet.

A door slammed.

Liam started and turned toward the sound. The "Fire Exit" sign glowed an angry red. Bolted to the ceiling tiles above it, the remains of the security camera dangled in a mass of broken glass and twisted metal. His nose picked up Jensen's fading corpse-stench. The trail led straight to the fire exit. Sprinting, Liam expected the stairwell to be locked, but it wasn't. He didn't stop to think of why. He threw the door wide and bolted up the stairs two at a time. At the top of the next riser, he was greeted by yet another broken camera. A loud bang echoed from above. Another set of alarms joined the shrill chorus a few beats off-cant from the first. Small weapons gunfire punctuated the screaming alarms, and someone shouted. Up there, someone emptied an entire clip of rounds. The gun battle paused. A long shriek of agony was cut off by another slamming door.

Liam paused. *Go the fuck back now. See to Father Murray. Needs you, he does. No one should have to die alone. He doesn't deserve that.*

What if he's dead already?

A more pragmatic aspect of himself took up the argument. *And if he is? There's fuck all you can do about it. Stay, and you're bound for Long Kesh.*

Without Father Murray, it's fucked you are. You know it. He knew it too. That's why he wanted you away. Your only chance is to get the fuck out.

Liam reached the door labelled "Ground Floor." Once there, he paused to zip up his coat. He wasn't winded. The daily run had its advantages, and while he hadn't worn his trainers for almost a week, he hadn't lost much of his stamina. Pushing the door open a crack, he peered through to gauge what he was up against.

Alarm lights flickered. The main entrance hall was empty. One of the paintings hung crookedly off its wire. He estimated the glass doors serving as the entrance to the building were about a hundred feet away, and if he ventured farther from his hiding place he'd see the street from where he stood. As it was, he had a good view of the hulking reception desk positioned against the back wall. On the left side of the desk, a riser of stairs led to the upper floors but didn't access the lower levels. *No one there.* Two steel elevators were located to the right of the reception desk. The lights above the sliding doors indicated that the elevators were unoccupied, or at least not in use. All was quiet. He would've risked bolting to the exit were it not for the crimson pool spreading across the grey-flecked tiles from under the desk. Electronics hissed and popped, hidden behind dark oak panels. The reception desk was as tall as a bar counter, and based upon what Liam had seen upon entering the facility, the two priests who manned the station regularly stood up in order to greet the guests entering the building. Liam had wondered about that on Sunday, until he'd turned and spied the television screens displaying security camera feedback inside.

He breathed in layered scents of spent bullets, sweat, fear and blood. Father Jensen's stench lingered among them. So, the screw was gone—otherwise the stench would've overpowered the others. Where were the guards? Liam had counted three on Sunday. At least one was dead. He knew that from the smell and the blood. Perhaps they were pursuing Father Jensen?

Far off sirens added to the cacophony. The Peelers were on the way. It wouldn't be long before the situation became more complicated.

Liam inched farther from his hiding place to get a better view of the exit. The floor-to-ceiling bullet-resistant panes of glass were cob-webbed with glittery cracks and circular pock marks. Somehow the glass on the far right had escaped damage and formed an empty black rectangle. Two bodies lay sprawled on the tiles. One was missing an arm. *The left.* Both appeared to have been ripped apart. Liam avoided looking at their faces and focused on the clear window for some sign of Father Jensen instead.

No moon, he thought. *It'll be dark.* But the lack of light wouldn't pose too much of a problem, not for the likes of him. Other factors would, however. *The bloody cold, for one. You'll freeze your bollocks off for certain.* Liam thought. *No time to do anything about that now. Go now while there's the chance. Think yourself a shadow. No trouble at all. It'll be no different than those late night strolls through the Shankill.*

Right. You thought that when you had that run-in with those smugglers. Look what happened?

Fuck that. Was angry. That's what it was. Stay calm. Keep your head. You'll do.

Taking a deep breath, he prayed himself invisible and concentrated until he felt his skin prickle with it. He tugged his coat closer and decided to look in on the dead at the reception desk. *What would be the harm?* Once he knew their fates, then he'd head for the exit.

He walked hunched inside his anorak with the laundry bag perched on his left shoulder and had gotten half across the room when he heard a groan and a scratching sound from behind the reception desk. Upon hearing a second moan, he rushed to the desk. A young priest sat slumped in the second of the two office chairs—the source of the oxygenated blood oozing across the floor. His upper body was sprawled across the desk's surface, and his right cheek lay against the paper blotter. The television screens in front of him were smashed. The young priest's hand twitched, and it took a moment for Liam to register the consciousness in the one pain-filled brown eye. Half of the man's face was lost in a mass of torn flesh.

Liam searched the top of the desk for what the young priest might want and winced at a sickening mound of gory viscera glistening on top of papers stacked in a file bin labelled "Out Box." His stomach did a lazy flip and the back of his throat grew slick.

What kind of sick bastard does something like that?

The monster was muzzled and trapped in the darkest corner of his brain and had been for days, but Liam somehow sensed its amusement nonetheless. His jaw tightened in disgust.

The priest let out another soft moan, and his fingernails scratched the desk. Liam finally understood that the man was reaching for the rosary draped over the appointment book. Pulling the rosary beads free, Liam placed them in the priest's hand with a gentle motion. An expression of relief poured over the man's features.

Liam sicked up a reassurance out of reflex. "H-help will be here soon. They'll have you right again before you know it." It was clear the poor man was a goner. As it was, Liam didn't know how it was he was still alive. *Dying alone is bad.*

He has his God. No time for this. Must go. It was the monster's distant whisper. Liam didn't understand why he felt relieved.

"I'm so sorry. Wish there was something else I could do for you," Liam said. *Must go. Now.*

Echoes of footsteps clamoring up the stairwell spurred him into action. He was almost to the door when a group of guards tumbled out of the stairwell door with a shuddering bang-thud of steel against drywall.

"Hey! You! Stop there!"

Shoving through the heavy glass exit, Liam legged it without much hope of escape. Belfast City Hospital was across the street, and the Peelers were on the way. He almost tripped over another body sprawled just outside the building. He didn't give it a glance but sprinted as fast as he could while shouldering the awkward and heavy cloth bag. It became quickly apparent that he should drop it if he were to make much distance. At the same time, he needed its contents if he was going to survive the cold.

He took the first opportunity to get off the Lisburn Road and made for the shadows between two university buildings. That was when his Uncle Sceolán stepped from under a nearby tree and waved him across the cement walk.

"Took you long enough to get out of there," Sceolán said.

Liam stumbled to his uncle's side and dropped the laundry bag. Gasping for breath, he bent over and grabbed his knees. He felt dizzy. His uncle placed a cool hand on his back, and then Queen's grew dim. At that moment, a group of the Church's guards rounded the building. Liam's skin tingled more fiercely than it had outside of his dreams in a week. He held his breath and waited to see what would happen—if the sensation would grow worse with the coming of the monster or if something altogether different would happen.

Four guards ran past, never having seen him or his uncle. Liam counted five heartbeats before allowing himself to breathe.

"Thank you," Liam whispered, breathing in great gulps of frozen air. He was warm for the moment, but he was also sweating from the run and the dread. Soon he'd be chilled. Trembling with the rush of fading adrenaline, he said, "You were—you were right."

"Am often enough. Ask your da." Uncle Sceolán paused and then arched his right eyebrow. "And what was it that I was right about this time?"

"Father Murray," Liam said, sniffing and then drawing in a big breath. He held it to slow his galloping heart. When he couldn't hold it any longer he blew the air out his cheeks. He didn't risk speaking again until he was sure he could do so without coughing. His lungs ached. "Father Murray has been shot. I did it. Was an accident. Missed the screw I was aiming for." He took another breath. "What if he's dead?" *Shouldn't have broken my word.*

"We lose friends in war."

"Stupid. Was fucking stupid. Why the fuck did I pick up that fucking gun?"

"Don't be so hard on yourself."

Sirens echoed off the buildings and flickering lights were reflected in window glass.

"Oh, that's just fucking grand. Peelers are here. They find me, and it won't matter if Father Murray lives or dies."

"All right, calm yourself."

"I am calm."

"You are?"

"Oh, shut your gob."

"Is that the thanks I get for saving yourself from yourself twice in one week?"

"I didn't ask you to."

"You didn't thank me much, either."

"Fuck off!" Liam's head was pounding. He wasn't being rational, he knew, but he couldn't seem to stop himself. "Get the fuck away from me!"

Uncle Sceolán nodded once and then stepped back into the shadow. He was gone in a gust of wind.

"Wait!" Liam was struck with a sudden memory of the dream Oran's words before it all had gone bad.

Better this way, Liam thought. *Less chance of others getting hurt.*

Chapter 10

Belfast, County Antrim, Northern Ireland
December 1977

Shamed and frustrated, Liam wrapped a fist around his anger and eased farther into the shadows—away from the riot of emergency lights splashing the Uni buildings. An army helicopter was on the way. He could hear it. Heart pounding, he willed himself to fade into the background as his uncle had done, but nothing seemed to happen. He gritted his teeth and concentrated all the more. Still the tell-tale prickling on his skin that he'd come to associate with magic refused to surface. *For fuck's sake. Why not now?*

You shot Father Murray. You killed him. You killed Oran too.

No. He's not dead. You heard him. He's only—

Another siren approached—this time, clearly heading his direction—he panicked and hid behind a nearby tree. The siren drew louder and closer until an ambulance sped past on the Lisburn Road, heading for Belfast City Hospital. Relief poured over him, and he released the breath he'd been holding with a shiver.

Father Murray is—

Don't. No time for that now. Liam shoved the frenzied thoughts down deep inside before they could break him apart. Panic fought its way back up his throat, tasting of bile. He swallowed, squeezed his eyes shut and deliberately slowed his breathing. *The hole in him—*

Stop it, damn you! You've done worse. Survive first!

Why am I the one who lives?

"I said, stop it!" The words came out in a hiss, and it surprised him. *Hold it together. Aye? Father Murray might be fine. Think about it later. Must get out of here now.* Liam waited until his heart stopped racing and held out his hand. If he squinted he could pretend he didn't see the fingers tremble. *Right, then. What are the options?*

There weren't many. First, there was returning to West Belfast. *Not the best idea, mate.* Someone was sure to recognize him. Second, staying near Queen's. *Forget it.* He didn't know the Uni area. He did know Andytown and the Lower Falls—well enough to hide away for an extended time. Of course, that would mean a freezing walk through Loyalist West Belfast. Even the shortest route would mean heading into Sandy Row until he could turn west and up the Falls. If he were lucky, the UDA would be focused on other amusements. However, if he was unlucky—

Peace on Earth, good will to all men, thought Liam, glaring northward. *Provided those men aren't Catholic, is that not so?*

Best get on with it.

There's Great Victoria Street. That'd be considerably safer and closer than the Lower Falls, aye? He didn't know Great Victoria Street as well as he did the Falls but the odds of his making it through Sandy Row without being rompered were next to none.

He hefted the laundry bag and made his way north, walking on the right-hand side of the street. Like most of Belfast, Queen's was different at this hour than it was during the day—sullen and quiet. Lamps bolted to the sides of the red brick Victorian buildings formed patches of brightness on the cement walk, and rows of black windows looked down on him from warm rooms. He attempted not to think of the cold, but the fingers of his left hand were growing stiff and painful. Pausing, he shifted the laundry bag to his right shoulder and stretched the ache from his freezing fingers inside his coat pocket.

He told himself he'd find somewhere to kip until morning. It might mean sleeping in a dustbin, provided he could find one. Since the bombing campaign dustbins were thin on the street in certain areas.

Leaving Queen's behind, he got as far as University Road when it started to snow, and he came to the realization that he was going to freeze to death if he didn't get to shelter soon. The wind was up, naturally, and it tore right through him. The fucking bloodstains had frozen on the thin pajama bottoms and were chafing something fierce. His legs were numb where they weren't being rubbed raw, and his teeth clattered inside his skull. With the ice forming on the ground, he had to be careful of where he stepped in addition to being aware of the street around him. With so much depending on his ability to concentrate, he struggled against exhaustion and the numbing cold. Getting to shelter would take more time than he imagined he had. He decided to risk changing into warmer clothes. Temporarily straying from the road, he found a fairly secluded spot in an alley. Having the use of both hands made the process easier and faster. The arm was healing well. He left his torn shirt on, but the cold was shocking fierce as he struggled into jeans and a pullover sweater. By the time he had gotten to re-lacing his boots, he was shivering with so much violence that he had trouble tying the knots. The adrenaline had worn off, that was clear. He zipped his anorak and felt better at once. The walk seemed almost possible now. He crammed the ruined pajama bottoms into the laundry bag. He'd burn them later. Shouldering the bag once more, he headed back onto the street. Although he could feel some small warmth seeping into his bones, his teeth wouldn't stop clattering. His boots crunched on Great Victoria Street's icy pavement. Sirens echoed off the buildings, and he thought again of the ambulance.

Is Father Murray dead? Did I kill him?

Not now. Can't. Get somewhere safe. Call St. Agnes's tomorrow. Will know then.

He focused on the sound of his footsteps, pushing himself onward. *Left. Right. Left. Right. Left—*

Shouldn't have picked up the gun. Broke my word. Why the fuck did I pick up the fucking gun?

Better to set his mind on the tangible—like not freezing to death, or getting rompered by Loyalists, for example. Slipping through a few alleys and back gardens to avoid being seen might be more practical. *Or it could get me shot for a prowler.* He was making up his mind when he noticed the car following him.

Fucking great, he thought. *That's all I fucking need.*

Checking the street without turning his head too much, he noted it was a green or grey Ford Cortina, probably a Mark III. It pulled up a bit more, and Liam could smell cigarette smoke coming from the car's open window. He tensed in anticipation of trouble but kept walking. His mouth felt dry. There was nothing for it. He'd have to drop the bag and rabbit. With some luck he might even find a place to hide before they'd turned the car around to catch up. Even so, Liam knew better than to think he could outrun a car or a bullet.

"You look awfully familiar, mate," the front passenger said, leaning out the open window. "My friend wants to know if you're Liam Kelly?"

Liam's heart jolted. He risked a glance at the car. There were four men in it, including the driver. All were wearing dark clothing, and he couldn't make out their faces without stopping.

Shouldn't have shaved the beard, Liam thought. "Who wants to know?"

"Frankie Donovan, that's who," a second voice said.

Liam halted and turned. "Frankie?"

"Liam? Is that you, mate?"

The Cortina stopped, and the passenger door swung open. Chaos erupted inside the car. A passenger in the back thumped the front seat, impatient to get out. The seat folded forward in spite of the protests from the crushed front passenger. A lanky blond man emerged. He stank of beer and staggered once before halting in front of Liam. Squinting upward, he paused until the frown of concentration broke into a smile. "It is you! I haven't seen you in a year!"

"Frankie? What the fuck are you doing here?" Liam asked. His shivering made the question hard to get out.

Frankie gave the surrounding street a quick look and then lowered his voice, "Same question could be asked of you. This is not a street you should be walking this time of night, if you've any thought for your health."

"Oh. I was—I was—"

"Relocating by the looks of things. Between engagements, are you? Aye?" Frankie asked with a nod to the laundry bag on Liam's shoulder. He winked. "Come on. Get in the car. You look a bit rough, not to mention half frozen."

Liam swallowed. Frankie had once been a close friend, and he seemed friendly enough, but there was something different about him. He seemed calmer, more serious. *Uncomfortable?* Liam wasn't sure if Frankie was aware of his current status with the Provos, but one thing was certain, chances were very high that Frankie was still active.

"Ah. Well, I don't know," Liam managed to say through chattering teeth. Frankie frowned again.

Liam glanced at the car. *On the other hand, not accepting might not be an option.*

Frankie may have had a few, but he was sober enough by his expression. He spoke carefully, his breath misting. "Don't stand there like an idiot, man. You'll have us all rompered if we stay here much longer. It's in a bad way, you are. And I'll not leave you. Go on. In with you."

With a sigh, Liam nodded. Frankie took the laundry bag from him and opened the Cortina's passenger door.

"Make some room, will you?" Frankie asked those inside.

An American rock band praised the qualities of a hotel in California through the Cortina's tinny speakers.

"Are you sure of him?" the driver asked.

Frankie nodded. "That I am."

"All right," the driver said. "Davy, get over."

Cigarette smoke perfumed with stale whiskey and beer huffed out from the car's interior as the front seat flopped forward yet again, this time to make room for Liam. The poor bald bastard in the front passenger seat muttered a half-hearted protest about being flattened. Settling into the back seat with a queasy knot forming in the pit of his stomach, Liam waited for a sign of what was to come. He nodded a greeting at the dark stocky man in the black wool hat sitting next to the window. He looked to be in his mid-twenties in spite of the heavy moustache that met with the thick sideburns on the sides of his sullen face. Thick wavy hair brushed the shoulders of his coat.

Frankie shoved in the laundry bag. It slammed Liam in the cheek, and he abandoned the conversation—or the worry over the lack of it—for the moment and worked to keep the heavy bundle from wrecking one and all. Once the bag was positioned to allow Frankie room, Frankie climbed in. Liam tried to shove the bag down onto his feet, but there wasn't space. Seeing his struggles, Frankie grabbed it and pulled the thing onto their laps. The door slammed, and the driver waited just long enough for the passenger seat to thump upright before taking off. The balding, lumpy man in the front passenger seat rolled up his window. The driver flipped a switch, and the Cortina's heater got serious.

Liam frowned. "Is something burning?"

"Ah. That'd be the heater," the driver said. "My youngest dropped something down inside the vent. Bit of food. Can't clean the fucking shite out."

"Oh." *I'm smelling Fallen everywhere now?* Liam thought.

"Where were you headed, Liam?" Frankie asked. His voice was quiet and measured. It barely rose above the strains of The Eagles's lead guitar.

"The Falls Road," Liam said. The car's heater combined with the lack of wind gusts began to loosen the tension in his muscles. His teeth slowed their clattering, but the shivering didn't.

"Ah, good. We were off to Davy's place in the New Lodge first and then the Falls," Frankie said. His wholesome face seemed utterly devoid of subterfuge. "I'm forgetting myself. Introductions. This here is Davy." He motioned to the sullen man with the moustache.

Davy continued his staring for four heartbeats. It was the longest anyone had held his gaze since Liam could remember. Davy's hard brown eyes revealed nothing of what he saw. Then he sniffed as if smelling something he didn't much care for, nodded, and turned to look out the fogging window.

"And up front, that's Michael," Frankie said.

Michael waved—an expression of drunken satisfaction on his chubby face now that he was no longer being flattened.

"And our driver there is Lucas," Frankie said.

Lucas transferred the cigarette he was holding to his mouth and then lifted the fingers of one hand off the steering wheel by way of a greeting. Liam had a view of curly brown hair, a partial profile with a strong chin, and the gray wool scarf covering the back of the man's neck.

"This here's my mate Liam. We were in Malone together," Frankie said. "Was Best Man at his wedding. I haven't seen him in… fuck… When was the last time I saw you?"

Liam swallowed. The juxtaposition between unease and relief from the freezing weather threw stark shadows in his mind. *How much does Frankie know?* "Was a few months after the wedding. You helped shift boxes from my father-in-law's car." It hadn't been easy getting the containers of Mary Kate's Uni books up three flights of stairs. He'd been grateful of Frankie's assistance. However, Mary Kate hadn't cared for Frankie, and if Liam were honest there'd been good reason at the time. Soon Frankie had stopped ringing, and life had quickly moved them in different directions. "We met a few times at the pub."

"Oh, aye. I remember now. You left early. A lovely bird took quite the shining to you. What was her name? Marie? That's it. Marie. A redhead too. You weren't having any of it, and I had to smooth things over as I recall. Proper and married, you were. Although, it wouldn't have mattered much to her."

"It did to me."

"Never did understand why Mary Kate went in for the likes of you. She's—she was quite the ride." The familiar easy smile on Frankie's face vanished and was replaced with genuine concern and sorrow. "Heard about what happened. Terrible thing, that. Rang soon as I heard, but your ma said you'd gone home to Derry after the funeral." The sympathy was raw in his voice.

Liam blinked. The weight of old grief was worsened by the fact that the Frankie Donovan Liam had known had been anything but serious. A mixture of warmth and gratitude knotted in his throat. No matter what, Frankie had been a good friend. *And if you were a real friend in turn, you'd leave now. People die around you—even the ones you don't kill.* The thought cut deep enough to make him wince. He swallowed the now painful lump.

"Are you just back, then?" Frankie asked.

Unsure of how much he should say, Liam nodded. "Oh, aye. Was staying with friends until I found a place."

"And where is this new place of yours?" Davy asked. His eyes narrowed.

Liam froze, but before his weary brain could form a good lie Frankie came to the rescue.

"That's no concern," Frankie said. "As he'll be staying with me tonight."

"No need. Drop me off at Divis Street," Liam said. "I can walk from there."

Frankie shook his head. "Wouldn't hear of it. We're having a few pints, you and me. It's been too long."

Checking his watch, Liam said, "It's half past four in the morning,

Frankie. I'm fucking knackered. Can we do it another time?"

"I insist," Frankie said and then leaned in to whisper. "You'd do the same for me. Stop your arguing."

Liam let out the breath he was holding and then nodded. *Only for a wee bit. Enough to sleep. Clean up. I'll find somewhere to hide tomorrow. Leave Frankie out of it. He's got troubles enough.*

With the exception of a short argument over which tape should go into the player next—Abba or Elvis Presley—the journey to the New Lodge carried on without further conversation. When they stopped in front of a tidy-looking row house off Dover, Davy crawled out of the car. Lucas waited for Davy to get inside the house before driving away.

"Poor sod," Lucas said, breaking the tension. "It'll take more than a few nights at The Pound to see him through, so it seems."

Michael said, "One night with your cousin Delores, and he'll be set to rights."

Lucas shook his head. "She's settled down. Engaged."

"More is the pity," Michael said.

Lucas turned the Cortina around and headed south. Michael turned up the volume as Elvis launched into "Way Down" and then produced an open bottle of whiskey, passing it back to Frankie who wiped off the mouth of the bottle with his sleeve and took a few sips. He held it out for Liam to take.

"Go on. You look like you could use it," Frankie said.

Liam accepted the bottle. Three long swallows burned off some of the dark mood. He passed it back to Frankie.

"You up for more, Lucas?" Frankie asked.

"Keep it. The wife will be having a fit as it is, what with us being so late," Lucas said.

Michael put a hand over the seat to retrieve the bottle. "For a good cause, so it was."

"Aye," said Lucas. "My Betty feels for Davy. That's the only thing keeping me from the sofa tonight. Even so, it's the straight and narrow for a couple of days. You two are on your own."

"Come on," Michael said. "How are we to get to The Pound without your car? We'll have to find a place to stay the night."

"Find another friend fool enough to take you. It'll not be me."

Lucas stopped at Frankie's place in the Falls next. Liam crawled out of the Cortina behind Frankie and the laundry bag. Frankie shouldered the bag. Apparently, he'd decided to hold onto it in case Liam had a change of heart. Resigned, Liam waved goodbye to Lucas and Michael as they drove away. In the distance, a dog barked. Liam took a deep breath of sharp Belfast winter and a violent shiver shuddered through him. Frankie's keys rattled in the door of his ground-floor flat. Although slightly newer, the place wasn't much different from the one Liam had rented two years ago. It was a shabby white box of an apartment block hastily constructed from cement cinder blocks and steel girders with terraces for the three floors above. Frankie threw open his door. Liam followed him inside, shutting the door and locking it.

The flat reeked of some sort of hippy incense and old cigarette smoke but was otherwise clean. The furniture consisted of a stained brown sofa and a small television resting on a painted wooden crate. A black telephone sat alone on the green-carpeted floor next to the sofa. Its cord traced a path to the wall near the kitchen. Liam stepped over it as Frankie made his way directly to the refrigerator. The walls were papered with film images and rock band posters, none of them local: The Rolling Stones, Pink Floyd, Led Zeppelin, and Motörhead. A James Bond poster was taped to one wall—obviously stolen from a theatre. Someone had scrawled the word "fucking wanker" across James Bond's face, leaving the blond crouched at his feet unmolested. There were a few candles and even a potted plant in good health on the window ledge in the kitchen.

Frankie retrieved a fresh can of beer from the refrigerator's interior. "Whiskey is yours," he said. "I assume you've not changed your unnatural feelings on beer." The can in his hands let out a pop and fizz. He sipped the foam until it stopped erupting from the top. Then he set it down on the counter and opened one of the bottom cabinets. "Have a seat. I'll bring the bottle."

"Frankie, I really should get some sleep." *If I can.* The truth of it was, Liam dreaded closing his eyes. He knew perfectly well what he'd see when he did. *The hole in him. Was bleeding something fierce. I killed him. I know—*

"Sleep. Aye," Frankie said. "And you will. After you tell me who beat three kinds of shite out of you and then threw you out on the street in the middle of the night."

"It wasn't like that."

"Oh, it wasn't, was it?" Frankie asked, entering the sitting room, setting the whiskey bottle and juice glass on the floor and then flopping on the sofa. "Well, then how was it?"

Liam remained standing where he was and sighed.

"If it was anyone but you I'd say this was about the Lord of the Castle coming home before you'd finished with the Mrs., but this is you. And I know better," Frankie said.

"It's not worth it."

"Let me be the one to decide."

"Come on, Frankie. I'm not a wean. My battles are my own."

"Aye." Frankie took another sip of his beer. "It's been a long time."

"Aye." Liam sighed and rounded the sofa. "It has." He was too tired and too upset to argue. Snatching the whiskey from the floor, he poured three fingers into the juice glass. Whiskey might dull the images—might wipe out the dreams. *Tomorrow. I'll know for sure tomorrow.*

"Tell me it wasn't the RUC," Frankie said.

"It wasn't the Peelers."

"Good." Frankie nodded. "It wasn't the Loyalists either?"

"Have some sense. If it was them, do you think you'd be talking to me now?" Liam drank half of what he'd poured in one go. The whiskey wasn't terribly good. He swallowed it anyway.

"You owe someone money, do you?"

"I said I didn't want to fucking talk about it."

Frankie held up a hand. "Fair enough. Fair enough."

Finishing off the last of the whiskey in his glass, Liam poured himself another.

"Where have you been all this time?" Frankie asked.

Liam paused.

"You can't say, can you?"

Liam decided to play along with Frankie's assumptions. "I shouldn't."

"Aye, well. I got nicked," Frankie said and swallowed more beer. "Few months ago. They couldn't make anything stick. So, here I am again."

Liam nodded. "What did they pick you up for?"

Frankie shrugged. "Jewelry shop was burgled. Was in Malone for burglary, you remember?"

"Aye," Liam said. "Did you do it this time?"

Smiling, Frankie winked and said, "That would be telling."

"Right." Liam poured the last of the glass down his throat. The whiskey was getting more tolerable. He poured another glass of whiskey and changed the subject to Gaelic football. It seemed safe enough. Then the two of them got serious about getting ruined.

Chapter 11

Belfast, County Antrim, Northern Ireland
December 1977

L iam slowly surfaced from familiar nightmares of blood, rage and anxiety to the smell of brewing coffee and the feeling that he wasn't alone. Concern for Father Murray nudged Liam closer to semi-consciousness, but a small cough jerked him to cold awareness. His eyes snapped open, and an explosion of icy terror sent his heart to hammering against his breastbone.

Three men stared at him from their self-appointed stations in Frankie's sitting room. One leaned against the defaced James Bond poster—the word "wanker" scrawled just above his head. Blinking, Liam recognized him from the night before—the sullen one with the bushy mustache and the long sideburns. *What is his name? Davy?* There was something about the man Liam didn't like. The second, a balding man with bushy black eyebrows and a red face, had taken up a guard's stance by the closed front door with his arms folded across his chest. The last of the lot, and most worrying, looked to be in his late thirties, had military bearing and wore an oversized military olive-drab anorak. He occupied Frankie's one and only kitchen chair with the back turned to front. His arms rested on the chair back, and he peered over them with hard brown eyes. His straight brown hair was cut in a conservative style that would've been typical for a constable or a BA officer. *Or someone who wished to invoke authority,* Liam thought.

"*Maidin mhaith. Tá tú go maith?*" the man in the chair asked in fair Irish in spite of the Munster accent. *Good morning. Are you well?*

Liam moved to check his watch. The man guarding the front door suddenly reached for something lethal strapped to the small of his back.

Freezing in place, Liam said, "Only looking for the time, mate." He was surprised at how calm his voice sounded. Keeping the empty hand in the air where the man could see it, he slowly turned the arm so he could read the dial strapped to the inside of his wrist. The low, fierce ache of a hangover lurked in the depths of his brain. He could feel it making ready for just the right instant to strike. It was going to be a bad one. He could tell.

"Afternoon, more like." Questions flashed through his bruised brain. *Who the fuck are these bastards? Paramilitaries not BAs. Right. Frankie is Provisional. Provos then. Aye, Provos. Calm yourself. Frankie doesn't keep company with any other sort. Right. So, where the fuck is Frankie? Or do I have it all wrong, and they're Loyalists, and they've done for him?* As if in answer, a cabinet door thumped.

"Will you have coffee, Liam?" Frankie asked from the kitchen. The casual and friendly tone seemed a wee bit overdone.

Why am I surprised? Of course, Frankie fucking rang his mates. Nonetheless, Liam thought he sensed tension under Frankie's demeanor, but it was tough to be certain as both the sofa back and a half wall blocked his view of the kitchen. "I'll have the tea, if you can spare it."

"Afraid not, mate," Frankie said. "Ma always said a good Republican wouldn't have anything to do with that shite."

"Oh, aye? In that case, I'll have the coffee then," Liam said. His heart was still galloping with an enthusiasm that was sure to give his anxiety away. The knowledge that nerves wouldn't give the right impression under the circumstances didn't help. The hangover, done lurking, took up arms and started to work. He winced as it clawed away at the tender insides of his skull. Massaging his temples didn't do much good.

The man in the chair said, "I understand there was quite a party last night."

"Hope you'll not mind my asking, but who the fuck are you?" Liam asked.

The man occupying Frankie's cheap kitchen chair placed his hands on his thighs. The stiffness in the action reminded Liam of his former unit lieutenant. Liam couldn't shake the familiar anticipation of a dressing down. Éamon hadn't been much for drunken antics—not that it had prevented a fucking thing.

"Ah, there now. I've been rude, haven't I? Can't be having that. Not if we're to be having a polite chat, you and I. I'm Séamus. And you're Liam Kelly, wheelman. Formerly of Éamon Walsh's unit."

A chipped white mug appeared from over the back of the sofa. The nutty scent of coffee steam flooded Liam's nose.

"Here you are," Frankie said. "It's black. The milk has gone over. And there's no sugar. Davy had the last of it."

"Mind if I sit up?" Liam asked Séamus, unwilling to make any sudden moves without giving one and all a warning.

"Go on," Séamus said.

Liam righted himself, and regretted it at once. When he could bring himself to move once more he shoved the sheet and blanket to his hips, exposing his bare chest. It was a bit cool for that, but he wanted one and all aware that he was unarmed and had every intention of keeping himself that way—at least for the moment. He gingerly turned to retrieve the mug from Frankie. "Can we get to the point? My head is a wee bit worse for wear. And I'm certain Frankie has better things in mind for his afternoon."

"Liam, these are friends," Frankie said.

"Oh, aye? Good friends, are they?" Liam asked. The headache was now doing a lively slam-dance to the drum beat of his racing heart. His skin tingled with the cold, and he wanted to be sick.

"Very good friends," Frankie said. "Relax, will you? They're not here to put the hurt on you."

"You're sure about that, are you?" Liam asked, warming his hands on the hot mug.

"I am," Frankie said. "Liam, I—I told them about Malone. The Kesh too."

Liam inwardly winced. "What did you say, exactly?"

"Níal Healy told me," Frankie said, his voice growing less confident. "You know, about the ones that got killed. After—after the hidings.

Christ, Liam. I saw that myself a time or two. At Malone. Everyone in the cage knew. And Níal... well... he said you were the best wheelman he's ever seen. Said nothing could stop you. Not BAs. Not barricades. Nothing. You'd slip through like it was magic."

"And how is it you know Níal Healy so well that he tells you shite about me?"

"Come on, Liam," Frankie said. "We've all been searching for you. We've been worried sick, so we have."

"Have you now?" Liam asked. "So, you save me from a rompering just to hand me over to a punishment squad? Is that it?"

"No one wants that," Frankie said.

"Isn't that nice? We're all not wanting anyone hurt," Liam said, not liking the sound of the situation. "So, what is it you do want?"

"HQ want to know what happened at the farm," Séamus said.

"What farm?" Liam asked.

"Don't play me. It won't go well for you," Séamus said.

Frankie cleared his throat.

Séamus sighed. "Éamon Walsh's farm. HQ want a report. You're for giving them what they want, aye?"

Taking a sip of bitter coffee, Liam settled his back against the sofa. He let the bald man with the gun interpret that how he would. Rough wool upholstery scratched his bare skin. With the hangover it was bloody torture, but he ignored it. Frankie's coffee tasted fucking awful. *Fucking Nescafé.* Liam wasn't sure he was going to keep it down. *At least it's warm,* he thought. The post-adrenaline shakes were setting in. He rested the hot mug on his thigh so Séamus wouldn't notice the tremors in the foul liquid. "Éamon Walsh was an informer."

"What?!" Frankie rushed around the sofa. "What are you saying?"

"I said, Éamon Walsh was a fucking tout."

Séamus's eyes narrowed. "There was an informer, all right. But it wasn't Éamon."

"Oh, aye. They told you about Oran, did they?" Liam asked, letting his anger slip. "Oran was fucked. Wasn't shite he could do. That cunt Éamon fed him to fucking MI5 to save his own fucking neck."

"And how do you know this?" Séamus asked.

"Oran told me before I fucking shot him," Liam said. "And then the fucking MI5 fuck posing as a fucking Peeler confirmed it before I did for him. How else?"

Séamus frowned.

Frankie said, "You'd believe a—"

"Don't!" Liam stood up. The coffee sloshed on the blankets and his jeans. The pain inside his head stepped it up a few more notches. He didn't want to shout anymore for fear of making it worse. He lowered his voice. "Don't you fucking say one word against Oran. I won't stand for it."

Frankie's face went a little pale, but he held Liam's gaze. Liam felt a little shiver of surprise, and his estimation of Frankie went up a wee bit.

"But Oran was a tout," Frankie said. "You said—"

"Aye. I did. And he paid for it. I shot him. Because it was the best I could do for him. Because there wasn't enough left of him worth sending home after Éamon was done giving him a seeing to. Because if I didn't, Éamon would've done the same to me. All to cover his fucking lying arse."

Séamus blinked.

"Well?" Liam asked. "Any more idiot questions?"

Frankie swallowed. "But—"

"That's enough, Frankie," Séamus said, reaching into his jacket pocket. "Why don't you take Davy and Steven to the shop? You've need of milk and sugar, if there's to be any more coffee. Pick up some tea too. Meanwhile, me and Liam here are going to have a quiet little chat. Alone." He paused. "Why don't you have a seat, Liam?"

Hesitating, Liam caught Frankie's quick glance. *Be careful,* it seemed to say. Liam suppressed an urge to punch him. *Be careful,* Liam thought. *My arse! Why the fuck did I trust you, you gobshite?* He knew well enough, and Frankie hadn't really done anything wrong. However, Liam had no patience for Séamus's fucking questions. He needed to be away. He needed to know whether Father Murray was dead or not.

"And Frankie?" Séamus asked, reaching out with a hand full of folded bills. "Get us some cigarettes while you're at it."

Frankie took the money, nodded and left. The others exited behind him. Séamus waited until the door closed and the footsteps receded before continuing.

"Sit, son," Séamus said. "You're not in any trouble."

Liam sat, wary.

"You've only confirmed a few things," Séamus said. "HQ had their suspicions. Éamon was a bit too tidy when it came to it. The funds collected were never short, however."

Collected? Isn't it stolen, you mean?

"Everything accounted for. So HQ were willing to let it rest a while. That is, until we knew for sure. And we had our ways of finding out."

Too neat. Too sloppy. Tell me something, old man, would you know an innocent man if you saw him? Or do the fucking British have you so paranoid you'd suspect your own arse? "Why are you bothering with telling me fuck all?"

"So you'll understand all is forgiven." Séamus rested an arm across the top of the chair back. "We want you back."

"Fuck you." The words burst out of his aching head before he knew it. His heart rammed his ribs, making him almost lose control of his stomach.

Séamus didn't blink. "Are you not willing to listen to my proposal?"

Liam's chest seized up on top of everything else. The room was suddenly too small. He wanted out of the flat. He had to get away from this man. Before he could bolt for the door, the memory of Father Murray's voice whispered in his mind. *You have a choice.*

Liam forced his deepest wish past the guilt and through clenched teeth. "I've done my bit. I'm out."

"You have done. There's none can deny it," Séamus said. "Suffered, you have. Made great sacrifices for the Cause. And you're right, that should be the end of it. And normally, it would be. But this is different."

"How is it different?"

"Ireland needs you, son."

"No. Not me. Someone else."

"The Brits are breathing down our necks. The streets are locked down with the barricades. We need a real driver. The best. Nial Healy swears you've some sort of power in you. Maybe he's fucking mad. Maybe he isn't. I don't give a fuck. We need an edge. Now more than ever we need the best. That's you."

Liam thought, *The best, my arse. Save your fucking speeches for the new recruits who don't know any better.*

"Your wife—"

"Don't you fucking bring her into this."

"We both know she worked for a free Ireland."

"She wanted human rights for Catholics. Jobs. Housing. That's what she wanted!"

"She wouldn't want you to give up the fight after she—"

"I said fucking leave her out!"

Séamus sighed. "All right. I can see you're tired. Take a holiday. A week or two. Get some rest. You've the need. Think it over. We'll see to it no one will bother you. There's no rush."

"Are you out of your fucking mind?" Liam was finding it increasingly difficult to breathe. *Have to get the fuck out of here.* "Are you not listening? I said no!"

"You'll have whatever you need—"

"I need you to fuck away off!" Liam stood up. "I'm saying no!"

Séamus nodded. "Nial Healy said you might say that."

"Fuck you! And fuck Nial too!"

Getting up from the chair, it became apparent that Séamus was a lot bigger than Liam had thought—more solid. Still, Liam was the taller, but the half a head difference in height didn't seem to matter much to Séamus. He stared up with his cold eyes and nodded a second time.

"Think on it." And with that, Séamus left.

"I'd rather you stayed," Frankie said.

His hair still wet from the shower, Liam continued to pack and tried not to let the force with which he did so give away his anger. Frankie had done him a service, letting him stay—no matter the social call from the Boys.

"Do you really have somewhere to stay?" Frankie asked.

"Does it matter?"

"Of course, it does, mate. I can't let you go out into—into—fucking hell. Why don't you stay?"

"Because I don't need any more fucking recruitment speeches from your man."

Frankie looked away. "Aye, well. I told Séamus not to bother with that load of bollocks, but he wouldn't listen."

"You didn't tell him so he'd hear."

"Do you blame me, then?"

Liam sighed again.

"Wasn't like I had a load of choice in the matter. I couldn't leave you for the fucking Butchers. Not after everything we've been through, you and me. But I had to ring him up. Fuck, you know what I'd be in for if I didn't?"

"You've said that before."

It was Frankie's turn to sigh. The worry on his face was plain to see. Liam had an urge to let him choke on it, but he couldn't. Frankie was a brother.

"I'm not angry with you, mate," Liam said. "I shouldn't have come here."

Frankie's shoulders dropped a wee bit and the tension in his face lessened. "I—I was only trying to do right by you. Only—"

"I know."

"I mean, back in Malone. You and me, was us against the others. Hell, it was us against fucking Jack. You remember Jack?"

Liam nodded. "Still have half of Shakespeare's entire fucking works clogging up my skull."

"The time he caught us cheating on the lessons—"

"Aye. And the time you set fire to his socks."

"That was an accident." Frankie looked away and a sly grin slid across his features.

"Oh, aye. But what were you doing with a fucking candle in the laundry hut? Weren't you supposed to be studying?"

"Was fucking cold, so it was," Frankie said. "Was warming my hands."

"Sure you were. With Jack's socks? Had you not a pair of your own?" Liam asked. "Was fucking cold, though. Made me half glad of Mary Kate's obsession with knitting, disastrous as that was."

"I always wondered if she thought your left arm was that much longer than your right. Or was it the Uni bastard she was doing on the side with the gorilla arm? She was too consistent for that to be a mistake."

"Shut your gob," Liam said. "At least I had someone willing to make the attempt. Unlike you."

"What makes you think I didn't?"

"Do I need to return your attention to Jack's doomed socks?" Liam asked, unaware of the smile that had crept on his face until he felt the twinge of the morning's betrayal. He wiped off the grin with the back of his hand and went back to his packing. "Wonder what's become of him? Brits shot him for a rebel, I suppose?"

"Jack? Still inside, so he is. He'll not see the light of day outside of bars, I'm thinking." Frankie shook his head. "Looking really bad inside. Not that it was any holiday before."

Liam nodded.

"Is that why?" Frankie asked. "Is it the chance of going back?"

Liam straightened and narrowed his eyes. The heat of his anger poured out of him.

Frankie took a step back. The acidic yellow scent of terror seeped into the air. Still, Frankie held his gaze. "Didn't mean to call you out for a coward. I—"

My eyes. Sees the monster burning in there, so he does. Father Murray didn't find a way to lock that down, did he? "Stop it." Liam forced himself to turn his rage at the wall. He combed the fingers of his right hand through his damp hair, knowing full well smoothing things down only meant they'd stand straight out all the more. "Look. I—I have to leave. People I care about have a way of dying fierce hard. I—I don't know if it's because of—" He stopped himself from saying the words. They sounded too mad even to him. "I—I can't stand the thought of having to see another of my own going through... well, what Oran and Mary Kate did." *And Father Murray. Aye?* "Broke my word yesterday. And it didn't go well. I can't see it happen again. You understand? You're the last. You and my ma."

Frankie nodded.

"Best everyone stay the fuck away. Especially you. So, don't come looking." Liam tied a knot into the laundry bag with a jerk, closing it. "Let Séamus do as he will. Whatever happens isn't on your hands." He shouldered the bag.

"Wait," Frankie said. He ran from the room and noises of drawers opening and shutting came from the bedroom.

Liam did his best to keep a tight rein on his anger. He didn't understand what was wrong. He'd been feeling a wee bit off since he'd let Father Murray hypnotize him, and it was only getting worse. With the exception of that brief moment chatting about the old times, Liam didn't feel he was himself anymore. It was as if he were one or two paces back from the action, looking on as a passenger. It was how he'd felt when the monster was in control. Only this was worse. There was no one, only a blank creature whose eyes burned at the slightest provocation and who didn't care about anyone or anything. On one hand, it was a comfort, the numbness. On the other, it terrified him. His control was slipping. He could feel it. With the creature put away, what was he to become now? Something worse? Could he face it if it was?

Frankie returned with a small cloth bag. He fished inside for its contents and pulled out some money. "It's my wee emergency fund. This is emergency enough."

"I can't."

"You can, and you will." Frankie pressed the thick roll of bills into his hand. "I'll not have you sleeping on the street."

"Frankie—"

"Take the money, Liam. Christ!"

Liam closed a fist around the bills.

"That'll hold you up for a month if you're careful. As you're not me, I expect it'll last twice that."

"Aye, well. I have my own socks for starters."

"Oh, fuck away off!" Frankie shook his head, smiling. He took a deep breath and lowered his voice. "There's a block of abandoned houses not far up the Falls. Families moved out. A wee bit too close to the Peace Line for comfort, see. You'll be safe enough. Séamus and the others won't go poking around there first thing when they decide to come calling. I'll see to it."

Liam nodded. Standing in front of the door, he knew there were a hundred things he should say. He just couldn't think of any of them. "Take care of yourself, Frankie."

"You too."

"I—"

"Oh, go on. You've not seen the last of me, and we both know it."

Liam nodded. Still, it was hard to go. It'd been a long time since he'd been among friends. Thinking back, everyone he cared about had let him down. Lied to him. His ma. His da. Oran. Even Mary Kate had had her secrets. Father Murray too, for that matter. And Frankie's wee message to the Boys hadn't ended in anyone dying, had it?

Not yet. Taking a deep breath, Liam turned and reached for the door.

"Promise me something," Frankie said.

Liam paused with his hand on the steel doorknob. "Aye?"

"Promise you won't let them bully you into joining up again."

"I promise."

Chapter 12

Belfast, County Antrim, Northern Ireland
December 1977

L iam headed for the pay telephones located at the front of Frankie's apartment building. Séamus and his boys would be watching, but Liam couldn't bring himself to wait any longer. Upon reaching the alcove with its graffiti-stained white concrete walls and its stench of damp and grit, he faced the very real prospect of bad news. Guilt, homesickness and loss slammed him all at once. The 23rd of December wasn't far away. The significance of the date made everything worse. *Christ, what if he's dead?* Liam half-dropped, half-tossed the laundry bag. Landing on the grimy concrete, it made a dull, heavy thump. He retrieved it and then set it leaning against the wall. The hand with which he picked up the phone receiver shook. He swallowed once, and took a deep breath. Cursing himself for a coward, he dialed the number to St. Agnes's parochial house. He'd memorized it years ago when Mary Kate had been alive, and he'd thought of Father Murray as the only friend he had in Belfast—not a Church assassin originally assigned to kill him. Listening to the distant tone, Liam held his breath. *What will I do if he's gone? Where will I go? He's probably dead. The hole in him. The blood. So much of it. So fast.* His heart thudded in his ears, and his shirt grew clammy with sweat. He'd almost reached out to disconnect the line when a male voice answered.

"This is Father Stephen of St. Agnes parish. May I help you?"

Liam tried to place the voice. He didn't think he knew the man.

"Hello? Is there someone there?"

"May I—" Liam cleared his throat. "May I please speak to Father Murray?"

There was a pause on the other end of the line. "Could you hold, please?"

"Aye." Liam closed his eyes and prayed. *Please, God, Jesus Christ, Mother Mary. Please. Don't let him be dead.* Given the pause, he could guess the answer, and his dread grew. His sides became slick with sweat, and the shaking grew worse with each passing second. Finally, the sounds of movement came through the other line.

"Hello?" The voice that reached Liam's ear was a whisper.

His heart stopped for a second time that day. "Father?" Liam asked. "Father Murray?"

"I'm sorry. He's in hospital. I'm Father Declan Thomas. Is there something perhaps I can help you with, my son?"

"Wait. Hospital?" *He's alive?*

"He was struck by a bullet while walking along the Lisburn Road."

Underneath the Lisburn Road, is more like it, Liam thought. "How bad was he hurt?"

"Bullet made a bit of a mess. Penetrated his shoulder and broke his arm. Not so terrible. Missed anything vital. Either the sniper was a very bad shot, or Father Murray wasn't the intended target," Father Thomas said. "Is this... is this..." He lowered his voice even further. "Liam Kelly?"

"That depends," Liam said.

"Then you made it out."

What? "Aye."

"We weren't sure, given... the situation. You might have been... someone else's guest."

Liam blinked. "How long will Father Murray be in hospital?"

"I'm told he'll be on his feet again soon. Should be released in a week. The authorities believe the shot may not have been intended for him, but they aren't entirely certain. There are men looking for the sniper. So I understand."

Liam released the breath he was holding. *He's alive.*

"And you? Are you hurt?"

"What?"

"Are you hurt?"

"Me? I'm—I'm fucking grand."

"You should stay out of sight for a few days," Father Thomas said. "There are… things that have to be seen to before you can return."

Return? He thinks I'm fucking going back to that fucking rat maze ever again? "Wait, I—"

"He'll meet you at the record shop on Great Victoria Street when he's released. He said you'd know the place by a pasteboard Elvis Presley standing on the walk out front. He said it specializes in your kind of music."

"Oh." Hot tears burned Liam's eyeballs. He blinked them back and swallowed. *What the fuck is the matter with me?*

He's alive. I didn't fucking murder him.

"Do you have someone to stay with?" Father Thomas asked. "I'm to make certain you'll not be alone. Father Murray made me promise. He said that it was important. He didn't say why."

Liam thought, *I'm not a wean for fuck's sake, Father.*

"Hello?"

"I'm still here," Liam said.

"You're to call upon your father. Father Murray said he'll make sure you've done so, and that you know he can. Don't go and blame yourself for what happened. It was an accident. Did you get all of that?"

"I did. I understand," Liam said.

"Good," Father Thomas said. "One more thing. This is from me."

"Aye?"

"Be careful." Father Thomas cleared his throat. "We're—they're still cleaning up the mess, if you understand my meaning. No one knows for certain how far the problem goes. There are men searching for… the sniper. Some may be none too gentle when he's found. Understand?"

The Church's assassins. Liam nodded. "Aye."

"Father Murray will let you know when it's safe to return. God be with you, son." Father Thomas rang off.

Liam stayed as he was for a moment or two. *Father Murray is alive.* Regardless of the hangover, his joints felt loose as if he'd downed half a bottle of the good stuff in one go. A vast weight had vanished from his shoulders in a flash, and he staggered under the rapid change in equilibrium. It was as if he'd been in the blackest of rooms, unaware of how terribly dark it was until someone had turned on the light. He was weightless—happier than he could remember having felt outside of a dream since Mary Kate's passing.

He drew in a deep breath and then blew the air out of his cheeks to steady his rioting stomach. *Think.* First, he'd find a good hiding place. Store his things away, and then venture out for a few supplies—blankets, food, tea, matches and the like. Abandoned housing wasn't the most comfortable in the dead of winter without water or electricity, but Frankie's suggestion was as good as any other. It wouldn't be his first Christmas alone in a derelict building. It wouldn't be his last either, so he reckoned.

Retrieving the laundry bag, he turned and headed for the Falls Road. It took an hour but he was lucky enough to find a place that hadn't been too badly damaged not far from the Clonard monastery—a red brick row house with an intact second floor, and a functional fireplace. Liam stared up at the patch of slate grey sky showing through the roof on the second-floor bedroom and breathed out a cloud of relief. Freezing wind laden with sleet pellets slapped him full in the face. *Functional for the most part,* he thought. The upper floor smelled of mold and damp. There wasn't a whole piece of window glass in the place. The wind barged in and out through the empty windows. The toilet was smashed as was the sink. Work boots crunching on glass shards and burned decay, he could almost taste the ghost of the chemical accelerant that had been used to set the place alight back in 1969. *That's fucking impossible.* He told himself he was imagining it. *No one has a nose that sensitive.* It wasn't until he'd sneezed that the imaginary smell dissipated. Shrugging off a sense of foreboding, he stowed the laundry bag away in a dry corner and then headed downstairs.

He was on his way out when a shadow moved in a back room that had once been the kitchen. Liam froze and held his breath. Listening for sounds of movement, he tilted his head. There was nothing. He eased one step toward the back of the place, and the sound came again, louder this time—a shuffling footfall. Someone was in the house with him. His heart drummed a warning in his ears. The petrol taste in the back of his throat grew stronger. *Have they come back to finish the job?* "Who's there?" Liam was startled and stopped himself from screaming when D.I. Haddock walked through the doorway. The half-strangled cry came out in a high-pitched yelp.

"Nice shit hole you got here, Paddy."

"Fuck you."

"You know, I wonder if your idiot mother is responsible for your pathetic vocabulary, or is it that you're too stupid to learn any other words?"

Liam turned his back on Haddock, made for the door and slammed it behind him. The sound echoed down the empty street, and Haddock's laughter upset a flock of pigeons.

You can't last it, you fuck, Liam thought. *Oran said all I have to do is wait you out.* Nonetheless, Liam hated the idea of living in the empty place with only Haddock for company. The memory of Haddock's dead hand clamped down on his nose and mouth sent a clammy shiver down Liam's back. Stomping down the overgrown walk, he desperately tried not to think about the near future or Haddock. His ears began to smart with the cold. So, he retrieved a black wool hat from the pocket of his anorak and jammed it on. Frozen rain slammed on the pavement, sometimes splashing, sometimes bouncing like a brick against corrugated tin. Little pin-pricks stabbed his exposed skin. People ran for shelter in the sleet. A group of British soldiers hunched miserably in their gear and attempted to take shelter from the onslaught against a brick wall. Someone shoved him from behind, and Liam landed on the pavement face-first. Luckily, he caught himself with his hands and knees before he smashed his nose again.

Haddock laughed.

"Fucking wanker!"

Several people fled past, giving him an odd look as he got to his feet. One of them was a woman with wavy light brown hair. His heart staggered.

Mary Kate?

As she got closer he caught her gaze. He blinked, and her image shifted. Her face wasn't Mary Kate's at all. Her hair wasn't the same shade either. He searched for the resemblance he'd spotted earlier and found none. The young woman noticed him staring, and frightened, crossed the street as if to avoid him.

"What's the matter, Paddy? Seeing things?"

Liam ignored Haddock's fresh peals of laughter, jammed stinging hands in his pockets, and reconsidered his decision to leave Frankie's place. With Frankie there, at least there'd be someone to help sort out reality from imagination, someone to keep him sane. *Bad idea, mate.* Frankie's flat may have been warm and ghost-free, but given a choice between Haddock and Séamus, he'd have to choose Haddock.

I'm out of the war, and it's out I'm staying. You'll not have me. Not again. Not ever. Given the things he'd done, he supposed Haddock's company was a light sentence.

A Saracen armored personnel carrier lumbered past with its requisite complement of BAs.

"I wonder how we'll pass the time, you and me?" Haddock asked. "Let's see. How about I punch your teeth in, and you do the screaming? Sounds a fair distribution of labor to me."

Liam shrugged inside his coat and whispered, "Fuck off." He continued down the walk to the corner.

"Suit yourself. Must say. Life is rather boring on the other side. But lucky for me, I've got you for entertainment," Haddock said. "And oh such fun we'll have, you and me. Maybe I'll smother you in your sleep. What do you think?"

The wind forcing its way through Liam didn't touch the angry lump wedged up against the back of his tongue. It burned, tasting of bitter ashes. Again, he attempted to focus on something else—anything else. "You're not real."

"We both know otherwise. Oh, come on. You're not getting into the spirit of things," Haddock said and laughed. "Spirit. Good one. Did you get that?"

Liam turned away. The light wouldn't last, and there wasn't much time. He'd need to lay in supplies and then start up a small fire in the hearth to keep from freezing to death. He mentally counted off a list of what he needed as he reached the Falls Road, but it didn't do much good. Torn between overwhelming dread and anger, he jumped at every shadow and every sound that might be another of Haddock's attacks. Not paying attention to where he was walking, Liam bumped into a young man smelling of cigarettes and leather. There was another scent mixed in. It was old, smoky, and reminded Liam of church for some reason. The familiar tingling sensation crawled up his arms, but instead of anger or fear he felt at peace. *Safe.*

The young man was wearing a black motorbike jacket and punk-clipped hair. He glanced in Liam's direction as if to see if he was okay. His eyes glimmered silver for a moment, and he nodded as if acknowledging an-other of his kind. Then he muttered an apology and hurried off. When Liam turned to apologize in return he spied the words *The System Might Have Got You But It Won't Get Me* inexpertly scrawled in white paint across the back of the black leather jacket. Underneath the defiant declaration, a row of home-made patches had been sewn onto the leather. Liam regis-tered images representing The Clash, The Ramones, and Sex Pistols before both young man and leather jacket reached the next corner and vanished.

"Hey!" Liam trotted to the corner. "Wait!" Reaching the end of the street, Liam searched for some sign of the leather jacket. The freezing rain gathered more strength, pelting him hard enough to make him flinch. Others around him made good their escape. Across the street, a city bus stopped. Three passengers exited the back and fled—one, a young man us-ing a cane, hobbled down the walk as fast as he could. Strangers sprinted for the bus, the punk in the leather jacket among them.

Liam felt someone push him into the busy street.

A car horn blared, and tires skidded across wet tarmac. Haddock's laughter joined the cacophony. Liam dodged a Volkswagen's bumper and a second car as well without any clear idea of how. Joining the queue to board the bus, he breathed in gasps while his heart hammered in his ears. Bus passengers stared down at him from the windows above in stunned disbelief. On the opposite side of the street, Haddock waved and chortled. Liam lowered his head, brought his shoulders up against his neck and fixed his gaze upon the bus's step.

The scent of well-used upholstery fabric and diesel exhaust flooded his nose and throat as Liam boarded. Passengers muttered to one another. Change rattled against the steel collection box. He searched his trousers pocket for the fare and prayed Haddock wouldn't follow. The driver wait-ed until the offering was made and found adequate. Then Liam staggered down the aisle as the bus lurched forward. He passed two more passengers holding walking canes as he went.

A cluster of punks occupied the seats at the rear of the bus. It came as a shock. *Five of them, there are.* Of course, Father Murray had told him about the riot of Bedford Street. The Clash had been scheduled to play the Ulster Hall back in October. The city politicians had cancelled the show at the last minute for fear of trouble, and trouble was what they got. The RUC were called in, a riot resulted, and in the end, the windows in the Ulster Hall were smashed. Liam hadn't known about any of it until recently because he'd been focused on other things at the time.

Killing that fucking bastard Haddock, for one.

Nonetheless, the story implied that there were others like himself—quite a few, in fact. He hadn't thought about what that meant until this moment. The rest of the bus passengers sat in silence, obviously ill at ease. He could almost smell it. They avoided looking at the punks. Liam, in turn, didn't gaze too long at the passengers' faces for fear of spotting Haddock among them. Liam was hit with the sudden realization that the other passengers were treating the punks as he'd been treated for most of his life—with a combination of disdain and apprehension. Also, not unlike himself, the distinctions between the punks and the other passengers were small—a safety pin here, a torn shirt there—yet those distinctions were large enough to account for the sour aroma of unease inside the bus.

One of the punks had used pins to fix patches in place on his olive drab coat. Another was wearing a black and white checked scarf. The fifth was female—an option Liam hadn't even considered possible. Long, shapely legs encased in black tights stuck out of the flaps of her long coat. One big brown work boot bobbed up and down in impatience. At twenty or twenty-one, the sullen young man wearing a spiked dog collar looked to be the oldest and most daring among the lot. Liam was pleased to note his choice of hairstyle almost matched his own. That is, it was, as Oran had once phrased it, "a post modern hatchet-job." Of course, the other young man had someone who had managed to make it appear more stylish. Liam had to make do for himself.

The punk in the black leather jacket laughed at some private joke with the chubby lad next to him.

Now that Liam was facing them, he didn't know what to say or do. It was the first time he'd seen proof that he wasn't the only punk in all of Northern Ireland, let alone Belfast. Nervous, he settled for dropping into a nearby seat and tugging off the wool hat in order to show himself as one of them. They stopped talking and stared at his hair. He felt foolish and stupid and looked away, wishing he hadn't removed his hat. In his rush, he'd blundered in where he might not be wanted. *I don't even know where the bus is going for fuck's sake.* His cheeks grew hot. Turning to gaze out the window, he determined the driver was headed east.

"In a hurry, are you?" the girl asked. Black makeup traced thick lines around her eyes in a fashion that made her look far older than her voice declared.

Unsure of what to say, Liam shrugged.

"Do you know who Joey Ramone is?" she asked.

"Of course I do," Liam said.

"What about Joe Strummer?" she asked.

"You're joking," Liam said. "Who doesn't know The Clash?"

"Going to the party tonight?" she asked.

Liam shrugged. "What party?"

"Daft Kevin is having a Christmas party," the lad in the leather jacket said. "You know about him, right?"

"Daft Kevin?" Liam asked.

The lad in the leather jacket nodded, waiting with a good-natured expression pinned on his face. Once again Liam got that feeling of peace and safety.

That's strange, he thought.

"Well?" the girl asked.

Liam briefly considered lying but decided it wouldn't be a good start if he was caught out. "Ah, no. Afraid, I don't know him."

"You going or not?" the girl asked. She seemed to be daring him.

"Wasn't invited," Liam said.

The girl huffed a small laugh. "It's Daft Kevin. If you're punk, you're invited."

The group stared at him, expectant but not exactly unwelcoming.

"Am, at that, I suppose," Liam said.

They appeared to relax.

"Best stick with us, then," the one in the dog collar said, motioning him over. "Bully boys will have you, otherwise."

Liam moved across the aisle and closer, resting his back against the window and laying his legs across the seat. Normally, he'd never do such a thing. The back of his head was exposed to snipers and the British troops on the street—not that it would make much difference were he facing forward. Nonetheless, he felt safer than he had in years. The steel of the seat rail was cold and solid against his palm as he realised he might not have to spend the night alone with Haddock's ghost after all. Liam hated himself for feeling relieved.

"My name is Paul." The young man with the dog collar held out a hand.

Liam shook it. "Call me Ronan." He didn't know why he gave that name other than out of the need to be someone else, even for a minute.

"Ronan? Like the wee seal?" the pretty girl asked.

The lad in the leather jacket laughed and shook his head.

"Don't wind him up, Alice," Paul said. "We don't know him near well enough for that."

Alice rolled her eyes. It looked a bit strange with the eyeliner. "You can't tell me what to do. You're not my brother, you know."

"Sure, and if I was, I'd have left you home," Paul said.

Alice asked, "You're not going to start with that shite again, are you? If you lot are safe enough, I'm safe enough."

"I'm Skinny Pete." The lumpy boy wearing the olive drab coat stuck out his hand. "Never mind her. She's only flirting with you."

Liam shook Skinny Pete's hand.

Alice pouted. "Am not."

"Oh, you are too," the kid in the leather jacket said. "I'm Conor."

"Good to meet you," Liam said.

"Are you a Uni student?" Alice asked.

Liam blinked. "Ah. No."

"Oh." The spark of interest winked out in Alice's brown eyes.

"Stop it, already. Will you?" Skinny Pete asked. "You'll scare him off with all your nonsense."

Alice stuck her tongue out at Skinny Pete.

"Serve you right, your face gets stuck like that," Skinny Pete said.

"What are you, twelve?" Alice asked.

Paul said, "Will you two settle down?"

"You don't have to be at Uni," Conor said. "Although, myself, Paul and Skinny Pete are studying at Queen's. Alice is still in school and so is Mark over there." Conor jabbed a thumb at the boy with the checked scarf.

"I'm going to Uni next year," Alice said.

"You don't look familiar," Paul said. "New to the Falls, are you?"

"Aye, that I am," Liam said, thinking about how much information he could afford to give.

"You're from Derry, then?" Skinny Pete asked. "You've the sound of it. I've an uncle from Derry. Family name is McCorry. Do you know him?"

"Afraid not." That was the truth to Liam's relief. He didn't see the point in denying he was from Derry, however. "I am from Derry. Living with friends until I get sorted."

"What's their name?" Alice asked. "We might know them."

"Ah. Don't think you do," Liam said, and then changed the subject. "You lot are the first punks I've seen."

"You don't have punks in Derry?" Skinny Pete asked.

"None I knew of," Liam said. "But I don't know for sure. Maybe?"

"You don't get out much, do you?" Conor asked with a smile.

"I suppose I don't at that," Liam said.

An uncomfortable expression crossed Paul's face as he took a closer look at Liam's anorak. Liam didn't have to guess. He knew what Paul was thinking. *Paramilitary.* The fact that Paul was right didn't make Liam any happier.

"Work," Liam blurted. *Don't mention you were a taxi man for fuck's sake. That'll only confirm his suspicions.* "Used to work down on the docks. Didn't have much time outside of that."

"Oh." The accusation faded from Paul's eyes, but his reservations seemed to linger. "Why are you in Belfast?"

"The job ran out a few weeks ago," Liam said. "My cousin said I could find something here. He's put in a good word for me. But I don't think it's helping."

That seemed to remove the biggest of Paul's concerns and the conversation took a turn to Christmas and the coming family holidays. Liam relaxed a bit, appearing to be getting on fine until the bus stopped at the city hall. Paul, obviously the group's leader, indicated it was time to go. Torn, Liam hesitated before finally following the punks off the bus. Concerned he'd be spotted by the Church's assassins, he tried to blend in, but he was the tallest among them. Hunching didn't seem to achieve much beyond making his neck and shoulders ache. The angry sleet had softened into a wintry mist. Paul led them around the building and seemed to be heading for the Bloomfield bus. Liam paused.

"Is something the matter?" Conor asked.

Liam glanced up at the sky. "It'll be dark soon. Are you sure this is wise?"

"What's wise?" Skinny Pete asked. "This is for fun."

"We've no worries, mate," Mark said. "Once we're at Daft Kevin's place everything will be fine."

"I've a friend meeting us," Paul said. "He has the use of his father's car tonight. And he agreed to take us home when the party is over. Sure, we'll probably get stopped at the checkpoints but that's not unusual, is it?"

"Should've asked before, but where exactly is this party?" Liam asked.

"Daft Kevin's," Alice said. "We told you."

"His parents' place. In East Belfast," Conor said. "They're away on holiday. Visiting his older sister in London. New baby. Kevin told them he needed some quiet to study." He winked.

"East Belfast?" Liam asked.

"That's what I said. Come on. We'll miss the bus if we don't hurry," Conor said.

Liam followed, regardless of the lead ball of anxiety nesting in his belly. He'd never been anywhere near East Belfast in his life. Bloomfield was where the Reverend Ian Paisley lived—the very Reverend Ian Paisley who had formed the Democratic Unionist Party. In Liam's opinion, the man was an infamous bigot. Bloomfield, in particular, was an affluent and decidedly Loyalist area. "How well do you know this Daft Kevin?"

Paul shrugged. "Well enough. He's in a new band with my brother. Plays drums."

"And this Draft Kevin lives in Bloomfield?" Liam asked.

"Aye," Conor said. "His father is doing well. Enough to put him and his sister through Uni."

Liam whispered, "That's not possible."

"What's not possible?" Skinny Pete asked.

"He lives in Bloomfield. And he's in a band with *your* brother?" Liam asked, keeping his voice low so that the other potential passengers couldn't hear. "Paul, you're a Catholic."

Conor leaned closer and asked, "Is there a problem?"

"He's a Prod," Liam said.

"Aye," Conor said. "But it's not all that shocking to know a Prod that plays the drums, is it?"

Alice laughed, but Liam thought he detected a hint of tension in her face.

"Look," Paul said, turning to face Liam.

Liam nearly walked into him.

"I thought you were into the music," Paul said, frowning.

"I am," Liam said.

"Fair enough," Paul said. "No one at that party is going to give a fuck about any of that political shite. You hear? You shouldn't care either. And if you do, you'll have to leave. That's the way it is."

"Fuck sectarianism," Conor said.

The others nodded.

"We won't live by the same stupid rules our parents do. We don't want the hate and the killing," Skinny Pete said. "We live our way."

"That's how it is?" Liam asked.

"Aye," Alice said. "It is. You for it or not?"

Liam paused. He thought again of the message scrawled on the back of Conor's leather jacket and wondered how his life might have been different if he'd known the likes of Paul when he was younger. *What would Mary Kate have made of this?* Liam knew exactly what she would've said. Raised among staunch Republicans, she'd have said their ideals were impossible but that peace was what was important. Ultimately, she'd have been for it. He made a decision. It might be too late for him to stay out of the war, but it wasn't for them, and he'd do what he could to defend their right to remain free of it. Besides, where else would be a better place to hide from both Séamus and Haddock?

Liam nodded.

"Good," Paul said.

"But—"

"But what?" Paul asked.

Liam felt the strength of Paul's gaze boring into him, and he was glad that the monster was trapped deep down and quiet in the dark. "What happens if… I mean… Are you sure of this Daft Kevin?"

"We are," Paul said. "More than we are of you."

Liam swallowed.

"Come on, Paul," Conor said. "He's fine."

And if it turns out you aren't as sure of Daft Kevin as you think, maybe I can do a few things you can't. Liam felt a guilty twinge. *Not killing. Not that. But a wee bit of bruising would be all right, wouldn't it? If it was called for.*

"All right, then." Paul turned on his heel and set off at a brisk walk bordering on a trot.

Alice, the smallest of the group, had to run to keep up. For Liam, it felt grand to move as he hadn't in a week. They stepped aboard the second bus. The reactions of the other passengers were no different than the first. As the bus thundered over the Lagan, Liam gazed through the window at East Belfast. Everything looked so very normal. It reminded him of the house where Haddock had lived, and that made him think of the woman he'd crippled in his attempt to get at Haddock.

What am I doing? I should be in Clonard, staying out of sight. I should be looking in on Elizabeth and the weans. I've responsibilities. But he couldn't bring himself to tell the others he wouldn't go with them. He licked his lips and swallowed. With Mary Kate gone, it'd been a very long time since he'd felt normal, let alone felt he'd had anything truly in common with anyone… well… normal. *Human.*

He glanced at Conor and wondered if he'd imagined that silver sheen in his eyes.

In any case, Liam didn't know when he'd ever feel normal again—if he could at all. He was sick of living like a fugitive or an insect pinned under a magnifying glass. He yearned to forget himself for a time, no matter how short. At least, that's what he told himself.

So it was that Liam followed the others off the second bus and down a side street with growing unease. It was as if he'd entered a foreign country. He didn't know the area, wouldn't know where to run if cornered. Even the smell of the place worried him. The air seemed too empty. There were no British troops, no Saracens, no piles of rubble, no rotting garbage left by city workers too frightened to pick it up. The only reassurance was the knowledge that, no matter what, he knew he could find the Lagan and once there, be safe. He couldn't have said why. Mentally shrugging, he added it to the long list of things he should ask his father and probably wouldn't.

And why is that? he asked himself. At that moment he understood he was afraid, and it made no real sense.

Chapter 13

Belfast, County Antrim, Northern Ireland
December 1977

Darkness swept across Belfast and the ice turned to snow. Liam pulled on the wool hat once more and shoved his hands in his pockets to keep them warm. The wind blew snowflakes down the back of his neck. His shirt was already clammy and clinging to his skin underneath his coat. He resigned himself to a long, miserable walk—his shoulders tightening more and more painfully against the chill and unease. To his great relief, it wasn't long before he sensed a party's distant roar. When they reached a brightly painted house surrounded by a hedge crowded with party-goers, Paul stopped and then opened the gate. The others moved into a front garden sugared with frost where students hadn't trodden. Music, light, guests and conversations spilled out the open door. Uni students from all over Belfast seemed to have packed themselves into the limited space. Liam paused, his chest suddenly tightening at the sight and instantly lost track of Paul and the others in the crush. Once again, he spotted Conor's jacket. So, Liam pushed through the throng, using the leather jacket once more as his lighthouse beacon. Conor plowed through with a gentle force, pausing here and there to shout a greeting or wave. "Ginny! Didn't think you'd make it!"

A statuesque redhead with an athletic build waved back. Liam blinked. She was as tall as he was which meant she towered over most of the room.

"No one knows I'm here." Her American accent also served to set her apart. "I don't think Sister Catherine would approve. This is cool, though. Fun."

"I'll never tell," Conor said, moving on. He didn't stop again until he entered what was obviously the kitchen.

A flood of smells invaded Liam's senses—cigarette smoke, perfume, incense, alcohol and something else that gave him pause. The scent was very familiar. At the same time, it didn't belong, at least not in this setting. He closed his eyes and concentrated. Punk music vibrated the wooden floor under his feet. Someone pressed their body up against his back, and he had to clamp down on an urge to rip them apart.

Calm yourself, mate. He took a deep breath and again focused on the smell. The guitar from "Pretty Vacant" by the Sex Pistols filtered through the rumble of party conversation. *Soap,* he thought. *It's soap.* He was instantly slammed with a powerful sense of hope and grief. Someone touched his arm. He jerked away before he could stop himself.

"Ronan? Are you all right, mate?" Conor asked.

Liam blinked, not understanding.

"Ronan?"

Right. He means me. "Yes?"

"Here," Conor said, handing him a can of beer. Liam's hand automatically accepted it before he could object. Conor opened his own can with a pop and a hiss. Then he held it up by way of a toast. "Your health."

Liam glanced at the can in his hand before tapping it against Conor's, unopened. He hadn't drunk any of the stuff since before Long Kesh. The thought of doing so now made his stomach do a queasy flip.

"What's the matter?" Conor asked. His questioning expression held an edge of concern.

"I—well… I can't," Liam said.

"You don't drink?"

"It's not that. I—"

A short Uni kid with red hair and freckles pushed past. "Con! You made it, mate! Thought you had other plans? What was her name? Angie?"

"She turned me down. Her parents, you know?" Conor shrugged, as if that explained everything.

"Is it because… well… you know… because you're from the other side of the wall?" the ginger kid asked.

"She said it wasn't that," Conor said. "It's because I'm studying art."

Ginger snorted. "Ah, well. Her ma has a point. Aren't you lot famous for starving? Told you to change to engineering. Like me. Much more impressive. Speaking of which, do you still have Angie's telephone number?"

"Fuck you," Conor said, shaking his head. "John, this here is Ronan."

John said, "Nice to meet you, Ronan."

Someone else pressed against his back, and once more Liam tensed up. The room seemed to be getting smaller—so much so, that he checked for the exit.

"He's a jumpy one," John said.

Fuck you, you fucking wanker, Liam thought.

John looked startled and then a bit frightened. Whatever it was that John saw, Conor seemed to have missed it.

Watch yourself, now. The monster may be buried, but it isn't dead.

"Relax, mate," Conor said. "John didn't mean anything by it."

"Sorry." Liam shrugged. "I'm—I'm not much for tight spaces." He switched the unopened beer to his other hand. "Good to meet you."

John shook, but his grip was weak, and he seemed in a hurry to end physical contact. He stayed focused on something down and to the right of Liam's shoulder which only called more attention to the fact that his smile didn't reach his eyes. "Well… I'd better look in on Terry. He said he was bringing in more beer." John left.

"Wonder what his problem is?" Conor asked.

Liam shrugged again, disgusted with himself.

"Come on," Conor said. "Let's introduce you to Daft Kevin."

Conor headed for the door, and Liam gave the beer to a lad who couldn't have been more than sixteen. The kid grinned up at him in thanks and then went back to chatting up the much older, taller, and quite shapely girl with long black hair leaning against the kitchen wall. Liam pretended not to see her deep brown eyes sparkle in interest as he turned away.

How long has it been? He felt himself stiffen inside his jeans.

Don't even fucking think about it.

Why not? One wee ride. What's the harm? What do you want to bet she's up for it?

What the fuck is the matter with you? You're not a Uni student on a lark.

He forced himself to follow Conor's jacket once again into the crowd but was distracted by a glimpse of light brown wavy hair done up in a style vaguely reminiscent of Bridget Bardot. *Mary Kate?* He looked again and then the specter was gone.

"Ronan!"

Liam turned.

"Don't they have pretty Uni girls where you come from?" Conor asked and winked. "Kevin is over there." He motioned toward a group consisting of pretty Uni girls sitting clustered around the record player. A boy of about nineteen or twenty sat in the middle of them.

Liam moved closer.

"Kevin," Conor said. "This here is Ronan."

Kevin stood up. He had dirty blond hair, squinty eyes and a square chin. Lipstick smears marked the side of his face. He didn't say a word, just nodded in Liam's direction by way of a greeting. Liam's first instinct was to punch him. Swallowing the burst of rage, he said hello instead. Kevin nodded again, over-compensated and then tumbled backward into the squealing girls who proceeded to fuss over Kevin's imagined injures.

"Come on," Conor said. "You've met the host. Let's go outside. You look like you could use a breather."

Once outside, Conor sat on the edge of the short brick wall framing the back porch. The temperature had dropped a few degrees in the past hour. It was still snowing, but that didn't seem to make a difference to the couples necking on the children's swings. Liam found himself avoiding looking at their faces. Feeling unbalanced and odd, he didn't want to risk seeing Mary Kate among them. He wasn't sure what he'd do if he did. Liam turned his back on the back garden as a strange and powerful sensation—one part ordinary and one part alien—settled on him. On the surface, he had much in common with those around him, the music, their age, the clothes, even the attitude in some respects. At the same time, judging by their faces, most hadn't lived through the things he had. He didn't resent their good fortune, quite the opposite. More than anything, he wished he could be one of them. He'd seen enough hardship and loss to last him. Hope and enthusiasm for the future came off them in waves.

He could almost smell it.

He perched next to Conor on the wall and did his best to ignore the sounds from the back garden. Falling snow muffled the darkness, giving it an isolated feel. Conor offered him a cigarette. Liam took it and retrieved his lighter from his pocket. He handed it to Conor, who studied the small rectangle of steel for a moment before using it. Conor returned it when finished, and Liam lit his cigarette, snapping the lighter shut with a flip of the wrist. He filled his lungs with smoke before blowing it out in one long breath. Gazing in at the party-goers crammed into the kitchen, he flinched each time he sensed a familiar face. *Was that Oran? No. Mary Kate, again? No.* Haddock was sure to appear. It was only a matter of time. Liam wrapped his hand around the steel warmth in his pocket and prayed for some peace. At least he could breathe, and the dizzy confusion of past and present dissipated a bit.

"Better?" Conor asked.

Liam nodded.

"You're not political?" Conor asked.

Liam shook his head. *Not any more, mate.*

"Mind telling me why it is you're carrying a lighter with a tricolor painted on it?"

Looking away, Liam tried to focus on the loud music pressing against the kitchen window. Unfortunately, that brought up images of the girl with the deep brown gaze and shining black hair. He shut his eyes and let Mary Kate's memory surface instead. Chaos crept back inside his skull, turning his stomach. "The lighter isn't mine."

"Oh?"

"It's—I mean, it was… my wife's."

"You're married?"

"Not anymore."

"She left you?"

"She's dead. It was my fault."

"Oh."

Liam took another long drag, swallowed nausea-coated rage and stared at the cement. "Was political once. I'm not now. I'm done with it."

Conor said, "How—"

"I don't want to talk about it. All right?" The words came out in a snarl.

Conor blinked.

Liam sighed. "I'm sorry." *You're fucking losing it.* He ran his fingers through his hair. "I shouldn't have come here." The glowing tip of the cigarette trembled in the dark.

"That's why you're in Belfast." Conor's words were stained with sympathy.

Liam slammed his burning eyes closed again. He was afraid to move lest he dislodge the mass of roiling emotions spinning in his brain. His left hand gripped the red bricks beneath him while he fought for some shred of control. Rough brick edges cut into his skin. The pain was real. It was something solid he could hold on to, and he squeezed harder, willing the confusion away. *What the fuck's the matter with me? Why now?* He was glad he couldn't see Conor's face.

"You needn't say anything more. I'll not tell the others," Conor said. There was another long pause. The Ramones stopped playing, and then The Damned went for a go round on the turntable. "It's good you came tonight."

Liam held on, praying the army of tears would stop building force under his eyelids.

"Stay here," Conor said. "I'll be right back."

Liam let him go without comment. He heard the kitchen door open and close—the party's roar rose and fell with the swinging door. He opened his eyes and cooling paths of grief traced lines down his cheeks. His gaze happened to drift to the kitchen window. The pretty girl with the deep brown eyes and wavy black hair stared back at him. He felt his face grow hot. Wiping his face with the back of his arm, he sniffed and looked up again. She was still there, staring. He couldn't shake the feeling that she could see right through him and down into the dark where the monster lay sleeping. It was then that he noticed something was a bit off about her too. Although her eyes were so brown as to be black, they gave off a silvery sheen when she moved her head. It was like moonlight glittering on the surface of a black pond. He blinked and the effect was gone, taking the strange feeling with it. She winked at him as if they shared a secret—one corner of her full mouth curling into a crooked smile.

He shivered and turned away. *Seeing things. First Conor. Now her.* Finishing his cigarette, he stubbed it out with a vengeance in a potted plant full of cigarette butts. When he returned to his spot on the porch and dared to look into the window again, she'd gone. He considered going inside to search for her, but he couldn't think of what he'd say to her if he did. Caught between his curiosity, embarrassment, and if he were honest, no small amount of lust, he decided it was best to stay where he was. It didn't matter that Mary Kate had been dead for a year—*No. Two years. She'll be two years gone in a week. Christmas eve, mate. How could you fucking forget?* Any thought of another woman had felt like betrayal for so long—it still did. *You need one another.* Oran's dream words echoed up from the darkness. *Fucking hold it together, will you?*

Conor returned and then handed him a short glass, uncorked a bottle of whiskey and poured.

"Why are you doing this?" Liam asked, giving Conor a look. "You don't know me."

Conor poured a short for himself and set the bottle on the concrete next to the wall. "I know enough." He tapped his glass against Liam's and then emptied it in one go. "It's hard to turn your back on that lot. Once you're in. You're in. I should know. I lost my brother. Neil."

Liam stared.

"Hurry up," Conor said. "You need to get a bit of that down you."

"Why?"

"Don't argue. Just do it already, will you?"

Liam decided to take Conor's unspoken apology and swallowed the whiskey. It was smooth, sweet, and tasted of molten sunshine with an edge of chocolate. He felt it melt the sour ball of lead in his belly. The tension in his shoulders loosened. He kept his eyes to the ground or Conor's face just the same. Conor poured another round.

"That's very good," Liam said.

"It should be," Conor said. "Took it out of Kevin's father's liquor cabinet."

"Is that not going to be a problem later?"

"Kevin doesn't mind. And like as not his father won't even notice."

"Is that so?"

"Doesn't drink a drop," Conor said.

"Then why have it?"

Conor shrugged. "Dinner parties."

"Won't his ma notice?"

"Of course she will," Conor said. "But since she does drink and doesn't want his da to know, she'll only replace the bottle and not say a word."

Liam blinked. "What of the expense?"

"Kevin says his father hasn't said anything so far."

Liam shook his head and drank a second glass, a third and then a fourth. He'd counted to six and was feeling good and warm when he heard a shout. Paul burst through the kitchen door.

"What is it?" Conor asked.

"Skinny Pete," Paul said. "He's being rompered."

"What?" Conor asked.

"Where?" Liam asked.

"Up the street," Paul said. "Said he was walking Karen home. I told him not to go alone, but he insisted. Have you seen Alice?"

Liam set his glass down on the wall.

"Where is it you think you're going?" Conor asked.

"Should be me does this," Liam said. "It's too late for me. Isn't for you. Aye?"

"Wait," Conor said. "Take my jacket, then. You've need of its protection."

Liam paused. *It is leather. It'll hold up better against knives, if they have them.*

"It won't do much against anything physical, but it'll shield you in other ways."

"What the fuck are you on about?" Liam said. "I have to go. Now."

"Wait. Please. Shite." Conor glanced around him and whispered. "Not enough time. Needs a sacrifice." His gaze settled on the brick wall. "That should work." Scraping the back of his hand until it bled, he tugged the sleeve over it and pressed the lining against the fresh wound with a hiss of pain. He closed his eyes and muttered something quick in Latin.

Liam thought of Father Murray and his Order. *Is he a Church assassin?* The skin along his arms prickled. "What are you?"

Conor slipped out of the jacket. "No time to explain. Take it. It's yours now. It's the best I can do."

Accepting the jacket from Conor, the lining felt silky and warm against Liam's skin. The sensation of the jacket's weight settling on his shoulders was odd and comforting at the same time. There wasn't time to register why. He rushed through the kitchen and out the front door. Conor and Paul weren't far behind. A crowd was already gathering at the windows and on the front lawn. He trotted through the gate and made for a group of thugs standing over someone curled up on the pavement. The gate squeaked a second time as someone followed him up the street. Liam didn't look back, assuming it was Paul.

"Help!"

"Shut him up," a voice said.

Liam ran. "Hey! Fuck away off, you!"

"And who the fuck are you?" a second voice asked.

"A friend," Liam said. "Get off him."

The questioner took two steps closer, and Liam saw that while the brute was a head shorter, he weighed twice as much. His hair was dark and his nose appeared to have been in one fight too many. "Are you going to make me?"

"Aye, I will, if I have to," Liam said. *There are four of them and one of me.* He heard the gate creak and slam behind him a third time. *All right. Maybe two of us.*

"All on your own, are you?" the brute with the flattened nose asked.

"He isn't. Not exactly," a female voice said from behind him.

Liam attempted to hide his shock.

"Well, isn't that nice?" Flat-nose asked. "And who are you?"

"Eirnín."

Glancing at the figure next to him, Liam saw it was the girl with the black hair from the kitchen. She was holding a cricket bat at the ready. Where she'd gotten it, he didn't know. *Another of Daft Kevin's provisions?*

Flat-nose laughed and his bully boys laughed with him. "Ermine? What kind of a fucking name is that?"

"I said Eirnín, you shite for brains. An ermine is a stoat."

"A stoat?" Flat nose asked.

"I think they make fancy fur coats out of them, Charlie," one of the bully boys said.

"Well, then, Ermine," Flat-nosed Charlie said. "I think you should fuck off and take your boyfriend with you before someone makes a coat of you." He drew a small caliber pistol. "Bullet beats bat, bitch."

A distant part of Liam took over, and he reacted without thinking, throwing himself at Flat-nosed Charlie. There was a loud bang, and he felt a hard thump in his side. *Fucker missed.* Liam didn't pause, determined to shove Flat-nosed Charlie down and disarm him before the bastard actually hurt someone. The two of them landed in a heap on the pavement. Liam sat up first, and punched Flat-nosed Charlie square in the face. A satisfying crunch told him the fuck's nose was broken. His knuckles hurt. Someone was shouting. Someone else screamed. Liam didn't have time to wonder who. Flatter-nosed Charlie was sitting up. Liam bruised the knuckles of his left hand on the thug's jaw and staggered to his feet.

That was when he knew something was wrong. He felt it the moment he straightened. Charlie tried to get up again, but Liam reared back and gave him a good solid kick in the chest. Charlie cried out. Liam staggered as two of Charlie's bully boys jumped him. Liam slammed to the pavement. The left knee of his jeans gave away. He felt a shock as the cold seeped through. His knee stung. He couldn't breathe. Eirnín swung the cricket bat. It connected with the first bully boy's shoulder, and he shrieked. Another swing and the bat landed against the side of the second bully's head with a sickening hollow thump. He dropped at once. Liam would've laughed except at that moment the last of Flat-nosed Charlie's mates planted his boot in Liam's side and an explosion of pain consumed his senses. The last of his breath came out in two words. "Fucking hell!" He shuddered in agony. Once again unable to breathe, gasping for any chance at air at all.

The next thing he knew he was staring up at Eirnín's face. Her head was framed in a cloudy night sky, and her eyes once again glinted silver. She smelled of blood, smoke and sulfur.

"Liam?" she asked.

How is it she knows my name? he thought. He tried to sit up but the pain knocked him flat again.

"Don't move," she said. "You've a bullet in you." She had a smudge of crimson on her cheek. He blinked when he understood the blood wasn't hers.

"Oh."

"That stupid shite shot you," she said. "You're lucky it was only a .22. What were you thinking?"

"Get away from him." It took Liam a moment to recognize the voice as Bran's.

Eirnín turned. "He's been shot."

"I know," Bran said.

"I can help him," Eirnín said.

"Do as I say, girl," Bran said. "Connacht has done enough for me and mine this evening, I'm thinking."

Liam watched Eirnín's expression change from concern to embarrassment. She looked down at him and whispered, "Your da is here for you. You'll be right now. I'm—I'm sorry. About this, I mean. It wasn't supposed to be you. I mean, no one was supposed to get hurt at all. So, why did you go and do that for?" Her soft lips burned his skin as she kissed him on the forehead. "Thank you, you brave idiot."

He felt his head lifted and then gently laid back on the pavement. Uncle Sceolán's face replaced Eirnín's.

"Finally succeeded in getting yourself shot, did you?" Sceolán asked.

"I—"

"Don't waste your breath," Sceolán said, bending down. "Save it for the screaming later when Bran cuts that shite out of you. Fuck's sake, you couldn't have let well enough alone, could you?"

Liam was shivering. Snow was getting into his eyes. He blinked, trying to clear his vision. A blanket appeared from somewhere, and his uncle tucked it around him. Liam felt warmer at once. Someone grabbed his ankles while Sceolán took his shoulders. Liam had the sensation of floating as he was carefully lifted from the street. Turning his head, he saw party-goers gathered around Skinny Pete and the others. The tall redhead was among them. Liam thought it strange that no one seemed to notice him being carried away by Bran and Sceolán—no one, that is, but Eirnín and Conor. He wasn't sure, but he thought Eirnín was crying. The sight of it tore at him, but he couldn't have said why.

"Brace yourself," Bran said. "This is going to hurt."

Liam's vision blurred and once again, he found himself thinking his father had a nasty habit of understating the truth.

Chapter 14

The Other Side

Drowsy and aching, Liam stared across the campfire at his father and attempted to keep his breathing shallow. Every time he forgot, his ribs punished him. There were other wounded lying on the ground nearby, casualties from an earlier battle. Which battle or with whom Liam hadn't had a chance to ask. In a field not far away the dead were laid out in neat rows. He'd thought something was odd about it when they passed among them as he was being carried into the camp. Now, he understood. The dead were close, too close. The stench was going to be horrific, if it wasn't already. *Surely, they know that?* The faces of the dead hadn't even been covered, and sight had been particularly bad because of the crows. While he couldn't see them now that night had fallen, he could certainly still hear them fighting over the remains. He shuddered and then winced.

A thick fog clung to the woods. Above, the stars were brighter than in Belfast. The moon bigger. The air both felt and smelled more crisp. *Clean.* Everything about the land where his father's people lived was, for the lack of a better word, *more.* Which was why it seemed strange to him that anyone would associate it with the word "twilight." That word brought up of images of declining civilizations, decay and death. The place where his father had brought him was anything but dead.

Those not wounded or tending to the wounded were feasting at the centermost campfire. The fian, Bran's warrior troop, numbered fewer than Liam would've thought—less than fifty he guessed. Again, what that meant he wasn't sure.

Someone plucked out a tune on a string instrument and a melancholy male voice joined the song in ancient Irish, or so Liam assumed since he only half understood it. Another added the soft thud of a bodhrán. The music drifted out into the still night and masked the sounds of the feasting crows. His uncle leaned against a big oak tree with his arms folded across his chest and a bronze-tipped spear at his side. He seemed to be on sentry duty.

The sound of pouring water returned Liam's attention to his father. This was the second time his da had patched him up. Kneeling, Bran cleaned the tools he'd used to operate not only on Liam but a number of the other wounded as well. There were dark circles under his eyes, and his fine linen shirt was stained with blood.

That's my da, Liam thought with no small amount of pride. It didn't matter how many times he saw Bran, he found the resemblance surprising. Warm light painted shadows on Bran's face as he worked, drawing the weary lines on his face in hard strokes. A barely perceptible scar traced a thin curve on the right side of his jaw, and beard stubble shaded his cheeks. His black hair was thick and brushed his shoulders, but the grey at his temples was the white of fresh snow.

Is that what I'll look like in twenty years or a few hundred?

As the blood was washed away, the soothing scent of burning wood and damp, black earth took precedence. The grass was soft under him. His head was pillowed on an extra bedroll. A blanket had been draped across his lap. He was shirtless but for the bandage encasing his abused ribs, and the heat of the fire warmed his aching body while the night air chilled his left shoulder. Nonetheless, he was comfortable—if for no other reason than no one was digging into him with blistering hot bronze. Mind you, that was blistering hot bronze that had to be re-straightened periodically. With the easy availability of modern anesthetics and painkillers, Liam didn't understand why the Fey stubbornly tended their own using primitive herbs and poultices. He supposed there was a reason, but no one had offered him one.

Fucking hell. What I'd give for one fucking Aspro Clear tablet.

Or some smack.

Don't even think it.

His eyelids grew too heavy, and he stopped fighting to keep them open. He listened to the music as disconnected thoughts drifted through his mind, and he floated in a comfortable haze until a hard thump on his leg jarred him awake.

Bran was gone. So was Sceolán. Looking up, Liam was relieved to see Oran standing over him.

"You're sleeping," Oran said, his face stern.

"Aye," Liam said. "I was."

"You are," Oran said, "and you can't. Not here."

"And why not?"

"It isn't safe," Oran said.

"Why?"

Oran shook his head. "If I can find you, so can that fucking bastard."

"Haddock?"

"Don't speak his name here. Don't use anyone's name here that you don't want to come calling. Understand?"

Liam frowned. "He's already tried his hand at killing me twice today. I thought you said he couldn't last it?"

Oran said, "That only applies over there. You're here now. The rules are different."

Liam swallowed, but his mouth had gone dry, and it hurt. He sat up. "How are the rules different?"

"Wake up, will you?" The anxiety deepened in Oran's voice. "I don't know how long they'll hold him off."

"Who?"

Oran kicked him in the leg again. "Wake the fuck up, I said! Now!"

Shadows under the trees condensed. The eyes of the crows gathered in the branches glittered like polished jet. A heavy sense of dread stirred in the mist. Liam smelled something like ozone, and he tasted tin. Somewhere in the back of his brain the monster stirred. He had the impression it was muttering a warning but Father Murray had buried the creature too far and deep for even that.

Haddock stepped out from under the oak where Sceolán had been before.

"Well, isn't this sweet?" Haddock asked. "Two for one."

"Leave the lad be," Oran said, turning to face Haddock.

"And why would I do that?" Haddock asked.

The muscles in Oran's jaw twitched, and he held up his fists. "You know I can make it very uncomfortable for you."

Haddock grinned and once again Liam was reminded of a shark. "You can try, you Fenian Fuckwit. You can try."

Liam struggled to his feet. It hurt something fierce—that seemed a strange thing to happen in a dream.

"Now just where do you think you're going?" Haddock asked. "And here I've come all this way for a nice chat."

Liam felt the monster stir again. There was something important he was forgetting. He'd remember it given enough time, but there wasn't time. Haddock was there. "I've nothing to say to you."

"That doesn't matter," Haddock said. "I've plenty to say to you."

"I told you to go the fuck away," Liam did his best to sound bored, but his heart hammered against his chest in protest against the lie.

Haddock cracked his knuckles. "Time to play."

Oran charged at Haddock with a roar, but Haddock sidestepped him. Liam aimed for Haddock's jaw, but somehow his already bruised knuckles didn't connect. Haddock shoved. Feeling as though he'd just been hit with a lorry, Liam stumbled and fell backward with a rib-jarring thump. Haddock was on him in a flash and planted a fist in Liam's wounded ribs. Something snapped inside him, and Liam screamed. Before he knew it, he'd been flipped onto his stomach and his left arm yanked up behind his back. He felt Haddock straddle him. Overwhelming terror surged through Liam's system.

"Get off me!" The panic became too much. Liam fought with everything he had, but it did no good. He couldn't reach Haddock, and Haddock was too heavy to buck off even if Liam could manage it past the agonizing sensation of bone grinding against bone. "Don't you fucking touch me! Fuck off! Get the fuck off me now! I'll fucking kill you!"

"Too late. I want what's mine," Haddock said, slamming his right hand down on Liam's bare back. The feel of the ghost's clammy palm against Liam's skin spiked his fear to new heights. "I'm taking it now, and you can't stop me."

Trapped. Can't get free. Got to get him off or he'll— The sense of helplessness made it much worse. The weight of shame, terror and rage became huge—impossible to bear. He was losing his grip on himself and knew it, but there was nothing that could be done. *Get him off me! NOW! Christ! What if he touches—* Liam could almost feel rough iron bars clamped in his clenched fists. *Cuffs! Oh, Jesus! He'll cuff me next. Fuck!* Instead, Haddock's hand remained pressed against Liam's back. The cold, dead thing had an ever so slightly yielding texture that was downright sickening all on its own. Suddenly, Liam had the sensation of something tugging at him, drawing energy from him. The sharp pain was transparent but no less painful for all that. Like the feel of a keen knife edge slicing through skin. Sucking—

No! Oh, God! Christ! No!

—penetration. Sucking. He wanted to be sick. He lost the entire concept of himself. He was only hate, rage and fear. He wanted to— *KILL, Rip. Tear. FUCK YOU! Kill you! Kill you NOW!*

Something huge, furry and heavy sprang on Haddock with a snarl. Haddock was knocked off him with a howl of frustration. Liam lifted his head in time to see a great brown wolfhound rip at Haddock's chest and throat. Haddock struggled to get something free of his coat. The flicker of silver was the only warning as Haddock produced a knife. A high-pitched yelp pierced the air, and Haddock shoved the hound away.

Staggering again to his feet, Liam glanced around for anything that he might use as a weapon. There was only Conor's leather jacket. Liam snatched it up. The leather was heavy in his hands. The lining seemed to glitter with thin runes. It wasn't much but might help him defend himself against the blade. *It won't protect you from the physical.*

What the fuck does it shield me against?

"I'm going to make you wish you'd never been born," Haddock said, holding up the bloody knife. Half of his face was a ruin. White jawbone shone through the torn cheek.

Liam's chest was filled with agony—enough to flatten him, but he forced himself to stand and tried not to breathe. He'd die before letting Haddock touch him again. Blinking away tears, Liam set his teeth against nausea, dizziness, terror and rage. He gripped the heavy jacket tight by the collar.

"Fuck you." Lacking anything else with which to strike, he swung the coat at Haddock with all his might. Steel-zippered leather slapped Haddock full in the face.

There came a bright flash. Haddock's expression transformed from amusement to shock and then he simply faded away as if he'd never been.

What? Why?

Sceolán lay on the ground beyond, his chest covered in blood. Bran was kneeling at his side.

"Speak to me," Bran said to Sceolán.

Sceolán smiled with crimson-stained teeth. "That really hurts."

Bran opened Sceolán's shirt. "You could've been more careful."

"Oh, aye?" Sceolán grimaced. "How was I to know he'd carry steel?"

"Liam?" Bran didn't look away from his brother.

Liam gasped enough air to reply. His whole body started to tremble. "Am I awake?"

"You are," Bran said.

Two warriors went out into the woods. A third warrior with braided blond hair brought a cloth bag to Bran.

Bran searched its contents. "Domhnall, bring some water."

"Aye," Domhnall said.

Bran pulled a cloth from the bag. "You mind telling me what's going on, Liam?"

"Was only a dream," Liam whispered.

"It was, was it?" Bran asked, cleaning Sceolán's wound. "Two spirits violated our perimeter."

"Don't know what you mean," Liam said. The shakes got worse. He couldn't get the feel of Haddock's cold dead skin out of his mind. The feeling of being trapped under—

Domhnall returned with a bowl of steaming water. Bran stopped mopping up blood long enough to pour liquid from a vial into the water. "Thank you, Domhnall. Check with Fearghal. Find out what he's learned, check the wards, and report back."

Once more Domhnall rushed off.

"You're going to tell me this had nothing to do with you?" Bran tossed the blood-soaked cloth in the water.

"Don't be so hard on the lad," Sceolán said in a pained whisper. "Was him that banished the thing."

"Did he now?" Bran asked.

Liam didn't answer. "Was only a dream." *It's done now.*

"It was more than that," Bran said. He doused Sceolán's wound with the steaming liquid.

Sceolán let out a hiss. "Could you be a bit more gentle? It's mortally wounded, I am."

"You'll be fine, I'm thinking. Shut up and hold this," Bran said, indicating a folded dry cloth.

Sceolán held the cloth while Bran fixed the bandage in place. "Are you ready for that talk yet, son? I'll warn you. I'm in no mood for patience. Not tonight."

Liam paused. *For fuck's sake, talk to the man.* He tried to think of anything to say that wouldn't make him feel like a bog idiot. The fire crackled, filling in the silence.

Bran sighed in disgust. "If you've no use for questions, stop blaming me for not giving you the crossed answers. Mind, I'm not the one who's endangering others by withholding information this time. I couldn't speak to you because of your mother's geas. What's your excuse?"

He's right. Can't put it off anymore, Liam thought. "I—I'm going mad. Am mad. It's… I'm seeing things that can't be. Ghosts. Fucking Haddock. Mary Kate. Oran. I—I don't know what's happening. Or why. There. It's out. Are you happy?"

Finishing with Sceolán's bandage, Bran stood up. His expression was careful and solemn when he turned to face Liam. "Among mortals the word 'fey' can also mean mad."

"Do you think I don't fucking know that?" Liam asked.

"There's a reason, son." Bran ran his fingers through his greying hair. "The fey-touched reside in two places at once. As such, they must learn to navigate both in ways that those wholly mortal or wholly fey do not."

Liam narrowed watering eyes. "So, I'm destined to be off my nut. Is that it?"

"Not at all," Bran said and moved closer. "Let's see the ribs."

Sitting was difficult, but Liam managed it without passing out. He didn't want anyone touching him—not now, but he didn't see any other way. If he protested his father would ask why.

"Life is more difficult for the fey-touched," Bran said. He gently tugged at the bandages. "There's nothing to be done about that. I'm sorry."

Attempting not to twitch, Liam glanced down and saw the blood seeping through the cloth.

Bran said, "You need training. Someone to teach you how to manage what lives inside you. Without it, chances are you'll not fare well. You'll not know one world from the other. Everything will... bleed together. What I don't understand is why it's happening so fast. Why now?"

"Can—" Liam winced as the last of the bandages came away. "Can you teach me?"

"Unfortunately, no. Not everything. I'm not like you."

"That's fucking grand." The shaking was starting to slow, but the dread remained.

"Being fey-touched has its advantages, you know," Sceolán said, rolling onto his side.

"Oh? Aye?" Liam asked. "So far it's been nothing short of fucking hell."

"Calm down," Bran said. "Listen."

"I am listening." Liam felt his stomach tighten, and the earth did a sickening lurch. He shut his eyes for a moment and tried to focus on the solidity of the soil beneath him.

Bran made a concerned noise. "Both ribs are broken now."

The blond warrior named Domhnall returned.

Bran got up off his knees. "Don't move, son."

Liam listened as his father spoke to Domhnall. The conversation was deliberately quiet, but Liam was able to understand that Fearghal didn't believe Connacht had sent the spirits to attack the camp. The source had to be something or someone from within the perimeter. A search was being conducted among the men, but everything seemed secure for now.

Sceolán got up awkwardly and then stopped at Liam's side. "Thank you."

"For what?" Liam asked in a whisper. His abused ribs were killing him.

Sceolán said, "For banishing the spirit."

Liam wasn't sure what to say. "The fuck was here for me. He would've killed me but for you."

Sceolán let out a short laugh that was somewhere between a wheeze and a snort. "Then I suppose that makes us even. How did you do it?"

"I don't know," Liam said. "Maybe in this place I can hurt him as much as he can hurt me?"

Shaking his head, Sceolán picked up Conor's jacket and then frowned. He held it up so that the words *The System Might Have Got You But It Won't Get Me* were easy to read. "Interesting."

"What is it?"

"Where did you get this coat?"

"A friend. Conor gave it to me. Was before I went out to meet the bully boys."

Sceolán looked thoughtful. "Is this Conor a magician?"

Liam started to laugh, but the seriousness of his uncle's expression and the memory of the silver sheen in Conor's eyes combined with what Conor had called a blood sacrifice killed the mirth in Liam's throat. "I don't know what he is."

"Interesting."

"You said that already," Liam said.

Finished giving Domhnall instructions, Bran returned and once again knelt down. He spent a few moments searching inside the cloth bag, and finally produced a small jar.

"I should go," Sceolán said. "See how Fearghal is fairing. Find out if the search has turned anything up."

Bran nodded, waited for Sceolán to leave and then continued. "Will you have the training, then?"

"What kind of training?" Liam asked.

"To become one of the Fianna."

"I'm done with the soldiering. I told you—"

"There's more to the Fianna than the warring," Bran said, his stern expression vanishing. "This will help."

"It will? How is that?" Liam stared at the open hope in his father's face. It was powerful stuff, that. *It's too fucking late for the good da act. Fuck this. It's grown, I am. I don't need your fucking approval. I don't need anything from you at all.*

"Cross it, you're out of time," Bran said. "You can't pretend you're mortal anymore. Be what you were born. Know what you are and be it, or don't, and be a danger to yourself and others. It's up to you."

Liam twitched as Bran applied the cold, evil-smelling goo to the bullet wound and the broken ribs. "What is it with you and Father Murray? Choices? What choices? I didn't ask to be born like this!"

Bran wiped his hands clean of the ointment. "I understand your fears."

"I'm not afraid!"

"You're crossed terrified. And you've got good reason to be. Any man in your place would be. That is, anyone with any sense. Hold still."

"Fuck! That burns!"

"It's going to. I'm sorry for that," Bran said. "But it'll pass soon enough." He picked up a bandage roll and started re-wrapping Liam's tortured ribs. "The thing I don't understand is why you didn't shape shift."

"When?" Liam asked.

"When you were attacked," Bran said. "It could've saved you some of this pain."

"I can't," Liam said.

Bran paused, and then asked, "What do you mean you can't?"

"Father Murray—"

"What in Dagda's name did you let that holy man do to you now?" Bran asked.

"Hypnotism. Father Murray said it would put the monster away. Said we had to. He was right. Otherwise I'd have killed someone," Liam said with a shrug. He regretted the movement at once.

"What monster?" Bran asked.

Liam swallowed. He wasn't sure how to talk about the Hound. It was mad, all of it. He knew that from the few conversations he'd had with Father Murray and the furtive looks from that other one, Father Stevenson. And maybe the reason why he'd been putting off talking to his father was that he was afraid of what it all actually meant. As long as there was some doubt—some way of blaming the Fey in him, he wouldn't have to admit he was mad. *Oh, for fuck's sake, you're not a wean. What does it matter?* "Remember Raven's Hill?"

Bran nodded.

"The thing that attacked you," Liam said, unable to meet his father's gaze. "That Hound."

"That was you."

"That fucking... *thing* isn't me."

Bran sighed. "All right." He prepared some sort of tea and handed him the cup. "Drink this."

Liam took the cup, feeling the warmth through the ceramic. He sipped. The stuff tasted foul and bitter.

"Drink all of it," Bran said. "Then let's go back to the dreams. Tell me about the dreams."

Hesitant at first, Liam started with the hunting dream, the deer, and Mary Kate. When that didn't seem to get much reaction, he found himself rambling about the nightmares—the faces of the ones he'd done for, the woman who'd been maimed in the explosion that had killed Haddock, Oran's warnings and Haddock's ghost. He talked for what seemed an eternity. Everything came out in a long, confusing jumble, including one or two of the dreams about Long Kesh. It was more than he'd been able to tell Father Murray with his calculated stares and psychological theories. Bran, however, listened and nothing else. Perhaps the reason Liam felt he could speak freely was because he had no sense that what he said would be scrutinized? He wasn't sure what it was, but outside of the occasional request for clarification, Bran didn't breathe a word. When it was finally done Liam's throat ached. There was more, most certainly more, but he let it lay. He was exhausted with the talking.

When it was clear he was finished, Bran nodded once, and after a long pause, said, "That is quite a load to be carrying."

Liam couldn't bring himself to respond or look his father in the face. Everything—nearly everything, anyway—was out. It was too late to take any of it back.

Bran said, "I feel all I ever do is apologize, much good as it does you."

Liam opened his mouth to speak, but Bran held up his hand.

"The dreams and the ghosts," Bran said with real sorrow in his eyes. "They're connected." He pulled a wool sweater from the pack. "Let's get this on you. And then your coat. It'll be cold tonight."

Liam let his father help him into the sweater. His ribs were already feeling better. The goo had stopped burning, and the pain was fading. The wound site felt warm.

"In the stories of the Good Folk that mortals tell, have you ever heard of one killing a mortal?" Bran asked.

"Well, of course—"

"Directly, I mean. Not through a curse or trickery. I mean, actually murdering a mortal."

Liam blinked.

"It happens, but it's rare, and generally only if the mortal in question asked for the fight to begin with. There's a reason for that, son," Bran said. "Mortal souls hold great power." He sighed. "It depends upon the mortal, of course. But… well." He paused. "We don't speak of this to mortals, not even to those that live among us. Not ever. They'd lose the proper respect, mind you. So, no matter what, don't be telling your holy man about this. Do you understand?"

Liam nodded. His stomach clenched, the violence of it threatening to force out the tea he'd just consumed. *Here it comes.*

"The truth is, the price of killing a mortal is to risk having their soul cleave to you." Bran stared at the fire. His eyes reflected the flames. "There are rules to it, of course. As I said, if they start the warring then the Fey is justified in the killing. The price will be paid. Also, the mortal has a choice in the matter. If they've no wish, no interest in haunting, then…" He shrugged. "Someone should've told you before now. Someone—I should've told you long ago. When you were a boy. Long before now. Before this. I'm so sorry."

Staggering to his feet, Liam stumbled to the outermost edge of the fire's warmth. He was dizzy and sick. *How many did I do for? Haddock. The Peeler outside that first bank we'd robbed. Oran. Éamon. Fuck. The Lads at the farm house. Those who'd murdered Mary Kate. How many? Fourteen? Fifteen?* And God alone knew how many the monster had done for. *Make it an even twenty.* Liam dropped to his knees with a jarring thump. The jagged ends of his broken ribs ground against one another like glass shards, and he lost control of his stomach. The pain was awful. He bent over with the strength of his stomach's rebellion, landing on one concrete-abraded palm.

"I'm sorry."

Liam spit out the last of the foul mess. "Right," he whispered and spit again, feeling a clump of it lodged in the back of his sinuses. He swallowed and fought an urge to be sick again. "Jesus Christ, I could've fucking lived without knowing that."

"It's good you told me."

"And why is that?"

"You can't sleep. Not here. Not now. Not yet."

"Oran said as much."

"Oran?"

"A friend. The second shade. He fought against the other one." What was it Oran had said? *I'm your friend. I always will be. Nothing will change that. I owe you. I'm here to help.* Does that mean he's haunting me or not?

Bran hesitated. "I've a question I need to ask. A personal one. Understand, I only ask because I need to know how it will affect my fian."

Liam swallowed and nodded.

"How many spirits have you seen?" Bran asked.

It wasn't the question Liam was expecting. He understood why and was grateful. "There have been three so far. Oran, the one just now, and Mary Kate."

"So far?" Bran asked, still not voicing his actual concern.

Liam knew what was being implied. *How many is it you've killed?* But Bran was a warrior. He wouldn't ask. He knew better. Taking life was part of soldiering. There was no denying it, but asking such a thing was unthinkable. Each carried their own burden—their own gallery of faces that haunted their sleep. That was the price you paid. If you were lucky and smart, every choice you made was a good one, and every life taken was only what was required. No more. No less. If you weren't careful or lucky—

Bran cleared his throat and looked away. "We'll have to send you back."

Only with the likes of me the price is higher, isn't it? "What about the training?" Liam asked.

"We'll handle as much as we can in your mother's world until I can acquire the proper talisman. As for the rest... well... we'll deal with it when we must," Bran said. "Right now, I need you to explain what you were doing with that girl."

"Which girl?"

"*Eirnín Ní Conmaicne Mara*, the merrow. *That* girl." Bran's frown deepened.

"She was at the party. I don't know her. Or didn't. Never saw her before." Liam forced himself not to shrug again. "Is there a problem?"

"Is there a problem? Aye. There's a problem. She's Connacht," Bran said, as if that explained everything.

"So?"

"Stay away from her, lad. You're Clan Baíscne. She's Morna," Bran said, obviously angry. "I'll not tell you a second time."

"Why?"

"Because she's trouble, that's why."

"And if I don't?" Liam found himself asking.

Bran blew air out his cheeks. "Then you'll be putting yourself in the middle of things of which you've no knowledge. Dangerous things. Politics. Ties and creatures that will kill you if you don't know what you're about."

"Oh, aye?" Liam asked. "And how is that any different than usual? Why am I bothering to ask? It isn't as if you'll explain shite anyway."

Straightening, Bran's expression grew stormy, and he appeared to be ready to start shouting. Liam tensed in anticipation for an attack out of old habit, but Bran seemed to sense the reaction. He paused. Hurt and surprise flitted across his features and then his shoulders dropped.

"All right," Bran said. Although his eyes still glittered red, his voice was calm. "I'll tell you of the war, our war, and how it affects you and yours. But I'll do it on the other side. You can't stay here."

"You'll take me back to Belfast?" Liam asked.

Bran nodded. "Sceolán can take charge until I return."

Chapter 15

Belfast, County Antrim, Northern Ireland
December 1977

"The other clans have decided not to interfere in the mortal world, but not us," Bran said later that night once they'd travelled back to the mortal realm. "In return, the High King declared all of Clan Baíscne renegades and traitors for our trouble. That's why I came to your holy man's council, if you want the truth of it. It was the reason I gambled on giving you over to them. When I said the war wasn't going well, I meant it. I couldn't see another way of convincing them outside of giving you over to them. Although, I would've found another way had you chosen not to go."

"I thought you were only fighting the Fallen." Liam watched the fire take to the peat inside the brick fireplace enclosure. It was strange to be talking about such things with Bran in the derelict house in Clonnard.

"We are. But we're also fighting our own."

"Oh." Liam remembered the murders and vendetta killings that had resulted when the IRA had split into the Official IRA and the Provisional IRA—not that matters were any more settled or clearly delineated now. The IRA wasn't the only Republican group either. There was the INLA too, and God alone knew how many tiny splinter groups after that. *In-*

fighting, he thought. *Even that's nothing new, is it?*

He breathed in the scent of peat smoke and wondered how long Bran would manage to stick around. Bran had suggested a stay with Liam's mother at first, but Liam refused. He didn't want Haddock, ghost or not, anywhere near her, especially after what had happened the last time she'd been pulled into his troubles. *Or was it I who'd been pulled into hers?* Regardless, Derry wasn't an ideal place to hide anyway. The Peelers wanted to speak to him about a few dead bodies that had turned up last autumn. Of course, Liam hadn't been the one to do for them, but that wasn't the deciding factor, was it? He was an ex-prisoner and a retired Provo. He knew better than to think that anything else would matter to a Loyalist constable. The prevalent thought being, as a terrorist—whether former or not could be debated—surely he'd been responsible for a murder somewhere, and wasn't that enough reason to convict? *And these days they don't have to have a body to put you away for good. All they need do is pin suspicion of membership on you.* Therefore, Liam had had nowhere else to go. It was here in this shite hole with his father—or back to the ever-so-eager arms of the 'Ra, and he wasn't going back to the 'Ra.

Bran hadn't said a word against the derelict house that Liam had chosen. Instead, Bran had quietly set up camp on the second floor, leaving Liam to sleep on a bed of blankets and furs brought over from the Other Side. Liam would've done more to help but for the fact that the longer he'd remained still, the more agonizing movement had become. He was still wearing Conor's leather jacket, half out of necessity and half because he dreaded the thought of removing it.

Liam asked, "Didn't you tell me the Fianna had returned to aid Ireland in her hour of need?"

Bran nodded. He sat Indian-style on the floor near the fire. Liam didn't have a chair to offer him. There was only the bare floor, the items Bran had thought to bring, and the contents of Liam's laundry bag.

"The High King isn't convinced there's need," Bran said. "It's said that the Fallen have spies in Tara, the High King's court. But there's no proof, and we've not been able to get anyone near the place with the ability to detect them. Not yet." There was a sly quality to Bran's sidelong look that bothered Liam.

He wants something else from me, Liam thought. "All right," he said, in an attempt to steer the conversation away from whatever it was his father wanted. "So, clan Morna is the enemy?"

"Aye, among the rest," Bran said, feeding more peat into the fire. "But they're among High King Cairbre's staunchest supporters. There has been much strife since Cairbre assumed the crown. He keeps the clans fearful and divided. He's proud and tight-fisted. Sees no reason to pay tribute to the Fianna. He claims we are too proud and greedy. Yet, he demands more and more tribute and then leaves the people to suffer. Clan Baíscne feel it's time for another to take the seat of the High King. For the good of the Fey. Uncle Fionn has challenged him, but Cairbre is a coward. He's refused challenge and won't step down as he should. He says the Fallen are too big a threat to risk changing leadership. Yet, he'll do nothing."

"Why does anyone listen to him?"

"The trouble is, there's some truth in some of the things Cairbre says. The Fallen are powerful. And as I've said before, they are difficult to detect among our kind. There aren't many who have the talent for it."

There it was again. That look. "How is it that Fionn mac Cumhaill is still alive?" Liam asked, remembering the stories his aunt Sheila had told him as a boy. "Didn't he die at the Ford of Brea? Or was it the Battle of Gabhra?"

"She has the gifts of a bard on her, that one," Bran said, nodding. "The stories she told you are true."

"Which one?"

"Both."

"I don't understand," Liam said.

"Fionn didn't die the final death in either battle. Took a bitty rest is all."

"So, you're telling me someone sounded the Dord Fiann? The hunting horn? To call Fionn mac Cumhaill and the Fianna? That's real?"

"Not exactly," Bran said, poking at the fire. "The horn is real. Only… no one sounded it. That's part of the problem, you see. It's gone missing. And without that we're having trouble convincing anyone the problem with the Fallen among mortals is serious."

Liam blinked.

"To make matters worse," Bran said. "I've not seen or heard from Uncle Fionn in some time. I don't know where he is."

"And how does any of this effect… here?" Liam asked, trying not to shiver because of how much it hurt. Snow fell through the hole in the ceiling and was accumulating in a patch on the floor. For his part, Bran seemed unconcerned about the falling temperature.

"The Other Side is not only a place of transition for mortal dead, it is tied to mortal dreaming. It is where the old stories live. Imagination. Myth. Thought. Spirit. Creativity. All are tied to the twilight," Bran said. He went to his pack and pulled out yet another blanket. Then he laid it around Liam's shoulders. "Should the twilight falter... should it become the realm of the Fallen... Well, the mortal world will not stand long after."

Liam felt warmer at once. "So, the two wars are connected."

"Aye."

"We're fucked."

Bran gave him a sad smile. "Aye."

"You don't have to agree."

"You wanted to know the truth." Bran returned to his pack and brought out cookware and the last of the blankets. Then he paused. "Where were you intending to get water?"

"Stand pipe two blocks south."

Picking up a copper kettle, Bran turned. "All right. I won't be long. Don't fall asleep until I return."

Liam nodded. "I won't."

"I'm serious."

"I heard you."

Bran left the room, his footfalls echoed up the stairwell and through the hallway. When they faded away into nothing Liam was left with the crackling fire for company. Bored to bits, he stared at the damaged plaster and listened to the jaded city of Belfast fitfully doze and twitch in nightmare sleep. Gunfire popped in the distance. An army helicopter chopped at the night sky. Through the broken window he could see its spotlight pinning down whatever poor soul had caught its interest. He had a fleeting urge to dig the book out of the laundry bag but any sort of movement would cost him too much to make it worthwhile. So, he stared into the flames and considered his situation. No matter which way he examined it, he was well and truly fucked.

At least Father Murray is alive. Even Haddock's ghost couldn't ruin that.

Somewhere below and outside he heard someone approach the building.

Bran? He didn't think so. Something about the rhythm of the steps crunching in the snow and ice said otherwise. *Séamus and his boys, then?* Would Frankie have sold him out? Liam didn't think so, not any more. Liam held his breath while the rush of adrenaline did its work, making his eyesight sharp, and his breathing short. His heart rioted under his sternum.

The light from the fire, that's what has brought them. He'd thought the room distant enough from the street to make the risk less dangerous. Not that he'd had much choice. It was either chance the fire or freeze to death. He checked his watch. *Four in the morning. Surely, too early for Séamus to come looking? Aye? If he shows, it'll only be with the intent of talking me into joining up again. Right?*

At that moment, the back door creaked open.

Whoever it fucking is, they can't be here for a nice wee visit. Liam scanned the room for a weapon. Dragging himself to the corner where he'd collected wood scraps for the fire, he pulled a length of board from the pile. The motion disrupted other broken bits and made a loud clatter. He gritted his teeth and used the nail-studded board to stand up.

"Liam? Are you here?" It was a woman's voice.

He swallowed. He wasn't about to answer. He stared into the empty hallway and prayed she'd give up and go away.

"It's Eirnín. You're upstairs. I can hear you. May I come up?"

Shite. "What the fuck do you want, *Eirnín Ní Conmaicne Mara?*" If she was Fey, the use of her full name would make her uncomfortable.

"I wanted to make sure you were safe, William Rónán mac Bran."

So, that's how it's to be, is it? That was a nice try, he thought. *But you've missed the mark as others have before you.* "Fair enough. You know I'm alive. Now fuck away off."

"Well, that wasn't the only reason I've come to see you." He could hear her step closer to the stairway. "I wanted to talk. It's important."

"Go away, will you?"

"Come on, Liam," she said. "Are you going to believe everything you hear about me?"

"Who says I've heard anything?"

"You're going to tell me that your da didn't warn you off?" She was at the bottom of the stairs.

"Aye, he did."

"Well then," she said, her voice acquiring a sultry quality. "Do you do everything your da tells you to do?"

"Actually, no," Liam said. "But I think I'll make an exception in this case."

She moved closer. "Oh, I like you."

"Oh, aye? And I think you should shove off."

She was taking the stairs slow. One step at a time. He moved to one side of the doorway to both hide himself and get a more advantageous view. So he told himself as he slowly shifted his weight to lean against the door. His ribs were aching, and standing wasn't helping.

"I don't think you really want me to go away."

"Oh, I think I do." He could see the top of her head. A bright red hair clip nested in the waves of her black hair. It was shaped like a feather. "Stop right there."

Freezing, she waited for a few heartbeats. "Do you know anything about merrows, Liam?"

"I know what my Aunt told me."

"Then you know that I can be very friendly. I'm very good at being friendly. Very. Good."

Liam couldn't prevent a rather provocative image from surfacing in his mind. *It's been so long.* "I understand your kind are very good at drowning people when it suits you too."

"There's no water here."

Once again, Liam couldn't help thinking the entire conversation was out of place in the middle of Clonard. "I don't imagine that would give you much pause if you set your mind to it."

She made a tsk tsk sound. "It's true. Merrows are water people. But so are púcas. I don't think you could drown if you wanted to."

Really? I'll have to ask father about that, he thought.

"So, what would you have to fear from me?" She seemed to find the courage to look around, and got up on her toes to peer over the splintering floorboards. "I can't see you. Where are you?"

"Doesn't matter. I can see you."

"How do I know you don't have a gun pointed at me right now?"

"You don't. But that'd be a safe assumption on your part." *An incorrect one, but a safe one.* He could smell her perfume—something with lilies in it—mingling with the peat smoke. The bullet wound in his side was working up to a good sharp pain. Soon it'd be bad enough that he wouldn't be able to stay on his feet. *Go the fuck away. Please. I don't want to hurt you.* An image of Eirnín with the cricket bat in hand sprang to mind. *I'd rather you didn't hurt me either, come to think of it.*

"Ah, if that's the case," she said, turning to the sound of his voice, "then you are every bit the bad boy they said you were."

"Who said?"

"You think you're the only one who was given parental warnings?" She grasped the edge of the floor and peeked at the doorway where he was hiding. "Let's stop playing games and talk like civilized people."

"Are we?"

"Are we what?"

"Civilized people?" he asked, leaning against the door. Although he was cold, he was sweating now, and his ribs were practically screaming. He could feel the beginnings of a tremor in his legs.

She smiled. He could tell by the way her brown eyes sparkled. "I'd say we were very civilized."

"And what makes you say that?"

"Well, for one thing, you haven't shot me yet." She'd spotted him. "Or is that only because you don't have a gun?" Taking another step up, her whole head was clear of the stairway now.

"Love, I don't think that's a gamble you want to make."

"Oh, you do like me, don't you?"

"Wouldn't go that far," he said. He was enjoying himself in spite of the glass shards of pain. He couldn't help it. Something about her made him feel much younger and free of his responsibilities. *It's the injuries. Aye? I'm not myself.* It'd been so very long since he'd spoken to an attractive woman, let alone flirted with one.

Mary Kate needs you. The thought ambushed him, and he slammed his eyelids shut for a moment. "All right. Say what it is you're going to say." His eyes stung as well as his conscience.

"Here?"

"Aye."

"You're not being very hospitable."

"Look," Liam said. "If you've come to tell me something, you'd best get around to it soon. We're about to have company."

"You're expecting someone?"

"My father. He went for water."

"Oh." Her face grew serious.

"Well?" Liam asked.

"Maybe this isn't the best time."

Liam sighed. It hurt, but what else was new? The room began to tilt ever so slightly.

"All right, all right," she said. "I wanted to talk to you about arranging a peaceful council between our clans. Or at least between my sept and yours. The Fallen and the Fomorians are both our enemies, after all."

"Fomorians? You're saying the Fomorians are in this too?"

She rolled her eyes. "And the whole of the Tuatha Dé Danann. Have they not told you anything, your father and your uncle?"

Liam sighed again. That hurt worse, and he let out a hiss of pain. He was exhausted, his legs were officially trembling, and he'd be lucky to get back to his bed before falling flat. He was well and truly out of time. If she was here to murder him there'd be fuck all he could do about it. "Come on up." He stumbled to the hearth, using the wooden plank as support.

Eirnín cautiously entered the room and took in her surroundings. He couldn't help noticing how graceful she was. Her hair was loose and reached down to her hips in waves. He fought an urge to touch it.

"Is this the best your da can do for you?" She sighed. "Clan Baíscne are worse off than I thought."

"Are you here to criticize my fine accommodations or talk?" Liam asked and settled back down into his bedding with another pain-filled hiss.

Concern flashed across her features. "How bad is it?"

"I'll do," Liam said. "Talk already, will you?"

"The clans must cooperate with one another. The fighting has to stop." She sat on the floor next to the fire and out of his reach.

"And exactly how do you propose to do such a thing?" He sorted his blankets. It suddenly came to him that he was feverish. *Maybe she's only a fever dream? Well, if I'm dreaming I'm fucked. Aye?*

"We could make an appeal to the High King."

Liam let out a grunt of disbelief from the back of his throat. He was so tired. "And if Cairbre Lifechair is half the arsehole in person as he is in the stories, that will go far."

"Do you have any better suggestions?"

He laid back and relaxed for a moment. The room attempted a slow and nauseating roll to the left. Now the blankets were too warm. His face itched. He wanted and needed a shower and a shave. "Let me think on it." The short trip to the doorway had taken its toll. His eyelids grew heavy. He reconsidered resting and peered through half-closed eyelids at Eirnín. His mind drifted. He found himself wondering what a merrow would look like naked. They were not much different than mermaids from what his aunt had told him. *Except they wear a red feathered cap to help them breathe under water.* Would she have scales and fins under those clothes? *Quit that, now.*

"Well, don't think too long," she said and then made a face. It did little to mar her good looks. "This place stinks."

"No plumbing."

"It's cold too. And dark."

"Energy efficient. No heat. No electric."

She pointed up at the hole in the roof. "I can see why you chose this place."

Staring up at the cloud-drenched sky, he said, "That? It's my wee observatory. I like to study the stars in my free time."

She shook her head. "You should come with me. You'll freeze to death here."

"No." He shivered. Now he was cold again. *For fuck's sake.* His mouth was dry. Where was his father?

"Why? You already know I won't harm you."

He gave her a look. "I've my reasons."

"Fine." She got up, offended. "I'd best go before your da gets back."

I have to know. "One last question," he said, the words slipping out before he knew it. *The fever talking, no doubt.* "If—if you don't mind."

She turned in the doorway to face him. The warm firelight did wonderful things to her complexion. Her eyes were big, dark, and wide. Her wavy black hair was pushed over her shoulders, and a bright red hair clip was fastened on each side of her head. She was wearing a blue coat over a sweater and skirt combo with white tights. He tried not to stare at her legs.

"You don't look like any merrow I heard of. Where are your webbed fingers?"

"And you don't look like a six-foot rabbit named Harvey. What's your point?"

"I'm only half."

"Half what?"

"Half púca. Half mortal."

"So am I," she said, smiling a little. "Half merrow, that is."

"You are?"

She rolled her eyes. "I said so, didn't I?"

"So, I'm not the only half-breed?"

"Of course not, you idiot," she said. The smile stayed in place on her full lips. She wasn't wearing lipstick. She didn't need to. "In fact, you'd be hard pressed to find a family in Ireland that didn't have Fey blood somewhere. Your da and uncle, they didn't tell you that either?" And with that, she ran down the stairs and outside.

Chapter 16

Belfast, County Antrim, Northern Ireland
December 1977

Father Murray sat propped up in a hospital bed with its worn, thin sheets and anemic white blankets, staring at Father Thomas in stunned silence.

"Joseph? Should I get the nurse?"

"That depends," Father Murray said, attempting to keep his voice low to prevent the others in the ward from overhearing. "Did you say Father Conroy is convinced?"

An elderly woman in the next bed said, "That's what he said, so he did. My legs may not work, but there's nothing wrong with *my* ears, Father."

Father Thomas's puffy face grew red.

Stifling a smile, Father Murray said, "Thank you, Mrs. Coogan."

"You're welcome, Father," she said.

Father Thomas stood up and then pulled his plastic chair as close as possible to Father Murray's bed. The steel legs let out a piercing squeak as they were dragged across the linoleum. Then he yanked the privacy curtain closed. With that done, Father Thomas bent nearer and whispered in Latin, "Those precise words weren't used but—"

"He discovered a discernible difference between the anomalies and...

previously collected data?" Father Murray asked, keeping his voice low and praying that Mrs. Coogan didn't have any Latin.

"His exact words were that there are anomalies that haven't been encountered before. They can't be attributed to a… genetic inheritance from the… mother. I asked."

Gerry couldn't categorize Liam as entirely human or Fallen, Father Murray thought.

Father Thomas continued. "He suggested further investigation. The recommendation has already been approved by the Prelate's secretary."

"The truce will be extended?"

Nodding, Father Thomas gave him a small smile.

"What about… His Holiness?"

"Bishop Avery is scheduled to visit Rome during the second week of January."

"Yes!" Father Murray forgot himself and threw his left arm up—or rather, tried to throw his left arm up. His enthusiasm was sharply hampered by the IV drip. His broken arm protested as well. "Shite!"

"Joseph, please. You're hurting yourself."

"That's brilliant news! Brilliant! Better than I'd hoped for!" Father Murray didn't care about the pain. They were about to achieve something he'd thought impossible. Father Murray looked again at Father Thomas's face. His expression was withdrawn, his lips were thin, and he was definitely sweating. He switched back to Latin. "All right. What's the catch?"

"I think we should focus on the positive right now," Father Thomas said. "You must concentrate on healing."

"Declan, you can't win," Father Murray said. "If you don't tell me, I'll only call Thad and get it from him."

Father Thomas slumped, paused and then settled into his chair. "I had hoped this could wait until the situation stabilized."

"You mean, until I'd located Liam."

"He telephoned by the way."

"He did?" Father Murray felt a rush of relief. *Thank you, Mary and Joseph.* "He's safe then?"

Nodding, Father Thomas said, "I gave him your message as you'd asked."

"Thank you. Did he say where he was?"

"He didn't," Father Thomas said. His expression acquired a sly quality.

Father Murray nodded. *He didn't ask. That way neither of us has to lie. And who is going to be curious about such things but—* A chill ran through him. "Monsignor Paul."

Father Thomas looked away.

"That's it, isn't it?" Father Murray asked, thinking again of Father Stevenson's warning.

"He has demanded a private interview," Father Thomas said. "With your Mr. Kelly."

"Shite," Father Murray said. "We can't allow that."

"We've no choice, Joseph."

Father Murray shook his head. "There's always a choice."

"If we don't, Monsignor Paul will find him without our help, and he's capable of doing so. You know he is. You also know no one wants that. Especially your Mr. Kelly."

"I'll have to discuss it with Liam beforehand."

"Do what you feel you must."

Father Murray sighed. "Let me think on it before I give an answer."

"Agreed." Father Thomas got up. "You should rest now." He walked to the end of the privacy curtain. "Should I leave it?"

Shaking his head, Father Murray whispered, "You needn't bother. It'll save Mrs. Coogan a death from overactive inquisitiveness."

When Father Thomas had gone Father Murray laid his head back on the flat hospital pillow and closed his eyes.

"If you don't mind my asking, Father," Mrs. Coogan asked from her perch. "What was the good news?"

"My sister Agatha had twins. Girls."

"Oh?" Mrs. Coogan shot him a disbelieving look. "That's… lovely, Father. May Mother Mary and Saint Gerard bless your sister and her wee girls."

"That is kind of you, Mrs. Coogan. Thank you." Father Murray pretended to fall asleep before she could ask their names. He felt guilty for lying to the poor woman, but it wasn't as if he could tell her the truth, and he knew better than to say he couldn't tell her. It would only pique her interest. She'd worry at him until he lied anyway which would make matters worse because the lie would have to be bigger and more complex. An old hand at dealing with the likes of Mrs. Coogan, he knew the small boring lie was best. Anything more elaborate would mean he'd have to lie to others—the nurse, a doctor, any number of others that Mrs. Coogan would share the news with. Father Murray told himself he'd seek forgiveness in the morning at confession. So, he feigned sleep, and after a while, one of his fictions became a fact.

"Do you mind explaining how it is that my son was found lying in a street with a bullet in him?" While Bran's face was set in a patient expression, his eyes glittered red.

"Is he alive? Is he safe?"

"He is."

"Thank the saints," Father Murray said, glancing around him. He wasn't sure where he was or how he'd gotten there. The hospital was gone. His right arm was still in its heavy cast and sling, and he was dressed in his red plaid pajama bottoms and a hospital gown. Instead of the bed, he was sitting on the soft grass inside a circle formed of several three-foot-high stones. Huge oaks bordered the ancient stone circle. A full moon rode a cloudless night sky. It took him a moment to recognize the place. *Raven's Hill. I'm on Raven's Hill.* "This is a dream."

"Aye," Bran said.

"Liam was shot? That part is real?"

Bran nodded.

"How bad is it?" Father Murray asked.

Bran shrugged, unconcerned. "He will be fine in a day or so. He heals slower than most of our kind, but he recovers fast enough."

"Do you know who did it?"

Frowning, Bran said, "That isn't important."

"Isn't it? He's your son."

"Do you think me unaware of that fact?" Bran folded his arms across his chest and the red glint in his eyes flared, filling his irises entirely. "You're avoiding my question."

"Security at the facility was compromised by the Fallen. We weren't aware that it was the case until it was too late."

"So my brother tells me. That is troubling," Bran said. "No matter. My son's blood will be paid for."

Father Murray knew there was no point in arguing or pleading for mercy. He'd made a promise, and it'd been broken regardless of who had broken it for him. That was how the Fey operated in the stories, and he was fairly certain that much was true. Honor meant everything to civilizations that didn't rely on paper contracts or lawyers. The Fey weren't the only people whose culture functioned that way—certainly not historically and not even within modern Ireland. "I understand."

Bran's expression underwent a subtle change. "Interesting." The tone of his voice changed. His expression softened. "I believe you do at that, priest."

"Does it make a difference to you that I did my best?"

Seeming to think, Bran paused. "To me it does. It will not change the consequences, however. I'm afraid there is nothing to be done about that."

Father Murray nodded.

Bran sat down in the grass. His eyes were that startling shade of blue once more. "I begin to like you, priest."

"Thank you," Father Murray said. "Is that why you're here? To speak about what happened at the facility?"

"Not entirely so." Bran combed the fingers of his right hand through his hair. It reminded Father Murray of Liam. "I've come to discuss the truce."

"It will be extended." Father Murray could have sworn he saw relief in Bran's face.

"Good. The other holy men," Bran said and then hesitated. "Did they find what they were looking for?"

"I believe they begin to understand my position in the matter at least. While they don't necessarily believe, they do begin to allow room for doubt."

Bran's shoulders dropped slightly. "Then it was worth the price paid by all, Joseph Murray."

"I think so—I hope so. Thank you," Father Murray said. "I need to ask… Where is Liam now?"

"He's safe."

"I understand but—" Father Murray thought about how to explain his concerns. "Christmas is approaching."

"Is there a problem?"

"This is a time of special significance for him."

Bran frowned. "Is this about one of your rituals, priest?"

"I'm not talking about that," Father Murray said. "Although, I do believe attending Christmas mass might help him. This is about the anniversary of his wife's death."

"Oh." Bran's eyes widened slightly.

"Exactly," Father Murray said. "It wouldn't be wise to leave him on his own."

"And why is that?"

In Father Murray's experience, it was difficult enough to talk to mortal parents about their children's emotional welfare. He wasn't exactly sure how he could explain the situation to a man who quite probably hadn't heard of psychology, let alone believe in it. "He's still grieving."

"That is easy to see," Bran said. "Nonetheless, there is another problem. A bigger one." Worry etched lines in the man's forehead. "He's haunted."

Father Murray blinked. The conversation with Father Stevenson popped to mind. *The Facility's security was breached by spirits and not only the Fallen.* Father Murray shivered. How was he going to explain this to Bishop Avery?

"I wanted to ask… I need to ask you if you have a spell. Some sort of ritual which might protect him?" Bran asked, embarrassed. "I've done what I can for him. I have a talisman, and it is enough for one of our kind, but he was raised in your religion. I'm not certain he will—" He sighed. "My son needs comfort. He needs to believe he is safe. It is important. Do you understand?"

Perhaps he hasn't heard the term "psychology" before, but apparently he has an understanding of the concept. Father Murray said out loud, "I think I do."

"Good." Bran ran his fingers through his hair again. "Do you have this thing?"

"I do."

"Is it… difficult? Would it require a high price? I will pay. Whatever it is."

"It would cost nothing." Father Murray resisted an urge to smile. "Nor is it difficult. A blessing might be enough. We should try that first."

Again Bran seemed to relax. "Very good. How long will it take to prepare?"

"Not long."

"Then we will go to him now."

"How?"

Bran tilted his head. "We will travel in the twilight. No harm will come to you. I will see to it."

"I don't think it will work if he thinks it's only a dream."

"All right," Bran said. "Then I will return for you later."

"It would be best if I saw him alone," Father Murray said. "Briefly."

Breathing deep, Bran hesitated again. "If this is required for the spell. When can you be ready?"

"In my world?"

"Aye."

"Tomorrow, I think."

Bran nodded. "Call upon me when you're ready. I'll bring him to you."

"In hospital?"

Nodding again, Bran looked resigned. "I will do what I must."

"Can you keep him with you?"

"If not me, Sceolán will do so. I have already been away from the fian too long."

"You don't have Liam... here?" Father Murray asked.

"It is problematic for him to remain here for too long."

Father Murray blinked. "Why is that?"

"It is safer for him to remain in your world until you've done your spell for him. That's all you need know."

"Do you know how he came to be... haunted?"

Bran's eyes acquired that glitter again. "Do you need to know for your ritual, priest?"

Father Murray briefly considered a lie but had a hunch that Bran would sense it, and he didn't want to chance destroying the rapport he'd worked so hard to maintain. "I'm merely curious."

Bran got up. "I know why it happened, and that is enough."

"I can accept that," Father Murray said.

"Good," Bran said. "I will see you tomorrow, priest."

And with that, Father Murray's dreams took different turns.

Chapter 17

L iam shivered and held up the leather cord his father had given him. "What the fuck is this?" The peat fire popped and fizzed in the hearth, its glow heating the four-foot radius nearby to a survivable temperature. The rest of the broken-down place was a frozen waste. He was exhausted, and a headache had wedged itself behind both his eyes. At least his ribs were no longer attempting to sand themselves flat against his nerve endings. *It's half past seven in the morning, for fuck's sake,* Liam thought. *What is so important?*

Glaring at the thin metal scrap hanging from the bit of cord, he noted the leather had been threaded through the narrow end which had, in turn, been twisted into a loop. Another thinner length of leather had been wrapped around the metal, leaving only the tiny knob on the wider end uncovered. It looked all the world like a horseshoe nail wrapped in leather.

"It's a horseshoe nail wrapped in leather." Bran went back to his breakfast.

The scent of boiled oats set Liam's mouth to watering. He suddenly realized he was hungry. He gazed into his own bowl of congealing muck

199

and thought the better of eating it. What he really wanted was a cup of strong coffee or tea. He settled for hot water and toast.

"Very powerful talisman, that. Keep the metal from your skin," Bran said. "Being half mortal, you've a certain resistance. But iron will eventually poison you, nonetheless."

"A fucking nail is supposed to protect me from Haddock's shade?"

Swallowing, Bran nodded.

"You're joking," Liam said.

"Not about something as serious as this, lad."

"I thought the Fey couldn't abide iron? That's what Aunt Sheila always said."

"We have the use of steel," Bran said, indignant as if he'd been accused of an intellectual failure. "Your Aunt Síle may be a powerful bard with great knowledge, but she doesn't know everything about us. And what she does know isn't always correct."

"Then why is it you lot carry bronze spears?"

Bran stared at the fire. The smoldering flames were reflected in his eyes. Liam thought, *Or is it the other way around?*

"Medicinal herbs can be used to heal, can they not?" Bran asked. "And they can be used to poison as well, aye?"

Liam paused, considered his experiences with drugs and then nodded.

"It's all in the intention, the proportions, and the doses, you understand," Bran said.

"It still doesn't answer my question. Why does iron poison the Fey?"

The wooden spoon stopped halfway on its journey to Bran's mouth. He returned it to the bowl. "Some will tell you it's because iron is not native to Ireland as the Fey are, but they'd be wrong." He swallowed. "In truth, the reason has to do with the forests."

"What?"

"In order to smelt iron, you need a hot fire. Wood and, more importantly, charcoal are required," Bran said. "The forests of Ireland were stripped by the English. So it was, we had very little steel. And so it is that the English won out against us long ago."

"But what has that to do with anything?"

"We failed to protect the land entrusted to us, *Éire*. The land we took from the Fir Bolg, in truth. Many creatures died with those forests—elk, golden eagles, wolves, bats, and spirits of the woods as well. That loss is our greatest failing. And eventually became our greatest weakness, our lack of iron. It brought us low." Bran set his ceramic bowl down on the freshly swept floor. The broken-down room had been rendered much more liveable as a result of his ministrations during the night. "The Fir Bolg number mighty magicians among their kind. One such placed a curse upon the Fey." Again, his eyes glittered crimson, but before Liam could ask more Bran continued. "So it is that iron burns and poisons us as a reminder. The Fir Bolg name it *Éire's* Revenge." He shrugged. "Upon occasion, our old enemies have quite the sense of humor."

"But you said—"

Bran held up a hand. "Steel is also sacred to us. Important. Our weapons are made of bronze because to war with steel would bring the final death among our kind. It happens from time to time. The Morrígan will have her due. But it doesn't happen often and not without sanction. Therefore, we reserve steel and iron—sky iron and Northman's steel are two such kinds—for particular needs. Magical needs. And some types of iron, like what I've given you, are more sacred than others."

"I don't understand."

"That nail is made of sky iron and came from the shoe of the Mac Cumhaill's horse."

"What makes that so special?"

Bran sighed. "Give me your lighter, son."

Liam fished his lighter out of Conor's jacket pocket.

Bran wrapped his hand in the end of his linen shirt and then accepted the lighter. He held it up with his now bandaged left hand. Next, he took the leather cord necklace with the nail twisted on it and moved it close to the lighter. The nail swung up toward the steel lighter and stuck to it with a click.

"It's magnetic," Liam said, unimpressed.

"Aye." Bran returned both lighter and necklace.

"And that's supposed to help, how?" Liam asked.

Bran's face acquired a patient expression. "When a mortal is killed by one of the Fey, a spiritual connection is formed. A bond. If the spirit chooses it to be so and the killing wasn't in self-defence." His father pointed at the horseshoe nail. "That will disrupt the connection for as long as you wear it. Mind, it won't cut the connection altogether, but it will disrupt it. It will make you more difficult to find on the Other Side."

Liam chewed his buttered toast drizzled with honey and thought of Oran and Mary Kate. "What if you've a… connection with a spirit that you don't wish to disrupt?"

Bran started clearing the breakfast dishes. Liam hadn't seen a man so concerned with cleaning in his life. He wasn't sure if he found it strange or not.

"What sort of spirit, exactly?" Bran asked.

"Mary Kate."

Bran's face grew pained. "That is a very bad idea, son."

"Why?"

"She needs to move on."

"She has moved on. She's fucking dead."

"Exactly the reason why you must leave her be. You can't hold her to you. It's a selfish thing and will come to harm you both in the end."

"Harm us how?"

Shaking his head, Bran sighed. "I can't force you to listen. But you'll come to regret it. I know."

It was Liam's turn to stare into the flames. "Oran said she needs me and I, her."

"The other spirit?"

Liam nodded. "Oran was—is a friend. If he says Mary Kate is in trouble, she's in trouble. I can't leave her like that. I—I just can't. She's hurting something fierce. I have to help her. I love her."

Bran shook his head. His eyes were filled with sympathy. "I understand why you feel you should, but you can't."

"You've yet to tell me the fuck why."

Sighing, Bran stopped packing and crouched next to him. "When the shade touched you last night, what happened?"

Liam shuddered at the memory. "I don't know."

"You do. Tell me."

"I don't want to."

"Well, then," Bran said. "Imagine how bad it would be if it were Mary Kate and not the other?"

"She'd never!"

"Or you to her? Understand, you can do the same to her that was done to you."

"I'd never hurt her! I love her!"

Bran nodded. "I know, son. That's the problem."

Liam blinked.

"Eat. It's going to be a long day."

"I'm not hungry anymore."

"Suit yourself," Bran said and went back to packing.

Liam stared at the now cold bowl of boiled oats. He'd lied. He was hungry. However, he didn't want to eat. He wasn't sure about putting on the necklace either. It came to him that such thoughts were a form of self-punishment. He was angry at forces outside himself. Forces which had hurt him and at which he couldn't strike back. He was angry with his father, his mother, Mary Kate, the Provos, and God as well, if the truth were told, and this was that anger turned against himself—the only target he had remaining. Suddenly, none of those feelings made any sense at all. So, he slipped the leather cord over his neck. Still, he didn't know what to do with any of his feelings. So, the resentment condensed into a hard knot in his belly, turning his stomach. He couldn't bring himself to eat the oats. Glaring at the congealing bowl, he compromised by finishing the last of the toast. "What do you have planned?"

"You're to start the training today. But first, we're visiting a friend of yours. One Joseph Murray, priest."

"He's in hospital."

"So he is." Bran walked across the room to the back wall and whispered something in ancient Irish before emptying the bowl of cold oatmeal out a broken window. From the sound of it, Liam guessed it was some sort of blessing or offering. Crow cries echoed off the shattered buildings. Bran turned his attentions to finishing the packing. Done with the dishes, he proceeded to the bedding.

"The hospital will be watched," Liam said, getting up to help. He was still exhausted and achy, but he felt a little better after the toast.

"That is of no consequence. The truce has been extended."

"It has?"

"Aye," Bran said with a small, prideful smile. "The Fey owe you a debt."

Liam shrugged.

"It was a brave thing done. I'm proud of you, son."

Swallowing a strange combination of joy and bitterness, Liam gritted his teeth. *I don't need your approval. I don't.* But the truth was, he did and he fucking well knew it.

"The holy man will meet us."

Liam paused. "He's well enough to leave hospital?"

"We will see him in the waiting place inside the building." Bran accepted the last of the bedding and returned it to its cloth bag in a tight roll.

Liam found himself in the Belfast City Hospital waiting room, fighting bad memories and wishing like hell he were anywhere else. The nightmares were sure to return. They always seemed to after he set foot inside a hospital building. He watched anxious strangers read books, pray for family members, or pace, and wanted to feel hope for them. The air vibrated with anticipation, fear, and worry, making his back muscles tense to the point of pain. Even the stench of hospital disinfectant made his stomach clench. "This is stupid. I should not have come here."

Bran appeared unconcerned.

"Did you not hear me? Why are we here?"

"No one will harm you. Not while I'm with you."

"I'm not afraid!"

Turning, Bran tilted his head by way of a question.

Liam's cheeks burned. "I hate hospitals."

At that moment, a set of double doors swung open, and Father Murray shuffled through. He was dressed in a white terrycloth robe, red plaid pajama trousers, a faded blue hospital gown and black slippers. His face was pale, and his lips were pressed together with the effort of walking. His right shoulder was swathed in bandages, and his arm was encased in a cast and sling. Jumping from his seat, Liam took the heavy satchel from Father Murray and helped him to one of the plastic and steel chairs.

"You look different, Father," Liam said, squinting as if studying the priest. "If I didn't know any better, I'd say you've taken to listening to The Sex Pistols."

Father Murray gave him a look—narrowed eyes and a slow frown stretched to hide a smile. Liam was relieved to see it. He watched as

Father Murray unsuccessfully smoothed his hair left-handed.

"Father Thomas neglected to bring a comb. I suppose I should be thankful he remembered the razor. Nice jacket. Planning on a motorbike journey with Brando later?"

Liam held up the hem of Conor's leather jacket. "This? It's the latest. Didn't you know? Thinking of having my photo snapped next to a chain-link fence in a bit. Care to join me? You'd fit right in."

Father Murray's stern expression transformed into a smile. "It's good to see you, Liam."

"You too, Father."

Bran got up. "I'll return when you've finished."

"You're leaving?" Liam asked.

"We should talk. Alone," Father Murray said. "For a little while."

"Go with the holy man," Bran said.

"Why?" Liam asked.

"Come, Liam. Let's sit in one of the prayer rooms where it's quiet." Father Murray got up with some effort.

Danger. Get out. Now, the monster snarled from shadowy depths. *Enemy.*

Liam thought back at it, *What is it? Why?*

"Come on," Father Murray said.

"I'd rather not stay." Liam watched his father vanish among the grieving and an uneasy feeling oozed down his spine.

"Believe me, I'd have met you far from here if I could," Father Murray said.

Liam was slammed with guilt. *Was me that put him here.* "It's all right, Father. I'll go with you."

"We'll keep this to a minimum," Father Murray said. "I promise."

"What's this about?" Liam asked, following Father Murray through another set of swinging doors and down a hallway. He hadn't walked far before a man in a black sport coat and tie bumped into him. For an instant, Liam's nose was clogged with the stink of old gore. He got an impression of burn scars not quite covered by beard stubble when the man passed. Liam turned to look at his retreating back. The stench vanished as if it'd never been.

It was a couple of seconds before Liam realised that Father Murray had gone on without him.

"I understand you've had another encounter with Haddock." Father Murray opened a door to one of the prayer rooms.

Liam could see through the doorway that it was plainly furnished with dark wooden pews and had faded white walls. A wooden cross was nailed to the wall opposite—positioned between two narrow windows. The place smelled one part mortuary and one part church. A lumpy priest dressed in vestments arranged a few items on the small make-shift altar positioned under the cross. An aura of quiet weighed the empty space enough to squeeze the air from Liam's chest.

"And if I did see him again? What of it?" Liam paused before entering.

"Your father felt we should chat about it."

Blinking, Liam said, "My father set you to head-shrinking me?"

Father Murray looked embarrassed. "Well, no. Not exactly. We should go inside before we discuss this further."

Liam understood Father Murray needed to sit. The man appeared to be ready to fall over as it was. So, Liam relented, eventually settling onto one of the hard wooden pews. It seemed ironic that such an uncomfortable room was used as a place to seek comfort.

Father Murray winced as he eased into a pew. "Talk to me."

Glancing to the front of the room, Liam said, "We're not exactly alone, Father."

"Sorry," Father Murray said. "I forgot you hadn't been introduced. Liam, this is Father Declan Thomas. Father Thomas, Liam Kelly."

The big priest turned around. "Hello. We spoke on the telephone."

"Oh." Liam asked, "Why is he here?"

"I needed some assistance with certain details," Father Murray said, slightly lifting his broken arm.

"Details?" Liam asked. "What details?"

"We'll get to that in a minute," Father Murray said. "Father Thomas, may we have a few moments alone?"

Father Thomas nodded and then headed for the door, locking it behind him.

Liam waited until the lock turned. "My da thinks I'm mental."

"Liam—"

Jumping up from the chair, Liam began pacing. "Barking mad, more like. Tell me, Father. If I hadn't gotten out of that… place when I did, I'd be in a padded room or worse, wouldn't I?"

"I wouldn't have condoned such a thing, neither would Father Stevenson."

"Right. Fucking mental tests." Liam pushed his hair out of his eyes.

"I trust Father Stevenson. And so should you," Father Murray said. "He's part of the reason the Church ruled to continue the truce. He testified in your behalf."

Pausing, Liam then turned to face Father Murray.

"They've more questions, of course," Father Murray said. "But we can deal with that later."

"I'll not be locked up. I'll not go back."

"I'm not asking you to."

"Good."

"Your father gave you a talisman," Father Murray said. "May I see it?"

Liam shrugged and then reached inside his shirt collar, drawing out the horseshoe nail.

"That's it?" Father Murray asked, incredulous. "May I have a closer look?"

"Aye." Liam tugged the leather thong off over his head and dropped the nail in Father Murray's open palm.

"What is it supposed to do?" Father Murray stared at the bit of leather-wrapped iron in his left hand.

Shrugging again, Liam said, "It disrupts Haddock's ability to find me." *That's close enough to the truth, so it is. And vague enough at the same time.* He was ashamed of lying to Father Murray, but he'd given his word. *Tell no mortal.*

"How?"

"It's fucking meteoric iron. Magnetic even. Don't ask. Makes no sense to me either." Liam smelled a change in the room. He breathed deep and knew what it was at once. *Mary Kate. Why should I smell her here?*

"—for a blessing. Maybe something more, if needed," Father Murray said.

Movement on the edge of Liam's vision attracted his attention. He turned to see what it was and found a blank, antiseptic white wall.

"You need help fending off Haddock."

Liam blinked. "You believe me?"

"Why shouldn't I?" Father Murray handed back the leather-wrapped nail.

Cramming the necklace in his jacket pocket, Liam asked, "And you don't think I'm mad?"

Father Murray took a slow breath and released it. "You're stronger than you think."

"And you're not answering the question." Liam tried not to flinch as Father Murray stared deep into his eyes.

"You've been able to hold yourself together when most people wouldn't."

A derisive sound snuck out of the back of Liam's throat. "And how would you know?"

"I've a PhD in psychology, remember?"

Liam sighed, feeling a little better. "You wouldn't lie to me, would you, Father? I mean, if I were going off my nut… you'd tell me?"

"I've watched you grow up. I consider you… well… family," Father Murray said. "If I felt you were psychotic, I would tell you. But you're not."

"I'm normal?" Liam heard a distant laugh. It came from the other side of the door—he was sure of it. Nonetheless, he didn't care for the sound or the timing and shivered.

"I wish you wouldn't use those words. 'Normal.' 'Mad.' We're discussing things which should be dealt with on more specific terms." Father Murray sighed. "I'd say you were a bit frayed about the edges, but normal enough. Do you want to know what Father Stevenson said regarding your test results?"

Liam combed his fingers through his hair. Faced with actually knowing, he wasn't sure he wanted the information after all.

He nodded.

"He said that you showed certain neurotic symptoms," Father Murray said. "However, nothing severe or unusual given the stress you've been under."

Feeling the tension in his shoulders loosen, Liam released the breath he didn't realise he'd been holding. He wanted to believe Father Murray in the worst way but couldn't bring himself to place his faith in the diagnosis. How could he when everything his father's people were—everything he was, hadn't existed for the Church until recently? *Officially, we still don't. Aye?*

"Why are you so worried about being insane?"

Liam didn't know what to believe any more. He swallowed again. "Because Bran said I should."

"He did? Why?"

"Because someone like me... He said half-breeds live part in this world and part the other. He said that can be... confusing." Again Liam thought he sensed a presence on the edge of his vision, and again he looked only to see nothing there. The hairs on the back of his neck stiffened.

"Oh."

"I—I don't think God can help me, Father. I think I have to make my own way." Liam felt equal parts excited and terrified by the prospect. For the first time in his life he was committing to thinking for himself, not simply believing what someone else—the Church, the 'Ra—told him to believe. There was more to the world than anyone knew, particularly the Church. There had to be. He had to believe it was so.

Because I'm not a fucking demon and neither is my da. He sat up a bit straighter.

"You're never beyond the help of God, Liam."

"Are you so certain of that?"

"I am," Father Murray said. "God wouldn't turn his back on any of his children."

"Am I—you think I'm—" Again someone laughed. The presence was closer. *Was Father Thomas talking to someone?* Liam glanced at the door.

"Of course you are," Father Murray said. A worried look gathered on his face, pinching a line between his eyebrows.

Liam nodded. It was comforting to hear Father Murray's words, no matter what. Again, the old stories his aunt Sheila used to tell came to mind. The questions asked of priests on lonely roads in the middle of the night. *What's to become of us when the end comes?*

Liam walked to the altar and stared out of one of the small windows. The city glared back, sullen. The sky was a gunmetal grey, and mist clouded the glass with frost. He watched blurry people scurry across and down the street on their way home or to the market or whatever errands a normal life set them upon. He couldn't help envying them. *If I'd been able to save Mary Kate, would she be a solicitor now? I'd have loved her more than anyone in the world. I'd have given her perfume and flowers. Whatever she wanted.*

I'd have seen to it she'd never had a worry in the world. I would've done whatever it took. We would've had our wee girl. And maybe another. And I would've seen them to school like all the other fathers.

I wouldn't be here talking about fucking ghosts and demons with an ex-holy assassin. He glanced up at the ceiling, searching for cameras. He didn't see any, but he couldn't shake the feeling they were being watched. He paced down the aisle running between the wooden pews, arrived again at the door and peered out through the narrow window set inside.

He felt a touch on his left shoulder.

"I'm behind you, you cracked Fenian bastard."

Liam whirled—the wrong direction as it turned out. Haddock stood just to his right, laughing. It was an old, childish game, but one that Haddock apparently delighted in. Liam checked an urge to punch the ghost. It was pointless.

"Is something wrong?" Father Murray asked.

"Not a thing," Haddock said. "Everything is exactly as I like it."

"Haddock is here," Liam said.

Haddock made a tsk-tsk sound with his tongue. "Oh, now. He'll only think you're losing your mind. On second thought, this is a hospital. The mental ward is only a few floors away. That's convenient. Isn't it? Go ahead." He made a hand motion indicating chattering.

"Fuck you."

Frowning, Father Murray got to his feet. "Liam, tell Father Thomas to come back. Now." He reached inside the pocket of his robe.

Liam was shoved against the door with a blow to the stomach. It knocked the breath out of him.

"Liam?"

Coughing and doubled over, Liam said, "Wasn't me. It was Haddock again."

"Lie down on one of the pews. Hurry. We have to start the exorcism."

Liam drew in as much breath as he could and straightened. "I'll try." Father Thomas was knocking on the other side of the door. Liam could feel the force of the blows against his back. Eyes watering, he glared at Haddock. "Fuck away off."

Haddock said, "Oh, I think I'll stay."

Father Murray produced a bottle of holy water and started muttering a prayer in Latin.

"The good Father thinks he can magic me away?" Haddock asked with a snort. "You can't bless away the long arm of the law."

"Why the fuck are you here, Haddock?" Liam asked, feeling Father Thomas hammer against the door with more urgency. Liam stayed where he was. He wasn't sure what would happen if he moved. "What do you want?"

Haddock smiled, showing all of his teeth. He faded a bit for a moment and then solidified. As he did, his clothes became scorched and his skin blackened. "You and me have a score to settle."

"You're here to kill me then?" Liam asked.

Laughing, Haddock shook his head. "That'd be too easy. You don't deserve easy. Not you. Not yet."

"What do you fucking want?" Liam asked. He inched his way sideways in hopes of clearing the door for Father Thomas.

"I want my life back, you piece of shit!" Haddock slammed a palm down on the door, closing it in Father Thomas's face. The violence of the action made Liam involuntarily jump.

"I can't fucking give it back!" Liam pushed at Haddock. For an instant, Conor's leather jacket felt warmer, and Liam caught the scent of incense. As his hands met Haddock's chest Liam expected to go right through him but met a solid form instead. However, like before, Haddock's skin gave away just a bit like cold jelly. *Or decayed flesh.* Liam's stomach did a nasty twist, and he jerked back in revulsion. "Sod off!"

Haddock staggered backward. A shocked expression flashed across his face and then vanished behind a veil of rage. Liam took the opportunity to move away from the door.

Father Thomas squeezed through and sidled past. "What's going on?"

"What did he say?" Father Murray asked.

Liam said, "He wants his fucking life back."

"I'm sure D.I. Haddock misses his family and those he loved," Father Murray said, signalling to Father Thomas.

Father Thomas rushed to the altar.

"Priests." Haddock laughed again. "You just don't fucking get it, do you?"

"He says you don't understand at all," Liam said.

"Why doesn't he explain it, then?" Father Murray asked, clearly attempting to stall Haddock.

"I put bad people behind bars! That was my life! Every day I'm like this is one more day one of you Fenian fucks walks free!"

"Bad people? Are you fucking joking? You tortured me!" At that, Liam had a hunch he was missing something. It had to do with what his father had told him.

"Asked a few hard questions," Haddock said. "I had a duty to the law."

"Duty?" Liam let out a disgusted huff.

Haddock smiled his malicious smile. "You were the one who decided not to talk. Nigel merely attempted to provide appropriate motivation." He harrumphed. "Seven days. Bloody lawyers. Civil rights. My arse. They should never have put in that stipulation. Terrorists deserve what they get. Fucking Paddies. Cromwell should've finished what he started and did us all a favor."

Liam spat at Haddock.

"What did he say?" Father Murray asked.

Liam said, "He says he was only doing his fucking job."

Haddock's nostrils flared. "Don't you wind me up, Paddy-boy. Don't you fucking dare. I'll break you. You know I can do it. And no one can fucking stop me. Not now."

Liam said, "You don't know shite. I didn't steal that fucking car. And I never did anything to you."

"Liam, what is he saying?" Father Murray asked.

"I can't do my job properly any more, but I can make damned certain you suffer every day you have left!"

"Liam—"

What was it Da said? Liam thought and then he remembered. "You started in on me first."

"Liam, what is—"

Haddock frowned. "You broke the law."

"You had no proof." Liam felt his shoulders drop as the realization set in. "You lifted me because I was at the mechanic's with Oran. You had fuck all. I didn't steal that fucking car."

"Sure you didn't."

"I didn't!" Liam stepped closer to Haddock.

"And what does that matter?" Haddock asked. "You'd done something to deserve being nicked. If it wasn't that car then it was something else. I'm right, aren't I? Fucking piece of shit."

"You started in on me first," Liam said. "Fuck away off. I mean it. You can't stay."

"No! You—"

"I have it now," Liam said. "I let you come back. It was me." *My guilt.* "Well, I'm done, you fucking hear?" He shoved Haddock again, and again. Haddock stumbled backward. Reaching into his pocket, Liam wrapped a fist around the horseshoe nail.

"You can't—"

"I can." Then Liam punched Haddock full in the face. His fist met empty air.

Haddock was gone.

Chapter 18

The Other Side
December 1977

"Pick that crossed spear up like I told you, trainee," the warrior Bran had introduced as Ceara said. The top of her head barely reached Liam's chest, and she had the stocky build of a bricklayer. Like many of the Fianna, she was dressed in a combination of leather, fur, and wool. Her sleeveless brown leather vest was fitted with bronze buttons. Her loose-fitting wool leggings were dyed blue and gathered in at the shins and ankles with leather thongs. She'd taken off her long green cloak and folded it neatly on the ground. Her muscled and scarred arms were bare and folded across her flat chest. She had shoulder-length light brown hair knotted into braids, and pale eyes, and he guessed her age to be somewhere around thirty. A scar ran from just under her left eye, across a badly set broken nose and ended on her right cheek. *Sword slash. A bad cut, that. Was lucky not to lose her nose,* Liam thought.

All in all, she was anything but beautiful and could've passed for a man but for her full lips and delicate jaw.

"The spear." Her voice was every bit as hard-edged as her demeanor.

"No," Liam said.

She scowled up at him. "And why not?"

"I'm not here to learn soldiering," Liam said.

Her scowl became a glare, and if he hadn't already faced down the likes of Éamon Walsh, Séamus and Haddock, Liam might have reconsidered his attitude in spite of her being so short.

She paced. "Your father ordered me to train you for the Fianna."

"Then you got the wrong impression," Liam said, mirroring her stance by folding his arms across his chest. He had to be careful how high he held his head, however, or he'd lose sight of her, and he had a hunch that'd be a very bad idea.

"What *are* you here for?" she asked, turning to walk toward him again.

"To learn about the Fey," Liam said.

"All right," she said. "What is it you'd like to know?"

"Everything."

To his surprise she laughed. The effect was dramatic. Hearty mirth cast a light across her blunted and scarred features, softening her slate-grey eyes. "Sure and wouldn't we all like to know so much? But you don't have that long before the start of your trials. And you've enough learning ahead of you as it is. Could you be a bit more specific?" She sat on the grass and motioned for him to join her.

He sat, the spear abandoned in the grass several feet from his left hand. The clearing around them smelled of forest and moist black dirt. Cold as it was in Belfast, here it was a warm, fine afternoon. He shed Conor's leather jacket. His ribs put up a half-hearted protest. "Trials?"

"Surely you didn't think you could join the Fianna and not pass the trials?"

"Never said I wanted to join," Liam said. "I did say I was done with soldiering, though. And I do mean it no matter what my father says."

She studied his face for long enough that Liam began to wonder what she saw. "Bran is known for being a bit stubborn. And on more than one occasion has proven to possess selective hearing—not that I would know for certain." She paused. A hint of mischief lurked behind her now stoney expression. "Nonetheless, I am charged to instruct you. And your failings will be mine. Bran is my *rígfénnid*. I can't go against him in this." She paused. "Well, not directly."

Feeling his jaw tighten, Liam said, "You're saying I've no choice?"

"Not at all. Only that I don't. You may inform Bran of your wish to withdraw at any time."

Liam got to his feet.

"But," she said, "I'm not so certain I'd do so just yet, if I were you."

"Why?"

"Well, he has more than a few things on his mind at the moment."

"Oh, aye?" Liam said. "Well, he isn't the only one."

She motioned for him to stop again. "You are a hot-headed one, aren't you? Take after your da, if the stories are true. Sit. Listen. There's more than one way of going about this."

"I don't want to go about it at all."

Nodding, again she gestured for him to sit. "Hear me out before you run, puppy."

"I'm not running, and I'm no puppy!"

"Sit and listen, then."

He opened his mouth to shout at her again but one thought stopped him. *I can get answers here and nowhere else.* He clamped his teeth together and sat.

She smiled a crooked smile, making the mischief more prominent in her eyes. "Before we begin, I've a question. Why refuse to fight? Are you a coward?"

"No!"

"I thought not," she said, undisturbed by his fury. Her voice was quiet and steady. "Would it have something to do with that bitty nail hanging from your neck?"

"And if it does?"

"I'd say you've more sense and wisdom about you than I first thought." She stared at him again, but her gaze was less judging the second time. "You have options. And I've ideas to discuss with you regarding the trials, but we will talk about that later. For now, understand you'll not have to serve as a soldier. Your kind make better scouts in any case."

"And what kind is that?"

"Púcas, of course," she said. "Has your da not told you the simplest of things? You're gifted with the ability to shape shift."

"I know."

"Then show me." She nodded at him. "Change form."

"I don't want to."

"Why not?"

Liam sighed. "I can't."

"You can't?" Ceara's face bunched into an incredulous expression.

"I haven't been able to call it up lately. And whenever I have in the past, I can't control it." Liam felt his face burn. "I know what it is that I am, but I don't know what it fucking means. Or how it works. Or why. No one has told me shite. How is it I'm supposed to know anything? And why would I want to? That fucking monster has brought me nothing but pain and trouble. And I wanted it gone. So, I sent it away. But now that it's gone half the time I feel like I'm falling apart. Nothing makes sense anymore. I see things. Nothing feels… right. I don't feel I'm myself."

"Oh." Ceara blinked.

"What the fuck do I do?"

Ceara took a deep breath and released it. "Come with me." She got to her feet and held out a hand to help him up.

He accepted her help, got to his feet and then retrieved Conor's leather jacket from the grass. "Where are we going?" he asked, slipping into the jacket.

"I know someone who should be able to help. A druid. His name is Lochlann."

"And what can he do?" Liam followed her to a path that traced a winding way up the old mountain. It was steep, and he had to run to catch up with her. All the while he wished he'd gotten more sleep.

"You'll see," she said. "He's a mortal. From the Other Side. Hasn't been here all that long, but he has great power and much knowledge of both worlds. It was one of the reasons he was brought over."

"There was another reason?" Liam asked, panting.

"It's a common enough story," Ceara said. "Róisín Nic Cuinn fell in love with him, and he with her."

In spite of Ceara's warning, the druid, Lochlann, was not what Liam had imagined at all. To begin with, he was young, younger than Father Murray. Lochlann was no older than his late twenties, if Liam were any judge. For another thing, he was wearing small, round, wire-frame glasses, blue jeans, work boots, and what looked like a white button-down shirt under his open, brown druid robe. He had long red hair that fell to the middle of his back, an untrimmed beard the likes of which a hermit would be envious of, and a Cork accent.

Lochlann signalled for them to take places near a small peat fire deeper inside the cave. A narrow crack in the ceiling allowed afternoon light to filter down, and the smoke to filter up and out. Tree roots and cobwebs hung from the ceiling. Creatures fluttered and shifted in the blackness that stretched out behind and beyond the peat fire's light. Somewhere water dripped onto stone, echoing up through the back passage and the depths below. Based upon the claw marks on the walls, Liam guessed the cavern's previous tenant had been a large bear.

"Quite a place you have here," Liam said.

Lochlann didn't rise to the jibe. Instead, he stared at Liam for several minutes without speaking. When he did finally speak his tone was almost bored. "Look into the copper bowl and tell me what you see." He pointed down at a large copper basin resting on a wide section of tree trunk obviously being used for a table. It was filled with water.

"Why?" Liam asked.

"It is up to you," Lochlann said with a shrug. "Stay or go."

Liam glanced at Ceara who nodded encouragement. He stepped closer to the tree trunk and gazed into the bowl. The light inside the cave was mirky at best, but he could make out details easily. "I see water, and the bottom of a fucking copper bowl. What the fuck is that supposed to do?"

Ceara started to protest, but Lochlann put up a hand to stop her.

"Look again," Lochlann said. "This time, take a slow breath before you do."

Peering into the bowl, Liam didn't expect to see anything different. Which was why when a horrible monster with the distorted face of a black wolfhound and red glowing eyes glared up at him, he jumped and stifled a scream.

"Is there a problem?" Lochlann asked in his musical Cork accent. Liam could have sworn the man was mocking him.

Wee fuck. Liam stepped farther away from the bowl. "What was that?"

"You know perfectly well," Lochlann said.

"No I don't," Liam said.

Lochlann shrugged. "Something you've hidden. Something you… run from. Something you're afraid of."

"I don't know what you're playing at," Liam said. "But you'd better stop with the fucking games, or I'm leaving."

Lochlann turned to Ceara. "We've work to do, he and I. It will go easier for him if you're not here to see it. This may take some time. Come back before dinner. If he's not finished by then he never will be."

"What?" Liam asked.

Ceara nodded and turned to go.

"Where are you going?" Liam asked.

Pausing, Ceara turned to face him. "Lochlann can help you. I can't do a thing with you until you get yourself sorted out. And he's the only one who can do it. Understand?"

Liam swallowed and combed his hair from his face with his fingers. "All right." He watched her leave with a sense of foreboding.

"Are you ready to begin?" Lochlann asked.

Liam shrugged. "Ceara didn't explain why I'm here."

"It's easy enough to see for anyone with the sight." Lochlann motioned him closer to the copper bowl.

Taking a position next to Lochlann, Liam was uneasy. "How is staring at that *thing* supposed to help?"

"It's time to start listening instead of talking," Lochlann said. He waved a hand over the bowl and whispered something Liam didn't catch.

The air inside the cave grew heavy and gathered intensity until Liam thought he'd hear it crackle like static. The hairs on the backs of his arms stood up on end. He had a hunch something bad was going to happen, and he didn't like it at all.

"Now," Lochlann said. "Look into the bowl again. This time, don't flinch. Don't pull away. Look and tell me what you see."

"You're sure this is going to help?"

Lochlann shrugged.

Holding his breath, Liam slowly leaned toward the bowl. The creature was there again. "I see a fucking monster." He sensed more than saw Lochlann nod.

"Ah," Lochlann said.

"What do you mean?"

"The creature reflected in that water is you," Lochlann said.

"Look. Don't you think I already know that?"

"So you say," Lochlann said. "You're a púca, a shape shifter. You assume shapes. The shapes aren't separate beings. It's as if you've emptied every bad feeling, every aspect of yourself you hate into another form and then you discarded it. That isn't normal."

Liam winced.

"Good and evil are part of all mortals. They are aspects of the Fey and all beings who reside in this world as well as the mortal world," Lochlann said. "None of us is whole without our strengths and weaknesses. You're… splintered."

"Don't you mean broken?"

"Not necessarily," Lochlann said. "But you can't remain like this for much longer. If you do, you'll go mad."

Liam laughed. It didn't do much to hold back the panic. "I'm not already?"

"Confused, perhaps, but not mad. Not yet," Lochlann said. "The problem is, if the situation continues as it is something will have to be done about you."

"What do you mean?"

"Ever wonder why so many mortal stories about the Fey are dark and made of nightmares? This is why." Lochlann pointed at Liam's chest and jabbed him over the heart. "You are why. Go mad and live. You'll be the nightmare. The rage will consume you. You'll destroy everything and murder everyone in your path. You'll kill until you're stopped."

"Stopped? How?"

"Bran, as *rígfénnid,* will be forced to execute you."

"And…" Liam paused and swallowed. "How do I prevent that from happening?"

Lochlann gave him a small smile. "You finally seem to comprehend the seriousness of the situation."

"You present a convincing argument."

Lochlann motioned toward the copper bowl. "Drink."

"How much?"

"All of it."

Liam touched the copper bowl and shuddered. Its metal surface was warm as if it'd been cooling some time after having been in the fire. There was something uncomfortable about it. Something sickening. He didn't like the feel of it. Regardless, he brought the rim of the bowl to his lips. For an instant it smelled of stale beer and cigarettes. The monster's reflection leered back at him. Liam closed his eyes.

"Don't," Lochlann said. "You must see the contents of the bowl as you drink."

For fuck's sake, Liam thought. *I'll choke if I have to stare at that fucking thing.*

"It won't work otherwise," Lochlann said.

Liam opened his eyes, once more brought the bowl to his lips and began to drink. It tasted nothing like it smelled. *Thank God,* he thought. In fact, it didn't taste at all. As he drank he felt the press of warm copper against his mouth and heard a distant roaring that reminded him of gushing water. It grew in pitch until it sounded as if the entire ocean were pouring into his brain. Something changed. His skin began to prickle. Now the water tasted flat and was slightly salty. He remembered the water he'd drunk in the facility, but then became distracted by the familiar whisper of the monster in the back of his brain.

You thought you could put me away, it said.

Fuck you. I did put you away, Liam thought back.

Only for a wee while. The creature snarled. *I'm back because you need me.*

I don't.

You do. Without me you would have let him—

Liam choked.

"Don't stop," Lochlann said. "Keep drinking."

Shut your fucking gob, Liam thought at the creature. *You don't know shite.*

The monster laughed.

In an instant, Liam found himself in a white room with rough iron bars. *Long Kesh,* he thought with panic. *I'm in Long Kesh. No. I'm in a cave with a hippie named Lochlann who styles himself a fucking druid.* But Liam knew the room. There was no denying it. He was in a cell, a part of the infirmary. Blood was smeared and splashed across one of the walls. He was standing over someone. A guard. The word "FAIRY" in crooked letters sliced deep into living flesh. Screams. Pain.

Saunders.

"I can't." The feeling of entrapment squeezed Liam's chest. He couldn't breathe.

It was Lochlann from somewhere in the distance. "What do you see?"

"Nothing! I see nothing!"

Lochlann's voice was insistent. "You must see something."

"I'll not fucking tell! I'll die first!"

"Did you kill someone?"

"I'll not tell!"

"Don't shy away from it," Lochlann's voice insisted. "Keep drinking. You can do this."

"I don't want to."

"You do."

"I can't."

"You can," Lochlann said. "As long as whatever this is stays in the dark, as long as you can't speak of it, this thing will tear you apart. Do you understand?"

"No! I won't! I can't! It's too—" *Painful. Awful. It can't be true. The shame of it.*

"What?" Lochlann asked.

Liam was facing the wall—leaning toward it, iron bars in his hands. He was balanced on his toes with his legs spread. Naked. Standard procedure for a strip search. Except this wasn't a strip search, he knew. A steel cuff clamped on one wrist. His heart rammed itself against his breastbone—fast, faster, fastest. He had to move. *Escape.* Before it was too late. Someone stood behind him now, pressing against his back. They reached up to place the second cuff around his other wrist.

"No!"

"You can do it."

Our little secret.

"NO!" Liam didn't understand that he'd thrown the bowl across the cave until he heard the sound of metal hitting rock. It rang out like something between a broken bell and a gong. It was darker in the cave. The peat fire was the only source of light. His clothes were soaked and he was cold, shivering. Lochlann was dripping as well, his druid's robe half on the floor.

"Well, that could've gone better," Lochlann said.

"What just happened?"

Lochlann took a deep breath and then gave him a half laugh. "You threw the bowl at me."

"Hello?" It was Ceara. "Is it finished?"

Liam turned to face Ceara.

"Come in, Ceara," Lochlann said. "It's as done as it's going to be for now."

"Will I stay sane?" Liam asked in a whisper.

Stooping, Lochlann sorted out his robe. Then he picked up the copper bowl. It was dented. "So much for that."

"You didn't answer me," Liam said.

"I don't know," Lochlann said. "But I suppose you could give it a good try. How do you feel?"

Liam closed his eyes. Something in the darkness within his skull shifted. A familiar shape filled the void. He could almost feel it sneer at him. He felt more whole, more himself than he had in some time. "Better. I think."

"Good enough," Lochlann said. "Bravely done."

Liam searched Lochlann's face. "Are you mocking me?"

"Not at all," Lochlann said, continuing to pick up the other items which had been thrown to the ground. "Not many have come as close to finishing as you. Most don't even start. Although, that's the first time I've ever thought I'd have my head stove in."

"What did I do?" Liam asked.

"You removed the hold the priest had on you," Lochlann said. "The hound shape is yours once more."

Chapter 19

L iam sprinted through the woods at a comfortable pace. It felt good to stretch his legs. He attempted to remain focused on that aspect of the morning rather than his other concerns. No matter what, he was rested and alert with the wind in his face. He breathed in an easy sense of freedom regardless of the winter chill clinging to the shadows under the trees. He'd have been content but for the pursuing howls, laughter, and horn blasts echoing through the forest. Breathing easy, he was confident the Fianna wouldn't catch him. This was, Ceara had assured him, only the first of his trials and the easiest for the likes of him, in spite of the fact that he'd not been long in the training. So far, she'd told the truth. The area under the trees had been effortless and free of underbrush—hardly a challenge. There were no obstacles, no dead branches to avoid. He hadn't had time to consider why this was so. He simply ran as was expected of him.

Of course, there'd been a bit of bother at the start because his hair had been too short to braid. This had led to more than a few jokes at his expense regarding porcupine quills which Liam had taken with uncharacteristic good humor and patience. That is, until some fucking joker named Angus suggested he wear a wig fashioned from horse hair. The fucking

224

thing was too big and itched something fierce. Frankly, Liam was glad Oran couldn't see him—or anyone else he'd known for that matter. With the wig secured to his head with a leather thong under his chin, he didn't have to have a mirror to know he looked ridiculous. He'd have yanked the fucking thing off and tossed it in the nearest stream but for Ceara's warnings. He wasn't to take the bastard off, nor let any of the braids come undone, and if they found any twigs or leaves caught in the thing he'd fail the test as well. To make things worse, they'd made it clear that if he was caught he'd be given a good hiding. He wasn't entirely certain of whether his father would stand for that last bit, but he'd heard enough of his aunt Sheila's stories to take the threat seriously.

Not there'd be much Bran could do about it if he had objected. Word had it he was away on some sort of clandestine mission Liam wasn't allowed to know about.

Leaping over a deadfall—the first he'd come to—Liam landed on the other side and fell back into the steady rhythm of running. Left. Right. Left. Right. Left. Right. His feet pounded the damp, soft earth. One. Two. One. Two. He let his thoughts drift into a calm numbness while his eyes focused on the terrain. Left. Right. Everything was going well until the trees thinned out.

Slowing to a stop, he came upon a deep gorge. Gazing down at the overgrown thicket of brambles, deadfalls, rocks, and dead leaves, he cursed.

It was too fucking easy, he thought. *You knew there'd be a trick to it, did you not?* They'd herded him to this place with their shouts and horn-blowing like a frightened deer, and he'd let them do it. *Stupid.*

"Ah, now," Sceolán said in a bored tone. "Looks like you're in a bit of a mess."

Liam fairly jumped out of his skin. He whirled with his heart slamming his tonsils and spied his uncle sitting in the grass with his back against a fallen tree ten feet away. He appeared to have been there for some time. He was carving a piece of wood using a small bronze knife. Pale shavings littered the ground around him. He paused to straighten the blade with his teeth as if he'd done so a million times and then went back to work.

He didn't look up from his carving. "Aye. You're in a bit of a fix, nephew mine."

"Bugger off," Liam said. "You haven't caught me."

Sceolán shrugged. "True enough." He appeared unconcerned about the prospect, nor did he move from his relaxed position. "Well." He sighed. "Not yet, anyway."

Liam edged away from his uncle. Then he risked gazing down at the gorge a second time. It was about a hundred feet deep and perhaps fifty or so wide. The drop off was as close to ninety degrees as to make little difference. Any attempt to crawl, walk or climb down would result in a bad fall and most likely death. The bramble bushes were the softest and most pleasant of the possible landing options, by the look of it, and regardless of whether or not he survived, he'd certainly lose the fucking wig in the end.

The sounds of his pursuers grew closer. Frustrated, he stared at a few crows circling in the sky to his right. He assumed something had attempted the jump and failed. The crows executed their lazy loops, drifting farther and farther down like autumn leaves.

"What will you do now?" Sceolán asked.

Liam was furious—angry with himself for being so stupid as to do what the Fianna had expected—and they had expected it, since his uncle had obviously been waiting for him. Liam was also angry at the Fianna for mocking him, and angry at Angus most of all. The whole situation was a fucking joke. They had no intention of taking him seriously. That had been the reason for the rush, not due to any orders on Bran's part. They didn't think him worthy. It didn't fucking matter that he'd served in the 'Ra. It didn't matter to them that he'd done time. It didn't matter that he'd killed to protect his mates. All that mattered was his ability to run through a fucking wood with a stupid fucking wig on his head.

A fucking joke, so it is. He clenched his teeth. Well, they weren't going to take him down without a fight. He'd had enough of their jokes. He didn't give a tinker's damn what they thought of him.

Glaring at the crows, an idea occurred to him. Ceara had whispered something in his ear just before the trial had started about how the main thing was reaching his destination without getting caught. His methods were his own. He was what he was and the Fianna wouldn't fault him for it. She seemed to be implying that displaying a certain level of creativity in his solutions to the challenges wouldn't be frowned upon.

There's only one way of knowing, he thought. And if they'd thrown him into a hopeless situation without any solution, then fuck the lot of them. They wouldn't have him.

His uncle Sceolán threw the bronze blade at the ground with a flick of his wrist. It stuck into the soft earth point first. Then he slowly got to his feet. "You're running out of time."

Determined and enraged, Liam backed far away from the ledge. The Fianna were close now. He could hear their cries and caught glimpses of them running under the trees, laughing.

If I die, I die. At least that'll be an end to it, Liam thought, resigning himself. *Either way. They won't have caught me. Fuck them and their fucking challenge.* He made his mind up, took a deep breath and just as the others broke through the tree line he sprinted as fast as he could for the ledge. His heart pounded out a frantic drumbeat in his ears. "Fuckfuckfuckfuck—"

"Liam! Don't!" His uncle Sceolán tore after him.

"—fuckfuck!" Reaching the edge, Liam jumped with all his might. "Fuck me! Fuckmefuck—" There was a dizzying moment as he seemed to hang in the sky forever. His stomach lurched, and his blood froze with the realization that there was no ground beneath him. He stretched his arms wide into the air and tried to focus his intent, but a rush of terrified thoughts sped through his skull, ripping away his concentration. Each chasing the other in a mad race of panic. *Bad-idea-mistake-I-was-wrong-I'm-fucking-dead!*

"Liam! No!" His uncle's terrified shout echoed off the gorge.

Liam's skin prickled.

Unlike any other time he'd attempted a change, it came upon him without pain or delay. In fact, he hardly registered the shift of bones and sinew. One moment he was Liam Kelly, screaming his defiance at the whole of the fianna, his uncle, his father and every soul, living and dead that ever held him down. In the next, his wings caught at a sunny winter sky that tugged him up and away from death and danger and swung him up above the trees. It wasn't the most graceful flight achieved in the avian world. He dove straight into the circling crows, sending them crashing into one another with squawks of protest. Two tumbled out of the air and almost slammed into the brambles and rocks below before catching themselves. Liam shot past, gliding over the treetops. In that breathless moment he understood flying was better than running had ever been. The wind sluiced over his face, head and wings and playfully ruffled his black feathers. He didn't know what kind of bird shape he'd assumed. It didn't actually matter, but he had a lengthy wingspan and knew himself to be bigger than the crows. He knifed through the air, riding the sensation of speed and elation, crying out in mad joy and defiance. They'd thought they had him. They'd thought him stupid, but they were wrong. He hadn't failed. He hadn't.

Drunk on the sensation of flight and success, he'd sped two thirds of his way toward his goal—a stone tower with a blood-red flag fluttering above it—when he registered he wasn't alone. Glancing left, he spied a large golden hawk. He didn't know how he knew, but it was his uncle.

I'm not done yet, Liam thought. It became obvious that the hawk was gaining on him. Liam swerved and dove down among the trees. His uncle followed. Dropping farther down, Liam resorted to dodging and swerving up and around the tree trunks and branches. He was able to gain at least some distance in that way, but it wasn't quite enough. Strangely, he found he was enjoying himself. *You may have been at this longer, old man. But I'm younger and faster.* He dared to cut the margins between himself and the trunks, branches and brush ever thinner. It reminded him of the rally racing, only he wasn't limited to the tolerances of engine, rubber, and steel. He calculated distances, wind direction, weight and speed without any conscious thought. Something inside him took over the mechanics of flight. He let it, and rode the air, beating his wings and pushing himself ever faster. If he could, he'd have laughed. The sensation was amazing.

His left wingtip painfully clipped the bark of an oak. Behind him, his uncle did the same. It occurred to Liam that his uncle was not as slender as he was—not even in bird form, and that gave Liam another idea.

He threw himself at a rowan tree, waiting until the very last instant to swing sideways so that he was flying perpendicular to the ground for a second. He whipped past the rowan's trunk and ducked a wee bit to avoid hitting his head. He didn't understand that he'd miscalculated until it was too late. Rough bark painfully raked down his back. The pain threw his judgement off ever so slightly, and he almost slammed square into a second rowan. He was so busy avoiding flying into the second tree that he almost missed the sound of a most satisfying thump.

Almost.

A sharp hawk-scream of pain, rage, and frustration pierced the air.

I got you, you bastard! Liam slowed, and after gliding a safe distance, landed. He transformed back into himself. Winded, his back felt bruised. He wondered at the state of his back and Conor's jacket for a moment, but he judged neither was in bad enough shape to warrant stopping. There wasn't time, anyway. He wouldn't have the advantage for long. The annoying wig was still balanced on his head, and as far as he could ascertain, it was in the same state as it had been when the challenge had begun. He decided to pause long enough to catch his breath. He bent, grabbing his knees and breathing in great gulps of air. His trembling arms felt weak and rubbery. He didn't think he could fly any more. The undergrowth had thinned out, and the spaces between the trees had grown wider. Re-orienting himself, he caught glimpses of the stone wall surrounding the tower between the undergrowth. The challenge was almost done. When he could breathe without coughing, he continued on at a brisk run. His uncle was sure to arrive at any moment.

Unless he hit that tree headfirst and hard enough to break his fucking neck. What if I killed him?

Then it serves him right, the monster thought from the depths of Liam's skull.

The thought froze both triumph and anger out of Liam's heart, and he stopped to listen for a sign that his uncle was still alive.

Someone was crying. Liam turned to the sound and that's when he saw *her* huddled under the shadow of an ash tree.

Mary Kate.

All thought of his uncle and the trials was lost in an instant. He started to run to her but then brought himself up short. *Must be careful.* He slowly edged into her peripheral vision instead, in the hope that he wouldn't startle and frighten her off. When she sensed his presence she lifted her head from her hands and turned toward him. Her eyes were red and puffy from crying, and her cheeks were wet and blotchy.

He risked a question. "Are—are you all right?"

She blinked at him. His heart ached.

This is my fault, somehow, isn't it? It was the way she died. I wasn't there. I didn't protect her. "Can I help?" He stepped closer. "Are you hurt?"

Drying her face with the back of her sleeve, she sniffed and got to her feet. She was wearing the same ragged, long, white dress as before, only this time it wasn't stained with blood. Her feet were muddy and bare. Her skin was so pale it was almost blue. She looked as though she'd been sleeping rough in the woods. The waves of her long, light brown hair were in tangles. She was thinner than he remembered too.

She tentatively stretched out a hand to him as if in question.

He risked getting closer yet until she was only a couple of feet away. "I'm Liam," he said, not daring to breathe lest she bolt. "Do you remember me?"

"You're... really here?" Her hand moved up to touch the awful horsehair wig with its mixture of brown, black, roan, white, and grey braids of varying thicknesses. She tilted her head, and the corners of her mouth turned upward.

"It's fucking stupid isn't it?" Liam reached up to pull it from his head but thought better of it. After everything he'd been through, he hated the thought of failing the test no matter the reason. "I can't take it off. Not yet." He glanced in the direction of the stone tower. "I should go. But I don't want to leave you here alone. If someone has hurt you—"

"Liam," she said. "It's really you."

The shock of hearing her speak his name outside of a dream for the first time in nearly two years sent a shiver of joy through him. He turned. The faint smell of her reached his nose. *I might still be dreaming.* "Aye. I am." He paused. "You're Mary Kate. Remember?"

"Of course I do." She tilted her head in the other direction. Then she said, "Mary Kate Gallagher."

He smiled and tenderly brushed a stray hair from her eyes. Remembering his father's warnings, he took extra care not to make contact with her skin. "Mary Kate Kelly. Mrs. Kelly. My Mrs. Kelly."

She laughed. He hadn't heard that sound in so long. The ache in his chest, the one that had been with him from the moment he first spotted her, was burned away in a flash by the warmth of her laughter.

"Mrs. Kelly," she said.

"So you are."

She hesitated and her expression grew serious. Shifting close enough that he felt the brush of dirty, white linen against his body, she said, "And you're my Mr. Kelly."

He swallowed. He wanted nothing more than to wrap her in his arms and keep her there forever, but he was terrified of what would happen if he did. *Would it hurt her?* He couldn't risk it. Wouldn't. "I love you, Mary Kate. Jesus, Mary and Joseph, I've missed you so much."

"You were gone. Lost," she said. "I couldn't find you."

"Is that why you were crying, love?" He resisted another urge to smooth her hair—to hold her, kiss her. *Anything.*

A howl ripped through the trees. Afraid the Fianna were upon them already, Liam turned to check. The howl was repeated and then joined by others, a series of horn blasts and shouts. Mary Kate bolted in the opposite direction.

"Don't!" He started after her. "They'll not hurt you! Please! Don't go!" He lost sight of her at once and then she was gone as if she'd never been there at all. For an instant he considered changing into the Hound to track her but dismissed the idea. Even if he could trust himself in that form there wasn't time. Torn, he didn't know what to do. He couldn't leave her. The Fianna crashed through the trees. They had his scent now, that was obvious. He paused, took stock of where he was, and understood he'd headed in the wrong direction. Unfortunately, the Fianna were now between him, the wall, and the tower.

"Fuck."

There was nothing left to do. She was gone and there was no bringing her back. He must finish the test, or the Fianna would finish it for him. *No other option. Survive now. Think later.* He'd hesitated too long. The only viable option was to risk flying, or he was done for. He took a deep breath, praying the change would be easy and fast—praying he could do it this time without the terror of falling. He closed his eyes and thought hard about what it'd felt like. To his surprise, the shift came to him with ease once again, and he was up and off in a flutter of wings. He flew over and past the Fianna, screeching a challenge upon seeing his uncle Sceolán. His uncle was after him in an instant.

Liam didn't waste time with tricks. He made for the stone wall and the tower with everything he had and reached his goal seconds before his uncle shot past. Landing at the bottom of the tower, Liam reverted to his human form once more. Exhausted emotionally and physically unable to stand, he fell back against the tower gasping his grief. She'd been with him. They'd spoken. And then the Fianna had come.

Stupid fucking test.

"That was some trick you pulled," Sceolán said, rounding the edge of the tower.

Glancing up, Liam noticed his uncle had a rather large, bleeding lump on his head. Liam looked away and focused on filling his lungs with air, and hiding his grief. He held his breath until his heart slowed a little and then released it. *Don't think about her now. Later.* "Are... you all right?" He swallowed his sorrow and dried his eyes with the back of his hand.

"Am." Sceolán touched the lump on his forehead and winced. "Should've known what was coming. But you should've been more careful."

"Careful?" Liam asked. "You'd have caught me."

Sceolán smiled. "Exactly."

Liam shook his head and took another long, deep breath. He forced the ache of losing Mary Kate again into a small, tight knot in the pit of his stomach where no one would see it. He could almost pretend it wasn't there.

"Well, you'll not need this anymore," Sceolán said, pulling the wig free.

"Just when I was beginning to like it," Liam said.

"Right. Pull the other one."

Chapter 20

Belfast, County Antrim, Northern Ireland
December 1977

L iam returned to Clonard alone that night. This, after he'd lied to his uncle Sceolán. The lie had been necessary. He'd have preferred to have left unannounced on his own and avoided the lie altogether, but he couldn't travel the border between the twilight and the mortal world by himself, and no one was willing to teach him the way of it, not yet. So, he'd made up a story about needing to see Father Murray. Sceolán, happy with the results of the trial and more concerned with whatever it was that Bran was up to, had agreed without taking much notice of the details. So it was that Liam had been able to return to the derelict with quite a lot of scrumpy and a strong urge to drink away memories of blood and death. It was better than giving in to heroin, so he told himself—not that smack was an option. As far as he knew there was none to be had in all of Belfast, not for the likes of him, anyway.

He didn't sleep well most nights, but speaking to Mary Kate's shade had brought the old horrors back with fresh force—the pain of her dying, the guilt and rage. The being with her for those few moments had ripped at old wounds, leaving him bleeding again. He wanted to stay with her. He didn't care how. So, he yanked the horseshoe nail from his neck and threw it across the room with all his might and drank, praying for sleep or death. The alcohol did its work, lulling him into a dreamless sleep. Although he caught the scent of her, she didn't return to him.

So it was that Liam woke to being roughly shaken.

"Cross you! Wake up!" It was Bran, and by the sound of his voice he was not happy.

Liam didn't bother to open his eyes. If he did, he'd be punished for it in ways he had no wish to suffer. "Fuck away off. I want to sleep."

Bran proved to be annoyingly persistent and wouldn't stop harassing him until Liam opened his eyes. Then Bran shoved the horseshoe nail in his face.

"Why are you not wearing this?"

Refusing to answer, Liam let his eyelids drop and relaxed as much as he could manage. *Don't give him anything. He'll give up and go away.* Liam was cold, freezing in fact, and a hangover dozed in his head and belly. It was going to be a real bastard, and he wanted to avoid meeting it face on as long as possible.

"Answer me!"

Liam pretended to pass out, not that being jostled made the pretense easy. His stomach was about to stage a protest that Bran wasn't going to like if he continued. Fortunately before Liam got sick, Bran dropped him. The force of Liam's skull thumping the floorboards spurred the hangover into instant action. An explosion of agony filled every corner of his skull. He moaned and grabbed his head. Ice-cold water slapped him in the face. And before he was aware, he was on his feet and bellowing. "Jesus Fucking Christ!"

"What is this? Do you want to die?"

"What the fuck does it matter?" Liam shoved Bran with both hands, but it was like throwing himself at one of the iron ore stones on Raven's Hill. Bran didn't budge.

"What is this?" he asked. "Sceolán said you were to stay with the priest. But Joseph Murray says he's not seen you."

"I said leave me be!"

"I don't understand. What's wrong? Sceolán said you passed your first trial."

"Aye," Liam said. "And that solves everything, doesn't it?" His brain throbbed with terrible agony. Squinting against the harsh light, he staggered to the hearth. The fire was long dead, but he'd left the remaining bottles of scrumpy where he'd slept. With some pain, he retrieved a bottle, removed the cap, and took a long drink, hoping to pacify the hangover even a wee bit. His stomach twisted at the first taste of fermented apples.

Bran said, "Talk to me."

Liam wiped his mouth on the back of his sleeve. "What do you want to hear?"

Bran sighed. "The priest warned me."

"What the fuck does that mean?"

"He said you weren't to be alone. I'll knock Sceolán's head in—"

"It wasn't Sceolán's fault." Resentful, Liam settled back down on the blankets. His stomach remained uncertain about its opinion of events.

"Then tell me what in Danu's name is going on," Bran said.

"You don't know something?" Liam let out a short, bitter laugh. "How does it feel?"

Frowning, Bran stepped closer. Worry and fear were raw in his face. Liam shied away from it.

"All right," Bran said. "This is punishment for something I've done, is it?"

Liam shook his head. "This has nothing whatsoever to do with you for a change."

"I'll not crossing leave. You'll have to talk."

It was Liam's turn to sigh. "What the fuck do you want from me?"

"I was about to ask you that question." Bran stretched a hand out for a scrumpy bottle. His eyebrow twitched by way of a request.

Liam nodded approval. He knew enough about the Fey now to know he shouldn't refuse. It was bad enough that he'd not made the offer to begin with. "Nothing. I want nothing from you, do you hear?" He tried to keep his voice even. The headache was finally fading to a tolerable level, and he preferred to keep it that way. As for his stomach, he had a hunch that any sudden moves would be regretted.

Bran stared at him for a couple of heartbeats. Liam attempted not to care.

"That's a lie. You do want something from me," Bran said. It was spoken less an accusation and more as a statement of dull fact.

Bran's display of patience only irritated Liam more. An urge to rip and claw at something—*anything*—took hold. "It doesn't matter! It's too fucking late!" Liam winced at the sharp flare of fresh pain inside his skull. *Bad idea, the shouting.*

Sitting down, Bran said, "That too is a lie, I'm thinking." He took another drink. "Tell me something."

Liam stared into the empty hearth so he wouldn't have to look at Bran. The monster skulking in the back of Liam's head didn't comment. With one exception, the creature had been strangely silent since Lochlann and the copper bowl. Liam hadn't given much thought as to why, but in many ways it was a relief to feel its presence and yet not be plagued by its constant muttering.

"Why is it the harder I try to be a father to you, the harder you try to drive me out?" Bran asked.

Liam decided he didn't want to know the answer—not that he'd have told Bran at this point anyway. All Liam wanted was blessed numbness. *Quiet.* He was tired of caring, tired of struggling with the guilt, tired of the memories and the nightmares, above all tired of the fucking pain. Something had to make it stop, or he'd go mad. *Not an option, mate.* As much as he wanted an end to it, the idea of causing more destruction was far worse. "You're fucking immortal. Don't you have other sons whose lives you can make a mess of?"

At that moment Liam saw something he never expected to see—a flash of deep regret and grief in Bran's face. Liam was sorry at once.

"The truth?" Bran set the scrumpy bottle down in front of Liam with a thump. The remaining alcohol inside sloshed. "I'd appreciate it if you kept this information to yourself. There's your mother's feelings to consider. Aye? I've never told her this," he said. "There were others. And I cared for every one of them. Maybe not as much as my Kathleen… your mother. I was young and foolish once. And made young and foolish mistakes. But no matter. I did love them." He paused. "As for sons, they're dead. Every one. Daughters too for that matter. None lived to bear children of their own. Even the ones that weren't half-mortal." He took a deep breath and released it. "You are the only child of mine that lives."

"What happened to them?" The question was out before Liam could stop it.

"Four died the final death in the wars, those that lived long enough to be of age. Two were murdered before they could walk. Most died by their own hand. Ten in all," Bran said, the pain evident in his eyes. "Then there was Daimhín. I had to—I had to end it for him. He'd—" He choked, got up and then walked to the far window. Keeping his back to the room, Bran didn't say anymore.

Liam didn't need to hear. He knew enough. Shuddering, he attempted to absorb the news. *Is that sixteen? Or ten total?* His heart thudded in his ears. *Does it matter? All the others are dead.* He resisted an urge to grab the bottle and down the last of it. *I'm the last.* The knowledge didn't put a stop to the hurt and grief, but it did force him to think of something else. "I'm... so sorry."

"For what?"

"For shouting. It wasn't... it isn't... fair." Liam tried to think of anything he could say that was worth saying. *I didn't know.* The urge to rend and tear, the rage, was gone. Again, he thought of Daimhín and wanted to be sick. *Is that how it starts?*

Bran shrugged. "Apology accepted."

"It wasn't you." Liam hesitated, then forcing himself past his trepidation he said, "This wasn't about anything you did. It was Mary Kate. I saw her again."

"Ah."

"I didn't know what to do. So, I—I came here." Liam prepared himself for a fresh bollocksing.

Bran was silent for a moment. "I understand."

"You do?" Liam blinked.

Another long pause stretched between the two of them. "Her name was Úna," Bran said, turning to face him. "And I'd save you from that pain if I could, but I understand why I can't. Some things must be learned on your own. I know." He combed his fingers through his hair. "Sometimes I think that's the hardest part of being a father, knowing when to let your children make their own way. It's even harder to do when you know the odds."

Outside, a cold wind blasted through Clonard and shoved its way through the broken windows. Crows called warnings to one another. Liam shivered.

"I owe you an apology too, it seems," Bran said.

The ache in Liam's brain had dwindled into a dull hurt, but his stomach still twisted in nauseating knots. *Most died by their own hand.*

That'll be me, if it comes to it. I'll not make Bran do it for me. They'll not lock me away either. I won't let them.

"Your friend, the priest, is free from the hospital. He wishes to meet with you. It's why I came looking for you. What shall I tell him?"

I'll not be like Daimhín. Liam swallowed again, feeling colder now than he had in his whole life. "I'll meet him today."

"You'll have to get cleaned up first. When was the last time you ate?"

"I don't much remember. Yesterday morning?"

"I'll have Angus scrounge up something for you."

The mere mention of Angus brought up images of the ridiculous wig. From the sound of it, that was one of Angus's lighter practical jokes. "Forget it. I'm not hungry."

"You have to eat."

"Aye. Well, I don't suppose the Fey have a magical cure for vicious hangovers, do you?"

"We do," Bran said. One corner of his mouth twitched. "But I don't think you'll care for it much."

"What is it?"

"You stand there," Bran said, pointing to the floor in front of him. "And I punch you in the balls."

"How is that supposed to help?"

"You'll certainly forget the hangover."

"Fuck that."

"Only trying to help, my son." Bran assumed the guise of ultimate fatherly wisdom.

"After centuries of drinking, you'd think you lot would come up with a better solution."

Due to a series of bomb scares, the buses weren't running, which, given that Bran was gone, left Liam with no practical alternative than to risk a black taxi. Having been a taxi man in West Belfast, he knew the likelihood of the driver having certain political connections was high—depending upon the taxi association of which the driver was a member.

Unfortunately, the number of taxi associations which accepted Catholics as members or even passengers was not vast. Still, it'd been almost two years since he'd last been a taxi man. There were sure to be new drivers, drivers who wouldn't know him, not as he was now. In any case, even if Séamus and his boys did find him, all Liam need do was refuse again. It was a legitimate answer. He'd thought about it as requested, but his answer was still no. He'd done his bit. No more need be discussed.

Then why is it I feel otherwise? Liam thought. *What is it about Séamus that has me jumping at shadows?* He couldn't think of a logical reason. So it was that he walked to the Falls Road and found a spot to wait until a taxi man signaled there was enough room for more passengers.

The Black Hack pulled up to the curb, and Liam climbed into the back, giving the driver's face a quick glance before doing so. *Don't recognise him. That's good. Aye?* He gave an address one block from his actual destination and settled onto the seat next to a woman holding a baby. There were four other passengers—four possible destinations. As these things were handled, the original passenger had determined the direction the taxi was headed, which was downtown. The others might need dropping off in between. It was likely he'd be the last. So, Liam rested his eyes and allowed the lively conversation about Christmas dinners, family visits and other holiday plans wash over him without comment.

At Bran's insistence, he'd eaten a bit of bread and cheese and drank some water. The hangover had receded enough to make the trip comfortable. He'd been in better shape, of course, but he'd do. After the second drop off and pick up, he helped the woman with the baby get her things out of the taxi. When he climbed back inside he caught the driver staring at him in the rearview mirror with a puzzled expression.

Shite. That's it. It's fucked, I am. For fuck's sake, don't let him see you're nervous. One more stop. That's all. You'll be fine.

Oh, stop it. All you need do is say no, and it's done. Aye?

Liam tried to tell himself it wouldn't matter what the driver reported, regardless. He'd be long gone before the news reached Séamus and his boys. Sweat oozed down Liam's back underneath Conor's leather jacket. *Driver won't do anything. He can't. You're fine. He pulls over to give the Boys a ring, leg it. Don't fucking matter where.*

As it turned out, Liam's stop was the third. He exited the black taxi on

Great Victoria Street and strolled up to a sweet shop with his hands in his pockets. Hunched against the wind and the snow, he attempted to hide his face with the jacket's collar, but it was pointless. The driver had made him. That was clear when the taxi man stopped at a newsagent's a block or so up the street and got out. Pretending to look at a holiday display in a shop window, Liam watched the taxi man check the street.

Fuck. Fuck. Fuck. Liam entered the busy sweet shop, and then immediately turned to gaze out the window. Then he took off Conor's jacket. He turned it inside out and bunched it up under his arm. It was snowing, and he'd be cold, but it might buy him some time. Once the driver was out of sight, Liam threw open the shop's door and ran. A couple hundred feet away a cardboard Elvis stood in the walk, pointing toward the entrance to a tiny, narrow record shop. Liam didn't know how he managed to sprint the distance without slipping in the ice and snow, but he did. Glancing once over his shoulder one last time, he bolted inside the instant he thought it safe. The bell on the door jangled. Teeth rattling in his head, Liam pulled the jacket back on. The clerk behind the counter paused in his work and gave Liam a suspicious look. When he didn't appear to be there to steal or throw anything, the clerk went back to sorting records. Breathing heavy from panic and exertion, Liam took in great lungfuls of the shop's air. He could have sworn he smelled old beer, cigarettes, and the ghost of marijuana spliffs past.

Prod part of town, aye?

He spied Father Murray at the back of the shop, flipping through the record albums with a perplexed look on his face. His right arm was still in a plaster cast, but he looked far better than he had in hospital. His skin was a healthy pink, and he appeared to be rested. He had a brown paper-wrapped package tucked under his arm. It was easy to see it was a record by the flat, rectangular shape.

Turning, Father Murray asked, "Did you run the whole way here?"

"Not exactly." Liam blew into his hands, scanned the shop and counted the exits.

"You look half frozen. Let's get something warm. I know a place."

Liam went to the window and again checked the street. The black taxi which had been parked at the newsagents was gone.

"Is something the matter?" Father Murray whispered.

"Everything's fucking rosy. Isn't it always? How far away is this place with the warm tea, Father?"

Father Murray blinked. "The café is a couple of blocks south."

Will there be time to get there and off the street before Séamus or his boys come looking? Liam sighed. *Better now than later, I suppose.* "Let's go, then." He opened the shop's door and followed Father Murray out of the record shop and onto the street.

"How are you feeling?" Father Murray asked.

"Bit hung over, is all."

"You look terrible."

"Thanks," Liam said.

"Have you been eating?"

Liam shrugged. "Why is it whenever anyone sees me they fucking ask if I've been eating?"

Father Murray gazed up at him. "Do you have to ask?"

Looking down at himself, Liam noticed that Conor's jacket was hanging on him a wee bit, the white undershirt was baggy, and his blue jeans were looser than usual.

"Well?"

"It's a wee hangover. Nothing more dire than that."

"And why were you drinking?"

Liam paused. "What's with the interrogation, Father?"

"Bran said—"

"I'll be twenty-three next month. How old do I have to be before you'll stop treating me like a wean?"

A hurt expression passed over Father Murray's face. "I've only your best interests in mind."

"I know, Father. I'm sorry." Liam sighed. He seemed to be apologizing a lot lately.

As it turned out, the word café was a bit upscale for the place. Liam would've called it a chip shop. It smelled of grease, coffee and stale cigarette smoke. Its usual clientele, Uni students, were noticeably absent—it being the Christmas holiday. Two customers occupied a booth to the far right, and there was only one waitress on duty by the look of things. She was plump, had long red hair, attractive eyes, freckles, and couldn't have been more than nineteen. Father Murray selected a table at the back. Liam settled into a position against the wall with a good view of the entrance. The nineteen-year-old waitress brought over the menus, and Liam found himself counting and memorizing the exits while Father Murray ordered.

"You can't only have the tea," Father Murray said.

Liam knew he needed to be more careful with his money if it was going to last. Besides, Father Murray's shopping had reminded Liam that Christmas was only a few days away. Liam would've preferred to give it a miss, but it was impossible to avoid. He couldn't help remembering that Mary Kate had been the one who'd had a knack for those sorts of things—finding the perfect gift—but she was gone. The holiday had creeped up on him again like an unwanted visitor. There was nothing for it. He'd need a part of the money that Frankie had given him to send some sweets to his mother and half-siblings in Derry. His mother had gone to all the trouble of sending the records. He had to do something in return. It wasn't about the obligation. She'd worry for him if he didn't acknowledge the holiday, and he didn't want her worrying. She had troubles enough. "The tea will do."

Acting as if he hadn't heard Liam's answer, Father Murray requested two orders of fish and chips, some cheese and onion pasties, and two cups of steaming tea with milk. The waitress picked up the menus and left.

"Will you tell me what's wrong now?" Father Murray asked, his voice lowered.

"I ran into an old friend while you were in hospital," Liam said.

The waitress returned with the tea, gave him a shy smile and left.

"Who?" Father Murray sipped his tea, winced and then blew in it.

Liam held the cup, warming his hands. It was scalding and really wasn't fit for much else just yet. "My old mate, Frankie Donovan."

"Oh."

Nervous, Liam added sugar to his tea and stirred it. "I was given an offer of employment."

"And what did you tell them?"

Whispering, Liam said, "What do you think?"

"And how did... Frankie take it?"

"Frankie was fine with it. Frankie isn't the fucking issue. His friend is."

"And?"

"Let's just say, he wasn't satisfied with my answer."

Father Murray seemed to go a bit pale. "That may be a problem."

"Aye. You think?"

The waitress came back with the food. "You have a care now. The plates are hot."

"Thank you," Liam said.

"Is there anything else you'll be needing?" She was blushing.

Liam said, "Ah, no."

"I'll be back to check on you later, then." She scurried off.

"Good service." Father Murray hid a smile. "Must be the jacket."

Sipping his tea, Liam made a non-committal noise in the back of his throat while Father Murray started in on his fish and chips. Unwilling to let the food go to waste, Liam decided to tuck in too. Once or twice he thought he saw Father Murray pause as if to say something and then give up.

"Is there something I need to know about?" Liam asked. "Wouldn't ask, only it's as if you were stalling a wee bit before telling me the bad news."

Father Murray blinked. Liam watched him take another sip of scalding hot tea.

"There is something we need to discuss," Father Murray said. "I'm not sure that I'd call it bad, necessarily."

"Out with it, then."

Father Murray stared at his cup as if he were afraid to look Liam in the face. "There's someone who wishes to speak with you."

This isn't going to be in any way good, Liam thought.

The door swung open, allowing in a fresh burst of freezing, snow-tainted air. Another priest entered the chip shop. Liam watched him shake out his black wool overcoat. He was older—in his early sixties, Liam guessed, with wispy white hair. The older priest's shoulders were square, and he carried himself with a sense of authority. He was medium in build, and average in height for a local, but something about the man said he wasn't entirely local. *The overcoat?* Liam saw him scan the café as if looking for someone.

The creature living in the blackest parts of Liam's brain shuddered. In all the time he'd been aware of the creature's existence, he'd never known it to show fear. It was more than a wee bit unsettling.

"Would it happen to be the someone that just walked in the door?"

Liam asked.

Father Murray turned and cursed under his breath. "He said he'd wait for me to ring him." He paused and then waved at the priest, motioning him over.

"Who is he, Father?" Liam asked. He didn't like the look of the man one bit. His eyes were too sharp, and his mouth was too thin.

"The Grand Inquisitor for the Northern Hemisphere," Father Murray muttered through clenched teeth and then smiled.

Liam kept his voice low. "I'm going to wish I stayed with Frankie and his friend, aren't I?"

"Be careful, Liam."

The Grand Inquisitor arrived at the table. "Hello, Father Murray. I see you're having lunch. Mind if I join you?"

"Not at all," Father Murray said. "Liam, this is Monsignor Paul."

Monsignor Paul took two chairs from an empty table, and arranged it so that Liam's exit was blocked. He took off his overcoat and draped it over the first chair and sat in the second. In that moment, Liam decided he liked Monsignor Paul even less than before.

"Hello, Mr. Kelly," Monsignor Paul said. "I've heard a great deal about you."

Liam's back tensed. "Don't you mean you've *read* a great deal about me?"

Monsignor Paul laughed and shook his head. "Oh, he's good."

"Was nice meeting you, Father. But I've got things I must see to." Liam started to get up, but Monsignor Paul trapped his wrist.

"Don't go just yet," Monsignor Paul said. "You haven't finished your food, and we have much to discuss."

"Get your fucking hand off me."

On her way over with two fresh cups of tea, the waitress stopped in her tracks—a shocked look on her freckled face.

"Liam—"

"I don't give a fuck who he is," Liam said, interrupting Father Murray. "Tell him to let me go."

Glancing at the waitress as if sending a signal to Monsignor Paul, Father Murray said, "I'm afraid Liam doesn't like being touched."

Monsignor Paul paused, appeared to remember where he was and then lifted his hand. "I apologize."

Liam got up from the table and bumped it in his hurry to get clear of Monsignor Paul. Dishes clattered and tea slopped onto the table.

Get the fuck out of here, the monster growled. *Now.*

"You really should consider staying to chat," Monsignor Paul said.

"And why is that?" Liam asked.

"First, because if you don't I'll recommend the peace agreement be cancelled. Effective immediately," Monsignor Paul said. "And, as I'm sure Father Murray has explained, my recommendations carry a great deal of weight." He paused and a small and ever-so-certain smile crept across his severe lips. "Second, there is an RUC prowl car waiting at the corner."

All the blood in Liam's body seemed to drop to his feet, and he felt sick. He glanced at the rear exit.

Out now, the monster snarled.

"That isn't an option either," Monsignor Paul said. "Father Dominic and a few trusted others are waiting for us at the service entrance."

Father Murray gaped. "Now wait one minute!"

"Hopefully," Monsignor Paul said, holding up a hand to hush Father Murray. "I don't need to be any more clear than that."

Sweat oozed down Liam's back and sides for a second time that day. It itched as it crawled its way down his skin. In a futile sense of rebellion he waited three heartbeats before he swallowed a retort he'd no doubt come to regret later and then sat.

Should've stayed with the Fianna, Liam thought. *At least then my biggest problems were that fucking wig.*

"There. I knew we could have a civilized conversation." Monsignor Paul signalled to the waitress. "Young lady, a cup of tea, please. Lemon. No milk."

She nodded and hurried off, this time without giving Liam so much as a glance.

"Am I to be arrested, then?" Liam asked.

"That isn't my intent," Monsignor Paul said. "I merely felt sufficient preparation for contingencies might be necessary. To guarantee your co-operation."

"What the fuck do you want?" Liam asked.

Monsignor Paul brushed invisible lint from his shoulder. "It isn't so much what I want. It's what you want that's important."

"I don't understand," Liam said, his unease growing worse.

"You would prefer not to go to prison," Monsignor Paul said. "Well, again, that is." He folded his hands on the table in front of him. "You would also prefer to be declared human, I believe."

Clearing her throat, the waitress set a steaming cup of tea in front of Monsignor Paul. Then she took up the empties and left two fresh cups of tea, giving Liam a sidelong glance brimming with curiosity.

"However, that is now impossible," Monsignor Paul said.

"What?" Liam asked and prepared to jump over the table, knock down Monsignor Paul, and bolt for the back door. He could take Father Dominic. He'd done it before. But the others. How many were there?

Get out now! Danger! Get out—

Shut your fucking gob! I have to concentrate, Liam thought back at the creature.

"Our recent data—data which you provided, thank you so very much, indicates that you aren't human," Monsignor Paul said.

Father Murray said, "His mother is human. He's half human."

Shaking his head, Monsignor Paul clucked like a teacher correcting a student. "Don't argue semantics with me, Guardian Joseph. You know better."

"What am I then?" Liam asked.

"A demon," Monsignor Paul said. "Unfortunately, I can't prove it. There isn't enough evidence. Not yet. Speaking of, perhaps we should examine the rest of your family. I understand your mother has exhibited a curious talent for attracting demons. You've a sister as well. Moira? Her teachers say she claims to see demons. I wonder what data we can collect from her?"

He's threatening my family. A ball of hatred tightened in Liam's gut. "Ma and Moira are not fucking demons. Nor am I."

"Really? What is it exactly that you think you are?" Monsignor Paul asked. "A normal young man, recently married to a beautiful woman who is pregnant with his child? No? A normal working man who drives a black taxi? A grieving widower? How about a criminal? A convict?" He lowered his head and leaned closer. Liam could smell cigarettes on his breath. "A... terrorist with a rather intriguing reputation? Or some sort of myth? Which is closer to the truth, do you think?"

Liam's jaw tightened. "Some would say demons are myths."

"Don't disappoint me, Mr. Kelly. I'm told you're intelligent." Monsignor Paul shook his head. "We both know demons exist."

"I still don't understand what it is you want from me," Liam said.

"Return to the Queen's facility. There I will collect new data. My way. And assure that it isn't contaminated."

Jesus Christ. Liam thought of Father Conroy's tray of knives and suppressed a shudder.

Run. Run now! The monster was in a frenzy of panic.

"Liam has already fulfilled the agreement," Father Murray said.

Monsignor Paul frowned. "No, he hasn't. He declared the terms under which the data was gathered."

"Are you saying you don't trust Father Conroy's work?" Father Murray asked.

"Father Gerald Conroy is a very talented research scientist," Monsignor Paul said. "However—"

"However what? However you don't agree with his conclusions? Therefore, you're going to rearrange the facts until you're happy? Is that it?" Father Murray said. "You'll not get away with that this time. Not while I'm here."

Monsignor Paul's eyes narrowed. "What exactly do you mean?"

"I think you know exactly what I mean," Father Murray said. "I know about Waterford. I was there, remember?"

Liam watched Monsignor Paul's face change color. "Yes, you were. And I was there too."

"I don't care what you say. Do your worst," Father Murray said. "But I'll take you down with me. And you'll fall much farther. John told me everything before he died. Everything. I got to him first. Remember? I'll tell them all that happened this time. Everything."

"How dare you!" Monsignor Paul slammed a fist on the table. Cups, spoons and plates rattled.

"Call off the RUC," Father Murray said.

Monsignor Paul glared at Father Murray and hissed, "You can't blackmail me."

"I'll not stand for this," Father Murray said. "It's unethical."

"Unethical? The ends justify the means," Monsignor Paul said. "I shouldn't have to explain that to a Guardian."

"He came to us of his own free will," Father Murray said.

An explosion rattled the windows. The sharp crack of live rounds went off somewhere outside. The waitress screamed. One of the two customers inside the chip shop went to the windows. Outside, someone shouted. Another exchange of gunfire pierced the air. A prowl car siren screeched, and a car shot past the café windows. It was a four door. *Grey.* Liam wasn't able to get the make. The prowl car rapidly followed after. He almost laughed. *Great timing, boys.* At the moment, he didn't care which side of the Peace Line they'd come from. *You saved my arse, God bless you.*

Monsignor Paul got up from the table. He looked like he wanted to hit someone.

A flicker of movement in the restaurant's windows drew Liam's attention. Four men with balaclavas pulled over their faces and carrying guns ran to the café's door and shoved their way through.

Oh, fuck, Liam thought.

"Get down on the floor! All of youse!"

Father Murray didn't hesitate. He kneeled and then lay down on the cold tiles. Liam followed suit. He didn't bother to see if Monsignor Paul was complying or not. Two of the men ran to the back of the chip shop.

"Get down on the floor, priest."

Monsignor Paul said, "I don't think—" His response was cut off with a blow.

"On the floor!"

"Don't shoot him!" It was one of the other masked men. The one closest to the door.

Liam thought he recognised the voice but couldn't quite place it. In truth, he didn't want to. He felt someone kick him in the side with a steel-toed work boot. It wasn't hard enough to do more than get his attention.

"You. Up."

Liam staggered to his feet and saw Father Murray was being forced to do the same. Before Liam could protest, a pistol was shoved into his side. The men grabbed him and Father Murray, and they were led to the door. Behind him, Liam heard a man shout a warning. The sounds of breaking dishes followed. A woman screamed. He had time to hope the freckled waitress wouldn't be harmed and then was strong-armed out onto Great

Victoria Street. A white panel van pulled up and skidded to a stop in the slush. The back doors were thrown open. He and Father Murray were shoved inside. Liam landed on a layer of filled laundry bags. Father Murray wasn't long after, thumping into Liam's back and briefly knocking the wind out of him. Just before the van's doors slammed shut Liam caught sight of a group of priests running toward the café.

Father Murray put up a short fight. Liam rolled over in time to see him slam the plaster cast into one of their captors' faces. Liam winced at the sound of breaking bone. The man Father Murray hit screamed and fell back, holding his nose. Two others threw themselves on top of Father Murray and shoved a black bag over his head but not before he got in a few solid kicks. Liam was about to join the fray and then he recognized the men struggling to subdue Father Murray without killing him. One was Frankie, and the other was Davy, he of the bushy mustache and sideburns.

Séamus and his boys had arrived.

Chapter 21

"Won't the UDA be happy to hear you lot pulled a job in their territory?" Liam asked loud enough for Father Murray to hear over his struggles. It was a risk, letting him know they were in the hands of the Provos. However, Liam felt it best for everyone to send the message that there was no immediate danger and to save the fight for later.

"Liam? Are you hurt?" Father Murray asked, landing a solid kick in Frankie's stomach.

Liam winced in sympathy. "I'm fine, Father. I think we're for having a wee chat, nothing more."

With that, Father Murray stopped his struggles. Davy took the opportunity to grab hold of Father Murray's good arm, and Frankie caught the priest's legs, effectively ending the altercation then and there.

"I don't like this," Frankie said. "You hit that other priest. The waitress saw. What are we doing? The Peelers will be hunting for us all the harder. We kidnapped a priest. You said it was only to be Liam. The Falls won't be behind us. They'll turn on us, and I can't blame them."

Séamus spoke from the front seat. "I'd prefer to hold the talk until we reached our destination, if you don't mind."

Frankie frowned and nodded.

"Oh, aye?" Liam asked, attempting to sound as calm as possible.

Davy and Frankie tied Father Murray's left arm to the cast on his right and then secured his legs. When that was finished, Frankie saw to the third man's bleeding nose. Liam tried to catch Frankie's attention. He wanted some indication of what to expect, but Frankie avoided looking him in the eye. Liam hoped he understood why and sympathized. Were he in Frankie's place he'd feel as if he'd betrayed a friend. However, Liam didn't blame Frankie a bit. Liam knew the way of things. In fact, he'd seen, even done, worse, and he hoped Frankie would understand that soon enough. Giving up on Frankie for the moment, Liam shifted his attention to Davy who was running the rope around Father Murray's chest and arms a few extra times with an angry expression.

Weren't expecting that much of a scrap from a wounded priest, were you? Liam thought, attempting not to grin.

Tires squealed. The driver stomped on the brakes with a curse. The van skidded and suddenly lurched to the right, causing one and all to scramble for something to hold on to. The back of Liam's head slammed into the panel van's side. "Shite!"

The tires finally grabbed the asphalt, and the van righted itself without flipping.

The van's driver, Liam decided, wasn't the most skilled. *Lucky for them the Peelers were gone,* he thought. He glanced at the back of Séamus's head. *Lucky? Think again, mate. That car was one of his. Sent as a distraction. Not a good sign, that, when you think about it. Séamus ran a complicated operation in Loyalist territory. No Provo does that without very good reason.* Liam shuddered, but he couldn't help feeling a certain admiration as well. Complicated or not, the operation had gone smoothly. *No one was hurt, not yet. Well, outside of Monsignor Paul.* Liam remembered the waitress's scream and hoped he was right in that regard at least. *And on short notice too. Aye? Séamus is a crafty one, so he is. Better fucking remember that, mate.*

They kidnapped Father Murray too. That was no accident, to be sure. But why?

Séamus means to motivate me, the bastard. Big mistake, that. Perhaps Frankie hasn't told Séamus everything he knows about yours truly, or has he?

Maybe Séamus isn't fucking listening.

But how would they know to grab Father Murray? The Grand Inquisitor was there too.

Their man at the newsagent was watching you, you idiot. Saw the two of you walk into the café together. Talking friendly-like. Aye? Otherwise, how would they know you were at the café? Not difficult to figure. Knew you were there. Saw the Peelers. Figured they couldn't wait. Moved in fast.

Aye, that's it.

All this and you still believe you can tell him to bugger off?

My choice. I fucking decide.

Liam glared at the back of Séamus's head. *Right. You keep on thinking that.*

Although it was early afternoon, it was already getting dark—not that it'd been a bright day to begin with. Liam attempted to relax, but it wasn't easy with his stomach churning. He reminded himself that, no matter what, this was about Séamus needing him. Nothing else. They wouldn't put the hurt to Father Murray. Everything would be fine. Worst come to worst, he'd have to drive for Séamus, but he'd not carry a gun. It wouldn't make sense for Séamus to trust him with one anyway. Liam settled into a comfortable spot, rested his arms on his knees so he'd be ready to catch himself if the bog idiot driver took another sharp turn in a vehicle that was in no way designed for such a thing.

We'll be fine, aye?

But it's Christmas soon. Isn't it? The thought hit him like a sniper, and he hated it. He didn't want to remember the significance of the date. He didn't want to think about it. He didn't want to think about anything, truth be told. *I should've stayed with Uncle Sceolán.* Liam took a long breath. *We'll be fine. Everything will be fine. It will all work out.*

Like it has so many times before, aye?

Liam focused on Father Murray lying among the laundry bags trussed up like bait on a hook. He seemed well enough, all things considered. Davy and Frankie hadn't been too rough on him. Liam was thankful for that much.

It wasn't long before the van executed another sharp turn and pulled into a car park situated behind a row of buildings. The driver stopped. The rear doors of the panel van were thrown open, and Liam spied the back of a warehouse. Icicles fringed the bottom of the roof, and rust marred the steel walls.

Steel. There's no calling for Bran or Uncle Sceolán, is there?

"Come on," Frankie said, offering to help him out by way of an apology. "This is our stop."

Liam accepted Frankie's hand up and scrambled out of the van. He caught Frankie's eye and wordlessly reassured him that there were no hard feelings. Frankie swallowed and nodded. Davy and the man with the blood-stained face and broken nose hefted Father Murray to his feet on the snow-covered pavement. Behind him, the van doors slammed shut, and Father Murray started a wee bit. Frankie removed the rope from Father Murray's legs. Séamus walked toward the warehouse, his footsteps making crunching sounds in the snow. The van sped off, Liam assumed, in order to continue its appointed rounds as a laundry service. He held his chin up and focused on taking in as much of his surroundings as he could manage without being obvious about it—the street, number of men present and so on. He didn't know where he was, and it became clear that escape wasn't likely, not without the monster, and even then he wasn't certain of the chances. That wouldn't have mattered much to him, except there was Father Murray to consider.

Liam bit down on smoldering rage. *And keep a civil tongue in your head too. For his sake, aye?*

A gust of freezing wind invaded the car park. Liam hunched inside Conor's jacket to protect his neck. The weather was getting worse. The sky was almost black now, and the snow was coming down in clumps. He prayed the planned job wasn't for later that night.

Frankie tugged at his arm. A man Liam didn't recognise held the warehouse door open. One whiff of the inside, and Liam knew he really didn't want to be there. The place smelled of petrol and engine oil mixed with rotting cloth and other ancient factory smells, but underneath it all was the stench of decaying flesh and old blood. His heart staggered, and he gave the man at the door a closer look as he passed. However, Liam didn't notice anything unusual about him. That done, Liam scanned the interior of the warehouse for the source of the stink. Heart thumping, he counted seven other men huddled near a row of empty offices along the far wall. One of them, a medium-sized man with long brown hair, and an ugly face, stopped talking and returned the stare. The man smiled with broken front teeth, turned and walked away, moving behind a row of cars parked near the big rolling doors. Liam had a very bad feeling, but Frankie urged him forward before he could comment.

There was no heat in the place from what Liam could tell, and the warehouse was empty of furnishings and machinery but for a number of wooden crates and the four cars—among them, a gleaming black RS2000 with new tires and wheels.

The outside door slammed shut with an ominous bang that echoed along with the sound of their footfalls. Séamus stopped and turned about. Then he signaled to Davy and the one with the broken nose. Davy nodded.

"Frankie, Liam, come with me," Séamus said, motioning to the stairs to the right which lead up to a windowed office space in the top of the warehouse.

Frankie headed up the steps.

"Where are they taking Father Murray?" Liam asked.

"Somewhere safe and comfortable, to be sure. No need for worry. He'll be fine," Séamus said. "Meanwhile, we need to have a chat, you and I."

"Where are they fucking taking him?" Liam asked again, not moving.

Frankie stopped six steps up, a concerned look on his face.

"I said we'll not hurt your friend." Séamus frowned. "Can we not trust one another that far? We're to be friends, after all."

Liam frowned. "Then why is it you've brought him?"

Séamus folded his arms across his chest. "Get upstairs before I lose my patience, son."

I'm not your fucking son, old man. Gritting his teeth, Liam followed Frankie up and into the office space. Meanwhile, Séamus went over to the men on the other side of the warehouse.

Frankie glanced out the windows and down at Séamus and whispered, "Sorry, mate. Wish it hadn't come to this. I do. I didn't know. I didn't. They didn't tell me they'd be for taking the priest too."

Liam shrugged.

The place smelled stale and was furnished with a couple of ancient wooden desks, a few battered chairs, a big, cluttered table, and a cracked chalkboard. Its green-grey surface was coated in smeared chalk writing.

Runs his unit like a classroom, does he? Much like the Grand Inquisitor, the more Liam saw of Séamus the less he liked him.

The room was lit with freshly installed fluorescent lighting which emitted a low-level buzz that irritated Liam's ears and set his teeth on edge. It did nothing for his mood. The surfaces of both desks were clear. *Tidy.* Unlike the big table in the center of the room which was stained and littered with crumpled paper and abandoned styrofoam coffee cups. The grey-speckled tile was filthy and gritty underfoot.

Séamus entered and closed the door. The window rattled in the upper half of its wooden frame. "Have a seat, lads." Then he made his way over to the desk.

Frankie settled into one of the stiff-backed wooden chairs. Liam walked to the chalkboard but remained standing. He squeezed his fists tight and then loosened them.

Calm. Stay calm. Father Murray is depending on you.

Frankie mouthed a warning. *Don't do it.*

Pulling open a drawer, the sounds of glass clinking against glass jarred the cold air. Séamus produced a bottle of whiskey and two relatively clean glasses. "I've been saving this for this moment."

Liam, unwilling to play Séamus's game, waited to hear the rest. Séamus held up an empty glass. Liam paused a few heartbeats before aiming a punch for Séamus's face. Séamus shuffled a few steps backward. Frankie leapt up from his seat and grabbed Liam's arm. The chair was knocked over with a clatter.

"Don't, Liam!" Frankie's grip was tight. "It'll do no good!"

"You fucking kidnapped us!"

"Calm down," Frankie said. "Listen to him! Will you?"

"Let me go, Frankie," Liam said. "I'm warning you."

Frankie said, "Be reasonable—"

"Reasonable?" Liam asked.

"We've got your friend," Séamus said in a steady voice. He wiped blood from his lip. "Don't you care what happens to him?"

A chill passed through Liam's belly. *Fuck. You've bolloxed it up already. Stupid.* He nodded and then yanked his right arm free from Frankie's grip.

"Now, I apologize for the abruptness of our arrival. I'd intended a much more gentle introduction. However, it seems you're better at hiding away than I'd believed possible," Séamus said, making a second attempt at handing off the glass. "Where were you all this time?"

"Around," Liam said. His jaw was so tight it hurt. With a deep breath, he accepted the glass.

"Ah, I see," Séamus said. "You prefer to keep your secrets, so you do." He poured two fingers of whiskey into Liam's glass and then followed it up with two for himself. No offer was made to Frankie. "I can respect that in a man, provided he can keep his secrets regardless of provocation."

"What is it you fucking want from me?" Liam asked. The smell of whiskey didn't do anything good for his stomach at the moment. "Because from here it looks like you've gone to a fucking lot of trouble just to have me tell you to sod off."

"Again, he gets to the point. It's consistent, you are," Séamus said. "I like that too. Well, then." He emptied his glass. "You've given my proposal consideration."

"Aye. I have. And I've no wish to join up again," Liam said. "As I said before. I've done my bit."

Séamus nodded. "Is that your final answer?"

"Is this the part where you threaten Father Murray?" Liam asked.

"I'm afraid it is," Séamus said, pouring another drink. "Drink up. You may need it before the evening is through."

Liam handed his glass to Frankie. "I only drink with mates."

Pausing, the corner of Séamus's mouth twitched. "I understand. We hardly know one another. And I'm not one for easily placing trust in others myself." He turned to Frankie but kept his gaze on Liam. "Bring another glass, will you, Frankie? There's a lad."

Unhappy, Frankie left. The sound of him trotting down the stairs was loud on the other side of the glass window. His receding footfalls were confused with another's as someone else made their way up.

"Don't make this any harder on yourself than it has to be," Séamus said. "Understand, I'll have what I want from you. One way or the other."

"So you say," Liam said and shrugged. His heart tapped out a rapid beat. *Stay calm. Remember Father Murray.*

"Big talk for a lad in your position," Séamus said.

"And what position is that?" Liam asked.

The man with the long brown hair and broken teeth entered the room. An invisible cloud of decay seemed to follow him. Liam scanned his scarred face, searching for a sign that he was one of the Fallen. It would explain why Séamus was so persistent. It would also explain why he'd been so reckless. Frankie had been right. The Nationalist community wouldn't stand for a priest being harmed. They'd do anything to see Father Murray safe—even if it meant turning on Séamus and his boys. Still, Liam detected nothing unusual—no hump, only the stink. *The stink is enough, isn't it?* In the back of his skull, the monster shifted. He got the feeling it was restless, watchful. *Was the same with Jensen, aye? Wait. Keep an eye on the ugly bastard.*

"You'll drive," Séamus said. "And my boys will take care of the rest."

Frankie returned with another glass and a second bottle of whiskey. The ugly man with the long brown hair motioned to Séamus.

"Stay here. Think about it," Séamus said.

"What's to think about if it's already fucking settled?" Liam asked.

Séamus's eyes narrowed. "Don't piss me about too much, lad." He crossed the room to where the ugly man was standing.

Straining for any hint of what was being said, Liam thought they might be discussing Father Murray, but he couldn't be sure. The longer the conversation went on, the more Liam didn't like the look of things. It was clear Séamus wasn't telling the whole of what was going on. Of course, when it came to it, Liam could trust fuck all.

Frankie whispered, "Tell him you'll do it. Please."

"Who is that man?" Liam asked, accepting the glass from Frankie.

"Him?" Frankie asked. "That's Mickey."

Liam asked, "And how well do you know this Mickey?"

"Not that well. Doesn't talk much. He's one of Séamus's mates. From Crossmaglen, so I'm told. Showed up when Séamus did. When Patrick was topped by the RUC last year. I came back from the Crum, and Séamus was our new OC," Frankie said. "You know something about Mickey I should know?"

Liam said, "Maybe."

"Is he a Peeler?" Frankie asked in a whisper.

Liam studied Frankie's face. He was scared, that was easy to see. "What makes you ask?"

The door slammed as Mickey left.

"Well?" Séamus asked, returning. "What have you to say for yourself?"

"What exactly do I get out of this?" Liam asked.

With his back to Séamus, Frankie gave Liam a pleading look. Liam presented him a quick wink in exchange.

"If a love for your country isn't enough of a reason," Séamus said. "I'm prepared to pay you a wee bonus."

"How much?" Liam didn't actually care, but there were things he might learn from Séamus's answer. *For example, how likely it is Father Murray and myself are going to see the other side of this.*

"How does one thousand quid sound?" Séamus asked.

Shite. "That's mighty generous of you. Are you certain HQ will be all right with such a thing? Doesn't that cut into their funding a wee bit?"

"It's generous because I feel we've a need to smooth things out. To make up for how you're being brought in. And if what's in the vault is as much as I understand, that's nothing," Séamus said. There was a gleam in his eye that Liam would've sworn couldn't be accounted for by mere patriotism. "Understand, I can also make certain arrangements in Derry. Get the RUC off your back. It'd be nice to see your ma, wouldn't it? Stop hiding? Get a decent place to sleep?"

That's not fucking possible. He's lying. "And if I don't accept?" Liam asked.

Séamus poured another round. "Then I don't think your friend will be saying Christmas mass ever again. Not that you'll be fit for much other than a funeral yourself. Mind, what they find of you will fit in a very small box once Davy and Mickey are done. Consider it a blessing in disguise. Will save your poor ma the cost of a casket."

"You can't mean to kill a—"

"Frankie, shut your gob," Séamus said. "I won't tell you again."

Something is very wrong. No Provo would kidnap a priest. "Driving isn't that rare a skill. I can't be the only driver in all of the Provisional IRA, for fuck's sake," Liam said.

Shrugging, Séamus said, "There are others, to be sure. But you're the one I want."

"Why?"

"Frankie, there, says you're the best." Séamus again emptied his glass.

Fuck that. This isn't about the best. Séamus wants someone good and more importantly, expendable. "All right," Liam said. "I'll do it. But I'll not carry a gun. I'll drive, but I won't kill for you," Liam said.

Séamus raised an eyebrow. "Very well. No gun." He poured more whiskey into his glass. "Welcome to the unit, Mr. Kelly. You'll find, as OC, I can be firm but easy to work with."

"As long as you have your way," Liam said.

"Frankie, see to it he's sorted," Séamus said, and tossed Frankie a key ring. The keys jangled as Frankie caught them. "Yes, sir." He got to his feet.

"And get rid of that stupid jacket," Séamus said. "It's unbecoming."

Who the fuck does he think he is? Liam felt Frankie grab his arm again.

"Come on, Liam."

"Where are we going?" Liam asked.

"To get some rest. Have you eaten?" Frankie asked. He waited to say more until they were both at the bottom of the stairs. "You shouldn't have pushed him so far."

"I don't like him." *There's a Fallen somewhere close. I know it.*

Frankie glanced up at the windows, and Liam spied Séamus looking down on them.

"I don't much either. But that doesn't fucking matter," Frankie said. "And you know it."

"Why is he for pulling this job, do you think?"

"Don't be stupid." Frankie started across the warehouse floor, his breath making little clouds in the cold.

The gritty cement floor was stained and cracked from years of abuse. Frost coated the few windows facing the outside. Liam glimpsed an empty field and a burned-out tenement building. The wind tugged at the trees. Winter was settling in for the night. The sound of the wind pushing and pulling at the warehouse's tin walls made Liam think of Long Kesh.

"Séamus is loyal to the Cause, is he?" Liam asked. "Because that's not the way it looks from here."

"Shut up." Frankie glanced up at Séamus again, who was still watching. "Are you trying to get yourself topped?"

"What's the point? That's where I'm headed isn't it? Once this is done."

"Don't say that." Frankie led him to the wall of offices on the opposite end of the warehouse. Another set of stairs led up to a loft on top. Liam counted four offices on the bottom—all with windows facing the inside space. In the office to the far left, Liam spied Father Murray sitting tied to a chair.

"Are they planning on leaving that fucking bag on his head the entire time?" Liam asked. *I need to warn him. Wonder if Frankie will give him a message for me?*

"You know as well as I do that it's best that it stays," Frankie said. "What he can't see, he can't report to the RUC or the army."

"Aye." Liam hated feeling powerless to help even if it was in the smallest way. "It's only that it's hard to breathe inside one of those fucking things."

Frankie stopped at the office door on the farthest right. Looking through the window, Liam saw they'd placed two mattresses on the floor. A sleeping bag was unrolled on top of each. It was also furnished with a couple of chairs and a table. The keys rattled as Frankie unlocked the door.

"I don't care for what's been done. It isn't right," Frankie whispered. "Davy is always telling anyone who'll hear that the Church doesn't fucking care how many innocents die in this war. They'd rather we surrendered to the British so they can go on taking money from the starving as they always have. Mickey is with him. Me, I don't know. Mind you, there've been times I can see the point, aye? But this? A kidnap? It's too far. So, why? Why is he so important to you?"

"Father Murray married us, my Mary Kate and me. I've known him longer than I've known you. Since I was practically a wean."

"You think that will matter to the priest, do you? When he finds out you volunteered again? Even if it is to save his neck?"

Liam said, "You call that volunteering? Because it looked a lot like blackmail to me."

Frankie sighed and then signaled with a sideways nod that Liam should enter the room. "Aye, well. Séamus can be a wee bit unreasonable from time to time."

"Unreasonable?" Liam stepped inside. "That's fucking brilliant. What is it he's got over you, Frankie? Because from what I remember of you he's not your sort at all."

"Don't be talking like that." Frankie closed the door and locked it. "I don't like anything about this job. I admit it. But Séamus got me out of some bother—"

"What kind of bother?"

"I owe him," Frankie said. "I'd still be in the fucking Crum if it weren't for him. Look—"

Liam held up a hand. "I get it. He can put you right back, aye? You don't have to say any more." He took in his new accommodations, trying hard not to remember the sound of the lock clicking into place. If it weren't for the windows, his skin would be crawling. *Marginally better than the place in Clonard. Cleaner. Roof is sound.*

"This is where you'll be staying for a wee while," Frankie said. "Well, you and me. Toilet is over there." He pointed to a door to the left.

"What day is it?" Liam asked.

"Thursday."

"No, I meant—"

"It's the 22nd," Frankie said, pocketing the keys and producing a deck of cards. He set them on the camp table. "Don't worry. I'll be with you the whole time."

"Don't worry? About what?"

"Fucking cold in here." Frankie went to the space heater plugged into the wall and turned it on. "Séamus. He'll not hurt you. Nor will he hurt your friend the priest."

"Aye, he'll have Davy and Mickey do it."

"He won't."

"Are you so sure about that?" Liam settled onto the mattress. That's when he noticed the familiar laundry bag resting in the corner.

"Brought your things for you," Frankie said. "Thought you might have need of them. Collected your shite myself. I didn't tell the others where you were. I wouldn't—"

"I know." *Relax. There'll be an opportunity to get a message to Father Murray about the Fallen. Let Frankie think you've settled in, aye?*

"I didn't."

"I believe you," Liam said. "So, when is the job?"

Frankie looked away. "I don't know."

"All right. Don't tell me, then." Liam got up again and dragged the laundry bag to the mattress.

"Want to play cards?"

"If you think Séamus will be all right with it."

"Oh, sod off. It isn't like that." Frankie sat down at the table.

Liam stood up. "The fuck it isn't."

"Are you picking a fight with me?" Frankie asked. "Because if you are, I'll not fall for it. You'll need your hands whole for the driving soon enough."

"Well, since I don't know where I'll be driving or when, what the fuck does it matter?"

"Come on. Don't be like that," Frankie said. "Sit. Play some cards. You'll feel better after taking a few quid off me."

"I can't play poker for shite, and you know it." Liam paused and then sat down at the table while the conversation slipped into familiar patterns.

"Fine, fine. We'll play for change, then," Frankie said.

"I'll not gamble with you. I'll only fucking lose."

Frankie fanned the cards in three different ways in quick succession and then shuffled. The flipping cards made a noise that reminded Liam of a playing card stuck in a child's bicycle wheel.

"I'll teach you how," Frankie said.

"You always say you will, and you never do. And I always end up the shorter for cash," Liam said. "Sod off."

"Aw, now. What better way to pass our time together? Old times. Aye?"

"Fuck that. I'd rather bust my knuckles on your jaw. At least I'd have a chance of winning at a fight."

"Liam, me old china." Frankie placed a hand over his heart and set his face in an innocent expression that had no doubt charmed the pants off of several nuns—if half the stories were true. "Your fundamental lack of trust wounds me." He dealt the cards with an unusual ease, speed and grace.

"You've been practicing."

"Correct me if I'm wrong, but are not the contents of your wallet mine in the first place?" Frankie asked with a wicked smile and a wink. "All right. Matches. We'll play for matches."

"Do you have any fucking matches? Because I don't."

Frankie shrugged. "Your lighter then."

"No."

"Cigs?"

"Two left. And I'm saving those for tomorrow."

"I've a carton. I'll split it with you."

"No."

Frankie stopped dealing and sighed. "You've become an old woman."

"I've become too wise for you, so I have." Liam lit his second to last cigarette and then picked up the cards he'd been dealt. He scanned the hand and blew out smoke. "I decide the game."

Frankie flashed a five-hundred-volt smile. "Great. What'll it be, mate? Five card stud?"

"Go Fish."

Chapter 22

Belfast, County Antrim, Northern Ireland
23 December 1977

Liam didn't sleep well. Although the warehouse was far warmer than the place in Clonard—the building actually served to keep the wind out—the rumbling violence of foul weather meeting corrugated tin brought dreams of Long Kesh. He felt awful for Frankie, not that Frankie would complain. He wouldn't even speak of the nightmares, let alone ask the cause. The dreams were one of many items from a long list of things that had passed unspoken between them over the years they'd served time together. It was part of what had cemented their friendship, that understanding silence. So it was that Liam prayed the nightmares would leave him for Frankie's sake. However, Liam knew the only thing that would help was a quick—*fix*—run. He needed it. *Bad.* A run would do him good. It would clear his mind, but the storm, the hour, and the fact that he was essentially a prisoner made the idea impossible. A drink would be more probable. *Surely, the boys have a bit of something?* It was a sure sign of his state that he'd almost make do with the black stuff, if he had to. *Almost.* But the stomach-turning taste of hops combined with being trapped within metal walls would not be anything like a good combination.

It's the 23rd, so it is. One more day, and it'll be the 24th. The thought once again began playing over and over inside his skull. The monster stirred in the shadows of his mind. He'd been blissfully free of its complaints for a time, but now it was back to its muttering and whispering.

Kill it. Now.

Who? Not Frankie? Liam thought back, but the creature didn't answer. "Would it be possible to leave the door open?" Liam asked. "A wee bit is all I need. I can't breathe." *You know,* he thought at the monster, *it'd be more helpful if you were more clear with what you fucking wanted. Maybe I could do something about it, aye?*

The creature retreated to its shadows in sullen silence.

"It'll let all the heat out, so it will."

Liam paused, briefly unsure of what Frankie meant. Then Liam remembered he'd asked Frankie to open the door. "Doesn't have to be much. A wee crack, is all."

After a moment's pause Frankie got up and pulled the door open so that a mere sliver of the main warehouse showed through. It was enough. Liam could breathe again. He then glanced at his watch in the dark and wasn't glad of his ability to see for once. *After midnight now. It's the 23rd of December. One more day.*

He needed a fix. He needed to be away from his thoughts.

One more day.

Doesn't mean a fucking thing. Christmas Eve is a day like any other. Nothing more. Doesn't factor into the current situation at all. Still, he couldn't shake the dread. *Please, Jesus, Mary and Joseph. Not this time. Please, God. I'll do whatever it is you want.* Unfortunately, he was too familiar with the fact that God wasn't much for cutting deals.

What if Father Murray is alone with one of the Fallen and doesn't know it? "Don't suppose I could look in on my friend?" Liam asked.

"Oh, for fuck's sake," Frankie said. "My ribs hurt. I feel like I been kicked by a horse. He flattened Henry's nose with a broken arm and the two of us sitting on him. The priest can handle himself."

"Fair enough."

"Now, if you don't shut your gob and go back to sleep I'll punch you in the head. I swear I will."

Liam didn't bother attempting sleep. He spent the rest of the night staring up at the ceiling, remembering and planning.

The next morning, Séamus sent for the pair of them. Liam left the little office space with dread weighing heavy on him. The nutty scent of fresh coffee and fried dough permeated the warehouse. He noticed a few members of their unit were missing. So was the grey Granada. Mickey was alone with Father Murray, but everything looked sound. Father Murray appeared to be sleeping. They'd removed the bag from his head and had replaced it with a blindfold.

"Liam!" Frankie whispered. "He's fine. Come on."

Turning back to the main area, the remaining men were gathered around a camp table set up near the cars. One of the boys had brought in coffee and a bag of gravy rings. As Liam reached for the last sprinkle-iced one, Frankie grabbed it and stuffed it in his mouth.

"Sore about last night, are you?" Liam asked, glancing again at the parked cars. A dented and rusty, midnight-blue Ford Escort RS1600 was parked next to the black RS2000. Seeing two cars of similar make and model side by side gave him an idea.

Frankie chewed while pouring himself a cup of coffee. "Sod off, you. I lost ten quid."

"Beginner's luck," Liam said, reaching for a cup.

"You aren't a beginner," Frankie said.

"Didn't say *I* was." Liam winked.

Frankie punched him on the arm.

"Good morning, gentlemen," Séamus said. "Everything is ready. Henry and the boys are in place. We hit the bank tonight."

"It's almost Christmas Eve," Liam said.

"All the better," Séamus said. "Most of the staff will be away on holiday. RUC. Army. They'll be thinking more of Christmas dinner with the family than watching for trouble. And with the shopping there's sure to be more money in the vault than usual. Perfect."

"I don't like it," Liam said. "The RUC are probably already on to us. You kidnapped a priest. And you weren't exactly unobtrusive about it, aye?"

With the exception of Mickey, worried looks passed between Frankie and the others, but no one made a sound. *They know something's wrong, so they do.* Their loyalty had been stretched to the limit. Liam could see it. He could feel it in his gut. If he had more time—if he knew the right thing to say, the others were sure to pull away from Séamus. However, there wasn't time. *And I sure as hell don't know the right thing to say.* He never had the right words when he needed them.

A flicker of confusion passed over Séamus's face so fast that Liam wasn't entirely certain he'd seen it. Séamus glanced at Mickey and the moment was gone. Séamus's expression changed to quiet rage. "Seeing as you're the newest member of our wee family," he said. "What you like doesn't factor in, son."

But what HQ thinks of it is another matter, isn't it? I can't imagine they're in favor. Do they even know? Liam guessed not. He shrugged. "And what of the weather?"

Séamus blinked. "Why should it matter to you?"

"Road conditions," Liam said. "I don't think you'd much care for me driving like a mad man on six centimeters of ice on those tires. Sliding sideways into a ditch cuts our chances of escape."

"Oh," Séamus said. "Smart." He nodded in grudging approval. "Snow stopped last night. Don't know when. The temperature dropped. That's all I know. I'll look into the forecast. Is that good enough for you?"

"Aye, it is," Liam said. "And where is this bank?"

"You'll drive where I tell you," Séamus said. "The fewer in the know, the fewer chances of information leaking."

"Frankie opens the fucking safe," Liam said. "I'm the wheelman. Davy is the muscle. What the fuck are you?"

Frankie tensed up, and Séamus's face grew red.

"I'm your fucking OC. That makes me the brains. Not you."

"And what happens if the brains get blown out?" Liam asked. "Me, Frankie and Davy and the funds are nicked because I don't know where the fuck I am, or where the fuck I'm headed?"

"I'm not telling you shite," Séamus said. "So, shut up and do what you're told like a good wee lad."

Winding the man up will not help things at all. So, stop it, you idiot. Calm yourself. Be smart about this. Father Murray is depending on you. Aye? Liam did his best to swallow his anger but held Séamus's gaze without so much as a flinch.

Séamus looked away.

Breathing deep, Liam tightened a fist on his anger until he was confident he could speak in an even voice. "Wanted to consult with you about an idea, sir." That "sir" had cost him, but it appeared to win some good grace. "Would you mind me telling you what it is?"

Séamus shot a sideways glance at the others. "Go on."

"Is it possible to get a couple more Ford Escort RS2000s before tonight? RS1600s would be fine. Even one extra would do. They should all be black like that one." Liam pointed to the parked RS. "Even midnight blue would work in the dark, I'm thinking."

Séamus blinked. "And why would you need such a thing?"

"If the take is to be as big as all that, and what with you kidnapping the priest—" Liam saw he might have gone a touch too far bringing that up again. So, he rushed through the rest before Séamus could shut him up. "—they'll be all the more determined to nick us. Decoys would help." Liam couldn't keep the excitement out of his voice. "In case we're spotted. Park a couple of black RSs along the route. We drive past. Get enough ahead to make a quick turn, aye? The decoy gets their attention. Leads the Peelers a merry chase. Better if there's more than one. In case they get too close. Third one leads them off. The first comes back. Like a shell game. Harder for the bastards to tell which black RS is the right black RS. Could have them chasing their tails all over Belfast."

One of the boys let out a low whistle. "Bloody hell."

"Fucking brilliant, that is," Frankie said.

"Back when I drove for my first unit, I'd place a Captain Beefheart sticker on the rear windscreen. To keep us nice and conspicuous. When I didn't want their attention any longer, I'd pull in somewhere and remove it. Change the plates, and we were clear. We could sticker the decoys, aye? Doesn't have to be Captain Beefheart. Anything easy to spot will do."

"Interesting," Séamus said. The room grew quiet while he seemed to consider the idea. Liam began to think he'd banjaxed it when Séamus turned to the others. "Davy? See to the details. Let me know as soon as possible."

Davy nodded and left.

Liam decided to push his luck a bit more. "I wish you'd reconsider letting me take the RS out for a test drive along the route."

Frowning, Séamus said, "I'll not have it."

"Look. I'm good at what I do. That's why you wanted me, aye? Part of that is I make dry runs. I take time to learn alternate routes. I study the streets. I know exactly where I'm fucking going beginning to end and exactly how long it will take. I know the area better than the fucking RUC and the BAs," Liam said. "It's my duty to know. You and the boys, you're counting on me."

The scowl on Séamus's face didn't budge.

"I've never driven that car," Liam said. "Never even looked at the fucking engine. How do I know what shape she's in, or what she'll do in a fix?"

"I'll not allow it." Séamus folded his arms across his chest.

"Why bother having me drive at all, then?" Liam asked, losing control. "Why not do it yourself?"

"He's right, Séamus," Frankie said. "It's the smart thing to do. A practice run. You know it is."

The others nodded and murmured agreements—again, with the exception of Mickey. Liam held his breath.

"All right! Shut it, youse!" Séamus reached into his jacket pocket and gave Frankie the keys. "Don't you two bollocks this up. You hear?"

Frankie said, "Yes, sir."

"And Frankie," Séamus said. "You stay with him. Every minute."

"I will."

Liam gulped his coffee, tossed the cup in the bin and grabbed another gravy ring before heading for the car. "Keys." He held up a hand.

"You're in a hurry," Frankie said, handing them over.

Reaching under the edge of the RS's hood, Liam popped the latch. "Let's see what you're hiding under there, love." He gazed down at the engine and felt his mouth fall open. Someone had gone to the trouble of dropping a 1.6 DOHC BDA engine from an RS1600 into it. While the RS2000 had its advantages in suspension improvements and such, in his opinion the engine hadn't been one of them. The old BDA was far more powerful than the standard SOHC engine found in the RS2000 model. It was smaller and substantially lighter too. Impressed, he grinned like an idiot.

Frankie stood next to him. "Should be in great shape. Davy's cousin is a mechanic. Rebuilt her from the ground up, I understand."

Liam left the hood open, went to the driver's side window and realised that the engine wasn't the only modification. There were indications that Davy's cousin may have also traded out the standard RS2000 transmission.

The only reason that Liam could think of for doing such a thing was to replace it with a RS1600 transmission, and the more he considered the situation, the more he realised that it would be required. With the transmission and the engine changed out, the driveshaft had probably followed. *So much beautiful work.* Liam reached out and gently ran a hand along the top of the car, caressing it. He hoped he wouldn't be ordered to burn it because doing so was going to hurt something fierce. What he was looking at was essentially a RS1600 disguised as a RS2000. The only car that would beat it in a rally was the RS1800. RS1800s were rare. Even if that weren't the case every single one also left the factory painted white with distinctive blue stripes and as such were as noticeable as the fucking Queen casually standing on a corner in the Falls.

He'd have given anything for Bobby to see the modified RS. *A fucking work of art, so it is.* But Bobby was still in prison. Liam considered asking Oran about Bobby the next time he saw him. "Tools?"

"They're in the trunk," Frankie said. "I knew you'd want to make adjustments."

Liam went to the driver's side door and climbed in. He hardly tasted the last sugary bite of gravy ring as he wiped the stickiness from his hands on his jeans, inserted the key and then cranked the engine. Its roar bounced off the warehouse walls and then dropped to a throaty purr when he let up on the accelerator. The passenger side door swung wide, and the car moved on its shocks as Frankie hopped in. The door thumped shut.

"Engine sounds fantastic," Liam said. "Should run her a bit rich. She'll use more petrol, but we'll have need of the power." He muttered to himself about several other adjustments he wanted to make.

Frankie nodded. "If you say so."

"What?"

"Nothing you've said for the past five minutes has made any sense at all," Frankie said.

"You're going to tell me you know fuck all about cars?"

"Aye, well," Frankie said. "You know fuck all about locks and safes."

"I need to run her, Frankie."

"I know," Frankie said. "But you'll have to wait until I've shut the hood and moved the Volkswagen." He jabbed a thumb over his shoulder at a white sedan.

"Why have you not done it already?"

"Because Séamus has the fucking keys. Now shut the engine off before you fill the fucking place with exhaust. And we all die choking."

Liam shook his head and turned the key off. "I thought you didn't know shite about cars?"

Frankie put out a hand. "Keys."

"Why?"

"I need to be certain you'll not ram the Volkswagen in your rush to go do your duty. It belongs to the OC."

Liam handed over the keys in disgust. "You're still punishing me for the tenner you lost."

"Every chance I get," Frankie said.

Liam watched Frankie approach Séamus about moving the Volkswagen sedan. Instead of giving Frankie the keys, Séamus opted to do it himself after handing Frankie a folded slip of paper. It took a few minutes for two men to open the steel roll-up delivery doors and get out of the way.

"She's the most beautiful thing I've ever seen. How did they know to get an RS1600?" Liam asked, backing into the car park as soon as it was clear.

Frankie smiled. "Asked Níal if you had a type. He said you were into the rally cars." He laid a hand on the dashboard. "Told Séamus. He found one that'd been wrecked. Davy and his cousin pulled the parts we needed. You've everything of that other car—"

"The RS1600."

"—that you need. Séamus thought it would sweeten the deal."

"The tires are new. So are the wheels."

"He told them to get the best they could find," Frankie said. "Got her set up to rally specifications. Níal said you used to run the rallies. Said you were good. Is that true?"

Liam nodded.

"Why did you quit?"

Shrugging, Liam said, "Had a bad accident."

"Oh." Frankie looked uncomfortable.

"Mechanical failure. Happens."

Relief passed over Frankie's face. "Oh."

"Are you ready?"

"I suppose."

Liam gave Frankie a sideways glance. "Wasn't asking you." Grinning, he spun the wheel and slammed the accelerator. The RS leapt forward with a powerful eagerness he'd not felt before. The tires slipped in the slush. They started to spin. Liam made rapid corrections to the accelerator and the steering and regained control.

Cursing, Frankie scrabbled to get his seatbelt sorted.

Liam raced to the car park exit and the street. The RS was twitchy—a little too eager to respond. He'd have to be careful of being heavy-handed, or he'd lose her. "Is something the matter?"

"What the fuck are you doing? You'll get us killed!"

"Stop your gurning. You're safe, you great wean," Liam said and turned onto the street. "Was only testing the tires and the suspension."

"Oh, aye?"

"Frightening you half to death was only a wee bonus."

"Fuck you."

"Know where we're going?"

Frankie smiled and then waved the folded paper in the air. "I've the directions, so I do."

"Let's see this bank. Aye?" Liam asked. "Then we'll go to the drop off and time the distance." Of course, he had no intention of making the full run that night—not with Séamus in the car. But he did need to see how long it'd take to get back to the warehouse. *A plan. I need a plan. Got to get back and free Father Murray. I'll work something out. It'll come to me.* Much as he wanted to believe otherwise, Liam knew better than to count on his father. He wasn't even certain as to why he'd thought to ask for help. *I'm on my own as I've always been.* All things considered, he'd be needing some insurance. Something that Séamus didn't know and didn't have a hand in. For the moment he concentrated on timing the drive from the warehouse to the bank. He wished he had another day or two. It was next to useless timing a run at the wrong time of day. The number of cars on the road would be inaccurate, but it'd served to get him out of that warehouse. If the Peelers were on to them, Liam didn't want to be anywhere near the place.

After the run to the bank was complete, another idea occurred to him. He decided to learn the area and search for that insurance while he was at it. In a short time he and the RS were getting to know one another very well indeed. Of course, Frankie had yet to unlatch his seatbelt.

"Been thinking about what you said about Séamus," Frankie said, staring hard out the windscreen. His voice had become more serious, reflecting an abrupt change in attitude.

"You have?"

"Aye, I have. Thought about it all night." Frankie sighed. "Have to admit, you're fucking right. There's something off about him. I don't—He's not a tout. It's not that. I don't think. It's…."

"Go on."

Frankie sighed again. "He's got that look about him sometimes. Like he's playing a scene in his head. From a film. You know the kind where everyone else gets topped, and a lone man takes a wee holiday in a foreign country with a big bag of money?"

"What do you plan to do about it?"

"Was going to ask you. You've always been one for the planning." Frankie gave him a quick look out of the corner of his eye. "Well, more so than me."

"That's not saying much."

"Fuck you."

"Told anyone else?"

"Are you off your nut? And get shot?" Frankie shook his head. "It's proper fucked, we are. Try to report it. HQ starts asking Séamus questions. We're topped. Don't report it. He takes the money and runs. Won't matter if he does for all of us or not. HQ will ask questions. We'll end up topped. Either way, it won't be pleasant, mate."

Liam found what he was looking for in a car park near Queen's University and pulled in to the space next to the black RS. He turned off the engine and threw open the door.

"What are you doing?" Frankie asked.

"Getting a screwdriver from the trunk."

"Why?"

"See that car?" Liam pointed out the black Ford Escort. It was an RS1600 and rusted, but it'd do.

"And?"

"I'm going to change the plates on that car with this one."

"Why?"

"Will make us harder to find later," Liam said. "I'll not tell Séamus. And don't you either."

"Why?"

"In case."

Frankie frowned. "In case of what?"

"In case you're wrong about him being a tout."

Nodding, Frankie swallowed. His face had gone a little green. "What the fuck are we going to do?"

"I don't know yet." Liam got out and went to the trunk. After retrieving a screw driver from the tool box, he removed the rear license plate on the RS2000 and then changed it out with the one on the RS1600. All the while, he thought himself unnoticeable—his skin tingling with the force of it. *Nothing to see here.* When he was done, he moved to the front and did the same. It was an easy enough job with Frankie for the lookout. Liam was quick about it, put away the screwdriver and climbed back in to the driver's seat. He started the car, pausing to listen to the engine rumble. "Beautiful sound, that."

"You're wasting petrol," Frankie said. "That shite doesn't come cheap."

"We'll have enough. Stop your worrying." *We could leave now but for Father Murray,* Liam thought. Gazing across the car park, he reconsidered.

"That's easy for you to say. You've a fucking angel or something looking after you, so you do."

Liam hesitated before pulling away. *Not an angel. Bran. Maybe the Fianna.* "How do you feel about a wee visit to a cemetery?"

"Whatever for?"

"Help, that's what for."

"You're mental."

"Not at all," Liam said. "Not yet."

Chapter 23

Father Murray shifted on the thin mattress. It had been a long night already and seemed to be only continuing the theme. He was awake and uncomfortable. His back ached, his hands and arms were numb, and his wrists were chafed raw from the ropes. To make matters worse, his skin itched like mad under the plaster cast, and he needed to go to the toilet. With the blindfold on, he couldn't be sure whether or not it was day or night, let alone of the time. His captors had been conscientious for the most part. Therefore, he hadn't been able to get free—not yet, but the opportunity would come. He had faith that this would be so. Because while they had been careful to avoid giving him any opportunity to strike out at them, they hadn't bothered to search him thoroughly—which meant he still had his dagger, among other things. Sleeping with the sheath digging into the small of his back hadn't been the most comfortable thing he'd ever done, but as long as he had the dagger there was a chance of escape. It was an advantage, the persistent belief that a priest wasn't likely to be armed, let alone dangerous, and was an assumption which had saved his life on a number of occasions. So he'd remained cooperative in order to avoid providing his captors an opportunity of discovering their mistake.

He should go back to sleep, he knew. There wasn't anything to do at this point but worry and worrying wouldn't help anyone. He didn't know for certain who had kidnapped them, but he had an idea given Liam's initial reaction. However, if a Republican group was responsible, then it was a splinter group, and if that was the case, then Liam and he weren't in the best situation—not that being kidnapped would ever be considered the best situation to begin with.

No one had bothered to explain why they had been taken, and this fact preyed upon Father Murray's mind. Although, that probably wasn't all that unusual. Unfortunately, he didn't know where they were either. He had only gotten a glimpse of the warehouse when the bag had been removed and then replaced with a blindfold during the night. He'd taken care not to see anyone's face. The fact that his captors had also been very careful to not reveal their identities was a good sign. Of course, it didn't stop him from observing other important information, provided his captors didn't take notice. The best thing to do, he felt, was to remain quiet, cooperative and alert for the time being. All in all, he was in fair shape, all things considered, and he wasn't much worried for himself. He was worried for Liam.

A door slammed.

"Good morning to you, Father."

It was a comfort, knowing the time of day. However, the speaker wasn't Liam, nor was he the man with the nasal voice who had sat with him the night before—the man whose nose he'd broken. This voice belonged to a younger man.

"Good morning," Father Murray said, returning the mundane courtesy. It was possible it was a lie, and they were attempting to confuse him about the time of day. However, he didn't see the point. *If everything is as it appears.*

"Would you care for breakfast?" the youthful voice asked. The tone was respectful, easy and happy. Which Father Murray took to mean that whatever they were up to was going well. "Are you hungry? I've brought you a couple of gravy rings. Didn't know what you'd want in your coffee. So, I've left it black with no sugar."

"No need to trouble yourself," Father Murray said. He was unable to avoid the irony in the statement and paused. "Ah, that will be fine."

"I'll be helping you sit up. Then I must untie your hands if you're to feed yourself," the voice said. "You'll not be for bashing my brains out, will you? Because the moment you try, my friend will have to put a bullet in you. I'm a good Catholic, Father. Such a thing would be a great sin, so it would—topping a priest. But my friend here says he's an atheist and doesn't mind pulling the trigger. Me? I don't much care for this situation—"

Someone cleared his throat.

"I… I'd rather we didn't risk angering the Lord Almighty. So, do us both a favor, will you, Father? Don't be for making any sudden moves."

"I won't," Father Murray said. *Not yet.*

"That's a relief to hear, so it is."

The man with the friendly voice helped him into a sitting position and then worked at the ropes. His hands were cold against Father Murray's skin.

He's been outside, he thought.

"After the breakfast I'll take you to use the bog," the friendly voice said. "You'll be wanting it soon, if you aren't already."

"Thank you," Father Murray said, working the blood back into his tingling fingers.

"Got everything working?" the friendly voice asked.

Father Murray nodded, and a hot cup of coffee was carefully placed in his hand. He took a wary sip. The coffee tasted strong and bitter, but it did its job. He hoped the gravy rings would come soon. He was quite hungry in spite of everything. There'd been no tea the night before. "How long will I be forced to stay here?"

"Not much longer," the friendly voice said. "You should be back to your flock tonight, if all goes well."

"Oh." Father Murray hesitated and then took a second drink. He swallowed and asked, "And Liam? Will he be freed?"

There was a long pause. Listening to the men breathing, he got the impression they were communicating to one another in gestures. The second man spoke, the atheist with the gun, Father Murray assumed.

"Liam is free." The atheist's voice was deeper, cold, and carried the hint of an accent. He also lisped. Father Murray tried to think of where he'd heard it before.

"You've released him already?" Father Murray asked, confused. A jolt of fear set his heart to racing. *Did Liam misunderstand the situation? Is this about me or the Order and not him? Are these men not paramilitaries at all?*

"He's safe, Father," the friendly voice said. "That's what Comrade— I mean, my friend means. You should not worry for him. He's among friends."

"Is he?" Father Murray asked. "Which friends?" He heard the distinct sound of a gun being cocked.

"Enough questions, priest," the man with the lisp said.

Father Murray took a deep breath to slow the sudden jumping of his heart. The coffee cup was taken away and a gravy ring replaced it.

"Why don't you eat something, Father?" the friendly voice asked. "You'll feel better for being outside of some breakfast."

"And it'll stop your yammering," the lisping voice said, and once again Father Murray was certain he'd heard it before.

Not recently, though, he thought. *Not at the Belfast facility.* Of that he was certain. *Where?*

Muffled sounds of camaraderie and laughter filtered through the window glass to his right. Father Murray focused on the taste of pleasantly greasy, sugary dough and listened for some hint of what was going on. He couldn't hear well enough to discern what was being said, nor who the speakers were—let alone if Liam was among them. He finished the first gravy ring in short order. As he'd not been offered a paper napkin, he indulged himself and licked his fingers clean.

"More coffee for you, Father?"

Father Murray nodded. The cup was handed to him again, and he drank. The coffee tasted better after the heavy sweetness of the gravy ring.

"Must be hard getting by with only the one good arm, Father."

Urging the conversation along, he said, "It has been somewhat difficult, I admit. But I've been adjusting." In truth, he wasn't right-handed, but the nuns at his primary school hadn't approved of left-handed children, and so, he'd trained over the years to compensate. When he'd become a Guardian being able to use both hands was a distinct advantage in combat—one he almost never allowed his opponents to note until it was too late.

"How did you come to break it?"

Father Murray considered what to say. He didn't want them to suspect him of being anything other than a harmless parish priest with a small talent for bar brawling. So, he kept his answer vague. "I fell. Slipped." *That's close enough to the truth.*

"Ah. Well, you have to watch yourself in the snow and ice, Father."

"That you do." He wanted the second man to speak. He was sure to remember where he knew the man from, given time, but Father Murray wasn't certain that was possible without risking being killed. Whatever they needed him for would be done soon. When that happened would they free him? Or would they kill him for fear of being caught?

On the other hand, Monsignor Paul would be searching for them—of that, Father Murray was certain. Normally, he wouldn't have been comforted by such a thought, and he couldn't help feeling chagrined by the irony. Monsignor Paul was ruthless and notoriously persistent, resourceful and thorough when it came to achieving his goals. It was one of the many reasons he'd been appointed to the position of Grand Inquisitor. *But is he a match for paramilitaries?* Father Murray paused. *Probably. At least when it comes to ruthlessness and organization.* Faced with the prospect of murdering priests, most Catholics hesitated—certainly even regular Republicans did. Monsignor Paul and his men wouldn't feel any such qualms about shooting parishioners—particularly if they got in the way of the greater good.

Or what Monsignor Paul deems the greater good, Father Murray thought. As far as he understood, Monsignor Paul didn't suffer the same conflicts of faith that plagued other members of the Order from time to time. It had long been one of Father Murray's issues with the man. *He's so bloody certain of everything.*

A loud car engine rattled the windows. He heard someone let out an exuberant shout. *Liam. Has to be.* Father Murray had heard that exclamation before. *Once. And it'd been about a car then too, yes?* While he was relieved to know that Liam was in fact alive, at the same time Father Murray became more concerned. *What have they pulled you into? What do they need you for so badly that they'd resort to kidnapping?* He wished he knew which group had them. He knew he should've taken more interest in which Republican group Liam had been involved with, but Father Murray hadn't because there had been more important matters at the time—or so he'd thought.

He finished the coffee with a twinge of guilt and set the empty cup on the concrete floor.

"Here, I'll take that. Would you like another cup, Father?" The man with the friendly voice stooped to take the empty away.

A deep rumbling sent a shudder through the concrete floor.

"What's that?" Father Murray asked.

"Nothing to worry yourself over. The boys are off for a wee drive is all." He heard a small thump and a grunt of pain.

"Ah, will you have another gravy ring while I get the coffee, Father?"

"If you don't mind." *A drive,* Father Murray thought. *Liam had enjoyed rally racing, hadn't he? Hadn't Mary Kate said so? He'd driven a taxi too. Maybe that wasn't a coincidence after all, the driving.* Previous to the move to Belfast Liam hadn't displayed much interest in automobiles. *What if the fondness was less by choice and more because he'd been ordered into it?* Father Murray considered that last bit. *So, they needed him to drive. Why? What for?* When given a second gravy ring Father Murray took a bite and remembered what he could of Liam's life before Mary Kate had died.

A door slammed.

As always, Father Murray felt a terrible guilt at the memory of Mary Kate. He'd been so sure, so certain the abortion had been the right thing to do. He'd been so focused on the possibility of Liam's progeny being demonic, and therefore, dangerous, that he'd missed important signs. Liam's friends, Oran, Bobby, Níal and Éamon. *Provos, all of them, probably. But what about this lot?* Of course, he was only guessing. The INLA—the Irish National Liberation Army—as well as the Official IRA were both socialist, and although Mary Kate had been active in socialist student groups, Liam hadn't shown any interest in such things. Quite the opposite. Liam had avoided politics and political groups.

And yet, he joined the Provisional IRA. Can there be any doubt of that now?

What about the jacket? He'd read the message on the back of it and had been glad of it. No Provo would've walked about with such a thing displayed on his back. *Anyone can have a change of heart.*

"Don't get too comfortable, priest." It was the lisping voice. "I'm going to cut your throat and watch you bleed." The atheist's accent was clearly from the south. He wasn't a Dub. That was easy enough to hear. The accent was too musical for Dublin.

But where is he from? Cork? Limerick? Father Murray didn't think it was either. "Have I done something to you personally? Or is it more a general grudge against the Church?"

"It's personal."

His heart froze inside his chest. "I see. Whatever it is that I've done to you, I'm very sorry."

"I rather doubt that."

Not Cork. Not Limerick. Eastern. Wexford? "What is it that I've done?"

The distinct clock-tick of a pistol's safety was the only reply. Click. *On.* Click. *Off.* Click. *On.* Click—

A door opened and then banged shut. "You're in luck, Father. The lads left us one last gravy ring. If you've need of it, it's—Christ, Mickey! What the fuck are you do—"

"I'm away for a smoke."

Waterford, Father Murray thought with a sinking feeling. *He's from Waterford.* And suddenly, it all fell into place. *Oh, shite. It's Mickey Hughes, the half-breed. We burned down the whole building and killed everyone inside, but Mickey got away.*

I let him get away.

The door slammed a third time. He felt a gentle hand on his shoulder. "Are you all right, Father?"

Chapter 24

L iam stopped the car in the newer section of Milltown Cemetery, Ballymurphy. He could've gone to Belfast City Cemetery, but he preferred to summon his father in a known Republican graveyard. It was safer. He was dead certain they were being followed, and stopping at Belfast City Cemetery wouldn't have sent a good message to the boys. Besides, Oran was buried in Milltown.

"Stay here," Liam said to Frankie.

"I can't." Frankie popped his seatbelt catch. The black web-belt rattled as it was retracted into the seat. "I've my orders."

"Fuck orders. Christ, you're going to do what that fuck says even if he's for topping all of us and then stealing the money?"

"Now, I don't like his methods. I hate what he's done to you. I don't like holding your friend, the priest, at all. And I hate what he's done to that poor—" Frankie stopped himself. "I'm not for defending the likes of Séamus. He's a ruthless fucking tight-arsed bastard. But HQ made him the OC. I took an oath. *We* took an oath. None of us is in this for ourselves, not you and I. Maybe Séamus is a traitor. Maybe he isn't. Maybe he's straying from the organization's idea of the straight and narrow. But we don't know anything for certain."

"We don't?" Liam raised an eyebrow. "So, you've changed your mind? You trust Séamus, then?"

"Not one wee bit. But I'm not certain enough to put a bullet in his skull and then face HQ for it. We need proof." Frankie sighed and glanced over his shoulder at the side mirror. "Anyway, they're watching us."

"Aye? You spotted them too, did you?" Liam threw open the door in frustration. "Please yourself."

Frankie jumped out of the car.

Liam paused. *Calm down, will you? Frankie is only being careful. He's doing what he must.* The idea of Frankie being the careful one was sobering. "Walk with me until I tell you to stop. Then stay where I tell you."

"I can't—"

Liam sighed. "I'll stay within sight. I'm not for scarpering. You've my word."

Frankie seemed relieved. "Thanks, mate."

Both doors thumped closed, and Liam locked the car. Then he turned up his collar against the winter wind and proceeded down the cement drive, his work boots crunching in the snow. He zipped Conor's jacket closed against a blast of cold and was glad he'd remembered his neck scarf. It wasn't snowing, but the sky was grey, and for some reason the decade-old The Mama's and the Papa's song "California Dreamin'" sprang to mind. It never failed to make him think of when he was thirteen and had thought to run away from home because of his stepfather. The hopelessness of it set in fast. That'd been the first time he'd met Father Murray. Liam willed the song away and out of his head, but the more he tried to forget it, the more the melancholy tune persisted.

He walked with the weight of bad memories tugging at him. The graveyard seemed forested with stone Celtic crosses of varying ages, heights, and sizes. The rare Victorian mausoleum squatted among them. Three funeral services were being conducted in three different plots not far away. Droning Latin and kind words regarding the dearly departed drifted on the air like dead leaves.

Liam knew precisely where Oran's grave was located, but he pretended to be uncertain, stalling for time. He wasn't sure his father would answer with Frankie so close by. Liam needed a spot not far from Oran's grave

284 ᴥ Stina Leicht

where Frankie could keep him in sight per the agreement and yet would provide Bran cover—that is, if Bran required such a thing. Liam didn't know. There were two big Celtic crosses close to Oran's grave. *If there's need, that will have to do, aye?*

"What are we doing here?" Frankie asked.

"Visiting an old mate," Liam said. "Oran."

"They buried him here? In a Republican cemetery? Even after—"

Liam whirled and shoved a finger in Frankie's face. "Don't you say another fucking word. You hear? I warned you once. I'll not do it again."

Frankie swallowed. Looking spooked, he nodded.

Liam combed his fingers through his hair and sighed. "Sorry, mate." He knew full well his reaction had less to do with Frankie's words and more to do with how Oran had died. "It isn't your fault."

"Shouldn't have said it," Frankie said, and once again Liam was impressed because Frankie stood fast, holding his gaze. "I'm sorry, mate."

Frankie is no coward. He's seen what he's seen and still counts me a friend. Suddenly, Liam knew he'd do anything to get Frankie out alive and whole. In Liam's experience, everyone shied away once they'd spied the monster lurking in his eyes. Even Oran and Mary Kate hadn't been able to look him in the face when he was angry. Not that Liam felt Oran or Mary Kate had been cowards—far from it. After having seen the creature reflected in that copper bowl, Liam couldn't blame anyone for retreating from it. Hell, he'd done it himself. *And I live with the fucking thing.*

The monster gave out a satisfied huff from the back of Liam's mind.

Not a "thing." Not "creature" or "demon" either. You're myself. You, you're nothing but myself. He realised at that moment that the more he hated the creature, the more he disowned it and thought of it as something separate, the more power it gained and the less control he had over it. The choice suddenly became clear—accept it and accept sanity, or reject it and be—

He swallowed. *Don't want to think about that now. Later. Stay whole now. Long enough to get Frankie and Father Murray out of this mess.*

"But I don't understand how a dead man is going to help," Frankie said, following a few steps behind. His shoulders were up a touch, but his chin was up, and his back, stiff.

"You'll not understand until much later," Liam said. "And maybe not even then. Probably for the best, all things considered."

"I don't like this. You're not making any sense at all." Frankie's eyes were wide.

Liam paused. "Do you trust me, Frankie?"

To Frankie's credit, his hesitation was almost imperceptible. "Aye, I do. We've always had one another's backs, you and I. And regardless of… well… Mary Kate not caring for me at all—"

"That's not true."

"It is, and you know it. You want the truth? I was jealous, mate. She was something. Beautiful. Smart. And she really loved you. I'll never have a bird like that." Frankie shrugged. "Doesn't matter." He sighed. "I trust you. But…."

Stopping next to a large, limestone Celtic cross, Liam said, "But?"

"This is madness," Frankie said. "A cemetery? For help? Are you for rounding up an army of the great Republican dead?"

Liam felt the corners of his mouth twitch. "You could call it that." *Only they're not Republican—at least, I don't think they are. Not Socialist, anyway.*

The fear and confusion on Frankie's face intensified in a flash and then dissipated. "Either you're winding me up, or you've gone stone mad."

Like Daimhín. And Bran will have to— "Frankie, mate, please. Stay here. Everything will be fine. I'll be over there for a wee while with Oran, aye? You can watch me from a safe distance."

"Safe is it?"

"You'll come to no harm. It will cost nothing for me to try this. And if it works… well, you might have somewhere safe to go when all this is done."

"And where might that be?"

"With my father's people."

"You have gone mental. You hate Patrick." Frankie frowned.

"My real father. Not my fucking stepfather."

"Thought he was a Proddy."

"He's not a Prod."

"A Catholic, is he?"

"He's neither."

"What is he, then? Jewish? Muslim?" Frankie asked. "Are you, Liam Kelly, secretly black? Your Da's not… He's not English is he?"

"For fuck's sake!"

"Well?"

"No, he's not English. He's Irish."

"If you say so."

"I do. Now, stop with the questions." Liam turned, walked to Oran's tombstone, and prayed. *Mother Mary, Joseph and all the saints, please let him hear me calling.* It seemed an odd thing to do when he thought about it—the praying. *I'm half Fey. If I can be baptised, where is the harm in praying to see my father? No matter what they say.* He stopped just to the left of Oran's grave and stared down at the carved words in the granite headstone.

Oran MacMahon, Beloved Husband and Father—

It'd been months since Liam had last visited Oran's grave. He'd attended the funeral. Granted, he'd been hiding far enough away that even he couldn't hear the service. He'd snuck back later and had stood watch over the new grave lest someone disturb Oran's rest. Liam had heard of such things happening, particularly if the dead man in question was known for a Republican soldier. *Died 23 April 1977.* So much had happened in eight months. So much had changed. Liam's vision blurred, and he blamed it on the wind.

Time to do what you've come to do. "Bran?" Liam hesitated, combing his fingers through his hair again to get his fringe out of his eyes. Forcing himself past his uncertainty, he faced Oran's tombstone and whispered again. "Da? Can you hear me? It's me. Liam. I need your help. I'm in a wee fix."

The answer rode a fresh wind gust.

"You've never called me Da before." There was a hollow echo in Bran's voice, and it sounded as if he were speaking from a long distance.

"I've never called anyone da before," Liam whispered. That was the raw truth. He'd always referred to his stepfather by his first name no matter how many times his ma had told him that he was being disrespectful—regardless of how many times Patrick had tried to beat the insolence out of him. Liam had known full well Patrick wasn't his father, and Patrick had made it clear there was no confusion on his part either.

"Is that so?" Bran sounded pleased.

Liam felt an unexpected warmth grow in his chest. "Aye," he said, regretting that circumstances forced him to change the subject. "A man called Séamus Sullivan is holding Father Murray hostage, and he'll kill him if I don't do what he wants."

"And what is it this foolish mortal wants from you, son?"

"I'm to help in a robbery," whispered Liam.

Another cold wind blasted its way between the tombstones and crosses. A woman shouted, and a wispy, dark blue scarf floated away into the sky, landing on the tin roof of a crypt. It swept over the smooth metal like a ghost but caught on a rough patch and trembled there, trapped and unable to pull itself free.

"And you've no wish to do this robbery?" Bran asked, his voice growing more solid.

"Of course not." Liam risked a glance to his left and searched for a glimpse of Bran. It seemed a shadow moved on the other side of one of the largest Celtic crosses. A restless footfall crunched in the grit. "I've no wish to volunteer for the 'Ra again," Liam said. "I've done with it. But he'll not listen. He'll have me for a wheelman whether I want it or not."

"Mortals," Bran said with a disapproving growl. "They should have respect. That's all we ask. For all we do for them. For all they don't know."

Liam looked over to his right. Frankie was exactly where he'd agreed to wait. At the moment, he was smoking a cigarette and alternating his attention between the different funerals in an effort to disguise the fact that he was watching the blue RS parked among the ranks of mourners.

"The answer is simple enough," Bran said. "Come home with me. Now."

The idea was tempting. *Very* tempting. Leave Séamus to carry on without him. Liam would be free of it. And not only that, but free from the Grand Inquisitor and his knives as well. "I can't," Liam said. "They're watching me. And Séamus will kill Father Murray if I do." *And what would happen to Frankie, then? Where will he go, assuming Séamus doesn't do for him? One day the Brits will have him, and he'll land in prison for life.*

"The holy man is a soldier. He knows it'll come to dying one day."

"Da, please. He's a friend."

"A friend, is he?" Bran asked. "Did he not hand you over to those butchers—"

"I volunteered. Do you not remember? For the peace."

"He murdered your wee child before it was born. My grandchild."

Liam paused. "Maybe your war is different. But this war, my war, turns people upon themselves. Flips everything. Makes the certain, uncertain, and the uncertain, certain. How do you navigate through the shifting lines and keep yourself whole? Father Murray thought he was doing what was right. And... I... I can't judge him. Not when I've done for others for similar reasons." *Sometimes with even less reason.* He thought of those months when he'd let the monster have its way. "If Father Murray is to die, then maybe it's right I should die too. Maybe it's best for you to leave me be."

"Don't do this, son," Bran said. "Come with me. And we'll discuss the matter. There are too many mortals here."

"I can't. My mate, Frankie, he's caught in this too. And I'll not leave him and Father Murray to suffer. Running isn't the answer." Liam blinked. Mary Kate would've been stunned to hear him speak those words.

Bran sighed.

"There's something else. If I don't do what Séamus wants, he might go after Ma," Liam said, keeping his voice low. "Even so. This world is as important as yours. The two are connected. Have you not said so?" He waited. He had one last convincing argument that his father couldn't and wouldn't deny. *The Fey owe me a favor.* Liam didn't want to use it because it would be rude to bring attention to the debt, but he would do it if he had to. *For Frankie and Father Murray.*

The shadow cast on the ground near the big stone cross finally nodded. "Aye." Bran paused. "You have the strength of your mother in you. It warms my heart to see it."

Liam blinked.

"So, what is it you'll have from me, then? I cannot bring the fian over to make war on this mortal."

"Why not?"

"We've war enough of our own with the Fallen, or have you not noticed?" Bran said.

"You'll not help, then?"

"I didn't say that."

"What are you saying?"

"I need time to think. Plan. Consult with Sceolán," Bran said. "I'll get back to you. Are you well enough for now?"

"Aye, that I am," Liam said. "But the job is tonight. Don't wait too long. I've a feeling Séamus may be for pulling up stakes after. And I don't think the rest of us will be along for the ride, if you catch my meaning."

"What?"

"Greed," Liam said. "Occupational hazard in my line of work. Aye?"

Bran paused. "I thought this wasn't your line of work anymore?"

Liam looked away. "It isn't."

"There's something you're not telling me," Bran said. "Or is it something you're not telling yourself?"

"What do you mean?"

"You like the robbing, is it?"

"I do not!" Liam checked to see if Frankie heard and then lowered his voice. "It's the driving. I love it more than anything I've ever done."

"Ah, I see."

"I don't know what I'll do when this is over," Liam said. "I'll miss the driving, so I will."

"We'll talk about it when the time comes," Bran said. "Goodbye, son. Danu be with you. And good luck."

"Same to you," Liam said. "One more thing. Frankie. I wanted to talk to you about Frankie Donovan, if I could."

"What about him?"

"Could you take him with you? Later, that is? He'll need to be away for a wee bit once this shite has gone down," Liam said. "I owe him."

"That can be complicated."

"I understand. I do. I wouldn't ask if it weren't necessary."

"I'll see what we can do then."

Car doors slammed. *Another of the funerals must have ended.* "Thanks, Da." Liam turned and saw that the blue RS was now parked in front of his car. Two men had emerged. Both had brown hair and black wool hats. One wore a wool navy coat, and the shorter of the two was dressed in a black anorak. Liam recognised both men from the warehouse.

"Frankie!"

Frankie turned to see where Liam had pointed. "Hello, Eugene. Hello, Ned. What are you doing here?"

"More importantly," the one in the anorak said, "what are the two of you doing here?"

"A quick visit with an old mate of mine," Liam said.

"Oh, aye?" the one in the navy coat asked. "Which one is that?"

Liam motioned to Oran's grave. "Oran MacMahon."

Navy coat walked to Oran's headstone and looked down to read it. "I see."

The one in the black anorak strolled over to the Celtic crosses, obviously searching for anyone Liam might have been talking to while standing at the grave. The man in the anorak walked around the nearest crosses and scanned the nearby graves for any evidence that someone else had been present.

"We always have a wee chat before a job, Oran and me," Liam said, lying. "For luck."

"Come on, Eugene," Frankie said. "We're ready to go back now. Aren't we, Liam?"

"Aye, that we are," Liam said. "Any objections?"

Ned finished his circuit of the area around the grave and unable to find anything amiss, shrugged.

Eugene said, "Suit yourself."

Liam nodded and headed for the black RS.

"Séamus doesn't much care for what you've scrawled on that jacket of yours," Eugene said, following. "I can't say I do either."

"I suppose it's good that the jacket isn't yours, then," Liam said. He unlocked the door to the RS.

"We're fucking watching you," Eugene said. "One mistake. Put one foot off, Kelly. We've orders to top you."

"Is that any way to talk to a mate?" Liam asked.

"Ned and me," Eugene said. "We don't know you. You're not our mate."

"Relax, will you? Everything is cool," Liam said and slammed the door shut.

Frankie followed suit, closing the door with force behind him. "We're so fucked."

"Proper fucked," Liam said, cranking up the engine and waving at Ned and Eugene.

"Royally fucked," Frankie said.

"Oh, I don't know if I'd go that far."

"Were you able to... do whatever it is you came here to do?"

Liam pulled into the main drive with Ned and Eugene following behind him in the midnight-blue RS. "I was. I think."

"You think?"

Unsure, Liam shrugged. The morning was filled with firsts. He'd never asked his father for anything before and wasn't entirely certain he trusted that his father would come through. Liam's stomach fluttered at the idea. *What was I thinking? I'm on my own. Just as I've always been. He'll not show. It's nothing but big talk. Don't be a fool. Don't bet your life on him. Worse, don't bet Father Murray's or Frankie's.* "Don't worry. I'll think of something."

"You said that before and that got us here. And you having a fine conversation with a gravestone."

"I mean it."

"Well, if you're going to do it, you'd better do it fast. We'll be back at the warehouse soon." Frankie shook his head. "I don't know how you'll do anything when you said you'll not carry a gun."

"I'm not killing for the Cause."

"So I heard." Frankie said, "I suppose that leaves it to me."

"There has to be another way."

"If there is, I'm not seeing it." Frankie lit up a cigarette.

"Give us one of those."

Frankie handed over a lit cigarette, and Liam rolled down the window to blow out the smoke. He spied the midnight-blue RS in the rearview mirror. "Will you have a gun tonight?"

"I will." Frankie rubbed his lip for the fifth time in an hour and then began to fidget with the radio. "We're not expecting trouble. Not once we're inside the bank. But I'll be armed."

"Something is bothering you. I can tell."

"Well, for a start, we took a priest off the street, and there's been no talk of it on the radio at all. No search either. Why? The Peelers should be going mad."

That is odd, Liam thought.

"Then there's the other thing."

"What other thing?"

"Have you not wondered where Henry and the others are?"

"Keeping watch at the bank," Liam said. "Right?"

Frankie shook his head. "Séamus got this bright idea, so he did. Watch the employees for a few days. Find a man with a family. Follow him."

Liam's stomach did a slow roll. "He didn't."

"He did," Frankie said. "They're holding a bank teller's wife and wean. As long as he cooperates they'll be safe. He lets us in after the bank is closed. The job is done, we're safe away, and Henry and the others will let them go unharmed."

"Except we'll not be safe away," Liam said. "We'll be topped or lifted. All of us. And what happens to that poor man's wife and wean?" *This gets better and better. Fuck.* He breathed in a great lungful of smoke and blew it out. It helped his nerves a wee bit but not enough to slow his heart. "When our Séamus gets himself an idea he uses it over and over, does he?"

"I told you I didn't like it," Frankie said. He looked miserable. "I'm not supposed to know. Séamus has been fucking secretive about the whole job. I swear I'd not know what kind of vault they had, if he could've avoided telling me until we were standing in front of it."

"So, how is it that you know about the second kidnap?"

"Henry told me."

"And why did he do that?"

Shrugging, Frankie flicked his cigarette end out the window and watched as it bounced off of the midnight-blue RS's windscreen. Ned, who was driving, honked the car horn. Eugene gave them the two fingers.

Frankie returned the gesture with a grin and said, "Because Henry can never keep his gob shut before a job. He can't stop himself. It's like diarrhea. He has to talk to someone the once. So, he tells me."

"Séamus wouldn't be happy to know that."

"Aye. But Séamus doesn't know. And he won't. I'm in Henry's unit. Better me than anyone. So, fuck Séamus. Séamus is an arsehole."

Chapter 25

Belfast, County Antrim, Northern Ireland
23 December 1977—7:55pm

"**K**eep your hands where I can see them," Ned McCoy said, pulling a pistol from his pocket. Something in his voice said he almost regretted the request.

Liam left his hands on the steering wheel of the idling RS, and attempted to hide his nerves behind his balaclava. He wasn't sure how successful he was. However, he supposed a certain amount of anxiety would be expected in anyone facing the business end of a gun. "Am thinking of having a cig. Is that all right with you?"

"Go ahead."

Liam didn't move to fish the cigarettes Frankie had given him from the jacket's inside pocket, not yet. "Will you have one?"

Ned paused. "I will at that."

Reaching inside Conor's jacket, Liam grabbed the cigarettes and offered one to Ned. Afterward, Liam glanced at the watch he wore turned so he could see the face on the inside of his wrist. *Eight o'clock.* Although the moon was nearly full, it was dark in the alley. He pulled his lighter out of his blue jeans pocket in order to offer Ned a light.

The gates wouldn't be locked until nine, but Belfast's lively city center had died with the setting sun. The frequency of maimings, killings and bombings had been growing steadily worse as the war ran headlong into a twisted, hateful deadlock of tit for tat. The city council had reacted by enclosing Belfast's center with a "ring of steel"—a circle of chain-link fences. Regardless, most people in the area kept to their homes after dark. There hadn't been a soul on the street in front of the bank when Liam had driven past. Belfast's night life was as dead as a rotting corpse. *For the most part.*

As he waited for Ned to finish with the lighter, Liam's mind drifted to Conor and the others. Liam wondered what they might be doing? They were Uni students on holiday. They were probably at another party somewhere or with their parents, having tea. Once again the differences between their lives and his yawned wider than a canyon. *I should return Conor's jacket before it acquires more bullet holes.*

"Liam?" Ned asked. "Are you awake over there?"

"Oh, aye," Liam said. *What the fuck is the matter with you? There are more important things at hand. Like how to get out of this without being exiled, or killing anyone, or being assassinated or visited by a punishment squad.*

Exhaling a great lungful of smoke at the two inches of space created by the lowered car window, he shivered as icy air seeped into the car via the opening. It was that or listen to Séamus complain of the smoke when he returned. The low rumble of the engine was soothing. The balaclava pulled down over his face was warm, but he hadn't been able to shave for a week or so, and the pressure of the mask on his skin made his beard itch. He resisted an urge to yank the thing off his head and stared out the windscreen. The pavement was slick, the snow having melted a bit during the day. He didn't see it as a good sign.

At least it isn't snowing, he thought.

He squeezed the steering wheel with his left hand. Time was running out. His blood pounded in his ears loud enough for Ned to hear it, and he was sweating under Conor's jacket. Liam had considered his options all afternoon and hadn't come up with a single choice he liked. The first was to banjax the job. Get rid of Ned. Lock all the doors. Allow Frankie in and no one else and then drive away off. The problem with that was that it would endanger Eugene and Ned—not only Séamus, leaving them for the Peelers to lift. *And what about the teller's family? Would Henry and the others hear of what happened, top them and run?* Liam couldn't have that on his conscience. Then there was the likelihood of such an action ending in exile or execution at the hands of the 'Ra, execution being the most likely of the two. Of course, now that it came down to acting on his words he wasn't absolutely certain that Séamus would turn on them—not certain enough to risk killing anyone and anger the Provos. The second option was to wait until they returned to the warehouse.

Liam couldn't help worrying for Father Murray. Would they kill him while he, Liam, was away on the job? Or had Mickey been told to wait until they returned? Liam had to admit that it made more sense for Mickey to top Father Murray while there was no chance of Liam stopping it. *It'd be smarter. If doing for Father Murray is on the agenda at all.*

Liam hated that thought. Wiping his hands on his jeans, he returned them to the steering wheel. In the corner of his eye, he caught the tension in Ned's body. He seemed poised to strike. "Relax, mate. I'm not for doing anything wrong." And at that moment Liam knew it was the truth. He couldn't leave the others behind to face prison, no matter what. Nor could he risk the teller's family. He released a shuddering breath. *So, it's the warehouse, then. Wait for Séamus to hit first.* Liam didn't like it. There were a million things that could go wrong, but there was fuck all he could do about it. His mind was made up.

"See that you don't," Ned said. Something in his voice said that he didn't care for the situation much himself.

Maybe Da will come through.

Right. Sure he will. And Mother Mary will come down from the sky and pluck us all safe and whole from danger at just the right moment.

Fuck. It's a fool, I am. "What's with the gun? Have I done something wrong?" Liam asked.

Ned shrugged and blew smoke out the passenger-side window. "Séamus said to watch you. So, I'm watching you."

Liam remembered something he'd forgotten. "Don't get worried, mate," he said to Ned before lifting his left hand from the steering wheel. "Only getting my music." He slowly reached inside Conor's jacket and produced the tape. After showing it to Ned, he slotted it into the stereo. With that, all was ready. Liam had but to turn on the stereo.

"What the fuck is that for?" Ned asked.

"Helps me focus on the drive."

Liam heard muffled gunshots. He scanned the area for the source. A siren went off. The bank's back door slammed open. Séamus and Frankie bolted outside. Blood stained Frankie's anorak.

Liam asked, "Whose blood is that?"

At the same time Ned said, "What are you—"

Frankie wrenched at the rear passenger side handle. Séamus scrabbled at the door workings on the opposite side. The RS's doors swung wide and the cold rushed in to do combat with the heater's efforts.

Séamus screamed. "Drive! Go!"

"What happened?" Ned asked.

"The Peelers were there! We're fucked! Eugene turned on me! He was a fucking tout! Peelers did for him. Happened too fast. I couldn't do shite! Fucking go!"

"Where's Eugene, Séamus?" Liam asked.

"Oh, Christ! He's dead! Do you hear me? Dead!"

Liam shifted from neutral to first gear. Ned stretched out a hand for Liam's left arm and gripped it.

"What are you doing?" Ned asked.

"Saving our necks," Liam said.

The bank's rear door flew open. Several Peelers rushed out, aiming guns.

Liam said, "Or would you rather do time?"

"Don't you move, you fucking Fenians!" One of them yelled. "Don't you fucking run!"

Ned let go. A bullet shattered the rear passenger window. Frankie drew his pistol, shoved at the broken glass and fired back. The sound of it was too big for the inside of the RS. Liam turned up the volume on the stereo. Ned gave him a look as if he'd lost his mind. Liam couldn't have explained why, but this was how it was done. Every time. He tossed his cigarette end out the window and then the opening drum beats of Sweet's "Ballroom Blitz" blasted through the speakers.

"What the fuck is that sh—"

Roaring guitars obliterated the rest of Séamus's protests. Liam gripped the steering wheel and urged the RS up the alley with a heavy boot. Behind them, gunfire lit up the alley like strobe lights. He reached the corner, paused long enough to shed the itching balaclava—he needed his peripheral vision—and then turned, speeding west toward the warehouse.

Nothing to see here, he thought at the world outside the car. His hands tingled with the force of it.

A hand slammed down on his shoulder, shattering his concentration.

"Turn that shite down now!" Séamus's face was red.

Ned reached over and lowered the volume.

"I'll not put up with much more of this, Kelly," Séamus said. "You'll do something about that attitude. And your appearance, too. Or I'll take steps, you understand?"

Sirens and flashing lights burst onto the street in the rearview mirror. Liam bit back a retort with a tight jaw. He needed to focus on the driving, not Séamus. Why did it matter? Should Séamus not be more concerned about the Peelers?

"I said, do you understand?"

"Séamus! Let him do what he has to. The Peelers are behind us!"

Fuck you, Séamus. Who is it you think you are? "I do."

"All right then," Séamus said and settled back into the seat.

Liam attempted to focus on the road and not how much he'd like to punch the smug look off of Séamus's face. He was letting Séamus get to him. It was a bad idea.

Frankie and Ned checked their pistols.

Most of the jobs with Oran and the boys went as planned, that is with the exception of the first; they went quiet and with little to no fuss. It'd been why they'd been so successful as a unit. Liam had hoped that this job would be the same, given all the planning that Séamus had put into things. *Unless he's a tout and this is just another set-up.*

Don't even think it.

He said Eugene grassed us. How much do the Peelers know? Liam was suddenly very glad he'd thought to change out the plates before the job.

The RS's rear tires slid on the wet pavement and then grabbed. The modified RS2000 launched itself down the street with an easy eagerness. *She's twitchy. Remember that. Pavement is slick. Remember that too,* he thought, feeling the tingling in his hands return as whatever it was that took over when he drove kicked in. *Barricade is a block ahead.* Short, white-painted concrete pillars were set on either side—dragon's teeth—spaced to allow the flow of foot traffic while blocking cars from driving up the walks. The Peelers and BAs at the checkpoint were readying their guns. Liam spied the school playground to his left and then steered off the street.

Someone screamed as the Peelers fired. The remains of the back wind-screen cracked again. Liam felt a hard thump in the back of the car and checked the rearview mirror. The prowl car was close—too close. Liam assumed they'd been rammed. He felt no real change to the handling as he stomped harder on the accelerator. Séamus shouted. Cold air rushed in through the back windows. Ned and Frankie returned fire. Liam ignored it all, and focused on dodging a big iron swing set and a row of worn but happy animals impaled on springs. The Peelers in the four-door dropped back but continued to follow. Liam gritted his teeth as the chain-link fence which signalled the end of the playground loomed ahead.

This is going to hurt, he thought at the RS. *Sorry, love.* The tingling in his hands spread up to his arms as he prayed they'd make it through.

The RS slammed into the fence with the force of an explosion. The steel links ripped like fabric but clawed and tore at the RS's paint. Liam felt the tires leave the ground as the RS ran out of slightly elevated playground turf. The car landed hard on the street, bouncing on its shocks. Liam tugged the steering wheel into a violent right as soon as he could. Again the tires squealed in the race to grab the slick pavement before they were sent into a spin. He grinned, making adjustments with the accelerator and steering without conscious thought. The joy that came to him when he drove blossomed in his chest and filled most of his awareness. A laugh bubbled up out of the euphoria. Christ, he'd missed it—the racing, but this, this was even better. The chase. *It's been so long.* The prickling had spread from his hands to his whole body. He heard but didn't hear the others. Ned muttered a prayer. A frantic voice crackled in Séamus's hand-held radio. Séamus screamed threats into it in reply.

"Leave it, Séamus. They're done for." Frankie rolled down the window and leaned half out it, aiming for the unmarked prowl car.

"Get the fuck inside, Frankie!" Liam warned. "It's going to be a tight fit!"

Frankie squeezed off two more shots before slipping back inside. Liam took a quick left and then shot up a walk for a couple hundred feet. He took out a few street signs along the way. Each new dent in the RS made him flinch, but the unmarked prowl car was nowhere in sight. *Not yet.*

He was gratified to see the midnight-blue RS pull into the street just as he took a sharp right. Up until that point, he hadn't been certain that Séamus had acted upon his advice. Liam proceeded another block and then crossed back to the main road leading to the warehouse. He couldn't waste time making certain the Peelers and the British Army had taken the bait. Father Murray was in danger, and Liam couldn't know if Séamus was going to play fair. Somewhere above, a helicopter beat at the night sky.

"Henry turned. Fucking Eugene got to him," Séamus said, throwing the radio at the back of the front seat in disgust. Liam felt it bounce off.

"What of the teller's family?" Frankie asked.

"How the fuck is it you know of that?" Séamus asked.

"Tell us, Séamus," Ned said. "Are they out of it? Safe?"

"What does it fucking matter?" Séamus asked.

One more go. One more chase. Just one. It was the same urge for a fix, and Liam knew it. The hunger was deep and overwhelming. Still, he fought it. *Fuck off. I can't play with the army and the Peelers any longer. Have to get back.*

A second siren whooped into life, and a prowl car pulled onto the street in front of him. He was going seventy miles an hour. There wasn't time to stop. Heart in his throat, he yanked the steering wheel to the left. Clipping a phone box, glass shattered. He cheered as the prowl car pulled in behind them.

In the seat next to him, Ned cursed in a long string of Irish and reloaded his gun.

And then a second prowl car appeared to his left, speeding at them from a cross street. Liam jerked the steering wheel to avoid the full impact. The prowl car caught the rear passenger door. Both men in the back seat were thrown against one another as the RS was flung into a spin. Tires skidded. Steel screeched. Men screamed. Liam fought against the car's momentum, but the RS hit a patch of ice. It seemed to take forever, but he finally got the RS under control and stopped.

The Peelers in the first prowl car got out, guns aimed at the RS and everyone inside. "Out of the car! Now!"

The second prowl car pulled up in front of them with its crumpled front end, blocking the road.

"Fuck! We're lifted!" It sounded like Séamus.

Not quite. Laughing, Liam smashed the accelerator. Séamus screamed.

Liam steered for the prowl car and turned at the last instant, whipping around it and once again heading up the walk. To his left was a small churchyard, denuded of trees by last summer's 12th of July bonfire. Liam turned off the road and onto the slush-covered grass, hitting the church's sign in the process. A shower of splintered wood peppered the ground behind them. Tires ripped through the soggy dirt and up the wee hill. There was room to pass between the Protestant chapel and the graveyard, but not much. On the other side of a short stone wall, grave markers whipped past. They cleared the building, and he slalomed around a stone marker and a statue and was out the other side before the prowl car was able to make the turn.

The car slammed down onto the pavement again with a jarring crunch.

He had to be careful. They were in a Protestant area now. Getting stranded wasn't an option. He listened to the car. It was making a few noises that didn't sound good, but in spite of the hit she'd taken, all seemed well enough. However, something was rubbing against the wheels, and there was no telling how long they'd hold up. The back end felt a wee bit unstable. It was clear she wouldn't last another go. He ejected the tape from the stereo and pocketed it.

"What are you doing?" Séamus roared. "Why are you slowing?"

"Car won't make it," Liam said, searching the street. The tingling on his skin hadn't receded—in fact, it'd grown more intense. He hoped that was a good sign. Then he caught a glimpse of a car parked behind a row of businesses. He stopped the RS, backed up and found exactly what he was looking for.

A Ford Cortina. Not his type, but she'd do.

"What do you mean the car won't make it?" Séamus asked.

"Do you not hear the state she's in?" Liam said, parking the RS next to the Cortina. *It's a two-door, but we'll make it work.* "Change of plan."

Séamus moved up to the front seat. "We don't change plans unless I say so."

"Look," Liam said. "The RS is done. Can go on, but the next time a prowl car makes us I can't promise she'll have enough for another go. Even so, that big fucking dent in the side will give us away." He got out of the RS and opened the trunk using the key. He found the tools he'd left there and selected a rag, screwdriver, hammer and wire-cutters. Leaving the trunk open, he headed over to the Cortina.

The passenger doors thumped.

"Get back in the car, Kelly," Séamus said. "Do it now."

Liam turned to face Séamus and found the man was pointing a pistol at him. *I'm doing everything I can to save his fucking arse, and he's threatening to shoot me?* "This won't take long."

"You're right. It won't. Get back inside the car, Kelly," Séamus said. "Or I'll shoot."

"You fucking prick! Fuck you! I'm fucking sick of this shite! You going to shoot me? Fine. Shoot! Fucking get it the fuck over with!" Then Liam shoved Séamus.

Frankie and Ned ran over and grabbed his arms, dragging him off Séamus. Liam fought it. "I fucking told you! We can't go on in the RS. Do you want to fucking kill us all? Is that it?"

Ned asked, "Are you sure?"

Liam jerked his arm free and pointed. "Rear wheel is done for. See for yourself. It'll blow, we put any more strain on it. I'm for getting us a new car. It's what I have to do. Now, will you lot let me do my job, or are you going to argue about it until the Peelers lift us?"

Séamus gave the rear of the RS a sideways glance, looked to Ned who nodded. Séamus sighed. "Go on."

Liam headed for the Ford Cortina and found it locked. Using the hammer, he smashed the driver's side window. Then he reached inside and unlocked the door. He used the rag to sweep most of the broken glass from the seat and climbed in. He took the screwdriver, rammed it into the ignition slot, and gave it a few taps with the hammer. He was prepared to break into the steering column if he had to, but often this was enough. He thought hard at the car. *Turn over, you bitch.* His hands tingled as he turned the screwdriver.

The car started.

Waving the boys over, he released the breath he was holding. He hated abandoning the RS, but there wasn't anything for it.

"Bring the tools, aye?" Liam asked.

Frankie nodded and brought them as well.

Ned wiped down the inside of the RS. Then everyone scrambled into the Cortina. Liam shut his door and headed toward the car park's exit.

He glanced into the rearview mirror. That's when he noticed Frankie was bleeding from a wound to the side of his head.

"You good, Frankie?" Liam asked. "Were you shot?"

"Bleeding bad, but it's only a graze. I'll do."

"Glad to hear it," Liam said. He got reoriented and then pulled onto the street. By his calculations they were three blocks from the warehouse. He proceeded as if it were the most natural thing in the world to be driving down the street with a broken window and three men—one of them bleeding. He slotted his music into the stereo, and focused on pretending they were headed home from a late party.

Séamus cleared his throat. "That was a good bit of thinking."

"Oh, aye?" Liam said. "Too bad you almost fucking topped me for it."

Chapter 26

Belfast, County Antrim, Northern Ireland
23 December 1977

"Didn't expect to see me here," Mickey Hughes said. The demon's voice was deep and distinctive with its lisp. "Did you?" Father Murray blinked in an attempt to adjust his vision to the light as the blindfold was roughly removed. A jolt of fear exploded in his chest when he saw that he was very much alone with Mickey Hughes. A quick sideways glance through the room's plate-glass window confirmed it. All the vehicles which had been parked inside the warehouse when he'd arrived were gone. Suddenly, he felt cold. "I can't say that I did."

"We've been watching you for some time."

"And who, exactly, might 'we' be?"

"Ah, that would be telling." Mickey smiled, revealing his broken front teeth. "But I'm thinking you could guess."

"Why would a Catholic priest be of any interest to the Provisionals?"

"Wrong guess." Mickey sighed as if bored. "There I was, watching you in hospital. And there you were, taking a bitty stroll. Imagine my surprise when Séamus's wheelman arrived with a Fey captain. And who do they stop to chat with, but you? I knew then I had to find a way of arranging this little meeting. Too good an opportunity to miss, aye?"

He—*No, it*, Father Murray thought—took a deep breath and then slowly released it.

Mickey asked, "Isn't it interesting that you're the one wearing cuffs this time?"

When Father Murray had seen Mickey Hughes last, he'd been a lad. *So, long ago.* Now that the blindfold was off, Father Murray noted that the only resemblance remaining to the boy was in the hate-filled blue eyes, the broken teeth, and the voice. All semblance of innocence had long been stripped away, leaving a big, scarred man-shell with shoulder-length, brown, wavy hair and a great deal of rage.

Images from that terrible night in Waterford surfaced in a flash—the open suffering in young faces that hadn't seen light or human kindness in months, possibly years. The horror of it. The knowledge that one of the Church's own was responsible.

They were children of the Fallen.

Does that excuse what was done to them? The answer to that question had haunted Father Murray most of his adult life. He hadn't admitted it to anyone, of course. That was unthinkable. His superiors would have retired him from active field duty at once. However, deep in his heart he understood that Waterford had been the reason for so many things that he'd done, both good and bad—not the least of which was not executing thirteen-year-old Liam Kelly on sight. One glimpse of that bruised face had changed everything.

Thank God, Father Murray thought.

There were long nights when he consoled himself with the suspicion that perhaps the reason why God led him to be there that horrifying night—the reason he'd lived through it and kept his sanity when others hadn't—was to save Liam, and ultimately, the Fey. *Man can't presume to understand the ways of God.* But sometimes the questions couldn't be helped, and sometimes, if one searched, God granted answers. "I had nothing to do with your being imprisoned in that place."

"And yet, you helped kill everyone," Mickey said.

What was done had to be done. At least it was done with compassion. So, Father Murray had told himself then and had continued to tell himself every day since. *I made it quick and painless. It was a mercy.* "I think you understand why."

"I wonder what your new allies would say? Were I to tell them that four of your victims that night were children of the Fey?"

Father Murray stopped breathing, and he felt the blood drain from his face.

"Ah," Mickey said. "So, such a thing never occurred to you. Did it?"

Closing his eyes, Father Murray swallowed. *It's a lie. All the children in that cellar were taken from the sanitarium—a sanitarium staffed by the Fallen.* A team of Guardians had been sent to destroy it. He heard. Later, he'd gotten an anonymous call about an orphanage with a secret chamber located underneath, frequented by an elite few—politicians, church officials and the rich. Why he'd gotten the call and not someone else, he'd never understood. He recalled how the foul smoke from the burning orphanage had blotted out the sky, how it had clogged his nose and choked his lungs. The orphanage vanished from the Church's records the very same night.

Those who could be saved were saved. As for the others—*What was done had to be done.* Unfortunately, the names of the clients died with his informant, a local parish priest, less than a week later. The priest had only been able to give two names before he died. *An important two.* The first had been Father Burren, who had operated the orphanage, and the second had been one Monsignor Clarence Paul, who had protected the entire operation. What price had been paid for that protection, Father Murray didn't wish to speculate. He'd found Father Burren had been tainted and had reported it. Monsignor Paul had insisted otherwise. Late one night, Father Murray had woken to find Father Burren standing over him with a gun. In the end, Father Burren murdered Father Jackson along with three others before he was finally neutralized.

Mickey is a demon. It thinks compassion a weakness. It's only doing what demons do. It's trying to twist you against yourself.

What if it isn't lying?

You can't save anyone if you let it control you now. You can't think about this. Not now. Not here. It isn't safe.

But the seeds of doubt were sown, and that doubt opened an unbalancing void in his stomach.

Jesus, Mary, and Joseph, help me. Father Murray took a long breath and opened his eyes, keeping his gaze from drifting directly to Mickey's own.

It couldn't see that it'd reached its target. "What do you plan to do?"

"Why should I tell you?"

"Because it would instill more fear. And your kind dines on fear and misery."

Mickey laughed. "Are you attempting to manipulate me, priest?"

"Seems fair," Father Murray said. "Since you were attempting the same."

"You doubt the truth?"

"I don't. It's you I doubt. You're a demon—"

Mickey held up its hand. "Half demon, thank you."

"Your sort don't deal in truths."

"Ah, but hurtful truths can be effective weapons. Particularly, if the target is taken unaware," Mickey said. "Your kind taught me that."

"Get to the point."

"You've never been one for patience," Mickey said.

"What would you know of me?" Father Murray asked. "Except what you were able to observe all those years ago? Humans change over time. And can you be certain of what it was you saw then? You were young as I recall."

"Young but hardly inexperienced." Mickey got up and went to a folding table with an open steel box in the center. "Do you want to see what it is that I've brought for you?" An old madness played at the edges of its expression. "I've been dreaming of this moment for years."

"Are you certain there's time?" Father Murray asked, gambling yet again. His heart hammered at the underside of his breastbone. *Keep it talking.* "What of the IRA?"

"Oh, young Jack was easy. Sent him home to his girl. Séamus won't be happy, not at all. But in the end, Jack will learn a valuable lesson. If he lives." Mickey shrugged. "You and I have an hour together. Possibly two, before the others get back." He selected a glass vial filled with an evil-looking liquid from the box and set it down on the folding table. "Ah, yes. First this." It reached inside the box and brought out a black leather-sheathed knife. "And this, I think, second." Last, it lifted up a jar for Father Murray to see. Inside, a shiny black beetle scurried for freedom. "And this. This… is for last."

"What is that?"

"A pet brought over from the Other Side," Mickey said. "I call it 'Soul

Eater.' It likes to burrow, you see. Under the skin. Consumes the brain from inside the skull and then works its way out. Slowly. Once this is inside you, it won't matter if they get you to hospital. Surgeon won't know what's wrong, and you won't be able to tell them. On account of you'll be too busy screaming."

"Why are you doing this?"

"Someone has to pay. Of all those I remember from that night, I found you first."

"I didn't have anything to do with what was done to you prior to that night," Father Murray said. "I ended the suffering."

"And I'll end yours, priest. After a time. Provided you beg nicely, of course." Mickey showed him jagged teeth again. "It'll be a mercy."

Father Murray blinked. Mickey knew him better than he wanted to admit, and the time for talking was at an end. He needed to get to the blade at the small of his back. Although his hands were cuffed together, the knife was just within reach of his good left hand if he twisted himself around, but with the cast on his right arm he couldn't do so quickly nor without being obvious about it.

Mickey picked up the vial. "Do you know what this is?"

"I don't." *If I could get it to turn its back, even for a moment—*

"A poison from the Other Side. Didn't ask what's in it. It doesn't matter," Mickey said, stepping closer. "It's the result that counts." It held up the vial. "One drop, and you'll be for drowning in your own sorrow. Let's do an experiment. Like was done on me. Let's see how much of it you can take. Better yet, I wonder what will happen if I feed you the whole thing?"

Father Murray went for the knife, but it caught in the lining of his coat, and Mickey was on him before he could get it free. Father Murray was thrown backward onto the concrete floor. Knife and sheath jabbed into his back. A hot flash of pain opened his mouth wide, but the wind was knocked out of him and no sound came out. Before he could move, Mickey landed on him again. Abandoning the knife, Father Murray swung his right arm, plaster cast and all, into the side of Mickey's face. But there wasn't enough momentum behind the blow due to the healing wound in his shoulder. Mickey dodged the heavy cast. The full force of a head-butt slammed Father Murray in the cheek. Pain detonated inside his skull. He didn't wait for it to fade, or thought he didn't. He bucked his body in an attempt to get Mickey off of him and get the knife free.

A horrible stench filled the air as Mickey uncorked the vial.

"Open your mouth," Mickey said, smashing a fist into Father Murray's jaw.

Again, the pain was terrific. Father Murray was reminded that half demons were physically stronger than humans. Dazed, he watched as if from a distance as the vial came closer. He moved his head, and the contents of the open vial met his cheek. The awful liquid oozed onto his skin in gritty clumps.

Mickey roared curses in frustration.

A compact explosion jarred the building, sending a vibration that could be felt through the concrete floor. Mickey turned. Sensing an opportunity, Father Murray scrabbled for his knife, but the hilt wasn't quite within reach and his torso ached too badly to allow him to twist. He grasped the weapon by the blade. The lining of his coat ripped as he wrenched the weapon free. He registered sharp pain as steel pierced the flesh of his palm and fingers, but there was no time to change his grip. Mickey smashed a hand down on his cheek, smearing the gritty sludge across his face. Father Murray plunged the blade between Mickey's ribs. Scrabbling for the hilt, Father Murray then shoved the blade deeper. Mickey howled in pain and exasperation.

Shouts echoed in the empty warehouse somewhere on the other side of the glass. The door burst open.

"Stop right there!" It was a woman's voice, and American, but it rang with authority.

Mickey punched again. Father Murray felt the blow knock his head back onto the concrete, and his mouth filled with blood and powerful bitterness, making him gag.

A gun went off. The sound was huge. Mickey's forehead and half its face disintegrated in a splash of gore. The force of the bullet toppled the big demon. It fell face-first on top of Father Murray. The remains of Mickey's head landed on the cement with a sickening smack. Eyes stinging, Father Murray shoved at Mickey's body, but he couldn't see or breathe. Strong, slim hands reached to help, and the dead weight shifted.

"Father Murray?"

Father Murray rolled away from the body and vomited. Warm fluid splashed on the icy concrete and splattered on his hands. The open cuts in his left palm and fingers stung something fierce. He jerked his wounded hand out of the muck. Balancing on his knees, he tried to clear his mouth and gagged again. It was almost impossible not to swallow. He didn't dare open his eyes, lest whatever it was that Mickey had attempted to poison him with got into his mucus membranes through his tear ducts. *Hopeless. This is hopeless. It's too late. Why am I bothering?* The thoughts felt foreign and heavy. *I've not much time.* "Water. I need water for my face."

"Ginny! Bring some water."

"Yes, Mother Superior." The second female voice was American as well.

"Sister Catherine?" Father Murray asked.

"Yes?" Sister Catherine asked.

"What are you doing here?" he asked and spat again. He felt the saliva ooze from his lips, tickling his chin as it went. The stink of vomit threatened to make him sick all over again, but the bitter taste of poison and bile faded until he no longer felt the need to gag. Unfortunately, the room appeared to be shifting of its own accord and the hopelessness of the situation intensified. *Not a good sign, he thought. It's too late. Much too late.* It occurred to him that he hadn't been able to accept the sacraments in more than twenty-four hours. He attempted a quick inventory of possible sins but discovered it was too difficult to think. *Oh, Christ. I'm lost.* A strange lethargy set in. Suddenly, he didn't have the energy to remain on his knees. *Nothing matters. I'm done.* He had an urge to lie on the ground and simply stop breathing, but the idea of pressing on the wound in his back seemed horrible.

A hand steadied him. "Don't move. Are you hurt?"

"I've cut my hand. And I've another in my back, but I don't know how bad it is." *The poison. Tell her about the poison.* He opened his mouth to do so, but then he felt her tug up his coat and shirt. Winter air rushed against his bare skin, deepening the pain. He attempted to shove her away. "What are you doing?"

"Assessing the damage. I'm trained as a combat nurse," she said. "Vietnam. Stand still."

"It's nothing."

"Hardly. Three inches higher, a bit deeper, and you'd be short a kidney," she said. "It isn't too bad from what I can tell here. I'll clean it, and get a field dressing on it. What's on your face?"

"Don't touch it. The demon tried to poison me with something infernal."

"Have you swallowed any of it?"

"Indirectly, I think. I can't be sure of how much. It's on my face and in my eyes." The burning sensation crawled down the back of his throat and into his nasal passages. He kept his breathing shallow and spat again. It was futile. *She isn't field trained. She isn't going to know what to do. I'm lost. And time is running out.*

"Mary, please get the holy water and anointing oil from the car. And the Eucharist too. He'll need the full kit as a caution. Hurry. Thank you," Sister Catherine said, the hardness in her voice unrelenting.

She's aware of the procedures at least, Father Murray thought with relief. "I'm so tired."

"You're safe for now," Sister Catherine said. "But we haven't finished securing the warehouse. Do you know how many Fallen are present?"

"I know only of the one," Father Murray said. Speaking was becoming an effort. He felt terrible. Everything hurt. "It's neutralized now. There may be more. I spent most of my time in this room, blindfolded."

He heard movement, and the dead body beside him shifted.

"Here," she said. "I've the handcuff key. It was in its pocket."

"You shot that thing in the head." He felt her remove the cuffs.

"Yes."

"It doesn't upset you?" His hands freed, he massaged feeling back into his wrists.

"Why? I've killed demons before."

He found her bored tone somewhat unsettling. "Has the Archbishop changed his mind about your Order's relationship with Milites Dei?"

"I don't know what you mean," Sister Catherine said, although it was quite clear she did. "The Order of St. Ursula serves in an administrative capacity. Nothing more."

The Order functions as such, as opposed to individual members? "Then what are you doing here?"

"I received a message from a friend stating that you might be found here and that you were in dire need of assistance."

"You informed Bishop Avery? Where are the others?"

"The Order of Milites Dei is currently operating under a truce with the Fey. Since we have no means of making a distinction between the proposed Fey and the Fallen, all active field units have been ordered to cease operations in the area until further notice," she said. "Father, the Bishop doesn't know you're here. Nor is he aware of what we're doing to assist you."

How can that be? We were taken from a café. Then it occurred to him that the RUC had probably been infiltrated by the Fallen. "You're here alone?"

He heard her stifle a derisive laugh. "I'm with two of my sisters and a very good friend who has helped us before. I'd hardly call that alone."

"Have you found Liam?" Kneeling had become too much to bear. He sat on the ice-cold floor. *Lie down. If only I could lie down and not move forever. So tired. What's the use?* His hand and back hurt but that was nothing compared to the ache in his chest. He hadn't understood that emotions could carry so much physical pain. It was hard to breathe. *End it. It has to stop. I could take the gun from her. Put it to my temple and—*

"Our information indicated that Kelly was here. He isn't?"

A door opened and closed. "Mother Superior, I've the water you wanted. I thought he might need a towel as well." The new voice was American and female like the others but much younger.

"Thank you, Ginny. Please check the perimeter and report back."

"Yes, Mother—"

"Call me Catherine when we're outside the Facility. Please. I've told you before."

"Yes, Mother-ma'am."

He used the water to rinse his face, and not long after Sister Mary arrived with soap and water and the rest of the supplies. He used the soap and then washed his face a second time with holy water. With that finished, he finally opened his eyes. To his surprise, he saw that Sister Catherine was dressed in military fatigues.

"Is there a problem?" Sister Catherine asked.

"You're wearing—"

"Trousers? Army surplus? You were expecting us to perform a covert operation dressed in wimples and skirts? Would you?"

"I suppose not."

Father Murray returned to performing the remaining emergency rituals under Sister Catherine's watchful gaze. It was a struggle to work against the crush of despair, and once or twice Sister Catherine reminded him of a missed line. After reciting the appropriate blessings in Latin, he swallowed the Eucharist and a measure of the pain, sadness and lethargy weighing on him faded—although not all of it.

"We should go," he said. "We must ring for more help."

"Weren't you listening?" Sister Catherine asked. "There isn't any help to get. We're it."

"But you aren't field trained—"

She frowned, making her features look older than her thirty years. "Mary, Virginia, and I studied karate at Caltech for three years. Mary and I served together in Vietnam for five years before taking our vows. Under combat conditions, I might add. Virginia earned an Expert badge as a sniper in the U.S. Army at eighteen. Although, the Army refused to deploy her. Their loss is our gain. Mary grew up in Japan and is a Kendo champion. I hold a doctorate in chemistry, but my hobby is small explosives. Is that enough? Or do I need to go on?"

"No need."

"I didn't think so," Sister Catherine said.

The door opened and a sturdy woman in her late twenties with dark skin and an afro entered the room. A curved Japanese katana sheathed in a black scabbard was belted to her waist. "Ginny says no one else is here."

"Are you certain?"

Sister Mary nodded.

Sister Catherine turned and addressed him. "Where are the other men we saw earlier?"

"Gone," Father Murray said. "There may be a bank robbery under way. Their leader coerced Liam Kelly into operating as their driver."

Sister Catherine sighed. "And when will they be back?"

A tall young woman with short red hair ran into the warehouse, opened the door and peered inside. "Mother Superior, a car just drove up. Conor says the one we're looking for is driving."

Chapter 27

Belfast, County Antrim, Northern Ireland
23 December 1977

As Liam stopped the Cortina in the car park behind the warehouse an uneasy feeling settled in. The creature in the back of his mind was restless, but hadn't expressed any dire warnings for a change. *Not in the last few minutes, anyway,* he thought. The Cortina's headlights illuminated the corrugated-steel warehouse wall and the door. He didn't see anyone, but he understood something was wrong. *What is it?* He briefly considered signalling Frankie to stay put, but that would've meant he'd have to explain why. In any case, he couldn't just drive off. He wouldn't leave without Father Murray. Liam watched Séamus, Frankie and Ned climb out of the car while his stomach knotted and fluttered.

When will Séamus make his move now? Or will he wait until the next job? Or am I getting as bad as he is with the paranoia?

"Planning to stay in there all night, Kelly?" Séamus asked.

Liam turned off the Cortina's engine and opened the door. He rested one foot on the tarmac, and the dread worsened. Séamus made his way around the car's hood. He stopped close to the Cortina's side, blocking Liam's path.

"I'll be for having that screwdriver now," Séamus said.

"Do I not have to burn her out?" Liam asked, remaining seated. "She's stolen. We can't leave her here. The RUC or the army—"

"Ned will take care of it. Give us the screwdriver." Séamus held out his hand.

Ned and Frankie stopped, turning around to watch the developing confrontation. Liam swallowed. The beast in the back of his brain began to whisper its customary warnings. The intensity behind the rising paranoia and terror made it hard to focus on the present situation. He rubbed sweat from his palms onto his jeans.

Kill him now. Don't wait. Now. Danger.

I'll not kill again. I won't, Liam thought back.

We're going to die, then.

Liam felt a frown tug at his lips. *No,* I'll *die. There is no fucking* we. *And I don't fucking care.*

I do, the monster murmured. *We must live.*

Why?

"Come on, lad. You've shown us what you're made of. Now, show you can do as you're told."

Must live. Mary Kate, she needs you.

Mary Kate is dead. And I can be with her.

Good luck getting her started again, you bastard. Yanking out the screwdriver, Liam slapped it into Séamus's palm with far more force than was necessary.

Séamus winced but otherwise pretended not to notice. "There's a good lad," he said, stepping aside. "Now, get inside with you."

Liam preferred to wait until Séamus was farther away. The space between the open car door and Séamus wasn't wide enough to suit Liam. Too easy to slip a knife between his ribs. The others wouldn't even see. It'd be too fast. He didn't want Séamus behind him either, but he didn't see a way of avoiding it without another squabble, and Ned and Frankie were staring.

Thought you didn't care about death? the monster thought.

"Give us some room? Don't want to hit you with the fucking door," Liam said, annoyance seeping into his tone.

Séamus shuffled another six inches or so backward.

Liam stood up and thumped his head on the edge of the Cortina's roof.

The pain was short and dull. *If I die, I die.* He slammed the door and headed toward where Frankie and Ned waited. Liam had passed Séamus when he noticed the doorknob was missing from the warehouse door and a sudden movement in the dark to his right drew his attention. Then the distinct click of a pistol safety from behind him brought him up short. Time slowed. Frankie shouted a warning and drew his gun. Ned followed suit. Liam whirled.

Séamus was pointing a pistol at him.

Fuck, Liam thought. *Why is he waiting?*

A shout came from across the car park. "Kill the fucking taigs!"

Séamus turned. Something metallic bounced and thumped into the back bumper of the Cortina with a loud clatter and ding. Liam had enough time to register what it was and take three running steps for cover before he was shoved to the ground by something heavy landing on his back. He fell face-first on the tarmac, biting his tongue and skinning his knee and chin in the process. An explosion lit up the car park. The sound of it was huge. He felt it inside his chest. Then a wave of intense heat rolled over him and whatever it was that had knocked him down. The pressure of the explosion held him there for a moment, crushing the air out of him like the hand of God. Then it was gone with a wind gust, leaving behind an eerie silence. Whatever weighed him down moved, and Liam was finally able to roll onto his side. Flames consumed what remained of the Cortina, lighting everything and everyone in an eerie red-orange glow. Chunks of burning steel rebounded on the tarmac in silence. Séamus thrashed on the ground in a feeble attempt to put out his clothes and hair.

Liam looked away. *Bad way to go, that.* His nose filled with a noxious mix of spent explosive, hot steel, petrol, rot, and burning flesh. It was too late for Séamus, even if Liam had wanted to help, and he wasn't entirely certain he did. Five men with hunched backs dressed in army fatigues charged across the car park with an assortment of pistols, rifles and knives. It all happened in the absolute quiet of a silent film.

Loyalists? Liam thought, confused. He breathed in a second time. *Is that decay I smell?*

Danger. Move. Now! Must live, the monster in his skull snarled. *Fallen.*

Liam started to get up, but something fuzzy and huge thumped him in the back. Twisting his torso, he spied one hundred-fifty pounds of shaggy black Irish wolfhound.

"Da?" Liam asked. His voice resonated strangely inside his own skull, unable to escape the oppressive quiet.

The big black hound blinked with one eye and then bounded over him, attacking an approaching Fallen. Liam watched as the hound—his father—downed the creature and ripped at its face and chest. He felt small bursts of air flit past. For an instant he thought they were insects. *Those are bullets, you idiot.* He got to his feet in a crouch. Muffled sounds drifted slowly back into the picture, his father's furious snarls mixed with the Fallen's screaming and staccato bursts of gunfire which punctured the warehouse wall.

"Liam! Over here!" It was Frankie. He'd taken cover behind a row of steel barrels positioned not far from the warehouse door.

Ned was lying on the ground, twitching. Half his head was a bleeding mess. Liam scurried toward Frankie, pausing to check on Ned first. Taking the man's pulse, Liam kept his head down as live rounds pierced the wall inches above. Ned convulsed one last time and was gone.

"So sorry, mate," Liam whispered. "I'll get word to your family." He closed Ned's eyelids and suddenly realized he didn't know if Ned had a family.

A powerful stench caused Liam to look up.

One of the Fallen stood over him with a 9mm Browning. Liam's heart stumbled.

"You and the priest are done, you hear? Die, taig." The creature's finger tightened on the trigger.

A shot went off, and a black dot appeared on the Fallen's cheek. It staggered and then dropped to the ground. Liam pushed the thing away from Ned's body and then spied the abandoned guns. Grabbing both, Liam checked each.

"Liam! Get the fuck over here!" Frankie reloaded his pistol. "I can't hold them off you forever. Not from here."

Frankie will need the ammunition. Liam paused. "Sorry, mate. No disrespect to you, you understand." He went through Ned's pockets until he found the extra ammo. He counted two dead Fallen lying on the ground. Both shot. A third dropped as it attempted to make its way to him.

"Liam, stop arsing around! I mean it!"

Two Fallen remained, but Bran was giving them a seeing to. With all the noise, the RUC or the army would be sure to show soon.

Father Murray, Liam thought. *Where is he?* He left Ned's body and scrambled to where Frankie was waiting.

"Where the fuck did the Loyalists come from?" Frankie asked, shooting at shadows.

They aren't fucking Loyalists, Liam thought as he reloaded Ned's pistol with fresh ammunition. "Stupid question, mate. You do know where the fuck we are, right?"

"Shite! What's that?"

A second, lighter-colored Irish wolfhound bounded across the car park. Bran was now flanked by the remaining Fallen. One had its back to Liam, Frankie and Sceolán. Liam watched as Sceolán lunged at the back of the Fallen's ankle, ripping the tendon. The Fallen howled, turned and staggered. Sceolán was on top of him in an instant. Bran tore at the body of the other Fallen, but something drew his attention, and he ceased worrying at the body, blood dripping from his muzzle.

"Who keeps dogs like that? Fucking monsters, they are," Frankie said, aiming at Sceolán.

Liam shoved Frankie's pistol arm. "Don't. They're killing the ones that attacked us." He was reluctant to call the Fallen Loyalists. "I'm thinking we leave them to it."

Frankie stared at Bran and Sceolán as they finished off the Fallen. "Are they Republicans, do you think?"

"You planning on asking them their politics?"

Frankie shook his head.

Liam stood up. "We should get Father Murray and then do a runner before the Peelers arrive."

An explosion at the front of the warehouse lit up the night sky. Liam sprinted for the door. Frankie wasn't long behind. A chill passed through Liam. *Should've thought of Father Murray sooner. Am I too late?* The moment he was inside, Liam saw the first of the rolling doors was half gone—a warped, gaping hole in the middle. A number of Fallen had entered through the ragged hole. Three women he didn't recognize—two white and one black—dressed in army fatigues fought the Fallen side by side. The black woman carried a curved sword, and the other two women had pistols. One was older and the other might have been the tall, athletic redhead from Daft Kevin's party. They weren't alone in holding the Fallen back. A young man with blond hair wielded a long sword with long-practiced ease and skill. The polished blade reflected light from the now burning warehouse as it beheaded the enemy, making the sword look as if it were on fire. The Fallen tumbled in a gout of dark and stinking gore. The smoke filling the inside of the warehouse thickened as the flames spread.

Frankie slowed to a stop and then aimed his pistol.

Sword, Liam thought and grabbed Frankie's arm. *I've only seen*— Liam recognized the jacket the young man with the sword was wearing. Then everything snapped into place when the young man turned his head. *Conor?* "Frankie, don't shoot!"

"Why?"

"They're friends," Liam said, searching the battle for Father Murray and not finding him. "Where's Father Murray? Do you see him? We need to get him out of here. Before the whole fucking place goes up."

One of the Fallen broke free of the fight. It started across the floor to the opposite wall, spied them and then changed course. The thing growled and charged at Liam. Frankie fired his Beretta, knocking the demon back. Liam counted three shots before the creature dropped. Liam knew it wasn't dead. He'd seen what had happened at Raven's Hill. In each case, the wounded fallen angel had to be burned or blessed by a member of Father Murray's Order, or they regenerated after a time.

Liam turned his head and eyed the rear door with its blasted handle. *How long do we have?*

"Hope you're right about the others being friends," Frankie said. "Because I've some bad news, mate." He used his pistol again when the Fallen showed signs of moving. The thing twitched with each shot. The blasts were lost in the sounds of battle. "I've two bullets left."

Liam pulled Ned's Beretta from his pocket and offered the freshly loaded pistol to Frankie. "Will this do?"

"Aye." Frankie checked it and nodded. "Back to work."

Searching again for Father Murray, Liam saw the woman with the short red hair fall. He pointed to her. "Frankie! Cover her!"

Frankie didn't hesitate. He turned and targeted the nearby Fallen before it could finish her off. To his amazement, Liam saw her sit up and resume firing. He wasn't sure how long she could stay conscious. She was losing a lot of blood.

"Where are you going?" Frankie asked.

"We have to get her out of there." Liam ran to the red-haired woman. "She's wounded."

"You'll be shot!"

For a moment Liam felt a similar joy running through the battle as he did the driving. *Is it the danger?* he thought, feeling a bullet buzz past. By some miracle, he made it to her side without getting hit. He crouched beside her. "Miss?" He sensed Frankie gunning down those that fired at them.

She started and swung the pistol around and pointed it at him. Her lips were pressed together in a grimace of pain. Her eyes were watering from either the smoke or the bullet wound.

"Don't! I'm here to help you!"

She blinked. "You're Liam Kelly?" she asked in an American accent.

"I am," Liam said. "Let's get you out of harm's way." He looked down and saw she'd been shot in the left thigh.

She laughed and then coughed. "Being in harm's way is sort of the point." She reloaded her gun and winced. Her bravado cost her, that was apparent by the paleness of her face.

"Do you know where Father Murray is?" Liam asked.

Indicating the room where the priest had been held prisoner with a nod, she said, "In there. He's wounded but safe."

"You're going to bleed to death," Liam said. He crouched, getting a shoulder under hers. She stifled a cry of pain, but she let him help. "Frankie, we're leaving."

"Where to?" Frankie asked.

Liam said, "Father Murray is in that room. The one where he was being held." The woman didn't seem to weigh much as he helped her limp across the concrete.

"Right." Frankie followed, covering their progress.

Peering through the glass before entering, Liam could see the priest lying on the mattress Séamus had provided. A blanket was draped over him, and he was shivering. The blindfold and the handcuffs were gone, but his eyes were closed, and he looked sick.

Liam awkwardly pushed through the door. "Father?"

Wincing, Father Murray slowly shifted onto his side and then sat up. "Liam?"

Frankie positioned himself near the door.

"This place is burning down. The RUC or the army can't be far off. Time to go," Liam said and lowered the young woman to the floor.

Once she was settled, she got out her pistols and ammunition and began reloading. Something about her fierce efficiency reminded him of Ceara, and if he hadn't spent what had seemed like weeks training under her watchful eye, Liam would've felt less sure of the redhead with the mod bob. He took off his belt.

"What do you think you're doing?" the woman asked.

"Tourniquet. Have to slow the bleeding," Liam said, kneeling down and then wrapping the belt around her wounded leg. "Who are you? And what are you and Conor doing here?"

"Helping you," she said and flinched as he tightened the belt around her thigh. "My name is Sister Ginny."

Liam paused. "Sister?"

"You're a nun?" Frankie asked, gaping.

"If you can accept soldier-priests why not combat nuns?" she asked, frowning.

"What?" Frankie asked and then glanced at Father Murray.

I'm touching a nun's bare—don't even think about it. Not now. Liam turned to Father Murray. "Conor is part of your Order, Father?"

"Conor isn't part of any Order. He's a friend," Sister Ginny said.

A friend, Liam thought. *What kind of friend?* "I need a knife to cut a notch in the belt."

"It's in my patch pocket," Sister Ginny said, fumbling with the buttoned pocket on her right thigh.

"Hold this tight, then." Liam accepted the knife from her and got to work on the belt. "Can you get far on foot do you think, Father?"

"I'm not sure," Father Murray said.

Liam heard a door thump.

"Liam?" Frankie asked.

"Aye?"

"We've got company," Frankie said. "Two men. Never seen them before. One looks like a fucking hippie."

"Oh, aye? Is he a big blond fucker? And the other has black hair like mine?"

"Aye, mate. They're headed this way."

"That'll be my uncle Sceolán and my da." Liam took the belt end from Sister Ginny and set the belt buckle to the new notch. Finished with the tourniquet, he stood up to get a view of the main room. Smoke made visibility out the front of the warehouse almost impossible. Bran and Sceolán were at the door.

"That's your da?" Frankie asked.

"Frankie will help you, Father," Liam said. "We'll go out the back."

Father Murray nodded. "Ginny, where are the others?"

Ginny said, "Holding off the Fallen, Father."

Bran and Sceolán entered, both coughing.

Liam sat back on his heels and started re-loading Frankie's pistol. "Hello, Da."

Bran said, "This place isn't safe."

"You're Liam's real da?" Frankie was clearly trying to keep focused on the battle but was having some trouble.

"Da, this is Frankie," Liam said. "He's the one I told you about before."

"You told him about me?" Frankie asked.

"I told him enough," Liam said.

Ginny checked the tourniquet and nodded satisfied. "Not bad for a demon."

"I'm not a—"

"I know." She smiled and put out a hand. "Officially, I'm Sister Lara Virginia Toner. But you can call me Ginny."

Liam blinked and then took her hand.

The muffled cry of sirens filtered through the glass.

"If we're leaving, we should get about it," Frankie said, turning away from the door and running over to Father Murray. "Peelers are here."

Liam snapped the clip into place and got up. He handed off the pistol and the remaining ammunition to Frankie.

Frankie said, "I'm going along with this for now. But once it's done I've a great number of questions for you, mate."

Liam gave him a reassuring look. "I imagine you will."

"Just so's we're clear." Frankie helped Father Murray to his feet.

Liam returned to Sister Ginny. "You're going unarmed?" Ginny asked.

"I am. But that doesn't mean I won't help you lot do what has to be done." Liam lifted her from the ground using his shoulder again. Once again the thought that he was touching a nun passed uncomfortably through his mind. "Ready, Frankie?"

"Aye."

With Frankie, Bran and Sceolán watching their backs, they hobbled to the back door. The other two women and Conor retreated, meeting them. All were coughing and covered in soot.

"What happened? Where are the Fallen?" Sister Ginny asked.

"They retreated when they heard the police sirens," the black woman said. "Ginny, you okay?"

"I'm fine for now."

Liam managed to get himself and Ginny through the back door without injuring her further. Frankie, Father Murray, the other two nuns and Conor weren't far behind. Uncertain where they'd go, Liam knew there wasn't much time to get away. He had to think of somewhere fast. He wasn't sure if his da would be willing to take so many mortals to the Other Side, but he didn't see much choice. The Peelers were sure to think of covering the back of the warehouse soon enough.

"Stop right there!"

Lifting his gaze from the tarmac, the sight of ten Fallen clustered in a semi-circle brought Liam up short. Most of them hadn't bothered to disguise themselves—their burned, cracked skin, hunched backs and flaming eyes were unmistakable. Among their number was the big blond named Jensen. Liam's chest tightened. He heard Frankie gasp. The stench was awful, and Liam was glad he wasn't stuck in an enclosed space with them. In the shadows behind the tallest, Liam sensed the presence of another entity but couldn't get a good view.

Frankie stumbled beside him and whispered, "What the fuck are those things?"

"Fallen angels. I'd recommend keeping quiet and not drawing their attention, if I were you," Ginny said in a low voice.

"I've been thinking about what I'd say to you when we finally met without disguises or ruses," the tallest Fallen said. "I've been thinking for years."

"Don't believe a damned thing that creature says," the black nun said.

Liam's eyes narrowed. "The Peelers are here," he said. "The time for the big speeches is done, don't you think?"

The tall one's appearance flickered between various parishioners from St. Agnes's in Belfast and St. Brendan's in Derry. "The priest isn't the only one who's been watching you, half-breed."

"Who the fuck are you? And what do you want?" Liam asked.

"As you have most astutely pointed out, we've unwelcome company on the way." The creature stepped forward. Its movements were a cross between a bird's and a lizard's. Graceful and halting at the same time. Its head twitched to the side. "You may call me Samuel."

"That isn't who you are," Conor said.

The creature calling itself Samuel rattled off a string of Latin that Liam didn't understand. The sound of Samuel's words did unpleasant things in Liam's mind, turning his stomach and stirring up rage, terror and violation. Shuddering, he swallowed a need to retch. Next to him, Frankie bent double and coughed. Ginny clamped her hands over her ears. None of the words made sense. Liam had never learned Latin. He'd had enough trouble with Irish and English. However, he recognized one word from the masses he'd attended as a child. It was "angelus."

Conor said something in Latin and then shrugged. "Go on, then."

"I'm here to make you an offer," the creature called Samuel said.

"Me? Why?" Liam asked, still struggling with anger. "I'm nothing. A fucking half-breed Fey. Aye?"

"They wish to bring an end to negotiations between the Church and the Fey," Conor said. "You've caused them considerable worry with your truce."

"True enough," Mary said.

Samuel glared at Conor, and Liam braced himself for another long string of foul Latin. "What would you say if I told you I could give you back your wife, half mortal?"

"I'd say you can't," Liam said.

"You don't really believe that, do you?" Samuel asked and made a motion with his hand. The figure that Liam had sensed moved from the darkness behind the row of Fallen. It was Mary Kate.

The sight of her standing in the ordinary car park hit him like an army Saracen. For a moment he couldn't breathe and all the blood in his body drained to his feet. He was cold, and all the weariness and hurt descended upon him at once.

"Liam?" Dressed in the torn white dress he'd seen before in his dreams, she held out her arms. "Is that you?"

He'd taken five steps toward her before he knew it.

"Don't!" It was Father Murray. "It's not her! It can't be!"

Liam stopped. "He's right. It isn't you." But the denial was uncertain in his throat.

"It's me," she said.

"All we ask," Samuel said, "is that you walk away. Do this, and she's yours again."

"What's the catch?" Liam asked. "There's always a catch with you lot. Isn't there?"

Samuel paused.

Conor said, "I told you it wouldn't work."

"Conor, what's going on?" Liam asked.

"We'll be together," she said. "That's all that matters."

"Will we?" Liam asked.

"Decide. Now," Samuel said.

Liam felt he was being torn apart. He knew she couldn't be real. It wasn't possible. He took another hesitant step toward her and reached out. He wanted to touch her to be sure. *One more time.*

"No!" Samuel swung a powerful hand at Liam.

But it was too late. Liam's fingertips brushed Mary Kate's cheek. Her skin was ice-cold and gritty like ash. He got the sense of filthy feathers and his nose filled with the stench of rot. Mary Kate's mouth opened, producing a piercing raptor scream. Then Samuel's fist rammed into Liam's face, sending Liam stumbling backward.

Liam didn't think. The sharp tingling sensation which signaled a transformation poured over him in seconds. Before he knew it, he'd become the Hound—a form he'd not dared to take in months. The experience had changed. Instead of feeling as if he were peering out of a mask, the monster's—*no, creature's*—body was more his own. He was conscious that Frankie was near and could see him shouting obscenities in shock and fear. Normally that would've mattered, but now it wasn't important. During the change, Liam registered that the Fallen had fired their guns. The wind of the passing bullets brushed his fur. Somewhere window glass shattered. Liam charged Samuel. Lowering his head, he barreled into the creature. The move knocked Samuel down. He landed on top of the fallen angel. Outraged that they would dare to impersonate someone he cared about, Liam howled. Like the gunfire, the sound of it expanded huge into the night air. His anger pressed against his eardrums. Tearing at the Fallen to keep it from getting up, his mouth filled with shreds of gritty cloth and an acrid and foul taste. Fetid reek penetrated his throat and skull. It turned his stomach, and he forced himself not to retch. He understood that someone was screaming. He felt Samuel clamp down on his wrist—*paw.* Liam checked an urge to tear its throat out. *I can't kill it. I won't.*

They're evil, the monster whispered in a voice that seemed more his own. *They don't matter.*

That isn't the point, Liam thought back, locking his jaws on the Fallen's arm in order to free himself. *I matter. My word matters.*

Samuel jerked its arm free, tearing cloth and skin on Liam's teeth.

"Liam! Get back!"

Silver flashed in an arc. Something slammed into his back, and he was crushed against Samuel. Someone landed a forceful kick in his side, and he was knocked off his paws. Crushing pain descended upon him, taking away any chance at oxygen. He lay on his side, stunned. He thought he saw Conor standing over him, but Liam knew it couldn't be Conor. This Conor was robed in a warm, bright light that made Liam's eyes hurt. More silver flashed. Someone shouted in Latin. One of the Fallen in a terrible voice filled with hate and filth. It was answered with a loud war cry in Irish.

"Fág an bealach!" *Clear the way!*

And then the pain in his back became too much and a numbing darkness swallowed him.

Chapter 28

The Other Side
24 December 1977, Christmas Eve

L iam woke to terrible pain and an argument. Bits of other information filtered through to consciousness. He was no longer in the
middle of a battle or even the car park outside the warehouse. He
was lying on his stomach. Lumps of soft cloth were wedged against his
body, cheeks and neck—each seemed to be supporting his head and body
in a particular alignment.

"Damn it. We shouldn't have moved him." It was a stern woman's voice.
She had an American accent like Sister Ginny's, but her voice was deeper.
"His spine may be injured."

"And what were we to do? Leave him for the Peelers to murder? They'd
have put a bullet in his skull and then swore he was shooting back!"

That was Frankie, Liam was sure of it. *He's safe,* he thought, relieved.
That's good. His legs were tingling.

"He should be in a hospital, not a tent in the middle of—"

"You've no understanding of what you're about, woman," Bran said.
"He's one of us. He'll heal, or he won't. The Goddess will decide. It's bad
enough we've kept him here. He should be outside with the others. Leave
him be."

326

"I don't know what you think you're doing. You can't heal severed nerves with herbs and mud poultices. In fact, you can't heal them at all," the stern woman with the deep voice said. "He should be dead after a blow like that. He'll be lucky if he can walk after this."

"He'll walk," Bran said, but Liam sensed a hint of doubt. "He's my son."

"Then get out of my way and let me get the bleeding stopped," the stern woman said. "Or let Mary do it."

Someone touched him and another sharp pain exploded in his back, raced up his spine and lodged itself inside his skull. "Oh, Jesus! Oh, fuck!" He gasped for air but every breath only made the pain worse. Hands held him down—shoulders, arms, legs, head. With the lumps of cloth so close to his face he couldn't see.

"Don't move!"

He yanked an arm free, but someone grabbed his hand and forced it down. "Get this shite off me! I can't breathe! Fuck!"

"I said, don't move!"

"He needs morphine. I'll get it." It was another woman—not Sister Ginny. Liam guessed it was Sister Mary.

"And what is that?" Bran asked.

"Da, please," Liam said through clenched teeth. He shook with the force it took to keep from screaming. "Oh, fuck it hurts!"

"All right, then," Bran said.

Liam didn't even feel the needle. The tiny pain was lost in the roaring of his nerve endings. Breathing through his teeth, he shivered as he waited for the pain to abate.

"Get a blanket on him. He's going into shock," the stern woman said. "What is that? Is it even clean?"

She's a bold one, Liam thought.

"It's clean enough," Bran said, the anger clear in his tone.

"Please, Sister Catherine." Father Murray sounded strange and a bit distant. "Don't make enemies of the Fey. We've worked very hard to form a positive—"

"You're right, Father. I'm very sorry. You did us a favor, bringing us here like you did. We owe you a debt. It's just that all this is so... sudden," Sister Catherine said and then let out a deep breath. "I don't suppose it'd be possible for you to check on Sister Ginny for me? Her leg needs a fresh bandage, and Mary is seeing to Father Murray."

"You're only trying to get me out," Bran said.

Sceolán said, "You are a wee bit in the way."

Bran replied with something rude in Irish.

"Let the woman do what she must, aye?" Sceolán asked. "You've done what you can for him."

Liam heard a sigh and then he felt a blanket drop onto him.

"Liam?" Sister Catherine asked in a whisper. "Can you feel your legs?"

"Aye." The pain wasn't gone, exactly, but it was beginning to feel more remote. "Can you take this shite off my face already? I can't see."

"I'm afraid not. Not yet. Don't try to move," she said. "I'm going to touch you, and I want you to tell me where you feel it. Okay?" Sister Catherine went through a series of checks—arms, hands, legs and feet. At the end of it she sounded relieved—that is, until he told her about the tingling. Nonetheless, she agreed to remove the cloths that anchored his head in place, and he was able to shift into a more comfortable position.

"Try to get some sleep," she said and then went away.

It wasn't long after that when Frankie appeared on the edge of his vision. "Are you all right, mate?"

"I'll do."

"You look fucking terrible."

"Aye, well. So would you, if someone tried to cut you in half."

Frankie paused. "I should go."

"Don't. Please. I'm not sleepy. I'll be dead bored with no one to talk to."

"All right," Frankie said, sitting on the ground close by. "You know, someone should explain what nuns are to your uncle."

"Why?"

"Because he's been chatting up Sister Ginny and Sister Mary both since we arrived," Frankie said. "And I haven't had the heart to tell him he doesn't stand a fucking chance."

"He'll work it out, I'm thinking," Liam said. "Either that or they'll shoot him. Either way, why spoil the fun?"

"Pound says Sister Catherine shoots him first."

"My money is on Sister Ginny."

"You're on."

"What happened at the warehouse?" Liam asked. "After I was hit. I don't remember much."

"Your father's people came just like you said they would," Frankie said. "Never seen anything like it. Those things, the Fallen, they rabbited off. Then the Peelers came, and your da and uncle sent all of us here."

"You seem to be coping with it rather well," Liam said.

"Been talking to Father Murray and the sisters a wee bit," Frankie said. "They've explained a few things. Still not entirely sure of any of it. Sounds fucking mad, but I don't know what else to make of it. I'm half certain I'll wake up in hospital tomorrow. The mental ward, I'm thinking."

"I suppose it takes a wee bit of getting used to." *Is it Christmas Eve?* Liam didn't want to look at his watch. He didn't want to move. *Hell, I don't want to know.*

Frankie nodded. "Are you still hurting?"

It's near enough to Christmas Eve, Liam thought. "Not as much."

"Should I get someone?"

"Why are you in such a hurry to go?" Liam asked.

Frankie shrugged. "I'm worried for you, mate. And I don't know what to say. Aye?"

"I'll do, I said."

"I wouldn't be so sure. This isn't a broken arm or a bullet in a kneecap. It's your fucking spine. Sister Catherine says—"

"Da is right. She doesn't understand how we work," Liam said. "I'll be on my feet tomorrow. You'll see." *So I hope,* Liam thought.

"It's true then?"

"What is?"

"You're one of them. You're a…" Frankie lowered his voice. "…a púca?"

"Aye. Half, anyway."

"Why didn't you… Why didn't I know until now?"

Liam resisted an urge to shrug. *Would you have believed me if I had told you?* "Didn't know myself until recently."

"Oh." Frankie paused.

"What happened to Henry, Davy and the others? And what about that teller and his family? Have you heard?"

"Henry, Davy and the rest were lifted. Fucking overheard it on Séamus's radio. The teller's wee family are safe, I'm thinking."

"Good. About the family," Liam said. "Sorry about Henry and the others."

"Fucking hope Henry can keep his gob shut."

"You shouldn't have to worry, mate. You're far out of it. Peelers won't be for finding you as long as you're here."

"Shite," Frankie said. "This is real."

"Aye. It is."

"You're one of them."

"Aye," Liam said with a yawn. "I am."

Frankie paused. "Well, then. I respectfully take back what I said about you cheating at cards."

Liam was sleepy at last. "I cheated."

"I fucking knew it! How did you do it? Magic, aye? You predicted the future?"

"Was magic, right enough," Liam said and let his eyelids close. "Saw your cards reflected in the fucking window behind you."

Chapter 29

The Derry street Liam found himself standing on had been abandoned about six months ago. He walked with Mary Kate in afternoon shadows cast by empty and broken council houses. Their shattered windows stared down at him like fractured eyes. One or two of the places were burned out. British troops loitered on the corner. Somewhere high above several helicopters flew past. Rubble littered the narrow street.

"That was a stupid thing you did, Liam Kelly," Mary Kate said. Her tone was brimming with admonishment and pride.

Liam was uncertain how to react. Walking with his hand in Mary Kate's, he glanced up at the afternoon sky. It was good to be home. He took in a deep breath of free clean air. He'd been away from Long Kesh for one whole day. On one hand, he couldn't believe his luck. Mary Kate had rung him the moment she'd heard he'd returned, and now, here he was walking with her. On the other hand, before he'd been lifted she'd agreed to go steady with him, but now he was sure she'd return his I.D. bracelet. He was an internee after all—a criminal. His former classmates stayed clear of him, not that they'd been all that friendly before. And as if that weren't enough, Patrick had made his thoughts known on the subject by persisting in calling him "Jailbird." So it was that the worry that this might be the last time he'd hold Mary Kate's hand cast a cloud over Liam's joy at seeing her. He couldn't help but be confused. When they'd talked on the

331

phone she'd all but called him a hero. However, now that he saw her he began to have his doubts. She was acting a wee bit strange—*nervous*—as if she had news for him she didn't think he'd like.

She's seeing someone else, aye? That's why she's taken me down this street. She wants to break it off with me in private-like. He supposed he should be thankful she'd not done it in a letter while he was in prison.

"You might have gone and crippled yourself for life," she said. "You'll have to be careful when you wake."

He didn't know what it was she was on about. Largely, it didn't matter. She could be worse than his mother with the worry sometimes.

He glanced down at her. She was so bloody beautiful. She could be with anyone. He didn't understand what she saw in him—even for the short time they'd been together. He'd quit school, being too stupid to finish. Her, she was brilliant. She'd go on to Uni one day. She was still wearing her school uniform—black blazer, white blouse and black pleated skirt, but she'd taken off the striped tie and unbuttoned her blouse to the fourth button in spite of the cold. Such a thing was a simple rebellion and one common enough. Some girls were known to roll up the waistbands of their skirts so that the hem ended above the knee.

All at once, it occurred to him that if he tilted his head just so, he could see underneath Mary Kate's blouse without her noticing. It was a nice view. The wind picked up, and opened her collar wide. He caught a glimpse of dark pink cresting the top of her left breast beneath the semi-transparent lace of her bra.

She pulled her coat shut.

His jeans suddenly felt tighter. It never took much to get him going when it came to Mary Kate. It never had. One glimpse and more than anything he wished she'd let him reach inside her shirt to touch that breast. She'd let him do it before Long Kesh. He remembered it well. The memory had practically been seared onto his brain. It was one of those moments he'd played over and over in his mind during his stay at the internment camp. But now—

They'll know you for a fairy.

"Are you listening to me?" she asked.

"Aye."

She turned her head to look up at him; a faint smile played on her lips.

"No, you're not listening. You were staring down my blouse."

He blushed and pulled his gaze up to her forehead. He couldn't bring himself to look her in the eye. "I am not."

"You were too," she said, placing a hand on her hip. "How many times have I told you? I'm not that kind of girl."

He dropped her hand. She'd tell him now. Any second she'd take off that cheap bracelet he'd given her, and that'd be the end.

"I'm so sorry," she said and lowered her voice. "I didn't mean to upset you."

He swallowed and lifted his chin. "You didn't."

"Something is wrong," she said. "You're different."

I can see it in you. Anyone can. It's easy enough. He shut the sights, smells and sounds from Long Kesh out of his mind. His stomach did a sickening flip.

"You look like you've seen a ghost," she said.

He shook his head. He couldn't say a word, or it'd all come spilling out, and if he went and did that she'd leave him for sure. Worse, she might tell someone else. He felt her tug his arm. *Monster. It's a monster, I am. Unnatural.*

"Stop it," she said.

"I didn't do anything."

"It's cold," she said with a sigh. "Let's go inside for a bit. Here. This place will do."

Stunned, he let her lead him through the half-boarded-up doorway of one of the derelict houses. Their feet crunched on broken glass and grit in the gloom. She took him to one of the back rooms. He could see the remains of a weed-choked garden through the broken window. It was a bit warmer but not by much. *At least the walls keep the wind off.* He looked around for a place to sit. His heart sped up a few more notches. He wasn't sure why she'd taken him here. It was the sort of place kids went when they wanted to sniff glue or have sex.

She's not that kind of girl.

"Stay right there," she said. "Just for a moment."

He did as she asked, struggling with his rising blood and galloping imagination. When she returned he saw she was carrying a folded blanket, and his heart suffered a jolt. He was shaking and prayed she couldn't see it. *She's not that kind of girl.*

"I—I thought we might like something to sit on," she said. "I brought this here yesterday. When I heard you were back."

"Oh." *She's been planning this?*

He watched her spread the blanket on the dirty floor. Then she sat down and patted the space next to her. "Come. Lay down for a moment. It'll be nice."

His heart drummed a rapid tattoo against his sternum, and his stomach felt cold. Afraid she'd take hesitation as an insult, he threw himself down and winced as he landed harder than he'd intended. He sorted himself out into a more comfortable position and accidentally kicked her. "I'm sorry. I—"

She leaned over and kissed him long and hard. Her hair made a curtain around his face, blocking out the shabby room. Her lips were soft and warm. After a while her tongue brushed against his.

Christ, that's wonderful, he thought. *Better than I remembered.* His hand was inside her blouse before he knew it. She moaned with her mouth on his. Then he pulled her closer and kissed her throat, edging lower.

"Liam."

Oh, please don't make me stop, he thought. His face was an inch from the edge of her bra. She smelled wonderful—soap and salt and some sort of spice he couldn't place. He waited, not moving. *Please. Let me go on this time. Please. Just a wee bit more.* If he could kiss that breast just once, he knew it'd be the most wonderful thing that'd ever happened to him. What would it taste like? How would her nipple feel against his tongue? He paused. "Aye?"

"I want to do something. With you. I want it more than anything in the world, but—" She paused and moved back. "I don't want you to think badly of me."

"Oh, Mary Kate. I'd never—"

She placed a finger on his lips. He resisted an urge to kiss it.

"I'm going to let you… I want you to…." She looked away, bit her lip and then started to unbutton her blouse.

Paralysed, he couldn't do anything but watch. He was afraid to breathe or move lest she come to her senses. *This can't be happening. I'm fucking dreaming.*

He blinked and swallowed. She untucked her blouse and pulled it open so that he could see her chest. She was wearing a white lace bra. If he didn't know any better, he'd have said it was new.

Oh, Jesus. Oh, Christ. It's happening. She's going to let me—

"You won't tell anyone will you?" she asked. "I'm not, you know, like that. It's just I want to be with you. No one else. Only you. Do you understand?"

He nodded.

"Swear you'll not tell."

"I swear, Mary Kate. Not a soul. I swear on my Gran's grave."

"Your Grandma? She's not dead."

"The other one."

"Oh." Mary Kate took off her blouse and then her bra, and he saw her bare breasts for the first time. She looked nothing like the women in the magazine photos that Hugh and Tom had sold. Her breasts were more round and set apart, not as big, and her nipples were small and pink. She sat there, topless and blushing while he stared. Her gaze was fixed to the blanket. "Well? Am I… am I all right, you think?"

"You're beautiful." It sounded so stupid gushing out of him like that. Beautiful wasn't anywhere close to describing what she was, but he was stupid and slow, and he didn't have the words. He never did and never would.

"I am?" She smiled at the blanket, pleased. She caught her lower lip in her teeth again. "I'm cold. Will you… will you hold me?"

He got up his courage, wrapped his arms around her and then kissed her. Finally, he risked letting his hand drift to her bare breast, reveling in the texture of her skin under his palm. She didn't stop him or pull away. Before long they were lying on the blanket together. Hesitant, he let his hand drift lower. She laughed.

He withdrew his hand. "Did I do something wrong?"

"No. Not at all."

Then she did something he never expected. She unbuttoned the top of his jeans and plunged her hand inside. He stopped breathing at once. A bolt of terror pinned him to the broken floor. He grabbed her hand and pushed her away. "Don't."

"What's wrong?" she asked.

He rolled onto his back and closed his eyes. The fear was terrible. He wanted to run. *Have to.* The knowledge that he'd never touch her again if he did was the only thing anchoring him to the floor.

She said, "I thought you'd wanted me to—"

"Don't."

"Don't what?" she asked.

"Don't touch me. Not like that."

She blinked and sat up. "Why not? I don't understand. What's wrong?"

I'm doing it wrong, he thought. *Jesus Christ, I'm ruining everything. I can't do this. There's something wrong with me. She'll know. She'll see. There's—*

"I shouldn't have," she said. "I'm so sorry."

He sat up. "No. I'm the one who's sorry, Mary Kate. I don't want to make a mess of this. I want this. I want you. But—"

"Shhh." She sat on his lap and then snuggled in closer, hugging him. "It's all right. But we have to talk about this."

He didn't know what to do. The fear was back, and it was overwhelming. He was afraid that Saunders, the things that—

There. Open that sweet mouth. Slowly. Don't—

—happened would intrude. He felt sick and angry. *It's always going to fucking be like this.*

There's something wrong with me. There always will be.

"It's all right. You're all right," she said again, smoothing her hand through his hair. "I'm here."

Liam's breath hitched. *I'll not cry. I'll not shame myself.*

It was at that moment that he knew something wasn't right. This wasn't how it had been that first time. They'd made love with their clothes on that day—well, as much as they could manage—and with the blanket covering them. It'd been too cold and uncomfortable to do it any other way. And the truth of it was, he'd been too frightened of what she'd see.

"You're dreaming you know." Her face was warm against his chest.

"I am?"

"You are," she said. "And you need to talk to me. Now."

"I do?"

"Tell me what happened."

"What do you mean?"

"Long Kesh," she said, hugging him tighter as if to trap him. "I want you to tell me about Long Kesh."

"I can't."

"You can. You must."

"Why?"

"Because if you don't it will unravel you. You'll go mad," she said.

And Bran will do for me. He'll have to, or I'll murder everyone.

"I can't let that happen," she said. "You have to tell someone. So tell me."

"No, Mary Kate. I'll not speak of it."

"Whatever it is they did to you. It's something terrible. I can tell." She pressed closer, if that were possible. "But it'll be all right, you know. It won't matter. Not to me. It never did. I love you exactly as you are. I always will. You never understood that, did you?"

His chest began to ache and his vision blurred. "Why did you have to die?"

"I didn't want to."

"I know. Shhhh." He touched her face.

"I didn't—I didn't mean to—I'm so sorry about the baby." Tears slid down her cheeks. "Oh, Christ, that wasn't how I wanted to say it at all."

He smoothed the tears away and that's when he noticed the scars on her face, around her mouth. "It's all right, love."

"You hate me. I killed our baby."

"I could never hate you."

She sniffed. "Never?"

"Never. The babe... well... you did what you thought you had to. I understand that now."

She began to sob. "I was so scared."

"I know. I was too."

She blinked up at him. "You were?"

"You were so sick. Was terrified you were going to die," he said. "And there was nothing I could do to help." Ultimately, that's exactly what had happened, but he pushed away the thought.

"You were angry with me," she said. "I don't blame you. You'll never forgive me. How could you? I—"

"I forgive you, Mary Kate. I do. With my whole heart. I do. I swear it." He leaned over and kissed the top of her head. "I was angry, but I'm not anymore. You did what you thought was right. You didn't know. Father Murray didn't know. He told you I was a demon, a monster. It doesn't matter."

They weren't in that derelict building anymore. They were in their flat in West Belfast. They were warm and safe and in bed together. He'd taken a day off from the taxi driving to be with her. *No. This is a dream,* he thought.

"Yes," she said. "A dream. I told you. But we've still got time yet." She pressed her wet face against his bare chest. "I miss you so."

"I miss you too." He held her in his arms, breathing in the soft scent of her—holding it in his lungs for as long as he could.

"Thank you," she said.

"For what?"

"For forgiving me. It's a relief, it is."

"Forgave you long ago, love. Only you never knew it," he said and then paused, holding his breath. "Do you forgive me?"

"Whatever did you do?"

"I didn't tell you what I was. I didn't know, of course, but I—I knew enough. I didn't tell you about the monster."

"You're not a monster!"

"I lied to you. I let you think I was normal—"

"You are normal," she said. "You're normal for one of the Fey. You're normal for you. That's all anyone should care about."

He paused. "What if I'm not?"

"What do you mean?"

"What if I'm mad? Or going mad? What if it's too late? Da said—"

She laid a finger against his lips for the second time. "Don't rip and tear at yourself so. Just tell me what happened in Long Kesh. Please."

"Don't make me. I can't."

"Please, Liam. Do this for me. Please," she said. "I promise I'll love you anyway. Whatever was done to you doesn't change who you are to me. It won't matter."

"How do you know it won't?"

"You know what happened to me, don't you?" she asked, getting off his chest and laying on her side. He could see the naked length of her now. The scars were the wounds of two years ago, healed. Her broken front teeth had been fixed. A pale line was etched low across her stomach where her insides had been patched up. None of it marred her beauty. It was as if he was seeing her as she'd have been had she survived, and he loved her all the more for it.

"You know what happened before I died?"

You were raped. He took in a deep breath and then nodded.

"And does it make a difference to you?" she asked. "Does it change how you feel about me?"

"It never will. It wasn't your fault, what was done."

"Then why should what was done to you make a difference to me?"

She knows. The thought hit him like a hard blow to the gut. He felt half-frozen, suddenly, and his breath came in gulps. *It isn't the same. She's a woman. I'm—it isn't natural.* His skin tingled, and he felt the monster stir in the darkness of his brain. *She knows.* He got out of the bed and was at the door when she stopped him with a question.

"Where are you going?"

"I have to leave." The stirring became a rage-filled roar in the back of his mind.

"Why?" She sat up.

"It's different!" The prickling of his skin intensified. The monster was pushing its way to the surface.

"How is it any different, Liam?"

"It is!" He could hardly hear her above the monster's raving. "It was—it was—"

"Torture," she said.

"Not natural!"

"What was done was torture," she said. "It turned you against yourself. Rape isn't sex, Liam. It's about power."

"You don't understand!"

"Then make me understand."

The change would be upon him soon. He had to get away or she'd see. She'd—

"But I want to see," she said, scooting to the end of the bed. "Show me this monster."

"Mary Kate, please." A sharp spasm knifed through him, and he bent double and screamed with the force of it.

Mary Kate stood up at the foot of the bed and wrapped the sheet around herself. "You have to stop running from it."

Shaking his head, he staggered backward into the sitting room which joined with the kitchen. He knocked over a wobbly kitchen chair in the process. It fell to the floor with a crash.

"What is it that you think I don't understand?" Mary Kate asked. "That you had no control over your own body? That he took something from you that you didn't think was possible?"

"I mean it! You have to leave!" Terrified, he struggled against the change with all his might and as he did the pain grew worse. *It's too late.* Falling, he caught himself before he smashed into the arm of the sofa. He was on his hands and knees. "Please go. Save yourself."

"I'm staying and so are you," she said, her voice calm. She went to the front door and locked it. Standing defiant, her head held high with her scarred mouth—a proud warrior queen with her sheet-robe trailing.

"I don't want to hurt you."

"You'll not."

There wasn't anything left. The change was upon him. He'd kept himself from it for as long as he could stand but now it swept over him. He understood now why transforming into the Hound had always been agony and the bird form hadn't been just before all possibility of thought dissolved. He roared out his anger and frustration at the pain. An eternity seemed to pass. When the grinding of bone against bone and the cramping-shifting of muscle ceased at last, he was able to breathe. Blinking, he stumbled to his feet—*paws.*

Terror flashed across her expression before she got control of herself. She swallowed. "Oh."

He felt a growl crawl up his throat before he was able to bury it deep in his chest. He couldn't bring himself to look her in the eyes. *This is me. It's part of who I am. Accept it.*

I don't want to.

I must.

She took a step toward him and put out a hand. "I'll come to you. All right? Don't be afraid. I'll not hurt you."

Afraid? Why would I fear her? But he knew she was right. He was afraid. He took a long breath and slowly released it in an attempt to quiet his heart. He trembled. A memory of Haddock's palm on his back sprang to mind, and it suddenly occurred to Liam that there very much was something to fear. She didn't stop until she was close. *Too close.* He was big enough as the Hound that his head was at the same level as her chest. He backed up a couple steps.

"Everything is all right. See? I won't turn away from you." She moved closer again.

Very slowly, she reached out and then her fingers brushed his fur before he could jerk away. He froze but for the quivering, anticipating that horrible feeling. Instead, her palm pressed against his cheek, and he sensed warmth. *What was I afraid of? Were we not together in the bed before? Nothing happened then, aye?*

She bent a little in order to stare him in the eyes and smiled. "Hello, Liam."

Something inside him snapped, and it all became too much. He collapsed on the floor. The gentle pressure of her hand on his back was the only thing holding him together. *She knows. She's seen.*

She soothed him. "There. Shhhh. It's going to be all right."

He shifted back into human form without pain or thought but stayed as he was on the floor. Covering his head with both arms, he cried for the second time in his life since Long Kesh. She left him long enough to grab the blanket off the bed. Then she draped it around him, tucking it in close.

"It's all right," she said and settled onto the floor next to him. She lifted his head into her lap and smoothed his hair with her fingers. "You've needed this for a long time."

He buried his face in the sheet and wept until there were no more tears left. His throat was scratchy and raw and his nose was running by the end of it. She held him as if he were a child until he was finished.

"How do you feel?" she asked.

"Like a right idiot."

"Don't," she said, wiping the tears from his cheek. "It's all right."

"Admit it." He sniffed and sat up. "You were afraid of me."

"I wasn't."

"You were."

"What were you going to do?" she asked. "I'm already dead, you big idiot." She threw her arms around his neck and kissed him. "Let's go back to bed."

He picked her up and carried her the few feet to the bed, noticing again how little they'd had. "I'm sorry I never gave you nice things—"

"Oh, who gives a shite about that? I had you," she said. "That's all I ever wanted."

He lay back down beside her on the bed and stared up at the ceiling. "I didn't keep you safe." It'd been painted a drab white to match the walls that were made of drab white cinderblock. "I was your husband. I should've protected you."

She sighed. "And what difference would it have made were you there? We'd both be dead."

Aye, he thought. *And we'd be together.*

"Don't be stupid," she said.

The room was hardly big enough for the bed. He had to stand on the mattress to open the cupboard or the chest of drawers. "I never want to leave this place."

"You hated it," she said. "You complained of it every chance you had."

"I wanted better for you, but I couldn't—"

"And I said none of that matters."

"You would've been left alone but for me. But for my father." He sighed. "The Redcap was my fault."

"You have to stop blaming yourself. Promise me."

Thinking, he didn't answer.

"Promise me," she said.

"I'll try."

She sighed. "I suppose that'll have to do." She attempted to smooth his hair.

"I'm tired of living without you."

"You have to stay in the mortal world a while longer," she said. "You've things to do."

"I don't care."

"You do too. And anyway, I want you to care," she said. "Which brings up another thing. You've shut off your feelings, Liam Kelly. You're walking about half dead. It has to stop."

"I don't know what you mean."

"You're thinking now," she said. "That's good. Used to be, all you ever did was feel everything with that great heart of yours. You'd run into the middle of danger and think after, if you thought at all. Now all you do is think. That's no good either. You need to do both. Think and feel."

"What does it matter?"

"Don't you see? You can do the things I wanted to. You can make Ireland a better place. You can do something."

"I can't. No one can. Everything is too fucked. And all it'll ever do is get worse."

"You've already done something," she said. "You've got the Church talking to the Fey."

"What fucking difference does that make?" he asked. "Hasn't stopped the war." He paused. "Either of them."

"You'll see," she said.

"I will, will I?"

"Aye." She sighed again. "I have to leave soon."

"Why can't we be like this forever?"

"Because that time is ended. You have to move on. It was what it was," she said. "And I'm glad we had it, no matter how short."

"Spent half of it fighting."

"I know." He felt her smile against his chest. She sat up, pulled back the blankets and kissed him on the belly. "I really do have to go soon."

"No, you don't. It's my dream, so it is."

"I do," she said. Her golden brown hair fell over her shoulders and hid half her face. She gave him a look. *That* look. The one that never failed to send a shiver through him. "Do you want to spend the last of our time together fighting?" She lowered her head and kissed him an inch below his navel. "Or would you rather make a better dream?" Then she kissed him again a half inch below that. "Hmmm?" And an inch below that.

He could feel her breath tickle the hairs very low on his belly. "Oh, Christ. Oh, please."

"Thought you'd never ask."

Chapter 30

Organ music blasted through the chapel, making the stained glass windows buzz inside their lead frames. Hot beeswax and burning incense spiced the air. Exhausted and anxious, Father Murray sought much-needed comfort in the ritual of mass. He attempted not to think of the ramifications of what was actually going on and failed. Glancing at Liam sitting at his right, Father Murray searched for signs of physical distress. He wished there had been more time for Liam to recover. It would've been better for everyone involved. However, Monsignor Alghisi, Pope Paul VI's personal secretary had unexpectedly arrived instead of the Prelate's representative. Monsignor Alghisi expressed a need to witness certain proofs for himself before authorizing a more permanent truce with the Fey.

Word of the potential treaty had obviously leaked among the local membership. Private services in the Order's chapel on the third floor of the Queen's facility were usually well attended. Daily mass was a requirement for all members of Milites Dei. Therefore, multiple services were conducted to accommodate various schedules which meant the chapel was rarely overcrowded. However, one wouldn't know that by the current state of things. The chapel was so packed that celebrants were standing shoulder-to-shoulder along the back wall. Father Murray couldn't bring himself to blame them. It was a historic moment after all, but it lent a certain unpleasant circus air to the occasion.

Liam hadn't wanted to re-enter the Facility, of course. Given everything that he'd previously suffered at the hands of the Order's security force, Father Murray sympathized. However, controlled conditions were necessary if any proofs were to stand. Therefore, it had been agreed that Liam would not only go to mass, but he was to take holy communion as well which, in turn, meant confession. That alone had been a battle. As a biased observer, Father Murray knew he wouldn't be considered appropriate. Originally, Monsignor Alghisi had thought to hear Liam's confession. However, security had disallowed it due to the high level of personal risk. None of Father Murray's arguments to the contrary had carried weight. Security had countered by citing Liam's violent history. After that, no one had been brave enough to volunteer. With only an hour remaining before the scheduled mass, Father Stevenson saved the day by stepping forward.

Not that a certain segment of the Order will ever be convinced, Father Murray thought upon spotting Monsignor Paul in the audience. Noting the dark purple bruise covering Monsignor Paul's right eye, Father Murray briefly wondered what had happened and then remembered the incident in the café.

Nervous, he glanced over his shoulder and up into the balcony and spotted the sniper that security had placed there. He took a deep breath. *Is that completely necessary?* He'd already counted five armed security team members in the surrounding pews. *Do they not understand how impossible the situation would be, given the numbers packed into such a small space?*

Liam leaned closer, winked and whispered, "What's the *craic,* Father?"

"Please, pay attention to the mass, or pretend to," Father Murray said. "It's important."

Dressed in a new black suit, white shirt and black tie provided for the occasion by Sceolán, Liam at least looked presentable. *But for the boots and the hair,* Father Murray thought. Liam had been adamant about refusing the haircut, reasoning that God wouldn't much care about the state of his hair. The fact that he was attending mass at all was sure to be good enough.

"Aye," Liam muttered, facing forward. "Behave or the nice men with the wee rifles in the balcony will put a bullet in the back of your skull."

There's more than one? "Liam, please."

"Don't worry, Father. I'll be a good wee lab rat. I promise not to burst into flames."

Father Murray swallowed. It was only the lad's way of covering his fear and had served to keep him alive. However, as coping mechanisms went, Father Murray would have preferred anything else at the moment.

Wincing, Liam got to his feet with the rest of the congregation in preparation for the reading of the Gospel. Kneeling and walking seemed to be harder on him. Due to the previous history with opiates, Sisters Catherine and Mary had refused to give Liam much in the way of pain killers after the initial dose of morphine which had left him far from comfortable. This added to Father Murray's anxiety—not only because of Liam's physical discomfort but because the potential for misinterpretation regarding the source of his pain. All things considered, he seemed to be doing well enough, even appearing not to notice that most of the crowd studied him as he followed along in the missal.

Bishop Avery finished reading the Gospel, and everyone sat for the homily. Liam flinched as his back made contact with the hard wooden pew. His bruises had already healed for the most part, leaving only the gash in his back. Regardless of the severity of the wound, even that was healing well and fast. Sceolán had explained that Liam's accelerated recovery time was due to his having shape-shifted in addition to the time spent on the Other Side. Nonetheless it was obvious it hadn't been enough, and Father Murray found himself anxious for mass to end for the first time since he was a young man.

Someone in the audience coughed. The abrupt sound caused a visceral shock, and he noticed he wasn't the only one startled. A nervous laugh came from the back of the chapel, and then two priests took up positions at the end of the pews in the center aisle. The time for communion had arrived. One row at a time was allowed to line up. Since he and Liam were seated on the last row, they were the last permitted to go to the altar. Father Murray allowed Liam to take a place in line ahead of him in case he needed assistance. Liam took careful steps toward the altar with his teeth clenched. Father Murray could feel everyone's eyes upon them as they approached the communion rail.

Liam paused.

Intent on showing everyone that all was normal, Father Murray jumped the line and knelt at the communion rail. Liam wasn't long behind. From the corner of his eye, Father Murray watched Liam fold his hands in prayer. Bishop Avery moved along the communion rail, dispensing the Eucharist. Father Murray's turn came. He accepted the host and allowed it to dissolve in his mouth, closing his eyes in prayer as if nothing were wrong. When finished, he made the sign of the cross and opened his eyes. The Bishop had stopped in front of Liam but hadn't proceeded any further. The expression on his face was unreadable. Father Murray caught Bishop Avery's eye and gave him an encouraging nod.

Go on, Father Murray thought. *He'll be fine. There's nothing to be afraid of.*

The tension in the chapel grew and swelled. A deafening hush pushed against his ears. He understood he wasn't helping by hesitating himself. So he got to his feet, leaving Liam alone at the communion rail.

Jesus, Mary and Joseph, please, let him make it back to the pew without falling.

Finally lifting the Eucharist in the air, Bishop Avery said, "Body of Christ."

"Amen." Liam's answering whisper practically echoed through the chapel.

Father Murray tried not to smile. Upon reaching his pew, he risked a glance down the aisle. Liam got to his feet, using the edge of the communion rail to steady himself. For a moment Father Murray considered going back to help, but then Liam turned around. After a short pause, he lifted his head and started the long return journey to the pew. Keeping his gaze locked to the deep red runner carpet, he slowly limped back to his seat. Father Murray released the smile tugging at the corners of his mouth.

Let them make what they will of that, he thought and sat down, leaving a space for Liam. *I've waited nine years for this.*

The tension in the room didn't disperse until Liam knelt again and prayed.

Father Murray waited until Liam sat down and whispered, "Well done."

"Oh, I don't know. I may yet burn," Liam said, keeping his voice low. "Incidentally, does it count if the source of combustion is one of security's wee grenades?"

"Don't even joke about that." Father Murray felt a gentle tap on his shoulder and turned around.

Father Thomas whispered, "Bishop Avery wishes to meet with you both in his office after mass."

Father Murray nodded. *Is this it? Are they finally willing to admit to a small doubt at least?* He waited to share the news with Liam until the mass had ended.

With a majority of the attendees gone, Father Murray stood with Liam at the elevator door. Father Murray felt a presence at his back.

"How did you do it?"

Turning, he discovered it was Monsignor Paul, the Grand Inquisitor. *That really is an impressive black eye,* Father Murray thought.

Liam placed his back to the wall as if readying himself for an attack.

Biting down on one of several retorts, Father Murray settled on something more politic. "What do you mean?"

"That had to be some sort of trick," Monsignor Paul said. "Children of the Fallen can't accept the sacraments."

"It wasn't a trick," Father Murray said. "Liam is half Fey. You wanted proof. You have your proof."

Monsignor Paul took a menacing step toward Liam, his eyes boring into Liam's. "How did you do it?"

"How do you?" Liam asked. His lips thinned into a straight line and his brows pinched together.

"Liam," Father Murray said. *Don't lose control of your temper now. Please. That's all we need.*

"Don't know why we've bothered with this," Liam said. "Won't matter what I do."

"It's what the Bishop believes that matters." Father Murray moved between Liam and Monsignor Paul. "And if the Bishop believes it's proof enough, it's proof enough."

"Are you so certain?" Monsignor Paul asked. His expression was intense with hate.

"What is it that Liam has done that makes you hate him so? Or is this about your grudge with me?" Father Murray asked. "Or perhaps you can't admit that Liam has a soul because if you did it would place everything you've done for Milites Dei in a terrible perspective. Whatever the case may be, you should review your motives." *And the Bishop and the Prelate will too, if I have my way.*

A bell rang, and the steel elevator door opened. Several stragglers entered, and Father Murray motioned for Liam to get inside. When Monsignor Paul attempted to crowd into the elevator as well, Father Murray held up a hand.

"I believe the elevator is full," Father Murray said.

The doors slid shut in Monsignor Paul's face. The tiny space inside the elevator swelled with a tense silence. Father Murray reached over to the right and pressed the appropriate floor button. It was possible Monsignor Paul would take the stairs in order to cross paths with them again. However, Father Murray wasn't sure Monsignor Paul was aware of the meeting with Bishop Avery. Upon reaching the second floor, Father Murray exited first. He paused in order to be certain the way was clear. There was no sign of Monsignor Paul. Father Murray signalled for Liam to follow him down the empty hall. Their footsteps echoed off the cinderblock walls.

"Weren't you pressing your luck back there a wee bit, Father?" Liam asked.

"I never said I had infinite patience." Father Murray stopped at Bishop Avery's office door. He knocked and then opened it wide, indicating Liam should go inside first with a nod. Father Murray checked the empty hallway one last time and then closed the door.

Since Father Thomas operated as Bishop Avery's assistant, his work area consisted of a small antechamber. Waiting to meet with Bishop Avery, Father Murray noted the work area was furnished with a grey metal desk, a short table and three elderly dark green upholstered chairs. A photo of Pope John VI hung on the wall behind the desk, and wooden bookcases and filing cabinets lined the walls on either side. Father Thomas entered the room from the door opposite and held it open.

"The Bishop will join you in a moment," Father Thomas said.

The next room was more luxurious with dark cherry-wood panelling and a large antique desk to match. Father Murray sat in one of the three black leather chairs and pondered the reasons why they'd been called to a meeting now. *Will the Bishop agree to a truce? Or is this a portent of another reaction all together?*

Obviously curious, Liam hobbled to the memorial wall lined with row upon row of black-framed photographs.

"You should sit," Father Murray said. "While you have a chance to rest." *Will Liam hold up? Or is he going to allow his emotions to get the better of him?*

"Who are they?"

"The Order's honored dead."

"Oh."

"Liam, please. Sit. You're tired." Father Murray watched him limp to the next chair and perch on the edge of the seat. "Do you need more aspirin? I can ask Father Thomas—"

The door swung open and Bishop Avery and Monsignor Alghisi entered the room. The Monsignor was a small bald man with a thick moustache. His expression was carefully neutral, whereas Bishop Avery appeared annoyed.

"Declan, please apologize to Monsignor Paul. Tell him I'll be available in the morning. Unless it's urgent, of course."

"He isn't going to like that, Your Grace," Father Thomas said.

"It's Christmas," Bishop Avery said, in Latin. "Surely the man can indulge me and wait for a more civilized hour before voicing his objections to this evening's events. Oh, one more thing, can you bring some tea? I'd like a little brandy to go with it, please. Monsignor Alghisi might like some wine. And perhaps something to eat for Mr. Kelly."

"Yes, Your Grace." Father Thomas closed the door with a quiet thump.

Out of respect, Father Murray stood. Liam remained sitting.

Bishop Avery said, "Happy Christmas, Mr. Kelly, Father Murray." His expression had changed. He seemed more relaxed. There was even a smile on his face.

Father Murray took that for a good sign. "Thank you, Your Grace. Happy Christmas to you as well."

"May I call you Liam?" Bishop Avery asked.

"Yes, sir."

"Liam, let me introduce you to Monsignor Alghisi. He is Secretary to

His Holiness, Pope Paul VI."

Father Murray watched Liam's face, praying that the lad would choose to be diplomatic. Liam shook hands with Monsignor Alghisi and Bishop Avery and then sat. Greetings were exchanged in English. However, Monsignor Alghisi's Italian accent apparently caused Liam some difficulty. When the Monsignor inquired about his family, and where Liam might plan to spend the Christmas holiday, Father Murray had to repeat the question.

"Was hoping to see my mother, ah, Father," Liam said. "But I don't know if that will be possible."

The Monsignor blinked. "Why shouldn't he—"

Bishop Avery leaned in and whispered in the Monsignor's ear.

"Oh. I see," the Monsignor said.

The Bishop and the Monsignor sat down in chairs positioned behind the desk. There came another knock on the door, and Father Thomas entered, carrying a tray.

"Very good," Bishop Avery said in English.

Father Murray got up and helped Father Thomas arrange the wine glasses, tea things and a dish of tiny sandwiches on the top of Bishop Avery's desk. Once everything was done, Father Thomas left.

"Liam, would you like tea? Or would you prefer wine?" Bishop Avery asked, uncorking the bottle.

Father Murray saw Liam glance his direction as if asking permission. He gave Liam a small nod. *Either way, it might put the lad at ease. That was smart of you, Robert.*

"I'll have the tea, sir," Liam said.

It took a bit of time to sort out the food and for everyone to settle back into their seats. Father Murray watched Liam drink his tea and hoped for the best.

"Liam, the Monsignor and I have two proposals," Bishop Avery said. "First, we have been authorized to offer an indefinite extension of the truce between the Church and the Fey."

Father Murray almost cheered.

There was a long pause while Liam's face remained expressionless. "For which diocese?"

Father Murray placed a hand on Liam's arm. "Liam, please—"

"This truce will be declared for the Republic of Ireland and all of Northern Ireland," Monsignor Alghisi said.

Liam blinked. "Oh."

"However, this leaves us with a particular problem," Bishop Avery said. "Very little is known of the Fey beyond what we have learned from you. Unfortunately, since you are half human—"

"Mortal, sir," Liam said. "With respect, the Fey prefer to use the word 'mortal.'"

Father Murray held his breath. *Please, Liam. Don't anger them. Not now. Not after everything we've been through.*

Bishop Avery paused. The Monsignor nodded his approval.

"All right. It is unfortunately unclear which characteristics are due to your... mortal heritage and which aren't," Bishop Avery said. "More to the point, there is no reliable means of determining whether or not a suspected Fallen is a demon or Fey. Do you understand?"

"You want me to help you judge whether or not someone is a demon," Liam said. "In other words, decide whether or not you're to murder them."

Father Murray said, "Liam—"

"That is what you're talking about, isn't it?" Liam asked.

Father Murray attempted to calm him. "Please, Liam—"

"I'll tell you the same I told Séamus. I'll have nothing to do with the killing," Liam said. "I'm done with it."

"That is an admirable and understandable position," Bishop Avery said.

"Perhaps one might consider the proposition another way," Monsignor Alghisi said. "The persons targeted would normally undergo immediate execution as Fallen without further inquiry. We merely ask your assistance in determining who we should save."

It was clear from the expression on Liam's face that he didn't like the idea at all.

"Think of the Fey that will be spared," Bishop Avery said.

"My Mary Kate—my wife was in Uni, Father," Liam said. "Heard of a man named George Orwell, have you?" He leaned forward. "Absolute power corrupts absolutely."

"You're saying you don't wish to help us?" Bishop Avery asked.

"I've no wish for the power of life and death," Liam said. "I told you I was done with it. And I fu—I mean it."

Oh, Jesus, Mary, and Joseph. He's going to throw it all away. "Liam—"

"I mean it," Liam said.

Monsignor Alghisi exchanged a look with Bishop Avery and then nodded.

"We do understand your position," Bishop Avery said. "However, we very much need your help."

"And my da is looking for the same sort of help, did you know? The Fey have a similar problem with Fallen hiding in their midst. But I'll not be anyone's Diplock judge," Liam said.

"No one is asking you to execute anyone," Father Murray said.

"Oh, aye?" Liam asked. "That's your place, isn't it?"

Father Murray felt he'd been kicked in the gut.

Liam sighed. "I'm sorry, Father. I didn't mean it."

"I deserve that," Father Murray said. "I do. We both know why."

Liam said, "Father—"

"But please believe me," Father Murray said and took a deep breath. "This is about saving lives. Not taking them. You're thinking about this all wrong."

"Am I?" Liam asked.

"If it makes you feel better, we'll look into some form of oversight," Bishop Avery said. "It might make the situation more palatable to certain objectors, in any case. You see, our Order has never before extended membership to a non-ordained member of the Church, even in a strictly associative capacity. But if that would make you feel better…." He shrugged.

"Who?" Liam asked.

"What do you mean?" Bishop Avery asked.

"Who would be the one checking up on me?" Liam asked.

"We can discuss that later," Bishop Avery said.

"Not Monsignor Paul. Aye?" Liam asked, setting his cup down.

Bishop Avery glanced at Monsignor Alghisi.

Monsignor Alghisi said, "Not Monsignor Paul."

"All right," Liam said. Father Murray watched Liam's knuckles turn white as he squeezed the arms of the leather chair. "I'm willing to hear you out."

"In exchange for your assistance," Bishop Avery said. "The Church is willing to extend the truce on an indefinite basis. Should you agree to work as part of a team—" He held up a hand as Liam started to protest.

"The Church will agree to pay you a consultant's fee. Also, you will be provided with a residence and new identification."

They're offering him a new life, Father Murray thought.

Liam blinked. "Wait. What?"

Bishop Avery said, "Your services could potentially be required outside of Northern Ireland. In which case, we can't afford to risk having you detained by the authorities."

Liam paused. "You can do that?"

Bishop Avery nodded.

"What about my mother?"

"What about her?" Bishop Avery asked.

"Are you planning on telling everyone I'm dead, or were you going to simply make me vanish?" Liam asked. "Either way, my mother is left grieving."

Smart, Father Murray thought.

Bishop Avery asked, "How is this arrangement different from your former associations?"

Father Murray clenched his fist. *Oh, Mother of God, you didn't say that, Robert.*

"I'll only agree if I'm allowed to tell my mother I'll be living with my Da's people for a time. And that I'll be allowed to visit her."

"We can certainly make such arrangements," Bishop Avery said.

Liam looked up at the ceiling and seemed to spy the camera mounted there.

Oh, shite, Father Murray thought. *He'll reject the offer and spit in their faces. He'll—*

"I'll take care of my own lodgings," Liam said.

"Why?" Bishop Avery asked.

"It isn't that I don't trust you, Father," Liam said. "But after living under conditions you lot deemed secure, I think I'd be safer on my own."

Father Murray attempted not to smile.

"Oh, I see," Bishop Avery said. He cleared his throat. "All right."

"Who am I to be working with?" Liam asked.

"We thought Guardian Murray would be most appropriate," Bishop Avery said.

"Only Father Murray?" Liam asked.

"For the time being," Bishop Avery said.

Liam stared into his tea. "I'd like part of the money sent to my mother and another to Elizabeth MacMahon. I'll give you the address, aye?"

Father Murray asked, "Who?"

"Elizabeth is Oran's widow," Liam said. "Promised Oran I'd look after his family, so I did."

"Very well," Bishop Avery said. "Whatever you need."

"Lastly, Monsignor Paul is to have nothing to do with us," Liam said.

"I understand your misgivings," Bishop Avery said.

"I don't trust him," Liam said. "I don't like him either. I'll not have him coming in at me when my back's turned, you hear? I'll not have him near me, or Father Murray."

"I'm not sure we can—"

"You'll have to, or I'm out," Liam said.

Unable to help himself, Father Murray rested an elbow on the arm of his chair and hid a smile with his hand.

Bishop Avery again looked to Monsignor Alghisi. The Italian's dark brown eyes glittered and then he shrugged. "I don't have the authority for such a thing. However, I can certainly look into the matter. I might need a few days before I can give you a definite answer," Bishop Avery said.

"Fair enough," Liam said. "I may need a few days to think it over, myself."

Chapter 31

Londonderry/Derry, County Londonderry, Northern Ireland
27 December 1977

"Hello?" Liam spoke into the pay phone and turned his back to it so he could watch the bustle of the afternoon street. The tension between his shoulder blades ratcheted up a couple notches when he spied the troops stopped at the corner. He didn't breathe until they moved on. He found himself listening for extra clicks on the telephone line. *Watch what you say, aye?*

"Hello." The voice on the other end was very young and female.

"Moira? Is that you?" Liam asked.

"Aye."

"Why aren't you in school?"

"It's Christmas holiday. There's no school. Don't you know that?"

"Ah, right you are." Liam sighed. It was such a normal conversation. He'd almost forgotten what that was like. *School. Christmas holiday. The scent of pine from the Christmas tree stuffed in the sitting room that had doubled as his room.*

"You're my brother Liam, aren't you?" Moira asked in even tones. "I remember you."

He could hear one of his sister Eileen's records playing. It took him a moment to recognize Rod Stewart bemoaning the fact that the first cut was the deepest. Listening, Liam found he was a little homesick. "How do you know it's me?" he asked, feeling a sad smile curl his lips. *Will I see any of them ever again? Is it Eileen playing the records or Moira? Moira wasn't old enough to care about records when I saw her last.* Then he remembered her solemn grey eyes and how she always seemed to be looking right through him—even when she was small.

Moira paused. "I just know."

I bet you do. He shivered, stuffed his left hand in his pocket and hunched inside Conor's jacket.

"The dog isn't as angry as he used to be, is he?" she asked in a whisper.

"What?" His fingers squeezed the receiver.

"It's all right," she said, keeping her voice low. She sounded far away. "You should listen to him sometimes. He's only scared. And he doesn't mean any harm. Not really. He wants to protect you, is all. He's not as bad as you think. He didn't do all the bad things you think he did."

"What are you on about?"

"I shouldn't have said that, should I?" she asked. Her tone changed. She sounded on the verge of tears. "I'm not supposed to know."

A cold wind blew hard up the street, sending bits of grit and paper whirling.

Get fucking control of yourself, man. He shut his eyes briefly. *She's only a wee girl.* "I'm sorry. I didn't mean—It's all right." *But how does she know this shite?*

"I'm sorry," she said.

"Please don't worry yourself. I'm not angry with you. I shouldn't have spoke to you like that."

"Everybody is afraid of me. I'm stupid—"

"Moira, love. You're not stupid. You're smarter than all of them. That's why they're afraid."

"Da says I'm mental—"

"You're not mad either. Don't you listen to the likes of him," he said, wishing he were there to help her. *And what would you do about it? Hit him? You'd be just as bad as he is.* "You hear me? Don't listen to him." *Patrick. Fucking arsehole.* "Moira?"

She sniffed. "I hear you."

"I know what you are. I do, and I love you." He suddenly realized that he really did. It also occurred to him in the same moment that Eileen probably wasn't home. The last he'd heard she'd gotten a job. "Does Eileen know you're using her record player?"

Moira gasped.

"Ach. Don't worry. I won't tell," Liam said. "Be careful, though. And don't scratch her records. She was always at me for that, you know."

"Oh. I won't."

He wished there was something he could do for her, but he was running out of time. "May I speak with Ma?"

"She's not here."

"Where is she?"

"Outside. Talking to Mrs. McKenna."

"Go get her for me, will you?" Liam asked. "I don't have much more change left for the phone."

"All right," she said. "Liam, I love you too." The phone clunked and rattled as she put it down.

While he was waiting the telephone chimed and the operator asked for more money. He inserted the last of his change. Just when he was sure he'd have to ring off, his ma picked up. She sounded out of breath.

"Liam? Is it really you? Liam? Are you there?"

He felt guilty at once. "Aye, Ma. It's me."

"Oh, thank—" She took a deep breath, and sniffed. Liam was concerned she'd start crying. "Where the hell have you been? Do you realize I thought you might be dead? Why have you not rang?"

"Ma, please," Liam said. "I don't have long."

"Well? What is it, then?" Her questions were tight bursts of worry, anger and frustration.

"I'm so sorry, Ma," he said. "I am."

"What is it you've done now?" The question swelled with whispered dread.

"Nothing—I—" He stopped himself, remembering that someone might be listening. "I'm going away. I—I wanted you to know."

"Going away. Where?"

"With Da's people. For a time." It was only half a lie. He was planning on staying with the Fey for a few days, maybe a week or so and then he'd go back to working with Father Murray.

"Oh."

The silence stretched across the miles for a bit. He was about to ask if she was still there when she whispered, "So, you've been with him, have you?"

"Aye." It was close enough to the truth.

"Good." She paused again. "You'll stay out of trouble?"

"I will, Ma."

"Not... like before?"

"I've—I'm... not... no. Not like before." *Not any more*, he thought. "That's done. I'm not going back."

He could hear her relief gush out in a short exhale. "Thank God."

"Ma?"

"I'm here."

"No matter what you hear... I'm all right."

She paused. "And what is it I might hear?"

The telephone tweeped its pre-recorded warning.

"Ma, I have to go."

"What's the number? I'll ring you back."

"I can't give you that. You know I can't."

"Liam!"

"Yes, Ma?"

"I love you." She was crying. He could hear it.

"I love you too. Try not to worry. I'll be all right. Goodbye, Ma." He wished it didn't sound so final. He planned to see her in a week or two. The problem was, he couldn't tell her—not now, not over the telephone. "Take care of yourself."

"I will," she said. "You—You be careful."

"I will."

He rang off and blinked until his vision cleared. Another gust of wind blew past as he told himself he'd see home soon. He wiped cooling tears from his face and then ran his fingers through his hair. *She'll be fine*, he thought. *Everything will be all right. I'll be seeing them soon.* A cold wind gusted down the street.

Holding Conor's jacket tight around him, he went to meet Father Murray.

❧

Acknowledgements

Novels such as this one may mainly be the product of one person's imagination, but they only come into being due to the contributing efforts of an army of people whose names don't appear on the cover. Contrary to popular belief, no one stays in publishing because they swim in fame and piles of cash Scrooge McDuck-style. They're in publishing because they love it with every fiber of their being. Books are the result of passionate love, hard work and little reward. That's why the acknowledgment list is often long and tedious. So, please bear with me.

First, there's my husband, Dane Caruthers, who sees to it that I've a roof over my head, food, electricity, medical insurance, and enough coffee to keep me writing. He's my best friend, first reader, cheerleader, and idea sounding-board. He believed in me when no one else did. Also, if Liam has said anything humorous, chances are Dane is the inspiration if not the originator. (Thanks, love!) I'd also like to thank Joe Monti who is still the best literary agent ever—this, in spite of my having cried all over the front of his t-shirt last summer. I'd like to add Barry Goldblatt and Tricia Ready to this list because they rock. There's also my kick-ass editor, Jeremy Lassen and the entire team at Night Shade Books (Jason Williams—founder, rescuer, and all around great guy; Ross Lockhart—who keeps everything on schedule; Tomra Palmer—who herds cats and—I imagine—does it Emma Peel style while not spilling a single drop of her martini; Liz Upson—who is not only a great publicist but is damned fun to drink with; Amy

Popovich—production manager; Dave Palumbo—art director; and the rest of Night Shade's amazing staff.) Thanks to Min Yum for doing such a brilliant job on the cover art for both of my books. Many, many thanks to Brian Magaoidh (again) and Nicholas Whyte for fact-checking my Irish history, culture, Belfast geography, and political information. (All errors are my fault, not theirs.) I wouldn't have had the confidence to do this again without them. And thanks to Gareth Kavanagh and Melissa Tyler, super-fast beta readers. Big, big thanks to my writing mentors Charles de Lint, Sharon Shinn, Holly Black, and Carrie Richerson. I truly wouldn't be here without their wisdom, inspiration, encouragement and support. Also, thanks to Charles Stross for introducing me to Nicholas Whyte, and Scott "Gentleman Bastard" Lynch for telling me I'm too mean to my characters. (That's a gold star I'll wear with pride forever.) Thank goodness for Joe McKinney who let me pick his brain regarding police procedures and car chases as they'd realistically occur in the mid-to late-1970s. Once more, thanks to Troy Hunt for the mechanical details of upgrading Liam's RS2000/RS1600 and other car geekery. Thanks to Jennifer "Penny" Danvers, good friend and sister art-geek, without whom I'd never have made it to WFC this year. Also, thanks again to Joe Strummer, Rory Gallagher, Pink Floyd, Stiff Little Fingers, The Undertones, The Pogues, and my entire '70s play list for the musical inspiration. Another round of thanks goes out to the Austin Gaelic League, the Philo-Celtic Society and Kathleen Douglas for sharing their knowledge of Ireland, Irish culture and the Irish language; BookPeople, the best bookstore on the planet; last but not least to Mom and Dad and my sisters and brother—Cathy, Celina and Fred.

Also, if you'd like to learn more about the history of Northern Ireland and the Troubles, it's a good idea to look into Tim Pat Coogan's books (*Ireland in the 20th Century, The IRA, 1916: The Easter Rising*), *Those are Real Bullets* by Peter Pringle and Philip Jacobson, *Derry Memories* by Philip Cunningham, *War as a Way of Life* by John Conroy, *This Troubled Land* by Patrick Michael Rucker, *Ten Men Dead* by David Beresford, *Cage Eleven* by Gerry Adams, *The Price of My Soul* by Bernadette Devlin, *Mister Are You a Priest?* by Edward Daly, *Ballymurphy and the Irish War* by Ciarán de Baróid, *Down North: Reflections of Ballymurphy and the Early Troubles* by Ciarán de Baróid, *Derry: The Troubled Years* by Eamon Melaugh and

No Go: A Photographic Record of Free Derry by Barney McMonagle. In addition, the University of Ulster maintains a wonderful archival website at http://cain.ulst.ac.uk/index.html. If Northern Ireland's punk scene is of interest, see *Hooleygan: Music, Mayhem, Good Vibrations* by Terri Hooley and Richard Sullivan as well as *It Makes You Want to Spit!: The Definitive Guide to Punk in Northern Ireland* by Sean O'Neill and Guy Trelford. If your interest is in Irish folk lore as it's known in Ireland, be sure to read *Meeting the Other Crowd* by Eddie Lenihan and Carolyn Eve Green. As for the Catholic side of things, read *The Rite* by Matt Baglio, and *Interview with an Exorcist* by Father José Antonio Fortea.

Night Shade Books is an Independent Publisher of Quality Science-Fiction, Fantasy and Horror

ISBN: 978-1-59780-213-0 ❦ $14.99 ❦ Look for it in e-Book

"Stina Leicht is one of my favourites among the new writers we have today. She writes with depth and heart and tells a story with all the resonance of an old whiskey: dark with an edgy flavour."

— Charles de Lint, author of *Forests of the Heart*

STINA LEICHT

of BLOOD and HONEY
A BOOK OF THE FEY AND THE FALLEN

Fallen angels and the fey clash against the backdrop of Irish/English conflicts of the 1970s in this stunning debut novel by Stina Leicht.

Liam never knew who his father was. The town of Derry had always assumed that he was the bastard of a protestant—His mother never spoke of him, and Liam assumed he was dead.

But when the war between the fallen, and the fey began to heat up, Liam and his family are pulled into a conflict that they didn't know existed. A centuries old conflict between supernatural forces seems to mirror the political divisions in 1970s era Ireland, and Liam is thrown headlong into both conflicts.

Only the direct intervention of Liam's real father, and a secret catholic order dedicated to fighting "The Fallen" can save Liam... from the mundane and supernatural forces around him, and from the darkness that lurks within him.

Night Shade Books is an Independent Publisher of Quality Science-Fiction, Fantasy and Horror

The only thing worse than war is revolution. Especially when you're already losing the war...

Nyx used to be a bel dame, a government-funded assassin with a talent for cutting off heads for cash. Her country's war rages on, but her assassin days are long over. Now she's babysitting diplomats to make ends meet and longing for the days when killing people was a lot more honorable.

When Nyx's former bel dame "sisters" lead a coup against the government that threatens to plunge the country into civil war, Nyx volunteers to stop them. The hunt takes Nyx and her inglorious team of mercenaries to one of the richest, most peaceful, and most contaminated countries on the planet—a country wholly unprepared to host a battle waged by the world's deadliest assassins.

In a rotten country of sweet-tongued politicians, giant bugs, and renegade shape shifters, Nyx will forge unlikely allies and rekindle old acquaintances. And the bodies she leaves scattered across the continent this time... may include her own.

Because no matter where you go or how far you run in this world, one thing is certain: the bloody bel dames will find you.

Night Shade Books is an Independent Publisher of Quality Science-Fiction, Fantasy and Horror

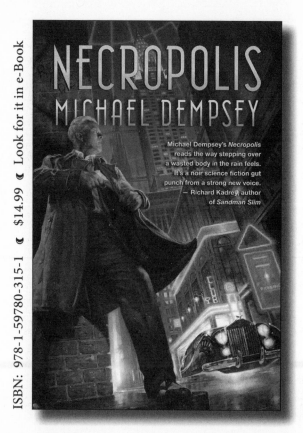

NECROPOLIS
MICHAEL DEMPSEY

Michael Dempsey's *Necropolis* reads the way stepping over a wasted body in the rain feels. It's a noir science fiction gut punch from a strong new voice.
— Richard Kadrey, author of *Sandman Slim*

Paul Donner is a NYPD detective struggling with a drinking problem and a marriage on the rocks. Then he and his wife get dead—shot to death in a "random" crime. Fifty years later, Donner is back—revived courtesy of the Shift, a process whereby inanimate DNA is re-activated.

This new "reborn" underclass is not only alive again, they're growing younger, destined for a second childhood. The freakish side-effect of a retroviral attack on New York, the Shift has turned the world upside down. Beneath the protective geodesic Blister, clocks run backwards, technology is hidden behind a noir facade, and you can see Bogart and DiCaprio in *The Maltese Falcon III*. In this unfamiliar retro-futurist world of flying Studebakers and plasma tommy guns, Donner must search for those responsible for the destruction of his life. His quest for retribution, aided by Maggie, his holographic *Girl Friday*, leads him to the heart of the mystery surrounding the Shift's origin and up against those who would use it to control a terrified nation.

Night Shade Books is an Independent Publisher of Quality Science-Fiction, Fantasy and Horror

ISBN: 978-1-59780-323-6 ❆ $24.99 ❆ Look for it in e-Book

"A hungry beast of a book, rippling with slaughter and sex, powerhouse action, surreal post-human horrors and bigger-than-life heroes. Amidst the carnage, Rob Ziegler's devastated future earth is shot with the surprising promise of redemption and rebirth. *SEED* pulses with life."
—Paolo Bacigalupi, Hugo Award-winning author of *The Windup Girl*

It's the dawn of the 22nd century, and the world has fallen apart. Decades of war and resource deple-tion have toppled governments. The ecosystem has collapsed. A new dust bowl sweeps the Ameri-can West. The United States has become a nation of migrants—starving masses of nomads roaming across wastelands and encamped outside government seed distribution warehouses.

In this new world, there is a new power: Satori. More than just a corporation, Satori is an intelli-gent, living city risen from the ruins of the heartland. She manufactures climate-resistant seed to feed humanity, and bio-engineers her own perfected castes of post-humans Designers, Advocates and La-borers. What remains of the United States government now exists solely to distribute Satori product; a defeated American military doles out bar-coded, single-use seed to the nation's hungry citizens.

Secret Service Agent Sienna Doss has watched her world collapse. Once an Army Ranger fighting wars across the globe, she now spends her days protecting glorified warlords and gangsters. As her country slides further into chaos, Doss feels her own life slipping into ruin.

When a Satori Designer goes rogue, Doss is tasked with hunting down the scientist-savant—a chance to break Satori's stranglehold on seed production and undo its dominance. In a race against Satori's genetically honed assassins, Doss's best chance at success lies in an unlikely alliance with Brood—orphan, scavenger and small-time thief—scraping by on the fringes of the wasteland, whose young brother may possess the key to unlocking Satori's power.

As events spin out of control, Sienna Doss and Brood find themselves at the heart of Satori, where an explosive finale promises to reshape the future of the world.

Night Shade Books is an Independent Publisher of Quality Science-Fiction, Fantasy and Horror

ISBN: 978-1-59780-205-5 ❦ $14.99 ❦ Look for it in e-Book

"Stackpole captures the grandeur and danger of the New World...."
— *Publishers Weekly*

THE SECOND BOOK OF THE CROWN COLONIES

OF *Limited Loyalty*

NEW YORK TIMES BESTSELLING AUTHOR

MICHAEL A. STACKPOLE

1767. In the three years since defeating the Tharyngians at Anvil Lake, The Crown Colonies of Mystria have prospered. Colonists, whether hunting for new land or the Promised Land of prophecy, have pushed beyond the bounds of charters granted by the Queen of Norisle. Some of these new communities have even had the temerity to tell the Crown they are no longer subject to its authorities. To survey the full extent of the western expansion, the Crown has sent Colonel Ian Rathfield to join Nathaniel Woods, Owen Strake and Kamiskwa on an expedition into the Mystrian interior.

They discover a land full of isolated and unique communities, each shaped in accord with the ideals of the founders. Conflicts abound among them, and old enemies show up at the least useful moments. Worse yet, lurking out there is a menace which the Twilight People only know from folklore as the Antedeluvians; and westward penetration stumbles into their lands and awakens them.

Alerted to this threat by his men, Prince Vlad petitions the Crown to send troops and supplies to destroy this new and terrifying enemy. The Crown refuses, citing massive debts from the last war. They dismiss Vlad's claims as fantasy, and impose a series of taxes on Mystrian trade to finance their own recovery.

Faced with fighting an inhuman foe in a land seething with resentment against the Crown, Vlad must unite the Colonies in a common cause, or preside over their complete destruction.

Night Shade Books is an Independent Publisher of Quality Science-Fiction, Fantasy and Horror

ISBN: 978-1-59780-332-8 ❦ $14.99 ❦ Look for it in e-Book

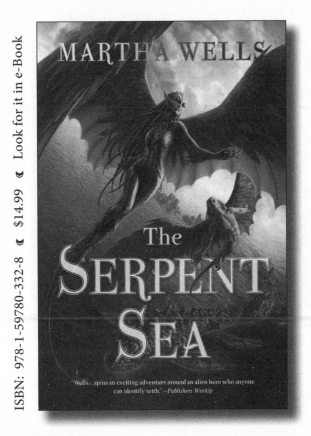

MARTHA WELLS

The SERPENT SEA

"Wells...spins an exciting adventure around an alien hero who anyone can identify with." —*Publishers Weekly*

Moon, once a solitary wanderer, has become consort to Jade, sister queen of the Indigo Cloud court. Together, they travel with their people on a pair of flying ships in hopes of finding a new home for their colony. Moon finally feels like he's found a tribe where he belongs.

But when the travelers reach the ancestral home of Indigo Cloud, shrouded within the trunk of a mountain-sized tree, they discover a blight infecting its core. Nearby they find the remains of the invaders who may be responsible, as well as evidence of a devastating theft. This discovery sends Moon and the hunters of Indigo Cloud on a quest for the heartstone of the tree—a quest that will lead them far away, across the Serpent Sea. . . .

In this followup to *The Cloud Roads*, Martha Wells returns with a world-spanning odyssey, a mystery that only provokes more questions--and the adventure of a lifetime.

Praise for *The Cloud Roads*:

"Wells...spins an exciting adventure around an alien hero who anyone can identify with."   —*Publishers Weekly*

"A starring light of the fantasy genre recaptures her mojo by going in a new direction."   —*SF Signal*

Night Shade Books is an Independent Publisher of Quality Science-Fiction, Fantasy and Horror

ISBN: 978-1-59780-335-9 ❦ $24.99 ❦ Look for it in e-Book

Two years ago, on the same day but miles apart, Finn Darby lost two of the most important people in his life: his wife Lorena, struck by lightning on the banks of the Chattahoochee River, and his abusive, alcoholic grandfather, Tom Darby, creator of the long-running newspaper comic strip *Toy Shop*.

Against his grandfather's dying wish, Finn has resurrected *Toy Shop*, adding new characters, and the strip is more popular than ever, bringing in fan letters, merchandising deals, and talk of TV specials. Finn has even started dating again.

When a terrorist attack decimates Atlanta, killing half a million souls, Finn begins blurting things in a strange voice beyond his control. The voice says things only his grandfather could know. Countless other residents of Atlanta are suffering a similar bizarre affliction. Is it mass hysteria, or have the dead returned to possess the living?

Finn soon realizes he has a hitcher within his skin... his grandfather. And Grandpa isn't terribly happy about the changes Finn has been making to *Toy Shop*. Together with a pair of possessed friends, an aging rock star and a waitress, Finn races against time to find a way to send the dead back to Deadland... or die trying.

Night Shade Books is an Independent Publisher of Quality Science-Fiction, Fantasy and Horror

ISBN: 978-1-59780-392-2 ❦ $14.99 ❦ Look for it in e-Book

"A forthright, alarmingly logical urban fairy tale with a very engaging protagonist. It balances its whimsy nicely with sarcasm and genuine emotion."
PAMELA DEAN, author of *Tam Lin* and *Juniper, Gentian, and Rosemary*

TOOTH *and* NAIL

jennifer SAFREY

Gemma Fae Cross, a tough-girl amateur boxer whose fiance is running for congress, has just made a startling discovery about herself. She is half faerie—and not just any faerie, but a tooth faerie.

A hybrid of fae and human, Gemma is destined to defend the Olde Way and protect the fae—who are incapable of committing violence—from threats to their peaceful and idyllic way of life, which must be maintained by distilling innocence collected from children's baby teeth.

But when a threat to the fae mission emerges, Gemma is called upon to protect her heritage, and become a legendary fae warrior... even if it means sacrificing everything she knows about being human.

About the Author

Stina Leicht currently lives in central Texas with her husband, their shared library, and a cat named Sebastian. She still sings too loud to punk music in her car, reads too much, and otherwise makes a general fool of herself because it's too much effort to take herself seriously.